THE WITCHES OF
PORT TOWNSEND
BOOK 2

WHICH WITCH Is Wicked?

CINDY STARK • KERRIGAN BYRNE
TIFFINIE HELMER • CYNTHIA ST. AUBIN

USA TODAY BESTSELLING AUTHORS

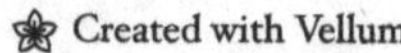 Created with Vellum

To our readers.

WHO MAGICALLY MAKE THE DREAM OF
WRITING A

reality.

CLAIRE

CINDY STARK

❧ I ❧

> Goddess of power, hear my plea
> Watch over those who pray to thee
> Grant the power, give it to me
> To protect those who are worthy
> By earth, air, fire and sea...

Energy crackled and hissed as Claire de Moray chanted the magical words.

A red haze colored her world and a loud crack filled the air. Claire blinked and glanced around, her gaze landing on shattered pieces of turquoise pottery that had once been a beautiful vase. Broken white roses lay mixed with the shards as a puddle of water seeped from the wreckage.

"Tierra's going to have your ass," Aerin said with a sassy smile. "She made that vase. Grew those roses."

Claire put a defeated hand over her face. "This will never work."

After a deep breath, she focused on Aerin, who'd joined her in the solarium. "Something is missing, but I can't figure it out. I need the damn Grimoire. Without it, how will we ever protect ourselves? Protect Tierra and her baby? Death might have spared Tierra, but that doesn't mean he wouldn't kill one of us. And it doesn't mean the other Horsemen won't try to end her life."

"Fucking thief sneaking into *our* house, taking *our* book." Aerin perched on the edge of the windowsill, staring into the cool morning air, a cup of heart-stopping coffee in her hand. The house had been hauntingly quiet for the past week since Nick had shot a deadly arrow at Moira and nearly killed Tierra instead. A thick, strangling gloom hung over all four sisters, mimicking the damp gray skies outside. "We need to figure out who took Grim and kick her ass."

"Agreed. And you and I are the perfect ones to do it." Claire wanted nothing more than to lash out at someone or something.

"Damn straight." Aerin leaned farther out the window and stared up at the sky with a frown on her face.

"Couldn't have been the guys who'd taken Grim," Claire continued. "We'd know if they'd gotten through our wards. Wasn't Justine because she was dead drunk. What about someone else in the coven?"

Aerin didn't answer, seeming preoccupied by something in the sky.

Claire stood and approached her sister. "What are you looking at?" Just as she reached the window, something sailed through the air, heading straight for the pink rhododendrons below. "*What the hell was that?*"

"Fish."

She leaned over Aerin's shoulder to see a salmon flopping on the ground in close proximity to several others. A frazzled bat swooped in through the open window and landed on Aerin's knee, his favorite spot to rest, barely escaping the next fish bomb.

"Oh, my God." Three seagulls came in for another round, all carrying squirming fish in their beaks. "Have they gone mad?"

"Bat-shit crazy." Aerin stood, leaving Doctor Lecter

to flutter about the room as she hurried to shut the window. Just as she did, the body of a fish smacked against the glass, leaving a blurry streak as it slid down the surface.

"But not as crazy as your sister." Aerin opened the window again. "Moira! What the hell are you doing out there? Get your ass inside before you get hit."

Claire watched as Moira dashed across the lawn to gather one, then another flopping body from the grass.

"Get your sweet ass out here and help me," she cried. "A'fore they all die!"

"Oh, hell." Claire hurried from the room, nearly colliding with Tierra as they reached the back door, both of them heading outside. "Don't ask because I don't know."

"They need water! Get a bucket or somethin'," Moira yelled as salmon smacked her head. "Damn it! Help me gather them up!"

"I'll get it." Tierra dodged a flying fish as she ran for the side of the raised porch.

Claire caught Aerin's questioning look and shrugged. "She's our sister. We have to help her." She grabbed the closest squirming body and tried to ignore the feel of slimy scales and thick, moving muscle in her hand. As she bent to capture another, one slapped her on the bottom.

"Ow!"

Aerin blurted out a laugh, and Claire straightened to send her a glare. "Shut up and help."

"I'm sorry, but the only way I touch fish is sturgeon caviar on a toast point." She shook her head as if questioning their sanity.

"Really?" Claire couldn't resist the temptation. She picked up the fish that had landed on her and tossed it at Aerin. Her sister grimaced as the large salmon fell squarely on one of her designer shoes. Before Claire could return her laugh, another bounced off the loose bun of hair on Aerin's head.

Aerin narrowed her gaze as though plotting a counter-attack. "You'll pay for that."

She lost her ability to execute her plan when more bodies began to pelt both of them. Sounds of screeching seagulls filled the air as the fish falling from the skies increased exponentially with each second.

"Help me," Moira called, tears in her eyes. "I can't do this myself."

Claire immediately shifted back to business. Surprisingly, Moira's emotions were enough to spur Aerin into action as well.

A moment later, Tierra came toting an aluminum basin. "I'll get the hose and fill it."

"Don't worry 'bout that. I've got it covered." Moira moved her lips in a silent prayer, and the skies opened above them. Rain and fish poured down on them like a vicious hailstorm. Only the fish were much bigger than hailstones, and a direct hit hurt like hell.

They scrambled to grab as many fish as they could and stuff them into the basin, even as the birds continued to deluge them.

"We need to figure out a way to stop the seagulls," Tierra called over the cacophony as she pushed sodden hair from her face.

Aerin snatched a salmon out of the air as she straightened and tossed it toward the mounding pile. "Oh, balls. Why didn't I think of that? I've got this one, sisters."

She lifted a finger and twirled it, whispering into the misty air.

Leaves in the surrounding trees rustled as though Aerin had roused the spirits inside them. Twigs and rose petals joined in the dance, swirling about them. Seconds later, the heavens screamed as the atmosphere shifted and swept powerful gusts of air toward the open water of the Puget Sound.

Claire could barely maintain her stance as Aerin's wind turned Moira's rain into stinging pelts, the force of it nearly knocking her over.

She knelt to the ground and helped cover the pile of fish along with Tierra and Moira. Frightened expressions marked their faces, and Claire grasped their hands. "We'll deal with this together."

Aerin conjured gale force winds for a good five minutes, knocking birds and fish out of the sky. When she stopped, the world came to a halt as an eerie silence cloaked them. They all glanced toward the skies and then at each other with wide eyes.

"Are they gone?" Aerin whispered.

"I think so." Tierra stood, her hair plastered to her face, her normally flowing skirt a sodden mess.

Soft sobs came from Moira's direction, her shoulders shaking as she wept. Claire scooted closer, wrapping an arm around her. "It's okay. They've stopped."

Moira lifted her gaze, black tears streaking her lovely face. "Why would the Horsemen do that? Hurt my babies like that? Isn't it enough that they're trying to kill us? Why hurt these poor creatures?"

"I don't know," Claire said softly as she took in the devastation covering their back lawn. "But look around. We saved most of the fish. There's no time for crying. We need to get them back to the Sound."

"We can't go out there." Fear burned in Tierra's eyes. "We're too vulnerable."

Claire met her gaze. "I'm not afraid. They might be some big, badass men, but look around. We're not average women."

"That's right." Aerin inhaled deeply, still looking like she owned the world despite her dripping clothes. "We're powerful witches. According to the prophecy, we're capable of ending the world, *so don't fuck with us*."

A tentative smile lit Moira's face as she glanced at each of her sisters. "Thank you."

"We'll all go." Tierra caught their enthusiasm and stood a little taller.

"Except you," Claire added, which flipped Tierra's smile to a pout.

"Yeah." Aerin sent her a commiserating look. "Momma and the kid need to stay safe at home."

Tierra rolled her eyes. "What happened to *witches powerful enough to end the world?*"

"It," Aerin answered with a disgusted sigh as she pointed toward Tierra's belly. "Kids ruin mojo every damn time."

"In fact, Moira should stay here with you." Claire glanced between the two, knowing they were both suffering from weakness at that moment which left them more vulnerable. "You can take care of each other while we get the salmon back to the Sound."

"Great idea," Aerin announced in a voice that said there would be no further discussion. "Let me change out of this mess, and we can go."

"Okay." Moira nodded in agreement as a soft rain began to fall. "I'll keep 'em wet until you get them all safely back home. Then we can bury the causalities."

"Or eat them," Tierra suggested, earning questioning looks from her sisters. "What? I'm pregnant, and I'm hungry."

Claire didn't bother to change. What would be the point? By the time they hauled that much fish back to the sea, she'd be a mess all over again.

So much for spending the afternoon practicing a spell. Perhaps that was the Horsemens' intent after all. Keep them all too busy fighting to protect themselves so they wouldn't have a chance to counter-attack. After all, Dru was a master of warfare. She'd come up against him once and won. She doubted she'd be that lucky again.

Didn't mean she wouldn't try though.

Yes. Come up against me again. Dru's voice whispered from somewhere in her head, sounding more like a sexy invitation than a challenge. Claire gritted her teeth and tried to shut out the sound. Again.

She didn't know what to make of it. Hadn't told her sisters. But ever since he'd owned her fire and she his sword, he seemed to hear and live inside her thoughts.

Couldn't really be so. She was certain it was her imagination. After all, a woman didn't have sex, even imaginary sex with a man like Drustan Geddes and remain the same afterward.

The voices were her libido talking. Nothing more.

Definitely nothing she'd ever act on. The man wanted her dead. He'd made it very clear. If she had her Fire, he was bound by some insane force to kill her. They'd never be friends like he'd promised. Certainly never lovers.

She shut down the ache inside her and concentrated on helping Moira. Then she'd focus on protecting her sisters. That's where her power lay. She'd remember and perfect that damn spell if it killed her.

❦ 2 ❦

Dru Geddes's boots crunched the twigs and dried leaves as he traversed the misty forest surrounding the obscure cabin deep in the woods outside Port Townsend, Washington. Fog shrouded the pines, wrapping him in silence and solitude. Something he sought regularly since he and the other three Horsemen had failed their missions.

Many things weighed heavy on his mind. First and foremost, Claire de Moray. Second, the fucking prophecy which proclaimed the end of the world.

Unfortunately, the two were intertwined, and, even using his most refined warfare tactics, he couldn't decipher a way to solve his dilemma. Kill the woman, or one of her sisters, which would be unforgivable in Claire's eyes, and save the world. Or save Claire and end the world.

Either way, he'd be damned. He'd never hold her in his arms again. Never know what it would be like to have her scream his name in the throes of passion as he buried himself deep inside her.

His existence might be tolerable if he could get the image of her out of his mind and the taste of her off his tongue. Worse, the sound of her out of his head and the feel of her fire out of his heart. Traces of her still burned deep inside, scars left from when he'd housed her essence.

His sword was no longer of the purest steel, honed by years of bloody battles. A woman's touch had altered the notorious blade and made it stronger.

Gods, he ached to have her do the same to him.

At times, when the world was quiet, he could hear her, experience her thoughts. Love and happiness for her newly-found sisters. Anger when she cursed him and his brothers. The soft sighs she made in her sleep he pretended he'd inspired.

Those he treasured.

When the darkness of night surrounded him, leaving him alone with his thoughts, her voice would come, and he could picture her lying next to him, fragile in sleep, stirring his desires, her fire warming his bed.

Unfortunately, when he reached out, all he found was cold sheets.

Fuck.

He sucked in a breath and increased his pace until he was full out running. His strong heart drove life-affirming blood through his body, and he filled his lungs with oxygen once again. He was alive, and so was she. Not once had he conceded a battle. Nor had he ever failed ultimately to complete a mission.

Gods be damned if he'd fail or concede this one. There had to be a way for them to be together.

If only Bane hadn't fucked up. If only he'd let Tierra die.

When the cabin came into view, Dru slowed his pace, allowing his heart rate to even out and his mind to settle. He and his fellow Horsemen had to solve their dilemma. Or someone would do it for them.

He found Nick outside, rapidly firing arrow after arrow into the trunk of a massive pine. The tree shuddered from the constant barrage.

"We've got problems," Dru said as he passed, not bothering to stop to impart further information as he continued toward the house.

Inside, Dru found Julian sitting in the leather armchair he'd claimed as his own. His eyes were closed. Dramatic classical music encompassed the silent spaces in the room, rising to a crescendo as Dru approached the stereo system. He hit the power button, bringing back the blessed silence.

Julian did not open his eyes.

"Do you really think what you've done was a wise idea, Roarke?" Dru asked.

"To what are you referring?" Julian asked, keeping his repose.

"What did he do?" Nick brought up the rear, and Dru was sure if he needed it, Nick would have his back.

"Damn pestilence and plagues," Dru nearly shouted at Julian. "I've just returned from doing recon on the witches' house. Imagine my surprise when a plague of seagulls dropped salmon bombs from the sky like they were bird shit. Appeared to be centered solely on ground zero." Dru tried to rein in his anger. "Now is not the time for petty games, Roarke. I'd like to know the expected outcome of that tactic."

Julian inhaled and straightened, pinning Dru with crystal blue eyes. "Sorry, chap. My plagues tend more toward toads and boils. Birds and fish lie in another purview altogether."

"It had to be you. Who else?"

Julian shrugged, seemingly uninterested and innocent, but Dru knew behind those eyes rested an infinite amount of knowledge and the power to wipe out entire civilizations. "Perhaps you'd care to impart more information so I might make an informed estimate," Julian replied.

"Could have been Bane." Nick grabbed an apple from the bar and claimed a seat on the leather couch.

"The Fourth Seal has been opened, bringing forth Hell and the beasts."

"Speaking of hell, where is Bane?" Dru asked. He should have been there with the rest of them trying to solve their problems. "He'd better not be out getting another piece of ass."

"He's collecting souls." Just as Nick answered, the front door opened, and Killian Bane strode in, his expression darker than the obsidian that washed up on the nearby shores.

He slammed the door behind him hard enough to rattle the paintings on the wall. "Fucking druggies. If women want to be reckless, they should be sterilized so they can't procreate."

"Another child casualty?" Julian drawled, and then smiled at the other men. "He's become so sensitive now that he's going to be a daddy."

"Fuck you," Bane spat as he headed straight for the bar.

"You've got to toughen up, Bane." Nick never could resist a good opportunity for provocation. It wasn't in his nature. "Can't have a soft spot for the kids. You need to man up. Take care of shit. Especially your own shit."

"Fuck you, too." He tossed back a shot of Silver Patrón and poured another.

Dru shook his head. "You shouldn't have intervened, Bane. Should have let them both die. The fates had interceded on our behalf, and you should have let it be. The world tried to correct itself, and you stopped it. Now who knows what kind of shit storm you've created with your selfishness."

Bane sent him a murderous look. "Don't make me take your soul, too."

"I wish you could." Dru eyed the man, understanding the depths of pain he experienced.

"The prophecy never mentioned a child." Julian

shifted, turning his pensive gaze out the window to the lush greenery surrounding them. "For all we know, it could be the spawn of Satan. A soulless wonder, to be sure."

The rest of them turned their gazes to Julian as a wave of uncertainty rolled through the room. "*Never mention her name*," Dru said.

The last thing they needed was Lucifer taking them to task for failing. She was a difficult bitch to handle on a good day.

"Dru's right." Nick spoke in lowered tones. "I'd swear the woman has listening devices planted across the universe informing her when she becomes the topic of conversation. I can't begin to imagine what would happen should she find out about Bane's offspring."

"She can't know." Bane drew his fingers through his ragged hair. "Ever."

Bingo, Dru thought. If Lucy discovered their failures, they were all doomed. "I didn't mention anything when I talked to her today. Told her we were in operations mode and that she shouldn't worry."

"If she finds out we failed, you know she'll have her hot ass down here in a second, and she'll take matters into her own hands." Nick blew out a breath in memory of his last meeting with her.

"Are you saying you wouldn't enjoy that...again?" Julian lifted a sarcastic brow. "Perhaps you should have used more discretion when dealing with the Devil."

Nick snorted. "Perhaps you should have fucked her and then you wouldn't still be a virgin. Beware the scorned woman."

Bane's expression turned tortured. "She'll kill them. All of them."

"Isn't that the ultimate goal here?" Julian asked. "To end this nightmarish Apocalypse?"

"They don't *all* have to die," Dru reminded them. "Only one."

"It's not going to be Tierra." Bane shot a glance at each of them, daring them to challenge him.

"Arguing is getting us nowhere, gentlemen." Julian regarded them with quiet disdain. "We need to find a way to stop the women from opening another seal and ending the world, all before incurring *her* wrath."

"You're right." Dru released a sigh heavy with frustration. "If she comes to Port Townsend, we're all screwed. We need to formulate an infallible plan."

His brothers murmured their agreement as he reached for the crystal bowl sitting on the mantelpiece and grabbed a handful of the tiny cinnamon candies and poured them into his mouth. The flavor sizzled against his tongue, bringing him a measure of reassurance.

"What's with the candies?" Nick asked with a condescending look.

"I thought you didn't pollute your body with that garbage."

"Yeah, that's what I thought, too." But he hadn't been able to deny the recent incessant craving.

❧ 3 ❧

Claire sat in a melon-colored Adirondack chair on the wide porch, staring toward the Puget Sound. Precious sun rained down on the hillside town for once, and she soaked it up like a dwindling fire inhaling fresh oxygen.

Below, in the yard, Tierra knelt near the holly, planting who knew what in the garden. The scene was far too domestic to be comfortable, and Claire itched to get on her motorcycle and let the glorious rays fall down on her. She hadn't ridden it nearly enough since they'd opened the Fourth Seal and all hell had broken loose; not to mention, her vitamin D levels had bottomed out.

She needed to escape before she went crazy.

She jumped to her feet and joined Tierra. "I'm going to see if I can find some more of those blueberry leaves. We used them all when we created that protective spell we put around the house, and I'm sure that's what is missing in the potion I tried to make the other day."

Tierra lifted a haughty brow. "Would that be the day you broke my favorite vase?"

Claire gave her a guilty smile. "Sorry. I didn't think you'd miss it. You have so many."

She climbed to her feet and dusted dirt from her

hands. "Excuse me? You didn't think I'd miss one of my babies? I know exactly how many I have and where each of them is placed in the house."

Aw, shit. "I just insulted you, didn't I? I'm so sorry. I didn't mean to disrespect what's important to you."

A grin broke over Tierra's face. "Okay. I didn't really miss it. Aerin told me—"

"*She what?*" Claire would be having words with that girl.

"That it was an accident. She apologized on your behalf. Said you were trying to remember a spell that would help us."

Claire worked to calm the residual emotion from her reaction. Learning to live with three women when she'd been isolated her entire life because of her affinity to Fire had its challenges. "I think I almost have it, and I can't sit around waiting for something to happen. We need to prepare now for future possibilities. I think I can figure it out, but I believe I need leaves."

"There are some wild ones growing near the rocks out by the old barracks." Tierra paused, worry settling in her expression. "I don't know if it's a good idea for you to go, though. Especially alone. Take Moira or Aerin with you."

Tierra had finally accepted it wasn't safe for her to leave the protection of the house. Not if she wanted to ensure her and her unborn baby's life.

"I'll be fine." As much as Claire loved her sisters, she found, at times, she craved the solitude she'd cursed all those years. "I'm just going to make a quick run on my bike. I'll zip up the street and over. No one will see me coming or going."

Tierra's expression remained uncertain, but Claire could sense her acquiescence.

"Really," she pressed. "I'll be back in thirty minutes or less."

"Okay, but take one of the fabric bags I made. It

won't suffocate the plants like plastic will. There are some in the garage."

"Sure," Claire said with a smile. Anything to appease her sister. "See you soon."

She stopped long enough to snag a bag from storage and headed straight for her bike. She didn't need the other two tossing out opposition for her going alone. It wasn't as though they could all do a spell together anyway should something bad happen. If they did, they might end up busting open another disastrous seal, bringing them that much closer to the Apocalypse. Whatever came her way, if anything, she'd handle it alone.

If she died trying? Well, then all their problems were solved, and her sisters could live a peaceful life without her. In all reality, it might be worth the sacrifice.

The anticipation of having heated power between her legs left her giddy. She zipped up her leather jacket and straddled the beast she'd secretly named War. If she couldn't have the man, she'd settle for this magnificent machine. Her bike was more trustworthy anyway and didn't have a desire to bring about her death.

As she backed out of the drive, she spotted Aerin frowning at her through the window. She gave her a quick wave as Aerin leaned out and then shifted her bike into gear, letting a spray of gravel kick up behind her. She knew her sister had a few choice words to say, but damn it, she needed freedom.

Warm sun soaked through her black leather and caressed her shoulders. She inhaled, enjoying the feel of her hair flowing behind her. She should have grabbed the helmet from her room, but there hadn't been time. Besides, with the end of the world resting on her shoulders, she had more important things to worry about.

She constantly flicked her gaze to her rearview mirror, very aware of anyone or anything that might have followed her as she headed up the hill. So far, nothing. Those Horsemen, as tough as they liked to think they were, couldn't be everywhere at once. So, she'd take the gift of aloneness and enjoy the hell out of it.

She parked her bike in the camping area at the Fort Worden State Park and hid it among the large pines before hiking her way to the bluff overlooking the bay. Soft yellow grasses danced in the breeze coming off the water as a few fluffy clouds drifted across the blue sky. She found the wild blueberries exactly where Tierra had said, and she bent, cutting them with a pocketknife she'd found in the house.

Someone had carved curious runes on the blade, and she'd received a weird, electric vibe from it when she'd picked it up. So, she'd claimed it. It wasn't like Tierra would bother tracking a knife anyway. She'd already explained that whatever was in the house belonged to all four of them. Family heirlooms, so to speak.

Weird, that. Having a family, having sisters who loved her and watched her back. It was a feeling she could definitely grow used to. Their love and acceptance conjured a warmth inside her that had nothing to do with her power.

With her task completed, Claire turned to retrace her steps toward her bike, but halted instead. A small red fox blocked in her path, staring at her with beautiful gray eyes. Claire inhaled a surprised breath, not sure if she should be afraid or not.

Suddenly, a steady stream of energy filled her like she'd not experienced before. Powerfully intense, but filled with love and compassion. On some unknown level, the fox reached out to her, and she wanted to respond in kind.

"Hello," she said as she crouched to its level. The

fox lifted its slender nose, sniffing the air. Claire held out a hand to indicate a desire for friendship.

The fox hesitated and then stood, its white-tipped tail unfurling behind it. With cautious steps, it approached. Claire waited while it sniffed her, its black leather nose wet against her fingertips. Then it rubbed its face against her, its fur warm against her hand.

"Oh..." she said on a sigh, delighting in the shared energy. She had the distinct impression he was a male.

"You are adorable." She ran her fingers down the flame-colored fur on his back and over his huge fluffy tail.

You're mine.

The thought came to Claire on the breeze, and she tilted her head. "Did you say that?" Foxes couldn't speak, any more than...

You're mine, and I am yours. The fox stared deeply into her eyes, sending a shiver racing over her.

She was well-accustomed to familiars by now. Each of her sisters had theirs. Tierra loved Jinx, the typical black cat famous in the lore for accompanying witches. There was Cheeto, of course, Moira's sweet little pig, and Aerin's bat, Lecter. Claire had just assumed the goddesses hadn't granted one to her.

But now...maybe so.

Claire stood and took several steps toward her bike as she glanced over her shoulder. The little fox trotted after her, his tail waving as he walked. She stopped. He stopped. She continued until she reached her bike, and he followed her the entire way.

As she straddled her motorcycle, the fox walked in front of her, stopping inches from her front tire. He glanced up at her as though to inform her she wasn't leaving without him. His gray eyes held steady until she laughed.

"Well, come on then." She patted the seat in front of her.

He didn't hesitate to race forward and jump. His back claws found purchase on her jeans as he climbed his way onto her seat. He settled his warm body between her legs and laid his head on her thigh.

"I'll be damned," she whispered, petting him between his ears. "Hang on tight...Kai." The name popped into her head. Kai, Scottish for *fire*. Perfect for a fire witch's red fox.

She started her bike and headed toward the house. When she was a block away, a cloying, depressive feeling clouded her. She couldn't go home. Not yet. She needed more freedom. More time with her little fox, and he seemed to be doing just fine riding on her bike.

Instead of going home, she headed toward the outskirts of town where she could open up the throttle and really fly. She infused her engine with fuel, skipping down the middle of the road, passing cars if they moved too slow. Kai gripped her with his claws, but not hard enough to hurt, and she was careful not to do anything drastic that might cause him to lose his seat.

When she'd released her excess energy, she pulled to the side of the road long enough to send her sisters a text, letting them know she'd be home soon. She needed space, but wouldn't make them worry.

Back in town, she eyed the street that led to their lovely Victorian home, but didn't slow or turn. More blocks of shops and structures flew past before she found herself in the quaint downtown area of Water Street. Brick buildings constructed back in the 1850s popped up around her, making her smile. Despite the pervasive misty weather, something about this town owned her. She'd definitely come home.

From the corner of her eye, she spotted a tall, dark-haired man approaching the doorway that led to Sirens Pub. Sizzling energy ripped through her. She'd know those muscles and that sexy walk anywhere. Dru.

The moment she thought his name, he stopped and

turned as though she'd called to him. Their eyes locked for an intense moment, stealing her breath. Then he blinked and focused on her fox. His expression grew darker as he narrowed his gaze.

"Shit," she hissed. She nailed the throttle on her bike and zipped around a corner, taking her away from the very one she desired and the deadly threat he posed.

A smart witch would hightail her ass home after a close encounter like that.

Then again, Claire always thought *smart* paled in comparison to sexy or dangerous.

Feeling brave, she circled around, slowly descending the quiet street again until she caught sight of Sirens' entrance. Disappointment and relief filled her. Dru was gone. He'd headed inside, maybe to meet with his brothers. If so, she may have stumbled upon the perfect scenario in which to spy.

Her sisters would be angry if they knew, but someone had to start fighting back. If they intended to win this battle, they couldn't be on the defensive the entire time.

Excitement pulsed through her as she parked her bike in an obscure spot behind a business. "You should stay here. Stay hidden," she murmured to Kai.

When he'd crouched down in a nearby clump of tall grass, she hurried to make her way across the street before anyone who might pose a threat could spot her. She peeked inside the glass door on the first floor below Sirens.

The entrance was empty.

Quietly, she opened the door and slipped inside. The stairs leading upward provided a few vulnerable moments, but she hurried and made her way toward the bar. As she neared the hallway, her heart stopped.

A window provided the perfect view into the back-room of the bar.

Death, Pestilence, Conquest. Where was—
"Looking for someone?"

Claire whirled around to find Dru, his dark gaze boring into hers like black nails into a coffin.

❧ 4 ❧

Claire fought to retain her composure. *Sweet Goddess in the heavens,* Drustan looked breathtakingly fine. His black, form-fitting t-shirt outlined pecs and biceps in tantalizing detail. Ripped jeans barely contained his powerful thighs, while sturdy military boots completed his ensemble. She didn't know of one woman who could see him and not want him. Certainly not her.

A dark shadow underscored his mesmerizing eyes leaving him with a haunted look that only made him sexier.

Claire took a step back, coming up hard against the window frame. She couldn't help but remember the last time he'd had her against a wall and the full-blown sensory onslaught that had followed. Even if he'd only conjured their intimacy, their encounter was still real in her mind. She could taste him, feel the exquisite sensations of his mouth on her breasts, his...

She blinked and refocused her gaze, wondering if he'd tried to seduce her again just now. A slow smile curved his lips, tightening her insides. He closed his eyes for a moment, and then nodded as though he could somehow sense her reaction to him.

"Stop it," she whispered. She drew her tongue across her bottom lip, searching for moisture. Dru caught the movement, watching her as though he'd pull her into his arms at any moment and kiss her. The idea intrigued and scared her at the same time.

"You look good." His deep voice slid over her senses like satin against her skin.

"No thanks to you." As much as she ached for him, she harbored serious resentment for what he'd done.

"I wouldn't have taken your Fire, you know, had I not thought you'd survive." His gaze drifted lower, down her neck toward her breasts. "I trusted sources when I shouldn't have."

Could he really have been concerned?

She raised a hand to her throat, certain he'd caressed her. But he hadn't moved.

Another skill of his.

"Liar," she said in a low voice. "Everything you've told me is a lie. Everything you've shown me is, too." She needed to remember the hard truth of that.

"No, Claire." Unexpected pain radiated from him, giving her a surprising slap. "I would have found another way had I known what it would do. You can't imagine what it was like to see you lying there..." Her heart inched toward him, her Fire urging her to forgive.

Traitor, she thought with a hiss. "I want to know what you've done to my power. Did your source tell about that as well? It was pure when you took it. It's not the same now. You've tainted my essence." The rawness, usually so apparent, had been soothed. *By his presence*, she realized. Molded by something older and stronger than her powers.

Feeling suddenly vulnerable, she glanced around, wondering if she'd make it to the stairwell before he caught her. Leaving the house unescorted had been a bad idea at best. Following him inside the building, walking straight into his trap for all she knew, may have been a deadly mistake.

"'Taint' is a harsh word, Claire." He took a step toward her, his body coming up hard against hers, leaving her no room to run.

His thighs molded to hers. Heat swirled, combining with an energy source radiating from him that she didn't remember from before. Familiar, yet masculine. Hot, potent masculinity that she ached to climb all over. But, upon their last encounter, she'd discovered her seductive powers didn't work on him.

She tried to breathe, but each attempt pressed her leather jacket tighter against his chest. Having him so close stole more of her oxygen, leaving her trapped in a vicious cycle.

He dropped his gaze to the swell of her breasts, and she couldn't help but inhale. "I have a theory, love."

"What? What theory?" She slipped her hands between them and flattened her palms against his chest, trying to focus on his words instead of the excitement and pleasure he generated inside her. They'd had such a short time together before the world had collapsed around them. Damn him. Damn this whole prophecy.

She shoved against him, but he didn't budge.

Slippery heat welled inside her, quickening her pulse. "I need to go." Run before he completely owned her.

He lifted a hand and traced a finger down her cheek. "You don't want to hear my theory?" She shook her head.

He stilled her movements by cupping her chin. Heat licked at her skin, and she fought to retain her current focus. "You scarred me," he said fiercely. "With your Fire. It burned a hole deep in my heart. Left traces of you inside me."

"No." She couldn't, wouldn't accept that. Her Fire was hers alone.

He leaned close, his lips a breath away. "I feel you," he whispered.

"Always. I hear you in my head. I want to touch you and take you..."

Her brain screamed for her to knee him in the nuts again and run, but this time, her heart, bolstered by the power of fire, firmly had control.

Her lips sparked when he brushed his mouth against hers, igniting a scorching sizzle that rushed through her. Cinnamon on his tongue burned her mouth as he teased his way inside. She wished to refuse him entrance, but she couldn't get past how much she wanted him. How much she ached for this.

She lifted a hand to stop his sweet assault, but instead of pushing him away, she slipped her fingers over his exquisitely carved chest and up the corded muscles of his neck.

He fisted his hands into her hair, bending her further to his will. She allowed it. Craved it within the depths of her soul.

Something inside her recognized him. Yearned for him more than life.

Horsemen, sisters, curses faded into the background as he wove a web of delicious desire around her. Crimson need turned black. She melted against him, shoving her resistance into a dark closet somewhere in the back her mind. Her body warmed and softened, and something powerfully older than time awakened inside her.

"Is this real?" she whispered when they parted for air.

He caught her gaze, his penetrating deep into her soul. God, he could have her so easily, she realized. Right here, right now. Anywhere, any time.

"It's real, Claire. This is as real as it gets." His eyes promised he spoke the truth, but an unwanted grain of doubt reminded her she'd believed him once before. He cupped her face and claimed her mouth, washing away any objections she might have had.

"*What the fuck?*" he said as he jerked away from her and glanced downward.

Surprised, Claire followed the direction he'd flung his curse and found Kai with his teeth firmly implanted in Dru's pants. He lifted a hand to strike.

"*No*. Stop!" Claire screamed as she dropped to her knees, pulling Kai protectively against her and away from Dru. She closed her eyes and braced for impact, but it never came.

"*Claire*." Dru pulled her to her feet, and she clung to her little fox. His gaze darkened as the sound of others approaching drew her attention. The rest of the Horsemen breached the exit of Sirens and advanced rapidly.

"*Is this what I fear it is?*" he asked as though she'd somehow betrayed him. He held her with a powerful grip. "Your familiar?"

Fear exploded inside her. She couldn't get away. Not from all of them.

Kai squirmed in her arms. They would hurt him too, she realized. If Kai truly was her familiar, he'd be a threat once she learned how to use him to enhance her powers. She jerked in Dru's grasp trying to get away.

When she failed, Kai stiffened, the fur on his tail fanning out in a beautiful plume. A shockwave followed. Dru dropped her and reached for the wall to steady himself as the other Horsemen did the same. Sounds of breaking glass filled the air with dramatic reverberations, and she froze.

Silence ensued. The men glared at her with murderous gazes as her heart thundered in her chest.

Run. The deep voice flooded her mind, stirring her into action. She flicked a quick glance at Dru. Couldn't tell if he'd warned her or not. But now was not the time to discover the truth.

She gripped Kai as she turned and raced down the stairs. A couple of masculine curses followed from behind, but she didn't slow to see who followed.

She burst out the front door on the lower level and collided with a woman. The impact knocked her to her ass. Kai scrambled from her, racing across the street, barely escaping screeching tires.

"Sorry," Claire said as she scrambled to her feet, surprised the collision hadn't knocked them both down.

The woman's carefully outlined, red lips turned into a patient smile as she brushed pretend dirt from her full-length black leather coat. Her skin was smooth and radiant like a cultured pearl, and everything about her screamed refined luxury. "Do be careful, love. You could get injured."

Claire glanced over the woman's shoulder to ensure none of the Horsemen were about to bust outside. "I'm sorry. I hope I didn't hurt you."

The woman snorted, a dismissive glint firing in icy blue eyes fringed by the longest lashes Claire had seen. "As if." She tossed luxurious blond curls over her shoulder as she turned toward the entrance to Sirens and left a cloud of highly sensual perfume in her wake.

Claire couldn't begin to form words to describe their encounter, so she turned and ran instead. She found Kai pacing the ground near her bike, and he glanced up with a startled expression when she approached.

Utter fear emanated from him, sending shivers coursing through her. Had the Horsemen scared him that badly? He hadn't seemed fearful in the hallway. In fact, she distinctly remembered experiencing his power and satisfaction as Kai had knocked down the Horsemen. Something had certainly set him off, though. Maybe it was a delayed reaction to using his surprising, awesome powers.

Either way, they both needed to get the hell off

Water Street and back to the safety of home. She straddled her bike and Kai jumped on her lap before she had the chance to invite him. His little body quaked against her as she fired up her engine, threw her bike into gear, and raced toward home.

D ru ducked as Nick threw a heavy fist in his direction. Nick clipped him on the side of the jaw, and Dru immediately retaliated with a similar attack. He missed his mark when he lost his focus while trying to trip Bane as he attempted to pass them in the hall outside Sirens.

Dru cussed as he fought to regain his position, stumbling, but managing to keep anyone from leaving the area. He had to stall them long enough to allow Claire to escape. They wouldn't hesitate to kill her if they caught her.

"What the *fuck* is your problem?" Nick slammed Dru into the same wall where he'd previously held Claire.

"I don't have a fucking problem." Dru shoved back, sending Nick barreling into Bane.

Julian's dry laugh mocked the three of them, effectively bringing their antics to a halt.

"What's so funny?" Bane asked.

"Don't you see? Dru's trying to protect his witch. The woman who stole his valiant sword along with his testicles."

Dru rounded on him. "Don't tell me you wouldn't do the same damn thing if we were after Aerin."

Julian scoffed. "If my memory serves me right, I'm the only one who actually carried out my task. I infected Aerin and fully expected her to die. How was I to anticipate she'd be the only person in the entire history of the universe who is immune to my touch?"

"Wait a second." Nick puffed out his chest. "I fully intended to pierce Moira with my arrow. It's not my fault Tierra stepped in front of it."

"I'm still going to fuck you up for that, Kingswood," Bane said.

You almost killed her and my—"

"*Boys.*"

The sultry, smooth sound of Lucy's voice brought terror into his friends' eyes. Dru inhaled and prepared to meet the one woman he feared.

He turned to find Satan walking slowly toward them, a smile on her ruby red lips, her long, leather coat unable to hide the sensual sway of her hips. Four-inch black heels accentuated her long, slender legs, and it was hard to tell, even with the deep vee of her coat, if she wore anything underneath or not.

Her lips turned into an inviting smile, and she cocked one brow as she approached him. "Drustan." His name slid off her lips like buttered rum.

"Lucy." He braced himself.

She wrapped one arm around his neck, pressing her abundant breasts against his chest. Her skin was flawless, like that of an angel, a contradiction to her soul. "It's good to see you." She pulled his face toward hers, and he caught the familiar scent of sweet candy a second before her lips touched his.

He endured her kiss, knowing what would happen if he rejected her. When she finished, she backed up, taking a moment to run her palm down his chest. "Mmm...cinnamon." She ran a wet tongue over her bottom lip. "You were my favorite, you know."

Nick coughed. "That's what you said to *me* last time."

She turned with a flourish, and Dru wiped his mouth as he watched the expression on Nick's face, knowing he immediately regretted his statement.

"Oh, Nicholas, darling. I'll never forget those lovely days we spent together. Some of my best, really." She repeated the kiss she'd given Dru before cupping his manhood. "Still a big boy, I see. But have you learned how to use it yet?"

Bane and Dru both snorted. Lucy laughed with them, drawing a bigger frown from Nick.

"Fuck all of you. That was a millennium ago." Nick started to leave, but she held up a hand.

"Not so fast. We have things to discuss, but first, I need to finish saying hello." Lucy glanced over her shoulder toward Bane.

"You'd better kiss me now, my dearest, sweetest death."

She forced him to walk to her, and while she kissed him, she reached around and firmly grabbed his ass. As she pulled away, Bane gave Dru and Nick a death glare.

"What have you been up to, Death? My sources tell me you've spilled the blood of a virgin witch, but I don't see that we have a soul to account for it." She said it as though he'd earned straight A's in school and yet failed to produce the report card.

Bane widened his eyes, and a palpable silence fell over the hallway.

"Perhaps because her blood was spilled as he absconded with her virtue, but not her soul." Julian leaned away from the wall and stepped forward.

The four of them held their breath and watched while Lucy processed the information. Julian had offered the perfect save, but would she buy it?

Her raucous laugh was over the top as far as reactions went, but more than welcome. "Well, isn't that divine? Was it everything you expected, my love? I do wonder why you'd want someone so inexperienced when you know you can call me any time."

Bane attempted to smile as he acknowledged her offer with a nod, but he wisely remained silent. Lucy watched him for a moment, and Dru prayed he'd keep his composure. One wrong look, one wrong thought, and the four of them would have hell to pay.

Literally.

She sighed and fixed her gaze on Julian. Instead of kissing him like she had the others, she sized him up with seductive eyes. "And what about you, my love?" she asked softly. "Have you reconsidered after all this time? Wouldn't you like to know what you're missing? One night with me, and I would grant you the power to have all the women you want, and not a single one of them would need to die from your touch."

Julian kept his gaze even and devoid of emotion, his smoking jacket giving the appearance of a man of leisure instead of one under fire. He stared at her, but didn't speak. All four of them had learned many millennia ago that she could and would use any words they spoke as weapons against them, if she chose.

"Certainly your virginity can't mean that much to you. In addition, it's been a desperately long time since I've had the pleasure of a new toy." She batted long eyelashes at him as she undid the top button on her coat, further exposing her voluptuous breasts. At least she wore a dress underneath. "One night out of the millennia you've been alive? It's not so much to ask, and I promise you won't regret it."

Julian's gaze slipped to Dru and then back to Lucy. He and Julian had had many conversations concerning the influence Lucy held over them. Personally, Dru hadn't minded the fuck, may have even enjoyed it, but Lucifer held a power strong enough to destroy a mortal man with just a glance if she chose. Fucking her had given him the strength to carry out his toughest missions, but damned if he didn't feel like he'd lost something of himself in the process.

Bane and Nick had agreed, and Dru couldn't help but wonder what would happen if she was able to tap into all four of their powers.

Out of all of them, Julian had been the strongest, refusing to succumb to her persuasion. He'd also suffered the most because of it.

No sex for thousands of years was a price no man should have to pay.

Julian moved forward, stopping within inches of Lucy. He studied her with a heavy-lidded, feral gaze. Excitement sparked in Lucy's eyes. She practically salivated, and Dru feared she'd win this time. Dru could only imagine the restraint Julian would require to turn her down once again, especially now that Aerin had caught his attention.

God knew, if given the chance, Dru intended to follow Bane's footsteps and make love with Claire. If the situation wasn't so dire, he would have cracked a joke about it. Hell, who would believe War would rather make love with a woman than fight?

Julian inhaled a deep breath and released it as though he'd made his decision. "Sadly madam, I shall have to decline once again."

The floor rumbled beneath their feet as a blast of Lucy's fiery disposition blew past them. His brothers held steady, knowing they couldn't defeat her, but also knowing she despised fear.

Then she snorted and turned a shoulder. "So it shall be, but know this my dear, virtuous horseman, I'm not one to trifle with. I can destroy you with a flick of my pinkie. The curse continues. If I can't have you, then no one shall."

Dru wanted to remind her she needed them to carry out the Prophecy and therefore couldn't destroy them, but it didn't seem like the time or place to piss her off any further. As if there ever was such a time or place.

She turned and fluttered her eyelashes. "Now that the niceties are over, I need a drink. Come sit with me, boys, and tell me everything you've been doing. I have no idea how you'll ever explain how four of the seven seals came to be opened, but it should be a delicious story to hear. Drustan, you may buy me the first drink."

CLAIRE'S HEART STILL POUNDED LIKE AN ANCIENT WAR drum when she pulled into the driveway and parked her motorcycle under the protective awning of their stately Victorian home. She stroked Kai's fur to reassure him he was safe, and she was surprised to find he'd stopped shaking.

"Are you all right, little fella?"

He jumped from the seat and trotted toward the front porch as though he owned the place, his tail swaying in the breeze. Claire noted his quick change in demeanor as she swung her leg over the bike, still puzzling over his earlier fright.

The front door opened, and Moira peered out. "Oh, my gawd. If that ain't cuter than a bug's behind. Just look at his adorable little face and that fluffy tail."

Claire smiled as she approached the porch, glad to see her familiar would be accepted into his new home.

"You come right on in." Moira held the door for Kai, but the second Claire ascended the steps, Moira stepped outside and slammed it shut behind her. She fixed an angry gaze on Claire. "*You* can sleep outside in the doghouse tonight for makin' all us worry about your sorry ass." She folded her arms beneath her breasts, looking like she might seriously put up a fight in order to keep Claire out.

Perhaps humor might defuse the situation. "We don't have a doghouse."

"Then I guess you better start building one unless you like sleepin' under the stars. I'm sure there's some lumber back there somewhere from when the guys busted down our house and we had to have those hot dudes come fix it."

Claire sighed. "Moira, come on. I'm sorry I ran out. I just need some alone time."

Moira snorted. "That weak shit ain't gonna fly with me, honey. You know we're all in danger any time we leave this house, and yet you just slide right outta here like a greased hen."

"Seriously. Things have been getting to me, messing with my head, and I needed some time to clear it." Dru's voice constantly haunting her thoughts for one. Was he right? Did they still own a part of each other?

God, could he hear her now?

Moira didn't budge.

"I found my familiar," Claire offered with a hopeful smile. She needed to get inside, needed to tell all her sisters what she'd learned.

"I already saw that, and he's already inside. So try again."

Claire shifted her stance, growing impatient. "Fine. I spied on the

Horsemen."

Moira widened her eyes. "*You what?* What did they say? Where were they?"

Finally. "I'm not going to tell you anything until you let me in."

Her sister narrowed her gaze, and Claire knew she'd won. "Okay, but don't think this gets you off the hook. You're on my shit list until notified otherwise."

Claire gave her a brief hug before passing her and entering the house. "Where are Tierra and Aerin? We all need to have a sit-down and discuss a few things.

Those guys sure aren't wasting any time plotting against us, and we need to have some countermeasures in place."

"Yes, we do," Moira said as she shut the door behind them and followed Claire upstairs.

Claire smiled, remembering how alone she used to feel before she'd met her sisters. Now, she couldn't picture life without them.

$\maltese$ 6 $\maltese$

Dru eyed each of his brother Horsemen as they sat in the dim backroom of Sirens Pub, all of them sharing the same concerned look. Lucy had taken her leave several moments before, but her threats remained along with her heady perfume. "Just because she's gone doesn't mean we're off the hook. You all know as well as I do she'll stick around and eventually figure things out."

"We need to take action." Nick loosened his tie and opened the first button on his gray silk shirt. "Enough of this bullshit arguing over whose witch will die. Here's the deal, and you're all going to sign off on it. The first witch any of us comes in contact with forfeits her life."

"Except—"

"*No.*" Nick slammed his fist on the wooden table, cutting off Bane's reply. "There will be no exceptions. You heard Lucy. We end this now. We have one commitment to fulfill, one reason to justify our existence. That fifth seal *cannot* be opened."

Dru and Bane shared a look, a silent reaffirmation that, if possible, neither of them would kill Claire or Tierra.

"Don't fuck with me," Nick said, catching the interaction. "We must all agree on this. You know the consequences of our failure."

"This is what we were born to do, gentlemen," Julian added. "A blood oath cannot be ignored."

Dru clenched his jaw, fighting to impart what he knew he must, knowing what his utterance would do to his reputation. "I am unable to kill Claire."

"You're a pussy, Drustan Geddes," Nick countered, disgust registering in his gaze. "What the hell happened to you?"

"*Fuck you.*" Dru stood, his heart thundering louder than the sound of his chair banging against the wall behind him. "It's *not* that I am unwilling. You and I have stood back-to-back through many battles. You know me." He placed a fisted hand over his heart. "The witch left a piece of her Fire burning inside me. I feel it still, and it has rendered me useless when I come up against her."

Julian snorted. "I have no such failures and will have no problem giving her or any of the others the kiss of death if need be."

Bane coughed.

"Oh, Jesus." Nick turned his repulsed gaze to Death. "You, too?"

The Taker of Souls raked a hand through his hair. "Tierra carries my seed."

A hint of derision lit Julian's pale eyes. "'Tis fortunate Lucy took her leave several minutes ago. Fortunate still, that two of us have not been rendered impotent."

Dru couldn't take another hit on his manhood. "Fuck you, Roarke.

You'd better hope it's not your witch who crosses my path first because I'll have no problem slicing her scrawny Fifth Avenue neck."

Julian arched a brow but didn't respond.

"*Enough.*" Nick spoke loud enough to draw the attention back to him. "One of the four has to die. The sooner, the better. I want concrete plans in place before sundown."

Bane tossed back his shot of tequila and stood. "I don't need plans. I need action. I'm going to find me a witch right now, and put an end to this once and for all. Then you can all get...off...my...*ass*." He strode from the room, the outline of wings showing through his white t-shirt.

Dru slumped back into his chair, wrapping a fist around a blessed shot of Johnny Walker Red. May the Gods help their damned souls. Either way, he feared an eternity of hell awaited them.

"I DON'T FEEL RIGHT LEAVING YOU ALONE IN THE house," Claire said as Tierra shooed her, Aerin and Moira toward the front door.

"I'll be fine," Tierra said. "We have this place locked down tighter than Knox. If not, you know as well as I do the Horsemen would have attacked again. Things have been quiet, and Goddess knows someone needs to attend to the teashop. Sunny has been a sweetheart taking care of things, but I can tell from her voice she needs time off."

"Tierra's right," Aerin said as she donned a full-length overcoat to shield her linen suit from the softly falling rain that had seeped from the skies during the past few days. "No one will protect our investments like we will. Stop being so frightened of everything. We're never going to win this fucking war otherwise. I have our website ready to launch. I know we need to do inventory, plus check our financials, which were shit before I came along. It's a wonder you made any money, Tierra."

Tierra frowned. "Everything in life isn't about money, Aerin.

Sometimes it's about helping people."

"Nothin' wrong with helpin' people," Moira chimed in.

Aerin snorted. "Don't fool yourselves. At the end of the day, it's always about the money." She threw open the door and stepped outside without looking back.

Claire shrugged and smiled. "What can I say? At least one of us has good business sense."

Tierra shook her head but returned Claire's gesture. "I suppose.

Either way, I do love her."

"We all do." Moira gave Tierra a quick hug. "You be sure to call us if'n anything strange or crazy starts happenin'. Don't question, just call, okay?"

"I'll be fine. It's you three that could be in danger." Tierra gave them both a small gauzy fabric pouch filled with herbs. "Angelica. For protection. Take one for Aerin, too. Hide it in her fancy handbag if she won't take it, okay?"

Claire accepted her sister's gifts with gratitude. Despite their differences, she could never deny the compelling, endearing bond between them.

A few moments and less than a mile later, Aerin parked Tierra's Prius in the alley near their teashop. They lived close enough to walk to the shop, but they were less of a target if they drove.

First on their agenda would be to ward their business against threats as well. It would be more difficult to protect, considering they had to allow the public to enter, but Moira had come up with something that would diminish any negative attacks, much like pouring water on fighting cats.

"Make sure y'all stay close," Moira said as they exited the vehicle. "I don't know if you've noticed none or not, but even if we ain't doing spells together, my powers seem stronger when y'all are nearby."

"I've sensed that, too." Claire had taken a great amount of reassurance in that fact.

"Agreed." Aerin linked arms with her sisters, and the three of them hurried around the corner and down the sidewalk toward their shop. The smart and savvy sister might not like to admit weakness, but she wasn't a fool, either. Claire respected her for that.

Claire eyed a scraggly man seated on the damp cement sidewalk, his back against the red brick of one of the downtown shops. His hair grew in a lanky, unkempt mess, complemented by stained jeans and a thin, once-white sweatshirt. He held a cardboard sign in his hands, but didn't look up as they approached.

"Since when has Port Townsend had panhandlers on the streets?" She hadn't lived in the quaint seaport village for long, but this was a new experience for her.

Aerin shrugged. "There's hunger everywhere, Claire. This is nothing new."

"I'll be a dog's conkers. His sign says *Hungry, Hungry Hobos*," Moira whispered with a snicker.

Aerin snorted and rolled her eyes. "He deserves a Jackson for being so creative." She slipped her wallet from her bag and stopped in front of him. Before she could retrieve a twenty-dollar bill, the beggar reached out and wrapped dirty fingers around Aerin's ankle.

"*Give me your soul.*" Icy blue eyes glanced over the three of them, sending a fright through Claire. Familiar, yet alien.

"Let go before I crush your balls." Aerin kicked, dislodging her foot. "How dare you?" Fear echoed through her words.

The man cackled a laugh and then fell into a coughing fit as he bent over.

Claire grasped her sister's arm in a protective gesture, prepared to slip her favorite dagger from the hidden spot near her waist and defend them if necessary. "Let's go," she whispered. "We're not safe out here." Aerin gave a quick nod, and the three nearly ran to their shop.

"What the fuck was that?" Aerin asked as calming scents of lavender greeted them. Her pupils were enlarged, and a slight blush colored her cheeks. Claire knew she didn't frighten easily, so their encounter must have really ruffled her.

"Hell if I know," Claire replied, waiting for her heart rate to return to normal. "Just a crazy guy, I guess. Probably didn't realize the effect of his words and actions."

"No." Moira shook her head, narrowing her aquamarine gaze. "Growin' up down in the bayou, I've seen crazy, and he wasn't it. *Possessed*. That's what he was."

"Possessed?" Claire shivered at the idea. She would have argued that possession wasn't real, but most didn't believe in witches, either.

Moira nodded. "By an evil spirit or some such thing. We're lucky he didn't get Aerin."

Aerin stared at Moira for a long moment, and then she blinked. "I need a smoke."

"Better take it upstairs, out on the balcony," said their friendly hired help as she navigated through the armchairs and café tables, her once-pink dreads now a shade of plum.

"Sunny," Claire said with a smile. "It's good to see you."

"It's good to see you all, too." She toyed with the piercing on her lower lip as she gave them all a quick perusal.

"Where's T? It's not like her to stay away for so long."

"Tierra's...incapacitated," Claire offered.

"Incapacitated?" Sunny lifted a well-drawn brow.

"She's caught a disease, and it's likely there's no cure," Aerin said with sarcasm.

Deep concern darkened Sunny's features. "Is she going to die?"

Claire snorted and shook her head. Leave it to Aerin to describe pregnancy in that manner. "No, she's not going to die. She just needs some extra rest, and she'll be fine. Why don't you give her a call, and she'll reassure you."

"Don't you worry none. She'll be just fine." Moira added. "Better yet, you sit yourself down, and let me bring you a cup of tea. Tierra's been teaching me all kinds of brews, and we're officially giving you a paid day off."

"Really?" Sunny glanced between them, her lips twisting into a smile that reduced the stress in her features. "That would be like...amazing."

"You've been working hard." Aerin made a shooing gesture. "Go relax your shit. We'll handle everything from here. I'll start with inventory."

Aerin headed toward the backroom as Moira made her way to the counter. Claire remained behind. "I'm curious, Sunny. Have we had any issues with panhandlers or hobos here at the shop?"

Sunny's usually bright expression fell, leaving behind signs of worry and stress. "I would say no because that's not really a problem here in Port Townsend. But..."

"What is it?" Claire could sense her hesitation.

"People are hurting, Claire. I've noticed. Others have, too. More sick people. Others losing jobs. Things like that. And this morning, we did have an old man come in here."

"Dirty white sweatshirt?"

Sunny nodded.

"What did he want? Did you give him anything?"

"Maybe just to get warm? He looked around for a bit, but when I approached to ask if I could assist him, he left." She shifted her stance.

"Crazy, weird eyes, though. Gave me the chills."

Claire nodded, similar unsettled feelings churning inside. "Thanks. Hopefully he found what he needed somewhere else. And thanks, too, for handling everything here. One of the smartest things Tierra did was to hire you."

"Uh...thanks." Sunny glanced away as though Claire's compliment embarrassed her. "I'm going to go help Moira before she wrecks everything."

Claire moved to the front door and glanced outside, looking for the signs of misfortune Sunny had mentioned. The Mexican restaurant that had been opened when she'd first arrived in Port Townsend had closed, along with a shop that carried knickknacks and souvenirs. And of course, the shops Nicholas Kingswood had run out of business.

Thank God Aerin and her attorneys had tied up that acquisition.

Other than those few things and an overhanging cloud of impending doom, things didn't seem that far out of the ordinary.

With a sigh, she turned and walked toward the storage room.

Inside, shelves of neatly stacked teas occupied one wall. Pots and jars of herbs and other potion ingredients lined another. Aerin had an electronic tablet already in hand, counting and entering supply information.

"Tierra really knows her stuff," Claire said, looking around.

"She knows the production part, and I know marketing. We're going to make a killing with this endeavor." Aerin flicked a quick glance in her direction. "We've already seen an uptake in general potions and brews for things like boils and depression. I'm sure as conditions continue to worsen, demand will skyrocket."

"So we're capitalizing on the impending Apocalypse that apparently we've created? Doesn't seem right." She unzipped her leather jacket and tossed it on a workbench.

"*We* did not create this. What we're doing will help those affected by this travesty. Make sure you keep the blame and the support in proper perspective." Aerin turned from the stock in front of her and gave Claire a warm smile.

"You're right. None of us asked for this, and the best thing we can do is try to help those in need. I'm at your service. What do you need me to do?"

Aerin paused. "Who I really need is Sunny. She's going to be able to make much more sense of some of this than I can. Would you mind enlisting her help?"

"No problem. I'll be right back." With a heavy heart, Claire reentered the shop, glancing across the quaint setting in search of purple dreadlocks and bright eyes. When she couldn't find her, she made her way to the counter where Moira studied a canister with a frown.

"Sunny says I screwed up the brew." Moira set down the container and picked up another. "I swore Tierra said rose petals."

"Did Sunny leave?" If she had a day off, she certainly wouldn't stick around.

"In the office," Moira said absentmindedly.

Claire circumvented the counter and opened the door that led to the small room behind it.

Sunny jerked her gaze upward with a startled glance, freezing midmotion. Claire halted at the look of horror on Sunny's face. An opened banker's bag rested on the desk, and Sunny had her fingers tucked into her bra, the edges of several bills still poking out.

"What are you doing?" Claire asked, though the scene in front of her was clear.

❀ 7 ❀

Claire stared at Sunny's heartbroken expression, wishing she hadn't walked in on their reliable, hired help pilfering the teashop's earnings.

"It's...I..." Sunny dissolved into wretched puddle on the leather office chair, setting the stolen money on the desk before dropping her head into her hands. "I'm so sorry. I know I shouldn't have taken it. But things have been really tough, and...and I've kept a running tally."

She slid open a drawer and pulled out a sheet of paper with several amounts written on it. "Tierra hasn't been around, so I couldn't ask her, but I fully intend to talk to her and discuss repaying her." She dropped her head into her hands. "I'm the worst person ever. You all believed in me. *Goddess*, Tierra trusted me, gave me a job when no one else would, and look how I've repaid her."

She peeked at Claire, black kohl liner smudged beneath her eyes, misery swimming in her watery gaze. "I'll get my stuff and go. Can I ask that you let me leave before you tell everyone what I've done? I don't think I can stand to see the heartbreak on Aerin's or Moira's faces. And I still promise to repay every cent."

"Not so fast." Claire held up a hand and walked closer to the other side of the desk, effectively trapping

Sunny in place. "You can't pull something like that and just walk away."

Sunny cowered, fear replacing self-loathing. "Please don't hurt me."

"What?" She frowned at her. "Seriously?"

She lifted a slender shoulder covered with intricate vine tattoos and let it drop. "Sorry. You are pretty bad ass."

Claire laughed, despite the unfortunate circumstances. "I guess I'll take that as a compliment." If only Dru was more afraid of her. She moved closer to the younger girl. "Before you run out of here with your tail between your legs, afraid I'm going to kick your ass, I'd like an explanation. I realize we haven't known each other long, but Tierra's ability to nail a person's character is uncanny. If she likes and trusts you, then I do, too. There had to be a reason for what you've done. I'll hear it now."

Sunny wiped forefingers beneath her eyes, drawing black streaks across her face. "My family." She sucked in a shaky breath. "It's like I said earlier. Bad shit's been happening. To more and more people every day. My dad lost his job at the paper mill. He's looking, but with so many others out of work, it's hard for him to find anything. My little brother requires expensive medication. Me and my mom are still working, but sometimes there's not enough money left at the end of our bills to buy food. I promise I didn't take much. Just twenty. If I'm careful, that can get us through a couple of days until my mom gets paid."

She started to cry in earnest then. "I'm sorry. I know there's never a good reason to steal. I really would understand if you wanted to kick my ass."

Claire's heart crumpled with empathy. She moved closer and wrapped an arm around the poor girl's shoulders. "Aw, Sunny. Don't cry. This is going to be okay."

"It's not," she said through a muffled sob. "The world is ending. My world, at least."

Little did she know. Sunny's proclamation brought their circumstances full circle. Had Claire and her sisters brought about this travesty?

"Sunny, listen. You're like family to us. Our little sister, so to speak. When you hurt, we hurt." Claire pushed a purple-hued strand of hair from her face. "I wish you would have said something to one of us. Let us help you."

"But it's not your problem." She searched Claire's face, a hint of hope shimmering in her moist eyes.

"You're wrong. We love you. Let us help you." She took the two ten-dollar bills Sunny had dropped and pulled another twenty from the bag. "Take this to buy a couple of days' worth of groceries. I know my sisters would agree with me."

"Thank you," Sunny said with a tremulous smile. "I don't deserve it."

Claire snorted. "Of course, you do. You've kept us afloat while we've dealt with personal issues. We owe you far more than this."

The gears in Claire's brain shifted. "I don't know how much Tierra has told you about our new Internet business, but Aerin's certain it's going to be huge. Already, we're struggling to keep up with orders, and as the world continues in a downward spiral, people will be begging for more and more of our affordable herbal and homeopathic teas, medicines, and supplies. We're going to need someone with some brawn to help with shipping and inventory. Do you think your dad might be interested? I know my sisters and I won't be able to handle everything, especially with Tierra—" she caught herself before she revealed more than she should— "being under the weather."

Sunny brightened by degrees. "Are you kidding? I

know he'd love it. And he's good with that sort of stuff. I'm sure he'd be happy to help with anything you'd ask of him."

"Okay, then." Claire gave her another hug before she headed toward the door. "Let me confirm with the others before you offer it to him. I'll let you know as soon as possible."

Sunny stood, wiping more black tears from her face. "Thank you, Claire. Give me a few minutes to clean up, and I'll get back to work."

"No, you won't. You have the day off. Though Aerin did have a question she'd like to ask. Tell you what. When you're ready, you come out. We'll see what Moira has been able to concoct for you tea-wise, and then you can help Aerin for a bit. After that, you have grocery shopping to do and your family to reassure. If we stick together, we'll get through this, Sunny."

Sunny nodded. "Thank you again. I'm so happy to call you all my sisters."

Claire smiled and left the room, feeling like one weight had been lifted from her, while five new ones now occupied her soul. She and her sisters might be able to help Sunny and her family, but how would they ever help all the residents of Port Townsend, let alone outsiders who might be affected by the shift in events?

Moira blocked Claire from escaping from behind the counter, her own eyes wet with unshed tears.

"What?" Claire asked, not sure she was ready for the next difficulty she might have to battle. "Did that crazy homeless man come in?"

Moira shook her head and sniffed. "I heard what you done told Sunny. That other stuff about you being on my shit list? It's all good." She gave a firm nod and turned back to an older woman waiting at the counter.

Claire raised her brows as the customer asked if Moira had anything to recommend for warts. She would have helped Sunny regardless, but the fact that she'd pleased Moira at the same time left a lighthearted fire burning inside her.

Dru followed his usual path through overgrown pines. The overcast day aided his covert mission as he headed toward the coven's headquarters.

A sudden rush of warmth filled him, causing him to halt mid-step.

Claire.

He inhaled a deep breath, closed his eyes, and savored the burning inside him. He wasn't sure what had just transpired, but she was happy.

He lived for those moments during the day, when she smiled or laughed. They gave him hope for the future, for a future with her, even when that seemed impossible. He had no idea how he'd reconcile the unfolding events, and, it seemed, the inevitable end of the world. But as long as Claire drew a breath, he'd keep fighting for their chance.

Refocusing on the duty at hand, he slipped into the coven's compound unnoticed. It wasn't that the Witches of Port Townsend hadn't highly secured their property. In fact, some of the most powerful wards kept out unwanted visitors, but, truth be told, he was wanted.

Some might consider messing with Gwen's affections a dangerous game. Dru deemed his time with the coven's leader a highly necessary, effective warfare tactic. Gwen had yet to discover his ability to conjure believable situations like Claire had during their first meeting. Then again, Claire was far superior to Gwen in beauty and talent, though she might not have realized it yet.

The other three Horsemen still believed the calamitous events of their recent days centered directly around the Apocalypse. Yes, the end of the world hung in the balance, teetering on their and the witches' actions, intended or otherwise. But he suspected there was more at play than the death of a witch.

No. *He knew it*.

They might take out Claire or one of her sisters in the current day, but this scenario would eventually come back around, and they'd face it again. Might be next year. Might be a millennia down the road.

He was tired of the fight. Tired of the endless days with no love and only death and destruction. His brothers had to be as well.

They needed to solve this predicament once and for all, or be faced with thousands of days of torture again. Claire's death might bring an end to the fire burning inside him, but knowing she no longer inhabited the earth would bring about a pain worse than death, worse than the raging fires of hell.

There was no other option for him.

If that brought him into the bedchamber of the lovely, cunning, yet chillingly cold coven leader, so be it.

As he neared the red brick mansion once owned by a highly profitable shipping magnate back in the 1850s, he slowed his steps. Claire's aunt would be inside as well, along with the rest of the coven. Though they were no match for his stealth and ingenuity, one careless step could out him, and he had no doubt Gwen would not give a blink to save him from their wrath.

He checked her bedroom window, and finding it unlocked, slipped inside.

The cool aquamarine and purples of the room bored him to distraction. Nearly lulled him to sleep, which, he supposed, was the point of a bedroom. At least to some.

He preferred rich, bold reds and oranges that excited his blood and his libido. Like Claire's room. He'd watched her many times through his high-powered rifle scope, brushing her hair, removing the leather sheath she liked to wear so often.

Beneath, he'd discovered she liked to wear black satin. No pink, yellow or green. Always black. Like his heart.

Or at least like his heart had been before he'd carried her Fire.

Voices in the hallway surprised him, and he quickly flattened his iron-toned body against an armoire, prepared to bring forth his sword if necessary. The doorknob sounded as someone twisted it, and a shaft of dim light entered from the hall, barely lighting the dark room.

"Why are you bothering me with visitors, Justine?" Gwen's voice carried the sharp edge of impatience.

Three steps into the room, Gwen caught sight of Dru. Her nostrils flared with surprise, and she halted abruptly, Justine bumping into her. Gwen twirled, coming face-to-face with Justine, forcing Claire's aunt to take a step backward, out of his view, meaning he was also out of hers.

"If you would let me finish." Excitement thrummed on each of Justine's words. "It's not Georgia like we expected. She's someone much higher up. I'm sure of it. If you meet her, you'll sense it as well. She has powers far beyond anyone in our coven. She's asked for temporary sanctuary. From whom, I'm not sure. But think of what we might learn from her. Even if she only stays a few days."

"This is risky at best, Justine." Gwen flashed a quick, concerned look in his direction, and Dru knew she didn't want him to overhear their conversation. "I will meet with her, but she cannot stay."

"But—"

"I've spoken. Take her to the conservatory, and I'll meet you there. I need a moment alone." Gwen's authoritative tone left no room for discussion.

"Of course."

A moment later, the door closed, and Gwen found him on the side of the armoire. She pressed her thin body against him, trapping him as a cloud of cloying perfume assaulted his nostrils.

"My love," she whispered. "I wasn't expecting you until later."

"My schedule changed, and I found myself with extra free time. Of course, I'd want to spend it with you."

He tolerated her kiss and then gently pulled from her, twisting until she occupied the corner. Her shivers of anticipation and delight reached out to him. "I don't have much time," she whispered. "Can we make this quick?"

He forced a chuckle. "A man like me never comes quick."

She laughed, the tinkle of her voice grating on him like the metal of a bobbing boat against a pier. "I suppose not. I do have something I need to attend to for a bit. Do you mind waiting? It shouldn't take too long."

He grinned, thinking she'd given him access to their lair while an important visitor was on site. "Why would I mind? Especially considering the possibilities of what might lay in store."

"This is why I love you." She gave him a quick kiss. "Shall I ward the door behind me?"

"Do you believe me incapable of hiding or protecting myself from your coven?"

"Never." She drew a finger down his cheek. "They haven't a clue how much danger lies in those delectable muscles, which is why I keep you around. You excite me."

Ah, gods. "Take care of what you must." While he did the same.

"Back soon."

He gave her ten seconds to disappear down the hall before he opened the door.

❦ 8 ❦

No wards or charms existed inside the walls of the coven's sanctuary. At least not that Dru could detect. Any mastermind protector would know never to use only a single line of defense. One fatal hit would leave the entire compound vulnerable. Lucky for him, the Witches of the Olympic Coven were more concerned about what transpired outside their area than inside the confines.

Transforming to a state where he wouldn't be detected for any length of time would require much from him, but the possible knowledge he'd receive would be worth the sacrifice.

Silently, invisibly, he stepped into the hall. Hushed whispers of excitement filled the house as others made their way in the same direction. Apparently, everyone was aware of the new visitor and yearned to know more.

The majority of the group passed the closed doors of the conservatory, continuing toward the end of the hall lit with flickering sconces where Dru knew the coven met as a group to chant, pray, and cast spells. Strong magic filtered from that room, reaching out toward him.

"She's called a meeting," one witch whispered.

"Report to the Hallowed Room," said another.

He followed the group of nearly twenty witches as they descended upon their gathering spot. At one point, he found himself sandwiched between three older witches, one of them Claire's aunt, Justine. He did his best to not touch any of them, hoping to remain undetected.

Unfortunately, Justine stopped abruptly outside the Hallowed Room's doors, and he couldn't avoid bumping her. The witch behind him plowed into him as well, resulting in a second collision with Justine.

Claire's aunt turned with a venomous glare. "Watch where you step, Martha. You don't need to be so close."

The grandmotherly Martha widened her eyes in offense. "I beg your pardon. You did this. Not me."

Dru flattened against the wall and slipped past them. The last thing he needed was for them to come to blows, only to realize an invisible object stood between them. No longer concerned for any noise he'd make in the cacophony of excited female whispers, he found his way into the conservatory, occupying space near a potted tree in the corner where no one else would likely stand.

Fearsome, dark energy blended with other light-hearted traces of past spells, reminding Dru these witches were capable of deadly deeds. Though many of the coven seemed dim-witted and easy to dupe, together, their powers could prove a difficult foe.

"Some are saying she's a high priestess," a short witch with a red pixie cut whispered to her equally short, dark-haired friend. "That she's come from back east."

"I'd heard she'd been banished, an outlaw looking for sanctuary," her friend replied.

Needless to say, the whisperings had piqued Dru's curiosity. He couldn't believe it was a coincidence that this notable witch, whoever she was, had arrived after Claire and her sisters had broken four of the Seals. Undoubtedly, four of seven broken seals would capture the attention of many interested parties around the world.

Gwen entered the room moments later, followed by a voluptuous woman, the sight of which kicked Dru squarely in the gut. She'd tamed her blond curls into submission and had toned down her glamorous makeup and clothing, but he recognized her immediately. *Lucy*.

What the hell was she doing pretending to be a witch?

At the thought of her name, she swiveled her head in his direction, scanning the crowded room full of witches. He froze. She narrowed her gaze as though pin-pointing him, but then continued her perusal of the area.

He allowed shallow breaths, but kept his thoughts blank.

Gwen stepped onto the dais, looking pale in comparison to her counterpart. "Welcome sisters to this impromptu meeting. Thank you for making yourselves available."

"As if we'd miss it," whispered red-headed pixie witch.

"The Goddesses have blessed us this day with a surprise gift unequalled in recent memory," Gwen continued. "This is high priestess Lucinda. She's traveled from The Brehon's Chair in Ireland, near the ancient druid ruins of some of our ancestors. She will be staying with us for the foreseeable future. Please make her welcome as she is our honored guest."

A rush of murmurs drew over the crowd in a wave. As far as Dru could tell, none guessed her true identity. He could only imagine what crazy, devilish plans she'd concocted.

Gwen stepped aside, giving deference to Lucy.

"Thank you, everyone, for opening your home to me. My hope is that I may be of as much of assistance to you as you've been gracious to me. I look forward to getting to know each and every one of you." She bestowed a warm smile, but Dru knew it went no further than the surface. Lucy would consider these women trivial, pawns in whatever game she had in mind. His immediate task would be to figure out what that was.

"As I've already discussed with your leader, I and others like me have a grave concern about the recent happenings in Port Townsend. The fact that four of your coven have been so willfully careless and selfish to have allowed four Seals to be broken is, dare I say, an abhorrent act of disobedience. I'm sorry to say, but we cannot allow these deeds to go unpunished. *You* cannot allow them to go unpunished." She flashed another brilliant smile. "However, we do realize we would be unfair to penalize the entire coven, and so I am here to offer my services to help you bring a stop to these errant witches."

"Technically, they're not part of our coven," Gwen pointed out, earning a silencing look from Lucy.

"Their mother was though, and their aunt continues to be, I believe. There are those who see them as your problem to solve. But, fear not. I am here to help." Lucy tilted her ruby lips in a smile sweeter than spun sugar.

"She means to kill Justine's nieces," the dark-haired witch whispered.

"They deserve it," murmured her red-headed friend with a vengeance. "Look what they've brought upon us. Better them than all of us."

"True."

How easy they turn on their own kind. Dru shook his head in distaste.

"I've had a long journey and shall retire for now." Lucy touched a weary hand to her brow. "But should any of you have ideas on how to...eliminate this problem before it progresses any further, please don't hesitate to stop by my room. I believe I'll be occupying

Gwen's room since she's assured me she wanted me to be as comfortable as possible." She tossed an expectant look at their leader who widened her eyes in surprise, which then quickly flipped to panic.

"Of course, Lucinda. Our house is yours. Give me a moment to make your room ready." Gwen made to step off the dais, but Lucy took her by the arm.

"No special treatment. Really. I'm sure it's fine as it is."

The alarm on Gwen's face deepened, and she pulled her arm from Lucy's grasp. "You'll need fresh sheets, and there are a few items I'd like to gather." Like *me*, Dru thought. Gwen forced a smile and then stepped away before Lucy could detain her further.

The group dissipated shortly after Lucy followed Gwen from the room, and Dru made haste toward the front door. His energy had dropped to an all-time low, and he needed to slip away before he lost his edge and someone discovered him.

When the coast was clear, he slipped outside the front door and closed it quietly behind him.

"Dru, darling," Lucy crooned before he took a step forward.

Her voice startled him, causing him to lose his shield.

"Fear not." She ran a hand up his chest, sending shivers of frigid energy shooting into him like frozen arrows. "Let me help you, love."

He drew from her power until he had enough to conceal himself again.

She turned and pressed her well-defined ass against him, pushing him until she'd pinned him between her and the door. To anyone on the street or watching from inside the house, it would appear she stood on the porch alone, perhaps to gain some of the Pacific Northwest's fresh air.

"Was that a wise move, mistress? Asking others to do our job?"

Her laugh carried a careful tinkle, and he wondered at her lackadaisical approach. "Why not? It's not as if you boys have accomplished your tasks. You know what they say about asking a woman if you want a job done correctly."

Annoyance burned inside him. "We will take care of this. To allow someone else goes against the very fibers which make up our universe."

She rubbed against him, pulling his arms around her. "Hold me, Dru. Won't you come back to Gwen's room and make love with me tonight? I know that's what she expected, but you should love me instead. It's been such a long time, and that sweet monk Julian won't give me any."

"I'm sorry, Lucy, but to allow myself to be distracted by your beauty and charms might deter me from completing my mission." It was as close to rejection as he could deliver and not be rendered mindless by her wrath.

"Oh, Dru." She turned as though she might be headed back into the house, still holding his invisible form against the door. "You were always a sweet-talker. We both know that Fire bitch ruined you. Yes, I smell her all over you. But know this, my delicious hunk of chiseled muscle, she will die, and you will come crawling back to me. When it comes, I shall savor the day. Be warned, I will torture you until you're a groveling mass, but eventually, I'll forgive you. Good night, dear Dru. Until we meet again."

She groped his crotch. "Mine," she whispered before she slipped around him and returned inside the compound.

Dru stood for a moment, experiencing uncertain fear for the first time in his life as the sun dipped closer to the horizon. The other Horsemen would certainly kill Claire if the opportunity presented itself. Lucy, on the other hand, would draw out and relish her death. There would be no honor in the act. Only desecration.

He had to find a way to warn her. If he directly outed Lucy, she'd know in an instant, so he'd need to keep his warning vague. Hopefully, Claire would be smart enough to piece together the rest and recognize the danger.

Jill Claire. If the opportunity presented itself for Lia to use the other hand, would Drew not and risk Lia's death? Dara would have no home in the act. Only destruction.

He had to find a way to stop her, if he didn't want Lia to see their world's end to hunt her, so he'd need to keep his warning sharp. Hopefully, Claire would be smart enough to persuade the seer to avoid catastrophe, the climax.

❧ 9 ☙

A fierce restlessness filled Claire, the likes of which she'd never known. She needed to *do* something. *Take* action. *Fix* the calamities piling up around them.

Yet, she sat in her room, staring out the window into the surrounding darkness, wishing she could eviscerate her longing to see Dru again. Since she and her sisters had discovered Tierra's pregnancy and had inadvertently opened the fourth Seal, an incessant need to see him, to touch him had grown uncontrollable. Incredible yet imaginary memories of Dru's touch and kiss constantly filled her mind. She closed her eyes and ran light fingers over her bare arms, pretending Dru touched her. She sensed his presence continually, and her body ached to have him near. To the point she'd considered her body a traitor against her mind.

She couldn't want him and save the world, too.

Goddess, she might go crazy before the end of everything became a certainty.

Feeling reckless, she lifted the screen from her second story window and slipped out onto the porch roof. Kai put his front paws on the windowsill and tried to follow.

She lifted the red fox, holding him against her chest as she stroked his soft fur. "So sorry, little buddy. I need to be alone for a while." She set him on the floor inside and closed the window behind her, refusing to allow his pleading black eyes to sway her.

Cool evening air caressed her heated skin, and her nipples puckered in response. The scent of pine tantalized her senses. It was as though the whole world encouraged her unrelenting needs. As though someone or something had ramped up her hormones to the point of driving her insane.

Over and over, she relived the kiss she'd shared with Dru outside Sirens. His lips on hers. The way her body had accommodated the hard angles of his. His promise that she couldn't hurt him. If only she could go back in time and savor that moment.

She blew out an agitated breath and carefully climbed to the widow's walk atop the house and stepped over the wrought iron railing that encompassed it. She wanted to dream and pretend her lover was there with her. She turned in a circle, the entire view of Port Townsend and the full moon glittering off the Puget Sound in the distance making her feel closer to Dru. He was out there, somewhere. Perhaps at his cabin. Perhaps at the Horsemen's lair in Sirens.

If only she could call him. Call a truce. Just for a night.

She couldn't imagine he wouldn't be agreeable.

She sighed and arched her neck, turning her gaze upon the mesmerizing starlit sky. He'd said he could hear her thoughts. Would he hear her now?

"Dru," she whispered. "Come to me."

Claire. I'm on my way. His voice, plain as day, echoed through her mind, sending her pulse racing.

The thoughts were all in her head, she knew. Conjured fantasies of a desperate woman, but she couldn't let them go.

I need you, she thought.

Ah, my love. I need you, too. I will be there soon.

Not soon enough. She cupped both breasts and emitted a soft gasp when her thumbs crested hardened peaks. She literally ached for his touch. Her skin burned with scorching need.

Yes, love. Do that again. Make me feel your need.

She had gone insane. No doubt. But she couldn't stop, not with overwhelming need thrumming between her thighs. She tugged on her nipples, rolling the tight buds between her fingers until an electrified sensation tightened her core.

Take off your shirt. I want to feel your skin.

The more they talked, the more real their conversation seemed. *You can't feel me.*

But I can. Take it off.

She closed her eyes, pretending Dru's hands tugged her black tank top from her body. She rubbed her fingers lightly over her lace bra, enjoying shivers of sensations. Moist summer air should have chilled her skin, but being bare stoked her internal furnace.

Nice. But I want skin.

Dru?

Yes?

Are you really there?

Yes, love. I'm here in your mind. I'll be there soon in person.

She trembled at the thought. Having him actually touch her was all she wanted.

Skin... he reminded her.

She reached behind her and unhooked her bra, letting it fall slack before she dropped it at her feet. She held her breasts and glanced down, the soft moonlight caressing her skin, making her glow.

A sharp distraction ripped through her thoughts, followed by a resounding *fuck*.

Dru? That *had not* been her imagination.

Sorry. I forgot how beautiful you were, and a damned pedestrian came out of nowhere.

You can see me? She glanced into the surrounding night, searching for a sign of him.

I can see what you see when your guard is down. Feel what you feel. Can you not sense me inside you? Close your eyes. Feel me. You'll find me.

She quivered in reaction as she closed her eyes. Behind her lids, she searched for the place she'd pretended didn't exist. The white hot center of need. A deep longing pierced her, sharpening to a red point somewhere beyond her eyelids where it pulsed like a heartbeat.

Drustan.

She flung open her eyes, and the crimson remained off in the distance like an X marking the spot on a treasure map.

A soft chuckle floated on the breeze. "Yes," it seemed to whisper. *If I were there already, you would no longer be in jeans. I want to see you, Claire. All of you. Take them off.*

She popped the button on her jeans and tugged them off her ass, caressing her thighs as she slid them down her legs.

Your skin is so soft. I've felt it a thousand times in my mind and can never get enough.

His sexy words caused a heated rush to pool between her legs. She stepped out of her jeans and then ran her hands across her stomach and over her black lace panties. "Have you felt this?" She ran her forefingers inside the elastic edge of her panties in a teasing gesture.

You're killing me, he groaned, bringing forth a similar response from her. *Don't stop, Claire. I want you to slip your hand down your panties. I want to feel your softness. I want to know how wet you are for me.*

"Oh, God," she whispered, knowing in that moment he owned her. She couldn't refuse if she wanted. Her hand shook with need as she followed his directions.

Every sensation from the smoothness of her skin to the texture of her lace registered in her mind with agonizing slowness. If he really could experience her consciousness, she wanted him to live this in detail.

"I want you, Dru." She traced her fingers over her mound and sought out the heated core hidden there. Moisture greeted her, and she trembled. She drew a solitary finger between her folds and gasped. She experienced his reaction to her touch, his essence burning deep inside her. A mini-orgasm rolled through her, and she pulled her hand back in surprise.

No, his voice roared through her mind. *Don't stop, Claire. Don't stop until I tell you to. Take off those panties. Then look at yourself. I want to see you naked.*

I don't want to do this without you.

You're not without me. I'm right there. Feel me.

She closed her eyes and searched for him again. And found him immediately.

Take off your panties. Touch yourself. Let me experience your exquisiteness.

Her thighs trembled as she removed her last piece of clothing. When she finished, she turned her gaze downward, looking at her body, wondering how much he could really see of her standing atop her house, naked in the moonlight, for the world to see.

My gods, you are beautiful.

She didn't wait for him to command her again. She kept her gaze focused on what she wanted him to see as she trailed her hand down her belly and searched out her aching core again. She inhaled sharply as she circled the edges, her nerves raw and exposed, her body pulsing with need.

She couldn't wait any longer.

She slipped a finger inside, and her muscles tightened in response.

Praise the gods. His deep voice rumbled inside her, increasing her passion.

Can you feel how much I want you?

Oh, yes. I can feel everything about you. Each heartbeat. Each quiver. You are excruciating perfection. Move your finger to the left side. Just a little farther.

She vocalized her pleasure when she found it. "Dru," she whispered, caught in the incredible sensation. "Oh, goddess."

Yes, there. I can feel it, too. Don't stop.

"You feel it?" The idea that he experienced her pleasure increased hers tenfold.

She panted as raging heat unfolded inside her. Hot. Blinding. Beyond what she'd known during the love-making Dru had conjured, more powerful than any encounter from her past.

She stroked, imaging he stroked her. During certain moments, she was positive he controlled her hand. Sensation upon sensation built, raging wildly through her mind and body, until she lost her breath.

When her pleasure broke, she grasped the wrought iron railing and held on as a massive tremor rolled through her body. She savored each wave as her heart thundered inside her.

Headlights flashed on the street below as Dru's Hummer came to a screeching stop in front of her house. He jumped from the driver's seat and raced toward the property only to come up short against the unseen wall of protection she and her sisters had laid.

He reached out a hand toward her, and she did the same, trying to regain enough power to stand on her own.

"I'll come to you," she whispered.

Just as she spoke, floodlights on the house cut through the sultry darkness, and her sisters raced out onto the lush lawn.

"Get the fuck out of here!" Aerin commanded.

"Yeah," Moira added. "Before we burn your balls. Claire don't want you."

His gaze jumped to Claire, bringing along the bewildered stares of her sisters. Claire slipped into her panties in an attempt to cover herself, but it was too late.

"Oh, hell." Tierra placed her hands on her hips as she glared up at Claire. "I was afraid of this. We need to cool this mess down immediately."

"*No.*" She tossed on her tank and climbed over the rail, not worried about her other clothes. "Just give me a moment with him." He couldn't leave without one real touch, one physical kiss.

"Got it covered, sister," Moira said to Tierra before she sent Claire a disappointed frown and opened the skies. Rain fell from the heavens, but surprisingly, Moira seemed to have the deluge of it focused on Claire and Dru.

Claire stopped trying to escape the slippery roof and sat as the water completely soaked her. Dru stood his ground for a moment, but then seemed to realize he needed to regroup and battle another day.

"This isn't over," he warned her sisters. He climbed into his Hummer, the engine engaging with a mighty roar. His tires screeched against the wet ground as he fled the scene of increasing chaos.

The moment he was gone, the rain ceased. Claire followed the direction his Hummer had taken, pacified to see the red pulse still beating.

❧ 10 ❧

"What the fuck were you thinking, Claire?" Aerin's cold anger swept upward to where Claire stood on the roof, a soaked, chilled mess thanks to Moira's shower. "Inviting him onto our property?"

"What the hell does it look like?" she shot back as she gathered the rest of her clothes and made her way to her bedroom window. Her well-intentioned sisters had just cost her what could have been the most incredible night of sex in her life. *They* were pissed?

She was furious and embarrassed. She climbed inside, ignoring Kai's chastising look as she stomped out into the hall and met her sisters near the bottom of the stairs. "Why can't you stay out of my business? Dru wasn't hurting you. He wasn't hurting *anyone*."

Moira widened her eyes in a surprised gesture, while Aerin's expression flipped from ire to concern. "Are you sick? Was Julian here with Dru? Did he touch you?"

"She's not sick," Tierra interjected. "It's what I feared. Look at her. Flushed cheeks, dilated pupils. She's...in heat...for lack of a better word."

"*Heat*?" Claire's question came out as an impatient barb.

"The fuck?" Aerin folded her arms over her white silk robe. "Would you care to explain?"

Tierra twisted one of her loose curls around a finger as though she hesitated to clarify further. "Claire's behavior is my fault."

"Have you all gone mad?" Claire tossed down to the lot of them. "My actions are not your fault. I make my own choices and pay my own consequences. I was about to have the most exquisite sex in my life, and you all ruined it. The only fault lies in your decisions, not mine."

Tierra cleared her throat as though that would wipe out Claire's declaration. "It has been known to happen from time to time...

Meaning, throughout history some witches will..."

"Oh my God. Out with it already." Aerin exhaled her displeasure, and Claire heartily agreed with her.

"Fine." Tierra pulled her finger from her curl. "When Earth witches become pregnant, things around them can display increasing degrees of fertility. That's why the grass needs to be mowed a couple of times during the week instead of once and why the rhododendrons have a riot of blooms this year."

"Oh my gawd," Moira exclaimed with a look of absurdity. "You're making us all horny?" She glanced at each of her sisters. "I don't think

I'm horny. Are you?"

Tierra wrapped her lips inward as though that would keep the hell yeah expression from her face.

Aerin turned her head toward the big bay window that looked out toward the Sound. "Not even."

"You all are insane." Claire stared at her three sisters whom she loved dearly, but, at the moment, would like to throttle.

Aerin faced her with a sardonic look on her face. "I beg your pardon. I'm not the one who diddled herself on the rooftop for a Horseman who'd like every other one of us dead. I'm also not the one who's soaking the carpet." She slipped her gaze to Moira. "Nice way to turn the hose on them, sis."

Moira grinned. "Been practicing that."

"It's pretty amazing," Tierra agreed.

Claire ground out a frustrated snarl. "Fine. Stand around and congratulate yourselves on how wonderful you are. I'm out of here!"

"Stay away from him, Claire," Aerin called as she ascended the stairs. "The least you'll get is trouble. You may end up with more than you can handle alone."

Claire turned an accusing glare on Tierra. "You mean like knocked up with Death's spawn that may or may not be the Antichrist?" She held up a hand as she continued upward. "Spare me the lecture."

"I'll talk to her tomorrow," she heard Tierra whisper as she reached her bedroom door.

Inside, Claire closed herself away from the rest of the world, her anger dissipating with each passing second. She peeled off her wet clothes in favor of a snuggly black hoodie and yoga pants. She threw a forceful glance at her fireplace and flames roared to life causing her to take a step backward.

"Whoa," she whispered. Her ability to conjure flames had always required more concentration in the past. Something had changed. Had her residual anger at her sisters given her extra power? Or maybe leftover passion from her...encounter with Dru?

She sat cross-legged in front of the fire and towel-dried her hair. Kai climbed onto her lap and curled into a ball as she worked through the snarls, bringing a measure of calm and reassurance to her.

"I know. I should have listened to you," she said to her familiar. "Then I wouldn't be all wet. I also wouldn't have experienced that amazing connection with a man I'm supposed to hate."

Kai lifted his head and met her gaze as though to question her sanity.

"You don't understand. None of you do. I know he's supposed to be all big and bad, which he is. Trust me. I've had firsthand contact with those muscles and that iron will. But there's something more. I can't explain it. Maybe he's right. Maybe it's because he held my fire and I stole his sword. But I know this, no matter what you or my sisters say,

I'll never be able to stay away from him. Never." Kai sighed and nuzzled tighter against her.

She breathed in the scent of burning logs and closed her eyes, searching for the part of her still connected to Dru. It wasn't as easy to find without him in her head, but after a moment, she recognized the red pulse.

Then it disappeared. Panicked, she dug deeper. This time, what she considered his heartbeat grew stronger. *Dru? Are you there?*

She sensed his presence, but he didn't respond. She thought his name again...but nothing.

When her phone rang, she nearly jumped out of her skin. She rolled and grabbed it from the bedside table, frowning at the unknown number. No one called her. Except her sisters.

"Hello?"

"Claire." Dru's voice came across the phone in a sexy rumble that rolled through her, leaving goose bumps on her skin.

"How did you get my number?"

"I've had your number from the moment we met, my petite warrior. A good soldier doesn't miss an opportunity to find out anything and everything about his target."

"You looked at my phone?"

"I've looked at everything you own."

A delicious shiver tickled her as she remembered their encounter less than an hour prior. "I'm sorry you had to leave."

"It was for the best. You and I are dangerous

together."

"I'm not afraid." Memories of saying that to him at their first meeting sparked in her mind. So much had happened since then. She should despise him, but she couldn't. "I wish we could sit and have a conversation like normal people."

He snorted. "I'm not sure I could be normal if I tried."

"Me, either." She smiled though he couldn't see. "I suppose we're kind of past that, aren't we?"

"Mmm..." He paused for a long moment. "Claire?"

"Yes, Dru?" She loved the sound of his name on her lips, the deep timbre of his voice in her ear.

"I've something to tell you. I need you to listen carefully because you will need to take the basic intel I give you and then continue to decipher on your own. I'll tell you what I can, but you cannot ask questions of me. It would put us both at grave risk. Ask your sisters for help if need be."

The way he phrased it left her curious and a little afraid. "What is it?"

"There is something in Port Townsend that's far more dangerous than anything you or your sisters have encountered."

"That's pretty vague. This thing is not you or the other Horsemen?"

"No questions, remember? I cannot tell you much, but I caution you to pay close attention to your encounters with others. Anyone could be lethal, even if he, she, or it doesn't appear to be so. Trust no one but your sisters."

A shiver unfurled inside her, along with a tremendous amount of confusion. "Can I trust you?"

"Yes, my love. You can trust me. You and I are bound to each other now. I think you know this. Listen to your heart. You'll find me there, and you can trust what it tells you."

Thoughts fired through her brain left and right. "Is that all you can say? I have so many questions."

"'Tis all. More, and I will be discovered. I will do my best to protect you, but this is a power greater than mine. Or yours. Do not ask more. Do not think of more when you're thinking of me. Do not forget we are linked."

"Okay. I will be watchful. But when I'm safe in my bed, I will think and dream only of you."

He chuckled. "I would enjoy that very much. With the gods' favor, perhaps one day we can put this behind us and have that casual conversation you desire. For now, I need to go before others discover me and discover what I've told you."

"I do have a question that has nothing to do with what you've told me. I need to know the truth. Did you or one of the other Horsemen steal Grim?"

"Grim? As in Grimoire? No, Claire, I did not, and as far as I know, none of the others have possession of it either."

She let his words settle, waiting for a sign of deception. When none came, a blessed wave of relief washed over her. "Okay. Good. It's hard enough to explain you to my sisters when you're trying to kill them. The missing Grimoire doesn't help."

"I understand."

She supposed he might. "One more thing. If I asked you not to kill any of them, either, could you promise me you won't?"

A drawn out silence crept through the airwaves, leaving her uneasy.

"It's not that simple, love. I'm honor bound to my duty to stop the Apocalypse. If the opportunity presents itself to do just that, I don't believe I could walk away. It's ingrained in my very essence."

"I thought you said I was now ingrained into your essence."

"'Tis true you are. Which is why you are safe from harm...at least from me."

"But not my sisters?"

"I do not wish to take their lives, Claire. To know the damage that would do to you pains me greatly. But I cannot guarantee their safety in my presence. I would like to think I could resist for your sake, but I might have to kill one of them to save you."

She released a weighted sigh. "I see."

"I cannot predict the outcome of unfolding events. My gut tells me what we know is only what's scratched on the surface. There is certainly more."

"More information that you know but can't say. More that none of us know. How do we fight that?" How did any of them make the world okay?

"The way any good soldier would. Make solid plans. Stay alert. Conduct surveillance. Strike when the enemy is weak, and, most importantly, never back down from a valiant cause."

"You're right. My sisters and I will stay strong. Though it seems we're on opposite sides from you and your Horsemen, I believe, ultimately, we're all fighting for the same thing."

"Exactly. Good night, Claire. Sweet dreams."

"Good night, Drustan." She didn't want their call to end...ever. But life moved forward, carrying all of them with it. Still, if she and Dru could find a way to communicate, perhaps the rest could as well. If they could find a way to work together instead of against each other, they all might have a chance. But that was like asking elements of fire and water to combine forces when neither could survive in the presence of the other. Though they did unite to create new forms of elements, which may not be a bad outcome after all.

Despite their continually darkening circumstances, a glimmer of hope burned brightly within in her heart.

❧ II ❧

Claire stood in the sunny kitchen and filled her cup nearly to the brim with her favorite chai tea. She still housed some resentment for her sisters interrupting her potentially thrilling evening, but she longed to have everything back to normal with them as well.

Still, they'd never understand her connection to Dru, never understand what it was like to suck out a person's soul and leave a loved one nothing more than a shell just because she showed her love. They had no idea how aching and empty that experience could leave a person.

Dru was immune to her destruction. She could love him, and he'd never die. Destiny seemed determined that they were a match. She had no desire to argue.

But how did she explain all that to her sisters? She supposed she had to try.

Tierra's singing drifted in from the solarium where her sister tended her plants while she crooned with Stevie Nicks. Claire should talk to her. Tierra obviously still harbored feelings for Killian, even if she didn't act on them. She carried his child, for heaven's sake.

Perhaps she would understand.

Just as Claire swiveled, she caught sight of a woman with long, blond hair walking toward the pathway leading to the front of the house. The same lady Claire had nearly knocked over the day she'd run from Sirens to escape the Horsemen.

The woman stopped as though stunned by the wards Claire and her sisters had placed around the house, and Claire set down her mug, prepared to sound an alarm. Then Aunt Justine appeared, smiled at her companion, and together they approached the house.

Apparently, neither of the women meant them any harm.

Otherwise, they wouldn't have been able to pass through the wards.

"The witch is here," Claire called out to Tierra and anyone else within hearing distance. The doorbell rang, and Claire made her way to the front door. Tierra joined her just as she opened it.

"Girls. How good to see you. I'd like you to meet a friend of mine," Justine said as she pushed her way into the house. She might have moved her things to the coven's compound, but she still acted as though she owned the mansion.

"You're not welcome here," Moira called from the stairs.

Tierra fired an admonishing look toward her before she turned back to their guests. "Hello." She stuck out her hand in greeting. "I'm Tierra de Moray. These are my sisters, Claire and Moira."

"How delightful." The classic blonde extended her hand as well, offering a weak handshake to Tierra and Claire. She nodded toward Moira, who only stared back.

"It's my pleasure to introduce High Priestess Lucinda, from The Brehon's Chair in Ireland." Justine acted as though she'd just presented Her Majesty, the Queen of England.

Claire lifted a brow, never one to be impressed by

titles or egos. Tierra, on the other hand, inhaled an excited breath as her eyes widened.

"Oh, my goodness." She took Lucinda's hand again and held it between hers. "This is such an honor."

"I knew you wouldn't want to miss the opportunity," Justine said with extreme gratification. "This is a once-in-a-lifetime visit. *Plus*, Lucinda has offered to share her knowledge with the coven."

Lucinda released a gracious chuckle as she placed her free hand over their joined ones. "And I see that you have other exciting news to share."

Tierra's face paled. "I'm sure I don't know what you mean." She pulled from Lucinda's grasp.

Lucinda gave her a puzzled expression as she studied Tierra's face, and then she suddenly smiled again. "Are you sure? I sense new life all around you. Are you—"

"It's all them new plants she's been growing." Moira bounded down the stairs and looped her arm around Tierra's elbow. "Her greenhouse is near to exploding with new life. Right, Tierra?"

"Would you care to see it?" Tierra asked, regaining some of her color.

"I would be delighted." Lucinda turned to Justine. "Shall we?"

"I'm coming, too," Moira said, not releasing Tierra. "Claire, you should start tea."

"Tea, but—"

Moira effectively silenced her reply with a cryptic look.

"I'll start tea," Claire said. "And find Aerin. I'm sure she'll want to meet our guest."

Moira nodded, pleased that Claire had caught on to her ambiguous directions. Moira didn't want tea. She wanted the four of them in the same room until they knew if they faced an enemy or not. Echoes of Dru's caution returned, and suspicion reared its distrustful head. The moment her sisters and the two guests entered the solarium, Claire raced up the stairs to Aerin's room. She knocked once and then entered.

She found Aerin in the adjoining bathroom, soaking in a frothy tub, headphones plugged into her ears. Aerin sat up with a start as she approached.

"The fuck, Claire? You scared the goddess out of me."

"Justine's here. With a guest. Some high priestess from chair in Ireland. I think she figured out Tierra's pregnant, but luckily didn't spill to Justine."

"God." Aerin's face blanched. "Hand me a towel. Wait. Chair from Ireland? Not Brehon's Chair."

"Yeah. Maybe. I don't remember. Tierra seemed pretty impressed with her." She held a fluffy blue towel to her sister and turned to give Aerin privacy.

"The fucking Brehon's Chair is supposed to be the judgment seat of the Archdruid, a very sacred Druidic site in Dublin County. If she's come all this way, this is serious shit, Claire."

She caught Aerin's gaze in the misty mirror. "What do we do?"

"I don't know. I'm sure she's here because we've opened four Seals. Certain people on this planet are going to recognize shit like that. It won't go unnoticed." She rushed from the bathroom into her bedroom and started pulling out clothes. "Our best option is damage control until we figure out what we're dealing with. Get back down there. Don't leave her alone with Tierra. *Ever*. I'm sure as shit she's figured out about the baby. We can't let her know who fathered the thing."

"No. That would be seriously bad. Goddess. Why the hell did I open the damn door?"

"You couldn't have known. Go back. Separate them if possible.

Keep this high priestess occupied and hopefully they won't stay long." She paused for a moment and nailed Claire with a look. "Whatever you do, don't act scared or guilty or anything she might pick up on. Calm, peaceful, happy. That's the only shit going on under this roof. Got it?"

"Got it."

"And don't tell Tierra or Moira what I just said until Justine and this woman have left. They're too kind-hearted and will give away their feelings in a second."

"Shit," Claire hissed as she raced back down the stairs. She stopped for a quick second to fill one of Tierra's pots with water and placed it on the stove. Then she made a beeline for the greenhouse.

Scents of moist dirt and greenery attacked the moment Claire entered the room. She spotted the four witches in the back corner and strolled nonchalantly toward them. Dru's red pulse thrummed inside her, and she forced it down with a calming breath. There was no reason to be alarmed. Justine and her friend hadn't threatened any of them. Yet. As far as she knew, this was a friendly visit. Acting alarmed might derail her and Aerin's intentions.

"What do you think?" Claire asked as she approached. She gave the group an easy smile. "Aren't Tierra's skills amazing? I wish I had her talent."

"Truly amazing," Lucinda agreed. "We could use someone of her skill back in Ireland."

Justine coughed, drawing attention away from Tierra. Normally, Claire would have called her for stealing the show, but this was exactly what they needed at the moment.

"I taught Tierra everything she knows. Isn't that right, dear? Practically raised her from a babe after her mother...died in childbirth." She blinked wide eyes and gave Tierra a fearful smile.

"That's right, Aunt Justine. You've taught me everything I know." Tierra grinned, and Claire could see right through her ruse. Smart of her sister not to give anything away. Then again, Tierra had a lot to hide.

"How's the tea coming?" Lucinda asked Claire. "I don't mean to sound rude, but it seems that Tierra has quite the extensive collection of brews. If you haven't chosen a particular one for my visit, I'd love to see her selection."

"Of course," Claire jumped in before anyone else could volunteer. "If you'd like to come with me, I'll show you the stash."

She strolled away from the group as though the occasion were nothing more than a girlfriend tea party, but inside, she said a prayer of thanks to Tierra's goddesses for protecting her. Lucinda's heels clicked on the kitchen tile as she followed behind until Claire stopped in front of a massive, hand-crafted cupboard that had once belonged to their mother. She pulled open both doors, displaying upwards of eighty different tea blends.

Lucinda released an excited breath. "My goodness. When she said she had a plethora, she was quite serious."

"If there's one thing Tierra is serious about, it's tea. While you're in town, you should stop into our shop. Ambrosia's Brews and Charms? It's down on Water Street."

"Yes, I believe I recall noticing the quaint little shop the day I ran into you on the street."

Claire lifted her brows. "You remember, then?"

"Of course." Lucinda chuckled. "I never forget a face or a circumstance, even if you and your sisters look very similar. You seemed to be in quite a hurry that day if I remember correctly." She pinned her with an exacting look.

Claire shrugged and gave a nonchalant laugh. "Late for an appointment. Again. I'm always forgetting something."

"Really?" Lucy lifted a sculpted brow. "I wouldn't

have pegged you for the type. If someone were to ask me to describe you after only knowing you a short time, I would say you're determined, calculating, and something of a risk-taker." She laughed, the sound tinkling through the air. "But then again, everyone knows you can't take initial reactions at face value. They're only correct fifty percent of the time."

Claire smiled, pretending to be good-humored along with their intriguing guest. "That's so true, isn't it? My first impression of you was someone who had an agenda, other than visiting for tea and getting to know the local witches. But anyone can see you're friendly and social, a warm person at heart."

Claire recognized the undercurrents of their tête-à-tête, knew she shouldn't do anything that might cause suspicion or bring forth the ire of their guest, but she couldn't resist letting this woman know she was on their turf now and Claire wasn't impressed with her credentials.

The friendliness faded from Lucinda's expression, and Claire braced for battle.

"You're an interesting witch, Claire de Moray."

"How so?"

"Harder than your other sisters, I'd say. Not much gets by you."

"Not much gets by them, either." She wouldn't let this friend of Justine's insult any of her sisters.

Lucinda laughed. "You misunderstand. Tierra and Moira seem to carry more of a nurturing spirit. Not meant to impugn you or them. Just an observation. You are more focused, less likely to be led astray."

Claire was sure her sisters would disagree after the previous evening's activities. "What's your point?"

She turned from Claire and studied the contents of the cupboard. "How about this one? It contains strawberries and grapefruit. Both good for fostering new relationships and trust." She grasped the container and presented it to Claire.

Claire smiled and took the offering. "As you wish." She scooped the contents into the tea infuser and poured in steaming water. She removed a red and orange ceramic mug from the cupboard as she prepared her next move. She wished to hell Aerin would hurry and strengthen their forces.

She placed everything on a tray and carried it to the table. She waited for Lucinda to sit before she took her seat.

"My point is, Claire, and let me be quite direct. I've studied you and your sisters for the past few months. I wasn't prepared to tip my hand quite yet, but I can see, we've reached an impasse, and our relationship will not progress further until I disclose full details."

"You would be correct." Satisfaction drilled through Claire. She knew she'd been right not to trust her. Dru had warned her of impending danger, and this woman with her timeless beauty and impeccable manners was one of them. "I'd like to know why you've been watching us. You and who else?"

Lucinda shrugged, her silk jacket sliding over her slender shoulders. "Only a handful of us. This thing is already out of hand, and the more that know, the worse it will be."

"This thing?" Claire poured tea into a cup and handed it to Lucinda.

"Four born of one. The breaking of the Seals. I'm sure you recognize the severity of your actions."

Claire nodded. She wouldn't mention the Horsemen or their failed attacks. Either Lucinda already knew, or she could figure it out on her own. Imparting that knowledge wouldn't help Claire or her sisters. "We did not plan to break the Seals. They were mistakes caused by a lack of knowledge on our part. We've put measures into place to prevent another broken Seal."

Lucinda nodded thoughtfully. "That's good to hear. It's always best to be prepared. Much better to prevent the pregnancy than try to figure out how to get rid of the baby afterward, I always say."

Claire fought to keep her breathing even. The woman knew. She could play her passive-aggressive games, but Claire wouldn't give any information. "I agree."

She snorted. "Ah, Claire. Such distrust. Really, you have nothing to fear from me. Truly, I come as a friend."

"If you say so."

"Listen." She tilted her head in a friendly manner. "I sensed Tierra's pregnancy the moment I took her hand. I also sensed she wasn't prepared to tell Justine yet. I'm not going to disclose her secret any more than I'm going to cause other harm to you or your sisters. *I'm here to help.* Can't you see?"

Claire studied her, watching for telltale signs of deception. "How can you help us?"

"I know things. Spells. Ways to protect against opening more Seals.

Ways to protect you and your sisters against the Horsemen."

"What do you know about the Horsemen?" She couldn't pass up the opportunity.

Lucinda laughed, a genuine, hearty laugh. "Too much, I'm afraid. They come across as deadly characters in some heroic effort to save the world, but they have their weaknesses, their Achilles heels."

"For instance?" Claire pressed.

Lucinda bent to retrieve her bag from the floor just as Aerin appeared at the entrance to the kitchen, just beyond Lucinda's view. Claire gave a slight shake of her head. She didn't want anyone or anything to interrupt Lucinda's flow of information.

Aerin signaled she would head toward the greenhouse, and Claire smiled, pretending the gesture was for their guest.

Lucinda pulled a rectangle wrapped in red velvet from her bag and set it on the table between the two of them. "This is a gift for you and your sisters. A sign of goodwill and hope for fostering good relations."

Claire stared at it, sensing the strong, almost familiar magic coming from the package. "What is it?"

"Something that's yours. Something I retrieved from a certain cabin in the woods just outside Port Townsend. I hope you will find it proof of my intent and my power to help you."

"Oh my goddess." Shivers erupted over her as Lucinda unwrapped the book. "*Grim*."

❧ 12 ❧

"**W**_here did you get this?_" Claire fired the question with along with an accusatory glare at Lucinda. "Who gave it to you?"

"Calm down." Lucinda lowered her hand toward the table as though that would take the fire out of Claire's veins. "As I explained, I'm here to help. I retrieved it from those incompetent Horsemen." She took Claire's hand and squeezed, sending a trusting warmth rushing through her.

"Dru?" Claire asked before she could stop herself. He'd said she could trust him. With only a few words, this woman had brought his credibility into serious question.

"He must have known, don't you think?" Lucy said. "A book as powerful as this hidden in the torture chamber in his basement? Anyone in the house couldn't ignore its existence."

Dru? Claire's fragile heart cracked as she remembered the room in the basement of his house where he'd first taken her when he'd kidnapped her. Immediately, she tried to summon his red pulse inside her, to question the validity of Lucinda's statement, but all she found was a cold, void. Had he known Lucinda had taken it back and then closed off the inexplicable connection between them? Surely all of the Horsemen would have recognized its disappearance. Her heart nearly crumbled as the fissures deepened.

"What is it, dear? What's brought that unfortunate look to your face?" She held up a hand. "Wait, don't tell me. I know Drustan Geddes. Have known him for many, many years. He's a handsome, virile man. Any unsuspecting witch or woman could easily fall for his charms. Is that what happened with you? It's okay. You can tell me."

Claire hardened everything inside her. "There's nothing to tell."

Lucinda compressed her lips, compassion hovering in her gaze. "Of course not. I shouldn't expect anyone could be as gullible as I was. Years ago, mind you. I've learned a thing or two since that time, thank the goddesses."

She sipped her tea, then set her cup down, meeting Claire's gaze. "I mistakenly assumed because Drustan has an affinity for Fire witches that perhaps he'd tried to seduce you as well. I do beg your pardon." Humiliation and distress churned into a nasty cocktail inside her.

Not again.

She'd trusted Dru once, and he'd stolen her Fire. She should have listened to her sisters when they'd warned her.

But, no. Instead of valuing their insight and wisdom, she'd fallen for Dru's lies once again, believed his honeyed words of connection and destiny. Goddess, she'd stripped herself bare for him, literally and emotionally.

The blood in her veins cooled to ice.

"I'm so sorry, dear Claire. I've upset you. I should take my leave." Lucinda pushed back from the table. "If there's anything I can do..."

"No." Claire held up a hand, unwilling to let the only person who might understand her feelings slip away. "It's not your fault. I should have known better. I should have listened. To my sisters. To my friends."

The compassion on Lucinda's face deepened. "I understand exactly how you feel. The shame, the degradation. It's a brutal realization to bear. I'd like to be your friend, Claire, if you'll allow it. I truly think I can help you and your sisters. Knowing I've helped to thwart the Horsemen will bring me great satisfaction."

Claire studied the woman, recognized the shared emotions behind her blue eyes, but she still hesitated. "Thank you for that. I appreciate your support."

"Trust me. I know how important support can be when a man knocks a woman to her knees. Our sisters and our girlfriends provide the backbone we need to get back on our feet." Lucinda reached out and covered Claire's hand, sending comforting warmth to her. "I never had friends growing up. Never was able to keep a lover around long either before he fell prey to my fiery charms."

Lucinda's declaration caught her attention. "How do you mean?" Claire asked.

She gave a self-deprecating smile. "It's embarrassing to speak of."

She paused for a moment. "But I feel I can be honest with you." Claire leaned forward.

"Unlike some, I did not have the benefit of a teacher while growing up, someone to help me control my powers. At first, I started fires unconsciously. Those around me punished me for my behavior, but as time passed, they became fearful and found excuses to push me off onto another family or home."

Claire nodded. "I had a similar experience." An excruciating one at that. Here was a woman who knew the depths of that agony.

"It's a hard way to grow up, isn't it?" She matched her expression to Claire's. "Then, I learned to use my fire to keep others at a distance. A protective measure, to be sure. But then... there was a boy." She smiled, her lips titling, giving her a wistful, youthful look. "We fell in love."

Claire smiled with her, remembering her own first love, trying to forget the tragic ending.

"Things were good for a while," Lucinda continued. "He wasn't afraid of my powers. In fact, he worshipped me. For a month, I lived in paradise, basking in his love, giving him all of mine. Then one day, he grew sick. Very, very sick."

"No," Claire whispered, reliving her own experience.

Lucinda met her gaze, blatant grief registering in her eyes. "I killed him, Claire. With my love."

"Oh goddess, no, Lucinda."

She nodded, tears filling her eyes. "I loved him so very much."

"I understand your suffering more than you realize. I, too, had a lover. A sweet man who was barely more than a boy when we met.

I...killed him as well."

Lucinda sniffed. "We can't be blamed, Claire. It wasn't our fault.

With no one to explain things to us, how were we to know?"

"That doesn't erase the pain." Claire swiped at her own tears.

"No, it doesn't." She blinked away the moisture in her eyes. "But the good news is, I've discovered a spell to help. It's brought an amazing amount of peace to my life. Perhaps it can help you, too."

"What does it do?" Claire sniffed, aching for something finally to bring peace to her tortured heart.

"It can bring back your loved one."

"No." Disbelief and alarm jumped to life inside her. "That sounds like black magic."

Lucinda waved her hand as though to dispel Claire's fears. "Don't worry. It doesn't actually bring back the person, but the apparition will look and sound exactly like your long-lost lover. You'll be surprised at the tremendous amount of absolution it will bring to your heart. You'll have the opportunity to apologize and explain your circumstances. You'll be able to love him and hug him, and though it's not real, it *feels* very real. In fact, the formula for this amazing spell can be found right here in your trusted Grim." She flipped to a page marked with a red heart.

"Trust me. You won't regret it."

Claire scanned the spell, recognizing the simple ingredients. Goddess, how she longed to see Tommy's face again. Especially in the light of Dru's betrayal. She needed someone to hug her, someone to love her. "Let's do it now."

Lucinda shook her head. "No, not now. You'll want to be alone for this one. It's powerfully overwhelming when you first look upon your loved one's face. You won't want any distractions."

"Okay. I understand." She didn't want Lucinda or her sisters to see her in such a vulnerable state. "Thank you for that warning."

"You should put the Grim in your room for now. Until you complete the spell. Then you can share its joyous return with your sisters. They will be so happy." Lucinda rewrapped the book before presenting it to Claire. "Take good care of this. It's important to all of you."

"I will." Claire clutched the book to her chest and stood. "I'll do that right now."

"Good." Lucinda stood as well. "I should take my leave now anyway. I'm sure Justine and I have overstayed our welcome. Plus, we wouldn't want your aunt to discover Tierra's secret just yet. I'll find her in the solarium and let her know I'm ready to leave."

"Thank you, Lucinda. Thank you for everything." Claire held out her hand to her newest friend.

Lucinda shook it, sending another warm wave through to Claire. "You are most welcome, my dear. We witches need to stick together.

Especially when devious men are involved."

"Yes." Especially then. She would need to devise a way to make Dru pay for his deceitfulness, but for now, she intended to soothe her soul first. "I look forward to speaking with you again. Perhaps you could come for dinner one night...without my aunt in tow. I know my sisters would love to spend time with you."

"Of course. Anytime. Just send a message to the coven's compound letting me know which day is good for you. Now, get that book to your room."

Claire complied, feeling lighter and happier than she had since she'd stepped off the plane in Seattle. Perhaps Lucinda was just what they needed to turn this war against the end of time to their favor.

✤

DRU STOOD ON THE CORNER OF WATER STREET AND Monroe, waiting for traffic to clear. The light changed, and just as he was about to step off the sidewalk, a red Civic squealed around the corner. He shot an angry look at the crazed woman behind the wheel. She responded by flipping him the bird before she plowed into the backend of a green pickup that was stopped at the next light.

"What the fuck?" Dru said to himself.

"The beasts of Hell have been released," Bane said, coming up next to him as they watched both drivers exit their vehicles. The woman approached the old man who'd been in the truck and released a string of invective a mile long. "Someone should help that guy."

Just as he said it, the old guy hauled off and punched the woman in the face.

"I need to get off the street." Dru picked up the

pace, heading toward Sirens. He wasn't sure how much of the world's atrocities he caused and how much was a result of four opened Seals.

Bane strode next to him. "Do you think you're doing this?"

"Hell if I know. But I doubt I'm helping in any case." He jerked open the glass door that led to Sirens staircase and stepped inside.

He took the first step and then bent forward as extreme pain slammed him. It was as though someone had thrust a cold dagger straight through his heart. He gripped the handrail, trying to catch his breath. He and his brothers might be immortal, but that didn't mean their bodies couldn't suffer a tremendous amount of agony.

"Jesus, Dru. What the hell is your problem?" Bane bent his head, peering into Dru's face.

"Fuck if I..." Then it registered. Claire. She was gone. The trace of fire still inside him cried out, begging to be reconnected with its mistress. "It's Claire. Something's wrong."

She wasn't dead, thank the Gods. If she had been, her fire would have been completely eradicated from his soul. But their connection had been severed.

"What is it? What do you think has happened to her?"

Dru leveled a hard look at his friend, sensing the hope in his voice. "She's not dead, if that's what you're wishing. Besides, you'd know that outcome as soon as I did." He sat on a step, trying to catch his breath.

He removed his phone and dialed her number.

As he feared, no answer.

Bane had the decency to look regretful. "Sorry, man. It's just...

Come to Sirens. Have a drink. Let's see if we can figure it out."

"I need to go there. To their house. I need to know she's okay."

Bane snorted. "You know as well as I do, you won't get the tip of your sword one inch inside that house without their permission. And they sure as hell won't roll out the welcome mat. Come on. Let's go up. Maybe the other guys will have a suggestion."

He gave a disdainful laugh. "A suggestion to save Claire? When Hell freezes over."

"Hey." Bane gave his shoulder an indignant shove. "Enough with the jokes."

Dru sucked in a breath as his body slowly accommodated the pain. He stood, then slowly made his way upward. Beads of sweat broke on his brow as he fell into his usual seat in the backroom of the bar.

By the time the Four Horsemen had gathered around the table with drinks in their hands, Dru managed regular, if shallow breaths.

"Claire's in trouble," Bane explained to the rest of them.

"I didn't do anything." Nick met Dru's gaze head on.

"Neither did I, so cast your accusatory stare elsewhere." Julian straightened his ascot.

Dru would have told them both to fuck off if he'd had any spare oxygen and wasn't so damn cold.

"What's this?" The sound of a delighted feminine voice tinkled behind him. "Are my boys fighting again?"

"Lucy." Nick stood and gave her a peck on the cheek. "Take my chair. I'll get another."

"Thank you, my dearest. You always were my favorite."

Nick grinned, and Dru wanted to remind them both that her favorite changed with each breath she took. Except for Julian. He'd never been her favorite. Yet.

"What's the problem here?" Lucy looked at each of

them, her attention stopping on Dru. "Oh, Dru, darling. Whatever is the matter? You look like death warmed over."

Bane huffed his displeasure but said nothing to Lucy about overused, unwanted jokes.

Dru focused on Lucy's icy blue eyes, finding too much pleasure in her gaze. "*What have you done?*"

"Me?" She unbuttoned the silk jacket she wore and removed it, revealing a sheer white blouse beneath. It was obvious she wore no bra. For a woman her age, her breasts were surprisingly pert. Then again, the devil never aged.

"You might be the ruler of the Underworld, but you suck at hiding your emotions." Dru inhaled a deep breath.

"You truly are suffering, aren't you?" A momentary look of concern stole over Lucy's face, but she quickly replaced it with admonition. "Perhaps one day, you'll learn not to mess with me."

Her eyes turned to crystallized wrath as she encompassed the group. "Not one of you *Horsemen* have fulfilled your duty. You're worthless, incapable of fulfilling your reason for existence. I should smite you all right now and eradicate your useless bodies from the face of the earth." The anger in her voice shook the glassware on the table.

"If your poor Claire is suffering right now, that's your fault, Dru," she continued. "She could have had a clean, pain-free death of your choosing. But you made a different choice, and now you'll both endure the consequences."

Fury burned through Dru's pain, giving him a shot of anger-infused energy. He stood abruptly, grasping Lucy's neck and pulling her to her feet. He ignored the sharp inhalations from his fellow brothers as he pinned her to the wall. "*What did you do to Claire?*"

Instead of anger, excitement sparked in Lucy's expression, her nostrils flaring. She rubbed her hand over his crotch. He released her, disgusted that he'd let her goad him into meaningless action.

She sucked in a breath and coughed. "You know how much I like rough play, Dru. If you want to come back to my room at the compound, we could spend a lovely afternoon together. I think you know the way."

Dru didn't check to see the reactions of his friends. They'd had no idea he'd been sneaking into the compound, scrutinizing the coven. Right now, he didn't care. Only one thing mattered. Claire. "Tell me what you did to her. Where is she?"

Lucy massaged her throat with crimson-nailed fingertips. "I haven't done a thing. She was safe and sound at home when I left her not long ago."

"You bitch."

The flare of anger in her eyes warned he'd crossed a line, but he didn't care. She could take his soul, damn it to eternal Hell if she wanted. But first, he'd do what he could to save Claire.

"Dru." Bane stood and put a hand on Dru's shoulder.

Dru shrugged him off, turned and strode toward the exit.

"Where are you going?" Nick called after him.

"It won't do you any good," Lucy said with a laugh.

He didn't waste time answering. Lucy could deny her involvement, but he knew. Something serious was about to go down, and he feared it wouldn't end well for the woman he loved.

Claire waited for her sisters to retire to their rooms. When the house grew quiet, she slipped from her room down to the kitchen. She rushed to gather ingredients for the awakening spell from Tierra's expansive stash, concealing them in her pockets. With stealthy steps, she hurried into her room and locked the door.

She hung a small cauldron on the hook in her fireplace and willed a fire into existence with barely a thought. Precious flames licked the kettle, caressing it with their touch. Peace settled over her, and she reassured herself this was the right thing to do.

With steady hands and an excited heart, she assembled the components on a table near the window and then pulled Grim from beneath her bed. Kai jumped on the book as though to deter her.

"No, baby. You need to stay out of the way." She gently pushed him away.

He whined, and she paused to scratch his ears.

"Don't worry. I know what I'm doing." She needed this closure in her life. Needed to heal so she would be less vulnerable to people like Dru. Needed to put the past behind her, because what lay ahead would require all of her attention.

Carefully, she reviewed each required element, each hallowed word. She could not screw this up.

With a nervous fingers, she added the correct amount of ingredients with the exception of one, stirring them with a wooden spoon. When the concoction bubbled, releasing fragrant spices into the room, she began to speak.

> *Goddess of fire, hear my plea.*
> *Bring back my love who is dear to me.*
> *Long been apart, unfairly so,*
> *Restore the love, make it glow.*
> *By earth, air, fire and sea...*

She took a deep breath and threw in the ginger. The walls began to shake, and Claire immediately cursed herself for not asking Lucinda what to expect. Kai growled and sought shelter under the bed. The idea of seeing Tommy again had been irresistible, but she hadn't meant to bring down the whole house or notify her sisters of the process. Really, she hadn't thought of anything beyond holding him again.

The contents of the cauldron caught fire, flames expanding until they reached outside the fireplace. The rock around the edges began to blacken, and Claire feared the fire would continue until it consumed her room. This spell was meant for outdoors.

"Hell." She had to do something before she burned them out of house and home. She mentally protected herself against fire as she opened her bedroom window. The rush of air enhanced the fire, the flames now reaching toward the wallpaper.

She raced toward the growing disaster and gripped the cauldron's handle just as her door burst open. Tierra stood wide-eyed in the doorway. "What in the name of the goddess are you doing?"

"Stay back," Claire yelled. Three-foot flames roared

out of the kettle as she ran for the window. As she climbed through the opening, her curtains caught fire.

"Moira! Aerin!" Tierra screamed behind her.

Claire didn't look back as she hurried across the porch roof and chucked the cauldron, contents and all, down onto the grass. She hoped the lack of a heat source and the moisture from the ground would stop the flames.

Instead, the blaze continued, the contents now beginning to take the shape of an undulating blob.

"Shit," Claire hissed. She turned to find her three sisters peering out the window behind her. Thankfully, her curtains no longer burned. She strode toward them, pushing through until she was back inside.

"What have you done?" Aerin asked, fear in all of their eyes.

"A spell. To bring back my first love. Lucinda recommended it."

"You trusted that lanky bitch?" Moira asked, reproach in her gaze.

"Look on the table. She brought back the Grimoire as an offer of friendship." Though Claire wondered now if she'd been too caught up in what Lucinda had said to pay attention to any inner warnings. "I sensed no evil about her. Why shouldn't I trust her? Why shouldn't we?

She could be the help we need to save everyone."

"You say this even as you try to burn down our house?" Tierra shook her head in disappointment. "Even I was smart enough to sense something was up with her."

Claire recoiled. "You didn't spend as much time with her as I did.

She only wants to be our friend."

"Uh-huh." Moira lifted a doubtful brow.

"I don't have time to argue." She shoved past them. "My cauldron is still burning in the yard. Whatever is *brewing* isn't done yet." She raced down the stairs and outside, her sisters hot on her trail.

"Oh, shit." Tierra said as the four of them came to halt at the edge of the lawn.

"What the fuck is that?" Aerin whispered.

The concoction had grown in size. The oily black blob continued to move and expand.

"I'd say it's Satan's spawn come to kick our ass." Moira linked her arms through Claire's and Tierra's.

"We have to stop it." Aerin opened the book she'd had clutched to her chest. "There must be a spell somewhere that can reverse it."

"I don't know where," Claire said.

"Find the original spell," Tierra suggested. "Sometimes reversals can be in small print at the bottom of the page."

Claire took the book, frantically looking for the page with the red heart. "Here! It's right here." Her hands shook as she tried to read the small lettering in the dim light from the porch.

"I can't see anything." Tierra grabbed the book and moved closer to the light. "Yes, there's one." She quickly chanted the words, and the four of them turned to watch the growing mass.

Tierra's spell failed to provide any obvious effect. "I'm not strong enough on my own."

"We can't join our powers, Tierra." Aerin shook her head decisively. "You know what will happen."

"Maybe just a couple of us can," Moira said. "Maybe me and Tierra since this is a fire spell. Water and earth ought to put it out, right?"

The four of them looked at each other, and then Tierra and Moira joined hands without waiting for an official decision.

At the end of their incantation, the form hissed and spit, but didn't diminish in size.

"Oh goddess. It's growing claws," Tierra shrieked.

"Kill it. Now." Panic colored Moira's voice. "Y'all have no idea what it could do by the time it's done growing. It might eat the entire town like Godzilla or something."

"Okay, three of us." Fear must have engaged inside Aerin as well because she quickly joined hands with Moira and Tierra.

As they chanted the spell, the black figure Claire had conjured tripled in size. It loomed over them, taking more of a human shape, though its arms and claws continued to grow. It had also gained mobility, and now inched across the grass toward them.

Unmitigated fear raged through Claire as her three sisters repeated the spell over and over. *What in the hell had she unleashed?*

Whatever it was had to be stopped. There was no guarantee the four of them working a spell together would break another Seal, but they'd already done it once. However, Claire was damn sure the present danger would overtake them any second if she did nothing.

She broke Tierra's and Moira's clasped hands, gripping them both with her own. With as much power as she could muster, she joined in the chant with her sisters.

The creature screamed, its howl piercing the night sky.

"Again!" Aerin yelled. "I think it's working."

They repeated the words, the spell becoming an enchanting, powerful song with a mystical rhythm. The leaves in the trees rustled in the stiff breeze as the ground beneath them shook. Electrical currents entered her body from one sister and quickly passed to another. Their energies had combined, creating a magnetic, formidable power.

Rain poured from the sky, sizzling the burning entity. It screeched and roared, but no longer crawled toward them.

Midway through another round, a powerful wave sent Claire and her sisters tumbling apart. The figure on the grass seized, a big, black mountain of frozen fear. Then it shattered. Pieces of what appeared to be obsidian broke away, leaving a man lying on the grass.

The women scrambled to their feet. Claire held her breath as Tierra grabbed her hand once again.

"We done birthed a demon," Moira whispered.

The young man groaned and slowly rose to his knees. He caught sight of them and halted, his expression full of confusion and distress. When his gaze landed on Claire, an elated smile erupted on his lips.

"Claire."

"*Tommy?*" Claire gasped as she dropped Tierra's hand.

"Claire," he said again. He jumped to his feet and ran toward her, throwing his arms around her, crushing her with his hug. "Where have you been? I've looked everywhere."

Claire pulled back and studied his features with anunearthly hunger. He looked exactly as he had before he'd become sick— blond hair, dazzling blue eyes that adored her. "I'm sorry, Tommy."

"I was so worried. But I've found you now. Thank God I've found you."

Aerin cleared her throat, drawing Claire's gaze away from her loved one's face.

"Who the hell is this?" Aerin asked as she cocked her hip and planted her hand on it.

"This is Tommy. He was my boyfriend."

Tommy sent her a hurtful, questioning look.

"He *is* my boyfriend," Claire corrected.

"I thought he was dead," Tierra whispered.

Moira shrugged. "Who says he isn't still?"

Dru parked a block from the Victorian mansion and stealthily made his way in the dark, his heart racing like a raging winter thunderstorm. If Lucy had harmed Claire in any way, he would see that she burned in the fires of Hell for an eternity. He didn't know how or when, but she'd pay for her crimes.

A loud, animalistic wail rang through the air as he neared, and he was forced to slow or lose his footing when the ground released a violent rumble.

Panic tightened his heart. Something in the universe had shifted, and he feared that only meant one thing.

Another Seal.

"Fuck," he yelled into the night and sprinted forward. There was no time for covert tactics. No time to waste. He needed to be by Claire's side now, before anything bad happened.

He had no idea what this event would bring about, but predictions decried the souls of the martyrs would to return to earth.

Lucy would be beyond pissed.

Light and voices gushed from the back of the house, drawing Dru in that direction. He skirted the edge of the protected fence, making his way between trees and bushes. When he caught the sight unfolding, he tripped on a large rock and stumbled into the fence, barely catching himself.

Claire's joy filled the air, a bright orange hue full of wonder. She jumped into a man's arms, and Dru could not mistake their connection. It far surpassed anything he'd built with her.

Was that why he'd lost their bond? He could sense she loved this man more than life. How could Dru ever compete?

He had no idea if Lucy had known that her ploy would open the Fifth Seal, or if she'd only meant to cause Dru excruciating pain. But two things were extremely clear. Lucy had won this battle. And Claire had given her heart to a dead man, leaving him to deal with pain and despair that would echo through the eternities.

What the hell could he do now?

AERIN

KERRIGAN BYRNE

❀ I ❀

"Earth to release me from the land
Water to guide the task at hand.
Flame to hasten my course ahead.
Air to be the path I tread.
By earth, fire, water and sky,
Goddess bless this broom to fly!"

Thwack. The broom hit the distressed wood of the kitchen floor with the loud, plastic sound of failure. Aerin de Moray gave a surreptitious glance around the empty room to make sure no one had seen her millionth unsuccessful attempt before she directed her frustration at the stubborn inanimate object. It was one of those light-as-a-feather blue and white plastic jobbers with polypropylene fibers arranged into yellow angled bristles with a matching attached dustpan that she gripped in her hand.

Waving the bladed rubber edge of the pan at the prostrate broom, she unleashed her wrath, "Listen up, motherfucker, I'm going to try this one more time, and if you don't at least levitate for a second, I'm going to have Claire melt you into a plastic dildo and give you as a Christmas present to Hank Miller down the street, and we all know what goes on in that house."

The broom couldn't have been more apathetic.

Aerin kicked it where she thought the kidneys would be.

"Unless this is *your* fault, Grim." She whirled on the ancient tome spread open on the table, distinctly emitting an air of innocence. The de Moray Grimoire had become a part of the family now that he'd been returned by Lucy. Aerin and her sisters all had the tendency to anthropomorphize the family spell book, going so far as to assign him a gender and nicknaming him "Grim." He was bound in human flesh, after all, and he was immensely helpful, even opening to the correct page upon request.

By himself.

After it stopped being spooky, it was pretty rad.

Aerin squinted down at the spell again, magically disambiguated for her. The first time she'd come across this page, it had been in some ancient form of Gaelic. She'd asked Grim to translate it for her and, at first, nothing had happened. But the next time she'd opened the book, there it was, in the Queen's own English.

It even rhymed.

She'd followed all the rules. Got a broom. Gathered four white fluffy dandelion heads and a puff of cottonwood, to which she was allergic, apparently, and blew them all over the damned kitchen and did the hokey pokey and turned herself about saying the spell.

And... nothing.

The book *specifically* said the air witch had to bless the broom before it could fly. That *she* had to go first. "So what gives?" she demanded of Grim. "Are you fucking with me?" A grimoire with a sense of humor could be a dangerous thing.

Aerin didn't trust ninety-nine-point-nine percent of people on a good day, and an ancient, sentient, rune-decorated, flesh book didn't exactly inspire confidence.

"Did you just yell at the Grimoire?" Tommy queried

as he sauntered down the stairs that led from the second floor to the kitchen.

"Did you just eat a raw steak?" Aerin made a sound of revulsion as Tommy rinsed a puddle of blood off the plate in his hands and put it in the dishwasher. He'd been around for two days, and they still hadn't landed on what exactly to do with him. Claire seemed to be ecstatic that her ex-boyfriend was back, and Aerin had to give it to the guy, he may or may not be undead, but at least he was a decent houseguest.

Still, Aerin didn't trust him, and not just because she prided herself on being a professional misanthrope. She couldn't read him. Couldn't feel any emotional vibrations coming from his body like she did with everyone else. Empathy was her ironic superpower, and Tommy was immune, which put him in the make-one-wrong-move-and-I'll-put-you-back-in-the-coffin category. At least, from Aerin's point of view.

Also, Tierra said he smelled weird. And at the moment, scent was *her* superpower. Not because she was a witch, but because she was knocked-up.

Aerin shuddered with revulsion again.

Tommy's blue eyes sparkled like the open sea. He had that kind of wide-shouldered, dimpled, all-American charm that belonged to sparkly-eyed men like Chris Pine and Channing Tatum. It was disarming and very, *very* different than Drustan's dark, exotic, dangerous, and otherworldly sex appeal. Claire's spectrum of men was quite varied.

Aerin had to give her sister that.

"I like my meat rare," Tommy said with a good-natured shrug.

There was *rare*, and then there was the fact that the stove hadn't been used, and neither had the grill as far as Aerin could tell. She supposed Claire could have roasted it with her uber fire powers, but she thought Claire was in the entertainment room with the others—

The high-pitched, terrified screams of her sisters was instantly drowned out by the pounding of adrenaline in her ears. Snatching the broom from the ground, Aerin raced down the hall, almost tripping on the Celtic-braided rug before skidding to a stop at the entry to the entertainment room.

"His boot still has brains on it!" Moira bounced up and down on the overstuffed sectional couch, crunching on another pork rind and pointing at the big screen TV. "Did y'all see that? Zombie's eye popped like a grape!"

"*My* eyes are still popping because the one with a crossbow took his shirt off." Claire wriggled her shapely eyebrows.

"Gross," Tierra moaned from where her face was buried in one of the couches' many throw pillows. "Tell me when I can look, you guys." Even in the ambient glow of the TV, she looked a little pale, maybe a little green, too.

Aerin lowered the broom she brandished, her breathing returning to normal. They'd all been on high-alert lately, and it must be getting to her more than she realized.

An impending Apocalypse will do that to a girl.

She knew how religious her sisters were about their Sunday night cable and that for the next hour, they would be glued to the tube, getting off on gore-porn and zombie killers.

"Why does the sweaty one in leather have a crossbow? Seems like an antiquated weapon with a high risk of running out of ammunition. Don't guns kill zombies in this show?" Aerin asked. "Everyone else is using a gun."

Three pairs of mutinous, incredulous eyes turned toward her in perfect synchronization. It was unsettling because each face was identical but for the color of their eyes, and it gave a distinct *Children of the Corn* vibe.

"The *sweaty* one?" Moira asked slowly, her aquamarine eyes narrowing.

"You mean the *hot* one," Claire corrected. "As in sexy. Also, that woman is using a katana, so not *everyone* has a gun."

"I prefer the leader," Tierra said, slightly off topic. "I like a rugged guy with a beard who's in charge and carries a big gun."

"But he's carrying a revolver," Aerin pointed out. "It only holds six bullets. What about the good-looking Asian with the AK47, doesn't it seem like he should be in charge? At the very least, he wins bullets."

"That so-called *sweaty one* is the melancholy backwoods badass loner with a tragic past and a heart of gold." Moira snorted her displeasure. "Almost every woman in this country would do him sideways from hell to breakfast."

"As long as they use protection," Aerin snarked. "It looks like his family tree doesn't have enough branches."

She gasped as a pork rind bounced off her face. "Hey!"

"Are you doing chores?" Tierra asked hopefully motioning to the broom Aerin still clutched with both hands.

Aerin looked down, feeling sheepish and at the same time wondering where the dustpan went. *Chores? Ha. Fat chance.* "I heard you guys scream, and I thought..."

"That we were being attacked and you were going to sweep them to death?" Moira chortled.

"If this was the zombiepocalypse, you'd totally die first," Tierra said.

"You know what? Never mind." Aerin brought the broom in closer to her chest, as though to shield it from their taunts. See if she came running to their rescue next time.

On the screen another zombie head exploded, and a

horde of gray, hissing, grotesque undead began ripping the limbs off a screaming victim.

"That's it!" Tierra held the back of her hand to her mouth, the silver backs of her rings catching the light from the TV as she squeezed her eyes shut. "Change the channel you guys, or I'm going to barf."

Moira grabbed the remote. "Okay, what else we got on Sunday night?"

"Hmmm." Claire pursed her lips. "There's Masterpiece Theatre presents historical soap operas, Sexy Highlanders on Starz, or boobs and dragons on HBO."

"I don't care." Teirra swallowed a few times. "Just switch it before you're wearing my dinner."

Moira hit a button on the remote and two newscasters, a man and a woman with impossibly white teeth and strikingly similar blowout hair styles, sat behind a gray desk.

"Whew, thank you." Tierra visibly relaxed.

"*... Officials are saying that they don't have any conclusive data as of yet to explain the cause of the recent rise in disturbingly violent crime in Seattle, but they did voice their growing concerns that it's spreading to other cities along the West Coast,*" the male newscaster explained in a solemn voice. "*Officials also refused to comment on the claims several victims have made that the perpetrators of assaults, violence, and even murder have been someone who was previously reported deceased.*"

They all wore identical looks of wide-eyed astonishment as they glanced at each other.

"Is this *another* zombie movie?" Aerin asked.

A horrified Tierra shook her head. "This is the channel five evening news. That's Kip Kipley and Sharon Trout, long-time local news anchors."

Cue Sharon with her red suit and chunky gold jewelry. "*We obtained some footage of the violence shot earlier today, and we have to warn you, this might be disturbing to some viewers. A local Tacoma man was brutally attacked at a coffee*

*shop by someone he'd claimed was a childhood friend who'd
drowned ten years ago when they were swimming together."*

A shaky video, obviously taken from a bystander
phone, showed a bloated teenager with soggy clothes
grab a man in a suit and chop the screaming guy's hand
off with a cleaver.

Coffee mingled with blood as chaos erupted, and
the cup, hand still attached, exploded all over the floor.

"Holy shit on a shingle," Moira breathed. She barely
noticed as Tierra ripped the bag of pork rinds from her
and heaved the contents of her stomach into it.

"So zombies, is that a thing?" The words rushed from Aerin's mouth into her Bluetooth the moment the click sounded indicating someone had picked up the other line. Sitting on the white trunk at the foot of her bed, she worried one of her silk cuffs and studied the black and white arabesque wallpaper.

"Aerin de Moray." Julian Roarke's British inflection wrapped her name in blood-red velvet, even through the phone. His cultured voice evoked luxurious Jaguar commercials and indulgent, delectable sins that would be illegal where Moira came from. "How did you get this number?"

"Not important." She tried to sound all clipped and business-like and shit. She'd swoon over the provocative surprise in his voice later. "Does this Apocalypse happen to be the zombiepocalypse?"

"You see," he continued, undeterred, "we bought this phone at a ubiquitous marketplace that seems to be off of every freeway exit these days. There was an astounding number of people in elastic-waist trousers or sporting what Nicholas called a "muffin top." He paused, and Aerin could almost hear him shudder. "Are you familiar with the term?"

"Yes, but I saw on the news—."

"Please, don't misunderstand me, I do so appreciate a voluptuous woman, but if ladies insist on wearing trousers in this century, then they should at least buy them in the correct size to avoid said phenomenon."

She couldn't agree with him more, truth-be-told, but she didn't have time to commiserate at the moment. Julian wasn't the sort of man who would be caught dead in sweatpants. He dressed exclusively in anachronistic suits that evoked Dracula movies and Brontë novels, complete with watch chains and cufflinks and buttoned vests.

Except for that once. When they'd enjoyed an evening ride through the forest on a black steed older than her last name. Where they'd kissed in the moonlight. He'd worn an open poet's shirt and loose trousers.

More Highlander than Hawthorne. He'd taken her breath and left her wanting way more than just one kiss.

She intended to remedy that. Eventually. If they didn't all die first.

"What does this have to do with zombies?" she demanded in that voice that always got her what she wanted.

He denied her. Again. "The point I was getting at is that I procured the phone from a gentleman, and I use that term *very* loosely, who assured me that it was untraceable, that no one could get the number."

Oh, now it made sense. "One thing you have to learn about the digital age, Julian, is that you can hide nothing. Especially from me. I own the clouds. All of them. Which means there is no information I can't find if I look hard enough."

"Indeed." He sounded sufficiently impressed, and Aerin had to swallow satisfaction. "May I ask why you expended so much of your expertise to seek me out, Aerin de Moray?"

"Because you know stuff." That was why. The only

reason why. Pretty much half of the only couple of reasons why.

His voice became dry enough to blow away in a sandstorm. "Duly noted. You inquired about zombies?"

"Yes, what do you know about them?"

He was silent a moment before answering. "Well, the genesis of the word itself is contested. It either comes from the Haitian or Creole French term *Zonbi,* which belongs to the Voodoo religion. They're historically human corpses reanimated by magic. Specifically, Necromancy. Though in popular culture of these modern days the consensus seems to be that the undead are corpses infected with a virus, which I find rather ridiculous as there is and never will be a virus that brings the dead back to life."

He should know. He was Pestilence, after all.

"Do zombies have anything to do with the prophecy?" she pressed. "If the dead start to come back to life, what does that mean?"

"Aerin..." A pregnant pause yawned in the chasm between them. "We shouldn't be talking about this. We're on other sides of this battle and—."

"Listen, bub, every last one of us is going to *be* on the 'other side' if we don't figure out how to stop this shit," Aerin interrupted. "I don't understand why we have to be in opposition. It's not like any of us *want* the end of the world to come about."

"That isn't *entirely* true."

This time it was Aerin's turn to pause. "Come the fuck again?"

"My brothers and I are divided on this issue," he confessed.

"Really?" This was news to her. "Where do you land?"

"I am...conflicted. I haven't *landed* on a side as of yet. It is all, up in the *air*, as it were." His soft chuckle washed over her like silk gliding over nude flesh.

Puns. Ugh.

"Har. Har," Aerin said acerbically. "Yuck it up, chuckles. But if there are those of you who want us to end the world, why are you still trying to kill us in order to stop it?"

"You know I can't answer that," he replied. "There are powers at play that you can't possibly—" He caught himself just in time and silence stretched between them once more.

She could see him in her mind as though she'd conjured him with a spell. His dark, gothic elegance underscored by a hint of archaic brutality. Beautiful features, artistically rendered with such flawless precision that even the staunchest atheist would have to admit only a god could sculpt such perfection. Pale as a vampire, strong as a mountain, and lethal as the plague. Literally.

That was Julian Roarke.

Maybe she shouldn't have fucking called him.

"I must admit," something warmed Pestilence's voice. Scotch, maybe, or laughter. Hard to tell. "After spending an infuriating half hour at said marketplace today, I lost what little faith I had left in humanity. I'm leaning toward complete planetary annihilation."

"A man like you shouldn't joke about that," Aerin said through a burst of laughter. "But I can't say I haven't experienced the same thing."

"You have a lovely laugh, Aerin de Moray." The sincerity in his tone sobered her immediately.

"Thanks." She brought a hand to her burning cheek. "Will you at least tell me why you're conflicted? I want to understand you."

"Have you ever looked up what the word Apocalypse means?"

"Don't try to change the subject on me, Julian," she warned.

"I can assure you, I'm not," he redressed. "Just indulge me for a moment whilst I explain."

"Okay," Aerin said carefully.

"If this prophecy is allowed to come to fruition, Aerin, it won't culminate in complete obliteration of the planet, or of humanity. As I was saying before, the word *Apocalypse*, when translated from Greek, its original language, literally means a revelation. A lifting of the veil, as it were. What we, the Horsemen bring about, would be mass devastation, there's no doubt of that. But it would be more of a cataclysm really, than true annihilation. It'll mean the gods of creation have forsaken mortals. That the planet would be on the open market, so to speak, for anyone with sufficient power to take hold of. To put it simply, no one wants to rule nothing. But scorched earth can easily be reseeded, and the outcome of that battle could be worse than anything our feeble minds could devise. On the other side of that argument, there is a chance for humanity to redeem itself. To start over. The strongest would survive the conquests, the wars, and finally the plagues. They would be ripe for the picking, ready to follow someone with enough power and—"

An idea straightened Aerin's spine. "Someone like us?" she posited.

"Like you?"

He made a wry sound. "Perish the thought... but yes."

Interesting...

"Though the likelihood would be more of the deity variety," he rushed on. "And none of them good. Listen, Aerin, there are those whose interests are directly tied to this prophecy. Who've waited literally millennia to swoop in and take over. To subjugate any who are left and to claim all errant power in this world for their own. Do you understand me? Some of them are *closer* than you *think*."

The hidden meaning in his voice could have choked a whale.

"Who do you mean?"

"I *can't* say," he repeated his earlier words. "But, who knows where we'll stand when the smoke clears?"

Who, indeed? Aerin thought. Something to consider. Might well-meaning, benevolent elemental witches make for some excellent overlords? *Hells yeah*. A damn sight better than the current fuckwads in power. If the de Moray Druids ruled the planet, would little kids starve? No. Would religious war devastate nations? Not on her watch. Everyone would be all happy and fed and shit. Plus, Druid magic made for one hell of a health plan.

Was that a terrible idea?

She was getting ahead of herself. First things first.

"So zombies are wreaking havoc and I don't think the problem is going to get any better." She shifted gears back to the problem at hand. "What do you think we should do? Do you know how to kill a zombie?"

That thoughtful, unhurried silence would be considered rude in this day and age, but Aerin understood that he had the patience of an immortal, not to mention the memory of one. That was a lot of files to flip through in the ol' noggin.

"I don't know that there's anything that can be done. Permit me to consult some texts. There exist many *many* myths about the dead coming back to life. The problem is, these are stories of those who conquered death himself and thereby become deities, or at least immortals. We've had this conversation before, you and I... Pantheons of your people. Demigods and luminaries who may or may not be deities but are supposed to have risen from the dead. For example, the Egyptian's Ra and Osiris. The Nordic God Baldr. The Greeks had Adonis. The Babylonians had Ishtar. And a myriad of others, Ba'al, Bacchus, Hermes,

Dionysus, Mithras, Orpheus, et cetera. Even the son

of the Christian God rose from the dead and the argument could be made that he's a zom—"

"*Dat!* – stop right there." Aerin held up a hand, forgetting that he couldn't see her through the phone line. "I might not be religious, but being raised in a Judeo-Christian society I still expect to get hit by lightning every time you wax so blasphemous."

That chuckle washed over her again, and the warm vibration made its way through her until it landed in her panties. "Lightning." Amusement made his voice a little deeper. Even sexier, if that was possible. "That's so charming coming from you."

"Why?"

"You'll find out, soon, I expect." A deep breath expelled too close to his side of the mouthpiece, and it made that unpleasant noise that wind did over the phone. "I'll look into this, Aerin de Moray. But this means I'll have to see you again."

Implications she dare not identify dripped from his cultured voice like expensive wine.

"You could call me," she ventured.

"You could meet me," he countered.

"So you can kill me? Please."

"What if I gave you my word that I wouldn't, this time?"

"Pff. Real romantic there, Casanova. But you have three brothers who'd love nothing more than to see my head on a spike."

"I won't tell them we're meeting. And I won't allow them to harm you. I—"

Aerin waited while he waged a silent battle with himself.

"I must see you again," he said darkly. "I must... touch you again... just to remind myself that it's possible. There's nothing so soft as your skin, Aerin. Nothing so beautiful as your face."

She snorted. "Except three other identical faces."

"They're not you," he insisted. "Their eyes don't flash liquid silver. Their mouths aren't hard and cynical. Their tongues are not so sharp. Their clothes are not so fine."

"Sycophancy."

"Not at all," he argued. "I want to feel your mouth soften. I like to think it only does that for me."

And she'd be goat-fucked if he didn't speak the absolute truth.

"Where?" she breathed. Suddenly feeling the damsel to his lord.

"The cliff where we kissed." His voice sounded breathier, as well. Husky with anticipation.

"When?"

"Tomorrow. Midnight."

She ended the call with a shaky breath. Of course it would be midnight.

The witching hour.

❋ 3 ❋

"They know even less than we thought," Bane mused, taking a drag of his beer.

"So it seems," Julian agreed after relating the particulars of his phone call with Aerin to his brothers. Well, the pertinent parts. They didn't know he and Aerin would meet on the morrow. They didn't know that, even now, the husky tones of her breezy voice vibrated in his ear. That his body and his heart ached with a hollow yearning he'd not encountered in a handful of millennia.

They didn't know... that he was falling for her.

"Didn't they read the prophecy?" Nicholas Kingswood tossed a cashew and caught it in his mouth as he sauntered toward the bar. His grey suit and burnished silver tie added a metallic bronze hue to his caramel hair. He looked like he belonged on Wall Street, though the last time he got involved with the stock market was nineteen-twenty-nine. Fairly recently to men such as they. "It says in their own Grimoire that when the fifth seal is broken, the blood of martyrs will be called forth and also the innocent, and they will rise up in vengeance."

"True, but theological scholars have been debating the meaning of that prophecy for thousands of years,"

Dru pointed out from where he ran a whet stone down his blade. The gritty sound it made a familiar, soothing melody for them all. Something from the past. A sound as perpetual as themselves. "From the Druids, to the Egyptians, to the Talmudic seers, and down through the Christians, they've all speculated about the last three seals. But very few have really witnessed an army of the undead. Or fought them. We can't expect a couple of modern-day, twenty-something witches to just know this shit. They're little more than babies."

"They're old enough to fuck," Nick countered. "Which means they're old enough to know."

"Not since Macbeth's successor, the Druid King, Malcolm de Moray and his sisters defeated the army of the undead raised by the Wyrd Sisters a thousand years past," Bane recalled.

"And before that, it had been five thousand years, at least." Julian leaned forward in his studded leather chair and swirled his wine. He'd had such a penchant for these dark-cherry colored reds these days. Touching each of his fellow Horsemen with a speculative glance, he also read their emotional signatures. Something they could all do. A bond they all relied upon and cursed in equal measure. "So the question arises along with this army of undead, gentlemen, do we sit by and let the de Moray sisters fight this battle on their own? Or do we help them?" He'd never sat among more conflicted souls in his life.

"That's a tough one." Nicholas touched his forehead with exhausted fingers. "On a good day, I lean toward letting this play out. Lighting a match and watching all these fat, fucking useless people of the world burn. When it comes to the Apocalypse, I say bring it." He paused, taking a sip from a martini glass.

"And yet?" Julian prompted.

"There's *her* to consider."

"Moira?" Dru queried.

Nicholas's eyes sharpened at the sound of the water witch's name, but he shook his head, regarding his drink as though salvation lie within.

"Lucifer."

A shudder passed through the room as the air was kissed with the evil chill of her name.

"Morning star, my dying ass," Dru muttered. "You know Nick and I have been leaning toward pro-Apocalypse for a few hundred years now. But we all know we have to stop it, or at least stall it until that evil bitch is handled."

"Indeed," Julian sipped his wine, allowing the velvet vintage to slide down his throat, taking all the moisture with it. "If eternity was a chess board, she'd be the black queen. Every advantage afforded her. Gaining power as more and more gods of light become obsolete."

"While we're on the subject, she could manipulate the de Moray sisters," Conquest pointed out. "She could draw them to her side, like she did the Wyrd Sisters. She's already infiltrated the local coven. Once she had the de Moray Druid magic in her control, it would be hellllloooooo to eternal darkness and suffering blah blah souls writhing, humans enslaved, creatures of the darkness unleashed, blah." He rolled his eyes skyward as he downed the last of his drink and reached for more vodka.

"There is that," Julian agreed, contemplating his conversation with Aerin just moments ago.

"Not Tierra," Bane insisted, a strange light in his midnight eyes. "She'd never allow her powers to be corrupted by the likes of Lucy. This earth means too much to her. She's a creature of the light. She's too...pure."

"Or *was* until you got your hands on her," Nicholas laughed.

"I will *end* you."

Dru jumped in, creating a much needed distraction.

"Claire has a shadowy side, but her heart is big. And good. I don't think she would knowingly allow herself to be manipulated by darkness."

"But can you be certain?" Julian asked.

"As certain as I am of anything these days." Dru's face shuddered, though his emotional signature ran hot. Hotter than usual.

"Moira's definitely a wild card," Nicholas speculated. "But I know she cares... she cares so damn much. She's more depth than darkness. But there's pain there, and fear. That can be exploited and fanned into hatred very easily."

Every man was silent for a moment, contemplating their futures, their desires.

Their duties.

"What about Aerin, brother?" Bane's deadly gaze captured his with meaning and maybe a little bit of sympathy.

"Speaking of bitches," Conquest muttered.

"I may not be able to kill you, Nicholas," Julian said rather glibly. "But it's damned uncomfortable to be an immortal with an incurable rash on your nethers." Standing, he set his empty wine glass on the sideboard and started off in the direction of the study.

Dru paused in his sword sharpening. "The risen, they'll be after the witches once their own vengeance is achieved. We let them do their thing? Let them consume one of the de Moray sisters?"

Nicholas gave a shrug that conveyed much fewer fucks than he actually gave. "Could possibly take the decision out of our hands."

"So, we've decided then." Dru blinked down, returning to his past time. "One of them still has to go unless we can figure out how to get rid of Lucy first."

"There is no 'getting rid' of Lucifer," Julian said.

"How would you know?" Nick challenged.

"What do you think I've been studying all these

centuries in isolation?" Julian hissed. "Unlike you, it hasn't been the many uses of my own cock."

"Jealous, much?"

"Not in the least."

Right before Julian quit the room, Bane stopped him with his dark voice.

"We still have to choose one of them to die," he stated bluntly. "You never answered the question, Julian. Is Aerin de Moray corruptible? Would she join forces with Lucy to overthrow humanity?"

Julian paused with his hand on the door jamb. "I think not." If anything, she'd overthrow humanity by herself.

"I've seen her soul... it's perturbing and opaque. Does she have a good heart?"

Julian was silent, every molecule in his body screaming to protect her. But he'd never lied to the faces of his brothers. Not in years beyond number. He was already hiding their rendezvous from them.

But an out and out falsehood? Honor wouldn't permit.

"I don't profess to know what is in Aerin de Moray's heart," he murmured, and quit the room, intending to find out.

❅ 4 ❅

"I just can't understand why it isn't working," Aerin grumbled, planting her forehead on the kitchen table. "I said the spell a million times. I've blown enough dandelions to impress a back alley whore. What else can I *do*?"

"Maybe you're using the wrong kind of broom. Perhaps it has to be made of all the elements," Tierra suggested from where her busy hands prepared lunch.

Aerin sat back up and squinted at the page again. "But polypropylene is just a thermoplastic polymer that comes from the earth. And when it's processed, it's liquefied and then heated with fire...should be good to go."

Skin-tight leather creaked as Claire leaned across the small table-for-four situated in the nook overlooking the sound. "That's quite a stretch, even for us." She wrinkled her nose. "Maybe you should try to make a broom that looks like the one in the book. A live branch, that would still have water inside of it, and then straw bristles that we can singe with fire."

"As suggestions go, it's a genius one." Moira's bare feet slapped against the floor as she wandered in with her little fire-breathing teacup pig, Cheeto, tucked under one arm. Once she set him on the floor, he rooted beneath the long lace tablecloth, content with chilling in the dark until scraps that he could pilfer fell from the table.

"I agree...what is this?" Aerin narrowed her eyes at the plate Tierra set in front of her. Luckily her sister missed her wince as she'd used her considerable waitressing abilities to carry all three of their plates at once and set identical ones in front of Claire and then Moira.

"It's an olive and feta soy cheese wrap with brined tofu and garden veggies. You guys are lucky, I found these wraps made of ground quinoa and coconut flour!" She turned to retrieve her own plate.

"Thanks." Aerin pasted on a fake smile that she hoped didn't show too much teeth.

"Delicious." Claire's amber eyes collided with hers in panic.

Moira blinked at it for a few seconds. "That looks as...green as a bullfrog in a blender."

"Aw, thanks!" Tierra beamed at them from back at the counter.

"That wasn't meant as a compliment," Moira muttered under her breath.

"Never can tell coming from you," Aerin whispered, and received a toe-jab to the shin.

The three giggled, but pulled straight faces when Tierra wandered back over. "Oh dammit," she grunted as she set her plate in her spot. "I forgot my prenatal vitamins. They're in my room. I'll be right back. Start without me, and when I come back down we'll talk more about flying on brooms."

The moment she disappeared up the stairs all three plates disappeared beneath the table.

"Looks like Cheeto is the only one having lunch," Claire muttered. "Think we have enough time to make something else?"

"Not before she comes back and catches us." Casting a longing look at the fridge, Aerin wondered why she even considered it. There was nothing edible in there. Fermented things that didn't get you drunk, so why bother? Cheeses without milk or the other proper components. Bread with no gluten or yeast. Meats with no animal parts. She'd thought Tierra was bad back before she'd gotten knocked up. This was approaching the surreal.

She'd bring about the Apocalypse if she could grill a decent filet mignon in hellfire. Tommy had eaten the last red meat left in the fridge last night.

"Zombies." Aerin blew out a heavy sigh of disgust. "How do you kill them?"

"Seems to me we oughta saw off a few shotguns and load them with ammo strong enough to blow their heads clean off their bodies." Moira suggested with apparent relish.

"Might not have to go that far. Maybe we could use more... magical means?" Claire's discomfort with the subject was written all over her face. "We're still not sure that killing is the best way to deal with them."

"You catch the news this morning?" Moira asked. "They're getting more and more violent. On TV, zombies are usually killed by chopping their heads off, or a crossbow bolt or bullet through the brain."

"We could try that." Aerin shrugged. "But the zombies on TV are made so by a virus. This is magic we're dealing with. There's no virus that could bring the dead back to life."

"How do you know that?" Claire asked alertly.

"Uh." She couldn't tell them she'd contacted Julian to get information. That they owed him a favor. And even though she trusted that his word was the truth, she knew they wouldn't. "If you kill something that's already dead, is it still murder?" Aerin redirected.

"I vote yes." Tommy sauntered into the kitchen, his fists punched into the front pocket of his jeans. For a dead guy, he looked pretty great in a tight white Tee and jeans. He leaned down and planted a kiss on Claire's up-turned lips before tossing a smile full of careless charm at Moira and Aerin.

"Gross." Tierra grimaced at the couple as she reappeared at the bottom of the steps, the bangles at her wrists and ankles tinkling at her approach. "You just kissed a corpse."

Tommy looked sheepish, but unperturbed.

"Says the woman who got knocked up by Death," Claire volleyed back.

Moira snorted with laughter.

"At least he smelled good," Tierra muttered. "Oh, hey! You guys sure finished lunch fast."

Claire didn't bat an eye. "My plate was licked clean."

"Yeah," Aerin jumped in. "My wrap was devoured."

"Scarfed, even," Moira supplied.

"Aw... I was afraid you wouldn't like them." Tierra smiled, looking utterly pleased.

An awkward silence burped into the kitchen. And was followed by the unapologetic rip of a fart and a smell so rank it evoked the sulphurous depths of hell.

Aerin clapped her hand over her nose. "Who in the several fucks is responsible for that?"

They all turned to look at Tommy, whose blue eyes widened in defense. "That wasn't me."

"I think I'm going to be sick." Tierra's chair scraped along the wood as she leapt up and fled the room, leaving her wrap untouched.

A mustard-colored puff of smoke filtered up from beneath the table, intensifying the nauseating aroma.

"Oh Goddess! It's Cheeto!" Claire cried, holding the collar of her black tank over nose and mouth.

"That's it," Aerin threatened. "I'm making bacon."

"No!" Moira reached beneath the table, but Cheeto shot out from beneath the cloth, his little hooves slipping and skidding on the polished wood floor. "He's laid some carpet bombs in his day, but never nothin' like that."

"Must be the food," Claire gagged, standing to claw at the latch to the windows.

Aerin grabbed the broom. "I'm chasing that thing *out* of here," she hissed, her words almost drowned out by another thunderous expulsion of smoke from beneath Cheeto's curly tail.

Ignoring Moira's defensive shouts, Aerin swept Cheeto toward the door and out into the gardens. Closing only the screen door, she flicked her fingers, circulating the air, watching the smoke inside the house dissipate in curling wisps of olfactory death as Cheeto let a fart so disastrous it lifted him off his feet and propelled him down the porch steps.

Beyond the lethal points of wrought iron enclosing *Maison de Moray*, a tall, wide black shadow lurked beneath a beech tree. Aerin couldn't make out the features from across the expanse of Tierra's splendid gardens, but she didn't need to. That cavernous loneliness reached through the sunlight filtering through dancing leaves. Beckoned her.

Julian.

Moira padded toward her. "I've got to make sure Cheeto don't dig up the yams and parsnips or Tierra will skin my hide."

"I'll do it," Aerin offered quickly.

Moira raised a skeptical eyebrow. "You just called my pig bacon."

Oh. Yeah. Shit. "I have to go get some damned branches and shit from those trees over there anyhow to make that cock-sucking broom. I might as well keep an eye on your pig."

Moira's other brow joined the first.

"If you're worried about it, take Doctor Lecter as collateral." Aerin threw some impatience into her voice, hoping between that and the enmity between Moira and the vampire bat, it would quell her sister's suspicion.

It worked. "Suit yourself." Moira turned away, wandering toward the fridge.

Aerin looked down at her storm cloud gray slacks and sighed. She'd said she was going to get a broom, so get one she must.

That meant an ax.

❧ 5 ❧

T he flagstone path to the tool shed helped to make sure her Manolo Blahniks didn't aerate the grass. The tool shed was surprisingly well stocked, and she found an ax hooked to the wall with two nails supporting the head.

Aerin was amazed how good it felt in her hands. Heavy and useful and dangerous. Now that she had to start thinking about zombiepocalypse weapons, this one was in first place.

Cheeto followed her cheerfully toward the fence, one of his gastric blasts propelling him to bump into her legs.

"Jesus H. Christ," she muttered, glancing around to see if she could stash the animal where it would do the least damage. She thought for a moment about putting it in the shed and locking the door, but after a few more of those methane-infused emissions, and the damn thing would probably explode.

Using the tippy, tippy toe of her pointed pump, she nudged the tiny critter toward the garden. "Hey little guy," she said in a bright voice people usually reserved for small animals and babies. "How about you go dig up some of those flowers? Doesn't that look fun?" She'd promised the safety of Tierra's tubers, but in her opinion, everything else in the garden was free game.

Intrigued, the little animal pranced across the grass toward the gardens, rhythmic little toots accompanying his happy gait.

That ought to keep him busy for a while.

When she turned back to the fence, Julian was nowhere to be seen, but she could feel him out there in the copse of trees that lined the property. He had an emotional signature like no one else she'd come across. It was an eternal stillness in a ruffling wind. A black smudge among a riot of color. Peace and patience amongst chaos. In a way, his lack of intensity made him very intense.

Closing the gate behind her, only pausing for a moment's hesitation, she stepped beyond the house's wards and plunged into the trees, the heavy ax secure in both hands.

Summer sunlight made the shadows dance beneath the tall trees, this particular swath of forest a collaboration of species. Oak, elm, pine, beech, and ash trees crowded around each other like gossiping neighbors, their boughs heavy with greenery and age. Aerin liked to think that the trees didn't have to compete for moisture here in the Northwest, and so they might be friendlier to each other in these plentiful groves. Underbrush and shrubberies that were foreign to her played at the ancient roots of the trees like unruly children. Tierra would be able to name them. Aerin avoided them.

She found Julian standing in the middle of a small break in the foliage with his back to her, the sunlight filtering down to shine off the silver strands in his otherwise ebony hair. He wore a thick black coat and leather gloves on his hands which were clasped behind him, even though the temperature topped the eighties. Wilting, dying leaves dropped to the earth around him like a rainstorm, and Aerin felt as though she could sense the trees throwing them at him, making it clear in no uncertain terms that he wasn't welcome among their summer bloom.

Famine. Desolation. Pestilence. It wasn't only humans he killed with his poisonous touch.

Aerin formed a breeze with her will, blowing the dead leaves away from him in a wild puff, uncovering the lush moss and grasses.

A small circle of brown and gray spread amongst the grass beneath his glossy shoes.

He turned to her, his sharp, masculine chin rasping against the high wool collar of his coat. In a forest of light and shadow, of greens and browns and tones of the earth, his brilliant blue eyes seemed to glow. A web of lines appeared at their corners as he smiled, and Aerin had to catch her breath. Those lines kept him from looking truly young. They whispered of a life harshly lived, like he'd been weathered on a sea where the clouds never broke. Where the sun never kissed him like it did in this grove. Sometime in a past so distant, it was unimaginable.

Even his fucking smile was inscrutable. *Beautiful.* There had never been formed in heaven or on earth a man more beautiful than this.

"If that weapon is meant for me, I surrender." He lifted his hands in a mock gesture of fear.

Aerin looked down at the ax in her grip, stunned to find out that she'd lifted it in a defensive gesture, as though to protect herself.

"It's not." She lowered it, trying to recover her wits.

"Then am I to assume you are going to use it on a tree, even in an Alexander McQueen cashmere suit?" Dark brows lifted in surprise.

"If I feel like it." She inspected the elm, which was closest, her neck craned to see if she could find a limb low enough to hack at. Which tree would be the most magical, she wondered. Which branch wanted to fly?

"Might I inquire as to your reasons for playing lumberjack?" He fell into step behind her, his hands still clasped tightly behind his back.

"We weren't supposed to meet until midnight." Aerin retreated from him a bit, unexpectedly uncertain, and pretended to consider the ash tree.

He was suddenly closer, his breath warm on her ear. "What is that intoxicating scent?" he queried.

"That, I believe, is a brined tofu soy pig fart." She slipped away from him. Or rather he allowed it as he paused.

"I—beg your pardon?" His voice colored with confusion, as though he thought he'd misheard her.

"It's your brother Bane who should be begging our pardon. He's the one that slipped it to my sister without using protection. Now she's pregnant and poisoning the atmosphere with dastardly consequences of a household fed on fuck-all but cruciferous vegetables." Aerin bitched. "Of which there are many."

He was quiet for a moment, and Aerin moved on to a pine tree, then dismissed it out of hand.

"You don't smell like a..." He cut himself off, and Aerin smiled as her back was to him. She knew he couldn't bring himself to say something so ridiculously vulgar. "I was referring to an aroma, not a stench. Your scent, it's changed to something warmer than when I saw you last. You smell...expensive."

"That's because I *am* expensive," she said, marveling at the fact that only Julian Roarke could discuss perfumes and still manage to sound masculine. How many men noticed when a woman changed her perfume?

"No doubt," he muttered.

I will not be charmed. I will not be impressed.

"What are you doing here, Julian? Did you learn

something about the zombies that couldn't wait until tonight?"

He turned toward her then. Slowly stalking the handful of yards between him and the beech tree beneath which she now stood. His hands were still behind him, as though bound, but it provided little comfort to her. His shoulders were so wide, his movements so impious and unapologetically predatory. The paradox of his placid features with the sinful intent in his blue eyes was astonishing. No, scratch that, terrifying.

"You shouldn't be here," she threatened, cringing at the note of hesitation that escaped her usually dynamic tone. "You shouldn't come to the house."

If he tried to seduce her, how could she resist him?

If he tried to kill her, *how could she resist him?*

He reached her, his towering height dwarfing her, even in her three-inch heels, causing Aerin to do something she'd never done before in her entire life.

She retreated a step. Then another. Then another. Until her back was up against the solid trunk of the beech tree.

"I came to warn you," he said in a voice that was ironically empty of warning and full of wickedness. Dark hair shot with silver fell over his face as he lowered it within inches of hers, placing his lips once again against her ear. "The undead... I have reason to believe they'll come for you, with the intent to do you harm."

He had yet to touch her, but their cheeks were so close she could almost feel the sharp rasp of the dark stubble there. Molecules vibrated on a more frenetic frequency in anticipation of their physical connection.

"For me?" she breathed, gasping as his hair caressed her collarbone.

"For you all."

"Yeah, well, they'll have to get in line." Her fingers tightened on the ax between them, but she didn't move.

"I urge you and your sisters to ward the house

against them. To seek answers within the Grimoire on how to defeat them."

Aerin grunted. "In all the spare time we have in between consulting it on how to defeat you?"

His sound of amusement was a puff of warmth against her neck.

"You're not frightened are you, Aerin de Moray?"

More like petrified. "I wouldn't tell you if I was."

"No, I don't expect you would." His hands finally came unlatched from behind him and landed on either side of her head against the tree trunk. The beech gave a great shudder of protest, or was that her own shudder as his body pressed closer?

"What—what other information do you have for me?"

"Not anything solid, as of yet. I promise to have more tonight." His lips skimmed the curve where her neck met her shoulder, light as a whisper. "I still can't believe..."

"*Aerin?*" Moira's bellow permeated the thick, seductive moment with some harsh reality. "Aerin, goddamnit, where did you get off to? You were supposed to be watching Cheeto."

"Fuck. Shit. Fuck." Aerin swore, ducking away from Julian. "I have to go. You have to go. I have to... leave." Why in the ninth circle of hell did she allow this man the power to seduce her like this? He was the damn virgin. Who the fuck did he think he was, emptying her head of thoughts?

"I'll wait until tonight then," he said with more than a little regret. "Though I would beg the answer, just what *were* you planning on doing with that ax?"

"Mother of all fucks," she cursed again. "I was supposed to chop a fucking tree branch big enough to make a broom." She'd never get it before Moira found her to chew her ass out.

"Allow me." Julian held his hand out, and Aerin surrendered the ax.

He pointed to a branch almost eye level with him and about the circumference of Aerin's wrist. She nodded and moved out of the way, expecting several hacks before the thing came down.

He swatted at it with one hand, the ax moving faster than the eye could see.

Aerin's mouth dropped open as he handed the ax back to her and stripped the limb of any sharp branches.

Holy fuck was he the sexiest thing that walked on two legs.

"I have to go," she repeated dumbly.

"As you say." He made no move away from her.

"I have lunch in the dryer. I mean—laundry in the fridge."

"Do you, indeed?" He gave her the branch, the perfect size and shape for a broom, with a knowing smile his lips.

"Yup." She backed away slowly, feeling wobbly on heels that had become like an extension of her own feet.

"I'll see you at midnight then, Aerin de Moray." He said, turning to disappear into the storm of wilting leaves. "Remember to be vigilant. They'll come for you."

Aerin retreated, trying not to think of the many meanings of the word *come*.

❧ 6 ❧

A zombie "came for them" much sooner than Aerin expected.

Like an hour after her tragically short conversation with Julian. Hell, her panties hadn't even had time to cool off yet.

Aerin sat on the covered porch off the parlor in the front yard, the afternoon sun warming her skin as she attempted to craft a broom. She felt at once peaceful and turbulent. For someone used to boardrooms and redeye flights, a quiet afternoon working with her hands was oddly peaceful. Her bare feet and discarded blazer were her only concessions to comfort. She'd never been the crafty type, magical or otherwise, but dammit, she was determined.

Moira was lurking about somewhere, still pissed that a neglected Cheeto had eaten nearly all Tierra's peppermint. Silver lining: it had seemed to fix his gastrointestinal expulsions. Tierra had gone to the shop in search of warding materials and had taken Claire and Tommy with her. Ironically, the pregnant lady was the safest when she left the house, as Death had made it pretty clear that his baby mama was off limits. At least, for the moment.

God, their lives were like a really bad reality TV show.

Up next on Survivor: Apocalypse. Will the sisters find out that Aerin has been secretly meeting with Pestilence? Will Claire forgive War for stealing the Grimoire? Is Tierra's baby the antichrist? Will Conquest seek revenge for a tidal wave?

Who will get the final rose? Who will be the next to break a Seal? Who will be voted off the island? Who wins a custody battle with Death?

Aerin pinched the bridge of her nose, a headache pricking behind her eyes. Probably from low blood sugar. What had the prophecy said?

When the reckoning comes, who shall be able to stand?

Who exactly would be the warring factions? Who were the enemies?

Who would be *left* standing once the smoke cleared? The proverbial King of the Mountain. Or, more accurately, the entire world. A god, essentially. Or goddess?

Goddesses? Maybe four?

A scream interrupted her dangerous questions. It came from the direction of the backyard.

Moira.

The broom clattered to the floor as Aerin bolted through the house. Through the wall of brand new windows in the kitchen, she watched in horror as Moira drove the heel of one of the stilettos Aerin had discarded by the door into a man's temple.

"*No!*" Aerin cried, grabbing the ax she'd also left leaning against the porch rail in case she'd needed a different branch.

Staggering back, the man, dressed in bell bottoms and a fringed vest the same brown as his stringy long hair, reached his hand up and tested the shoe sticking out of the side of his face. "Hey," he protested in a thick monotone ubiquitous amongst pot heads and surfers. "Uncool, man."

Aerin wasn't certain who she planned on using the

ax on until she reached them. "Yeah, Moira," she agreed with the walking corpse. "Unfucking-cool. That's my fucking shoe!"

"Peckerhead tried to eat me!" Moira pointed, her aquamarine eyes wide with disbelief.

"Who hasn't?" Aerin said acerbically as she turned to the zombie hippie. "Give me my heel back or I'll take it, along with your head."

"No need to be salty 'bout it baby," the man drawled with squinty-eyed passivity. "You seem like real fine chicks, and this sort of thing isn't my usual bag, but the lady fascist gave me no choice. It's like '*Nam* all over again, man."

"Who in the Sam hill you talkin' about?" Moira demanded.

The zombie ignored her. "Now which one of you groovy gals is the water witch? I'm a Scorpio, and I think I should stay with my sign, ya dig?"

Aerin stepped in front of Moira. "I'll dig your eyeballs out if you don't answer the question," she threatened, lifting the ax.

"Hey, I'll be the first cat to admit it's a real bummer. But making a meal of you chicks is the only way to save my immortal soul. But if you've been good, yours'll merge with the far out divine. Nothing more righteous than that." He put his lanky arms out in front of him, evoking the image of the quintessential zombie. "Now do me a solid, and hold still."

"Merge with this, *Daddy-o*." Aerin swung her ax like she'd seen in the Bronx when Horowitz, the bookie's Shylock used to swing bats to break kneecaps. Horowitz was old school.

It embedded in about half- way into his neck with an oddly fibrous sound and stuck there. As in, Aerin couldn't pull it out no matter how hard she tried.

"Yeouch," the Zombie wailed as he was yanked this

way and that. In Aerin's frenzy, she nearly knocked over Moira in their awkward, lethal tug of war.

Thinking fast, Moira managed to grab onto her shoe and pry it out of his face.

Arms slack with a bit of relief, Aerin didn't realize the extent of the man's strength until he gave a mighty tug and the handle of the ax was ripped out of her hands.

"Catch!" Moira snapped as she tossed the shoe at Aerin and lunged for the anachronistic zombie. "I got this."

Grabbing the handle, Moira kicked out at the man and used his chest for leverage as she yanked the ax out of his throat.

Aerin didn't know what she expected, perhaps a bit more arterial spray, but all that oozed from the wound was a foamy goo of indeterminate color.

She shuddered and swallowed some bile that threatened the back of her throat.

"Not gonna work, lady," the zombie taunted, his voice not at all affected by the fact that his vocal cords had been severed. "Can't kill a cat who's been dead forty years."

"Can't eat a 'chick' if you have no head," Moira volleyed back, swinging the ax one more time, her aim suggesting she'd done this before. Probably not with people, but one never knew.

His head bounced twice off the grass and rolled to a stop against the gate. "You're being a real drag about this, man," he accused, spitting grass out of his mouth. His body, still dripping with fringe and goo, stumbled forward, arms out and bending to grope for the head.

"Gitcha undead ass out of here or we'll start hacking limbs," Moira spat. Though Aerin could see that she was shaken. Or, rather, *shaking*.

The corpse picked up his own head and jogged toward the gate. "Don't take it so personal," he said as a parting shot. "This is our one chance."

"Your one chance to what?" Aerin started after him, but for a dead guy, his skinny legs ran pretty fast. "And who is the lady fascist?" she yelled.

"Later, witches." His answer was lost in the breeze that was picking up into a wind. Aerin took a moment to wonder if he'd meant witch as a slight or a title.

Hippie ass clown.

Moira stood on the grass, the ax dripping with blood, and... other.

Aerin whirled on her, her blood singing with fear and violence with no outlet. "What have we learned?" she demanded.

Moira blinked. Then blinked again. Her wild auburn hair ruffling across her face. "That...zombies are a damn sight harder to kill than they are on TV," she panted.

"No!" Aerin waved the shoe at her face, the heel stained with whatever resided inside a zombie's skull. "No, we learned that you grab the fucking ax to fight zombies, not my several-hundred-dollar shoes!"

Moira wrinkled her nose at Aerin's ruined sole, then shrugged. "They looked like any old high-heeled shoes to me, and I didn't see the ax lying there, or I'd have grabbed for it first. I wasn't exactly thinking clearly on account of the *zombie in the backyard*."

Aerin's mouth dropped open. "Any...old..." That's it, she was going to lose it. "These are Manolo Blahnik grey crocodile BB pumps.

Their stitching is worth more than one of your backwater pontoons—"

"That ain't no crocodile skin," Moira said skeptically. "I'd know."

"It's crocodile *print*. People don't wear crocodile skin anymore. It's not in fashion to actually wear animals these days."

Moira's eyes darkened from aquamarine to blueberry. "Excuse me, Yankee, but where I come from we're smarter'n to let some store with a name no one can pronounce talk us into spending a ridiculous amount of money for a shoe that looks like something you can buy at Payless."

"Payless?" Aerin gasped, her head jerking like she'd been slapped as she hid the shoe behind her as though to protect it from one not worthy. "Take. That. Back."

"And for your information, if you're tough enough to skin a gator where I come from, you wear that shit any old way you want." She looked Aerin up and down. "You wouldn't last a minute."

"I should have let him eat you," Aerin bitched, turning to inspect the damage done to one of her favorite shoes. Breathing deep, she did her best to slow down the heart that hadn't stopped racing since the moment Moira screamed. If anything had happened to her sister... well... She cleared suspicious weight out of her throat.

"Well, you didn't...let him, that is." Moira caught up to her, her bare toenails shimmering red against the green of the lush grass, the soiled ax swinging at her side. "I suppose I owe you for that and for the shoe... How 'bout I make you a real gator purse to go with it by way of repayment?"

Aerin didn't even have to think about it. "Make me chicken."

"Say what?"

"Fried chicken." Aerin's mouth violently watered. It said something about her appetite that she still had one after what they'd just seen.

"With a crispy shell," she quickly added.

"Chicken? Fried Chicken?" Moira was looking at her sideways.

"You heard me."

"I make some damn good fried chicken, but I don't

know as anyone's ever offered to pay me hundreds of dollars for it," Moira said modestly.

"At this point, I will," Aerin argued. "And I want it extra fatty. *Extra* crispy. If I have to eat one more of Tierra's goddamned vegan wraps I'm going to punch all the soy on the planet and shave off every hipster beard in this city."

Moira dropped the ax and scooped up Aerin into a spontaneous hug. Aerin froze. She knew her sister was prone to spastic outbursts of affection, but hugs were still something she was getting used to. "We really are sisters," Moira sniffed.

Aerin gave her sister a hesitant pat on her braless back, wishing she'd learn the art of air kisses and handshakes. "Of course we are," she said. And meant it.

Moira released her. "One mess of fried chicken, coming up faster than a greased pole cat."

Aerin nearly quivered with anticipation. "Wash your hands first." She motioned to some zombie gunk that had splattered onto Moira's hands.

"We should both wash up." Moira gestured at the front of Aerin's cream blouse, also splattered with gore.

Ew.

They turned toward the house. "And just so you know," Moira continued, "Skunk McQuee's pontoon cost a whole bunch on account of the gilded horns he had made special in Kentucky..."

Moira's voice faded as an easterly wind gathered strength, bringing a portent of danger and caution. They needed to ward their house against the undead like *yesterday*, and pray to whatever god hadn't forsaken them that it worked.

So this was their lives now... Before today, the only blood on her hands had been proverbial.

Maybe it still was, but it certainly didn't feel like it.

❈ 7 ❈

Rhythm, he had it.

Julian Roarke rode a horse like Fred Astaire danced. Like Shakespeare wrote. Like Michael Jordan basketballed. Before the underwear commercials, of course.

Light from a nearly-full waxing moon cast the glade at the end of Leighton road in an ambient silver that lent the witching hour an enchanted feel. Aerin stood next to the lush meadow and watched the two sleek, dark beings, horse and rider, race through the night toward her.

Julian's black hair would have matched that of his horse if not for the strands of silver laced throughout. Tonight, his tresses flowed free of their usual restraint of a slick queue at the nape of his neck that hid its tendency to curl.

Pale eyes, burnished with excitement, flashed down at her from the immense prancing stallion. Muscles flexed beneath the thin linen shirt he wore as he reined in his beast.

"Aerin de Moray." He said her name with an edge of anticipation that thrilled her like a jolt from a Taser. Sidling his horse sideways, he held his hand out in invitation.

She took it without hesitation, and using his preternatural strength, he pulled her astride behind him. Her arms automatically locked around his lean waist, and she rested her chin against the cords of his strong back.

"I have some information to share with you," he said lightly.

"Ride first. Talk later," Aerin demanded.

She felt, rather than saw him smile. "As you wish."

Julian didn't have to kick Archimedes into a gallop so much as allow him some slack in the reins. The horse knew what his riders wanted, could taste the reckless frenzy on the air and the need to race it until they ran out of land.

It amazed Aerin that riding a horse was so similar to riding a man. The roll of her hips synchronized with the beast's rhythmic strides, the clench of her thighs, the thrill low in her belly, it was all familiar.

The wind on her face coaxed an elated smile from her and she couldn't hold back the small, very unfamiliar squeal that escaped her when Julian had ordered her to hold on tight before they went sailing over a fence.

They could have ridden for a couple minutes or a couple hours for all Aerin knew. Eventually they both ducked low as trees and branches whizzed past them through a forest, and then they broke onto the clearing that rose above the water. Not quite a cliff, but tall enough to give Aerin vertigo.

This was *their* place. A moonlit meadow where the sparkling Puget Sound stretched below grass that laconically twitched in the ever-present ocean breeze.

"This place reminds me of a fairy land," Aerin breathed. Then stalled, embarrassed for vocalizing something so trite. "Does that make me sound ridiculous?"

"A little," Julian rumbled, as though amused. "But only because you've never actually met a Faerie."

Julian kicked his leg over Archimedes's back and jumped down, turning to reach for Aerin.

"You mean there's such things as—" The moment she was in his arms, he melded his mouth to hers. The kiss was nearly unbearable in its intensity, but Aerin instantly locked her arms around his neck, levering herself closer to him. Their blood was high at the thrill of the swift ride, and their desires more illicit because of their forbidden nature.

This was why they needed to meet. This was what they'd come here for tonight. After she got him naked, after she took him inside her, then they'd talk. Then they'd worry about the future. But first she would claim him. She would allow him to claim her, because if anything was destined, it was their joining.

She was suddenly consumed with the feel of him, his broadness, his strength, his careful deference. Even now, with need and lust rolling between them like a violent storm, he was gentle, painstakingly so.

She bit at his lip and he groaned, his hands lowering on her body in a long, torturous journey. Her shoulder blades, the dip of her waist, the flare of her hips. His kiss was like poetry against her mouth. It was as though he described every emotion she evoked in a language that even William Blake could not have comprehended. But she understood every word. Every insinuation.

The first of which was wonder.

Julian Roarke had never had the pleasure of exploring a woman's shape with his hands. Of searching for soft curves in a place where his body had angles and raw, hard muscle. If he touched a woman she died. Horribly.

But not Aerin. She was immune to his lethal powers. Though she could feel them trying to work on her. It was as though her very molecules battled the toxicity of his and won. It made her feel feverish. It made her heart pump faster, her blood work harder. It made her feel like every time he touched her, she became stronger for fighting him. And stronger for surrendering.

When he filled his large hands with her ass and dragged her against him, the movement sent a shock of lust straight through her loins. She was mindless with it. Overwhelmed by the barrel of his desire pressed against her belly.

Her hands, suddenly greedy for his flesh, fumbled with his shirt buttons until they fell away and she splayed her palms against the hard muscle and hot, smooth skin of his chest.

She heard the breathless sound he made low in his throat, but was too absorbed and delighted in how his muscles twitched and tightened beneath her touch.

Breaking their kiss, she pulled back to regard his sharp features, made more vague by the kindness of moonlight. Liquid heat gathered inside her and so did something else. Something hotter than fire. Something darker than desire. Something dangerous and bleak, but also possessive and feral. Aerin could no longer tell which emotions were hers and which belonged to him. What passed between them in that moment surpassed the present and hinted at the infinite, and her mortal brain struggled to comprehend it.

"I always wondered what it would be like to touch someone," he whispered, grazing her cheek with his knuckles. "But, I never dared allow myself to contemplate what it would be like for someone to reach for me. To touch me. Aerin...I—"

"Shut up and kiss me." Aerin tugged at his shirt, bringing his mouth against hers once more. This was safer. This was better. She'd stopped him from saying something that was too dangerous. That would make this more than it was.

That would make her fall for him.

She took in a sharp, shocked breath and he took advantage. His tongue lapping at the inside of her mouth, curling over hers, exploring the moist depths of her in a parody of what was to come next. His hands cupped her face like it was made of the most precious glass. His lips were searing and tender and everything that filled his heart spilled into her, magnified by her empathic abilities until she was swept along in a tidal wave of unfamiliar emotion.

In that moment, Aerin opened herself to him. Her mouth, her magic, her heart. Somehow, for some reason, her defenses dropped. Her walls crumbled and she was alone, like a specter beneath a streetlamp, for all the world to see.

And right away, she knew she'd made a gigantic mistake.

Whatever pulsed between Julian and Aerin morphed from tender to malevolent. Suddenly Julian's grip on her face was no longer gentle, but painful. And this time when she bit his lip, it drew blood.

Lust still surged through them, but it became something else too. Not possessive any longer, but dominant. Not searing, but seething. They were going to fuck each other. And it was going to hurt. It wouldn't be the kind of give and take sex that would leave them on equal ground.

This kind of fucking would have winner and a loser. And the loser might give up something they were not ready to have taken from them.

With a raw sound Julian pried his mouth from hers and peeled his body away, almost pushing her into where Archimedes stood observing them with mild disinterest.

He stalked to the edge of the cliff, scrubbing his face with his hands until he sighed and let them drop, staring off over the ocean.

Aerin took a few deep, steadying breaths. Willing herself to calm, trying to regain control over whatever situation had just arisen between them.

Putting her barriers back into place.

"What just happened?" she demanded, shocked at the hoarse note in her voice.

The breeze turned into a wind that lifted the corners of Julian's shirt still hanging open, causing it to flare out behind him.

She looked away. He'd sought refuge from her in the right place. He knew she was afraid of heights. That she wouldn't follow him to the edge.

"You have to go," he rasped. "We should not be here."

Aerin couldn't shake the darkness. Her skin slithered with unease and her blood boiled with irritation. "What the fuck, Julian? *You* called me out here. *You* kissed me. Now you're pushing me away? My balls are turning blue here. What gives?"

He didn't look at her. "You have to leave. Now."

"Like hell I do." She crossed her arms over her chest, then uncrossed them and let them hang at her sides, hands curling into fists. Rule number four of corporate warfare: don't make defensive gestures.

Don't show him how confused you are.

Don't show him that he hurt you.

"I came out here to butt-fuck Egypt because you promised me information. I'm not leaving without it." She'd process the feeling of her guts spilling onto the ground later. Right now, she had shit to handle. "If you're finished being a dick tease, then tell me what you found out about the undead."

He turned to her, his dark brows drawn down to shadow his pale blue eyes. "In order to be a dick tease, wouldn't you have to have a—"

"It's a fucking expression. Just tell me what the fuck with the zombies, Julian, so I don't have to look at you anymore."

His jaw clenched and he glanced at the ground as

though summoning his immortal patience. "You are cruel when you are hurt," he accused.

"If you think I'm the cruel one here, you are sadly mistaken," she all but snarled. "Now do you actually know anything or did you lure me out here just to be an ass?"

"You should not call a man's honor into question so lightly, Aerin," he warned.

"Then cough up what you promised me, Julian," she volleyed back. "I was attacked by one of those squirrely motherfuckers today and even chopping off his head didn't stop him."

Julian took a step forward and put his hand out before he stopped.

"Are you... all right? He didn't hurt you?"

"Don't pretend you care," she said coldly.

"I do care," he gritted through clenched teeth, his voice low and soft as though he didn't want them overheard. "I just *can't*. You don't know what I'm up against, Aerin. Or with *whom* I am dealing."

"Well at the moment, you're dealing with me, so keep your end of the bargain."

Regarding her from beneath his lashes, he took a deep breath, seeming to come to a decision. She could feel how conflicted he was. How aroused and aching. And beneath all that, she could sense something else. Something that distracted her from her ire. Fear.

What in the world would an immortal like Julian Roarke be afraid of?

"From what I read, the rules of necromancy are surprisingly simple," he began. "There are two kinds of undead, the astral kind and the physical kind. Essentially, they're a body or a soul that is ripped away from each other, but remains on this plane bereft of its other half."

Aerin tried to think past her pounding heart and her throbbing nethers. God she was going to hate him for this, for a good long time. She was going to hold a grudge that would make the Hatfields and the

McCoys proud. "So, these zombies are just bodies without souls?"

"Correct."

"And so if it's just a soul without a body, they're like... ghosts?"

"Essentially, as you mortals understand them, yes."

Aerin thought for a moment, trying to ignore the way his pale, muscled chest gleamed in the moonlight. Her fingers twitched and she turned away to stare out at the cold, lonely ocean.

"So all we would have to do is reunite the body with the soul and the problem would be solved," she mused.

"That's quite impossible." he said.

"Why?"

"Because their souls have moved on. Bane has delivered them to their eternal reward. When the fifth seal broke, they rose to take their vengeance, but it is not the power of the seal that keeps them animated. It is something else." He caught her eyes, regret and powerful meaning flashing in their fathomless, sea-colored depths. "*Someone* else."

"Who?"

"I *cannot* say." He lifted a brow at her. "But I learned how they can regain a soul, and a second chance at mortality which is why they are after you."

He paused, looking off into the trees in the distance, as though searching through the shadows there.

"Don't leave me hanging."

Julian took another step forward. "If they consume the source of your power, your life force... they'll absorb that power. They'll absorb your soul, and you'll be lost. The prophecy states that those who are martyred will return, but don't assume that all who returned are innocent. Not every one of their souls was sent to heaven when they died." His eyes positively burned into hers now, and each word was delivered with such annunciation, that she felt as though Julian was trying to talk to a stupid child. "Who are the most powerful mortal beings in existence, Aerin? Powerful enough to end the world?" *Witches*.

"Holy fuck." Her eyes widened as the truth of it all hit her like a cartoon anvil, threatening to pound her into the dirt.

"The souls in their heavens are at peace, Aerin. Once the seal was broken and vengeance was wrought, they returned to their graves."

A new horror reared its head. "That means...anyone who is left...'"

"Is beyond redemption, because their souls are writhing in the depths of hell," Julian finished for her. "They are the souls of the damned, and they are after you and your sisters' powers." *No*. That meant... *Tommy*.

"*Claire*!" Without thinking, Aerin ran and leapt atop Archimedes, and spun him around. If only she had a broom that worked. If only she wasn't such a goddamned failure at being a witch.

If only she'd make it back in time to stop anything bad from happening to her sisters.

The stallion wouldn't move, not without his master's go-ahead.

"Let me go," she commanded. *"Let me go!"* The second time came out as a plea.

"Take her to her vehicle," Julian acquiesced.

Aerin didn't look back to thank him. She didn't allow herself to look back at all.

JULIAN STOOD ON THE EDGE OF THE LAND, THE OCEAN swirling below him, and watched her plunge into the night. A part of him hoped she succeeded in her endeavor to rescue her sisters.

A part of him hoped she'd fail. That all this would be over.

"Are you going to lurk in the shadows all night, or show yourself to look in my eyes as you torment me?" he queried.

A black and yellow snake slithered through grass, tonguing the toe of his boot before climbing his leg with its sinuous body.

Even the brightness of the moon, that orb from which the

Goddess drew her power, seemed to dim in the presence of the serpent.

A mist crept through the meadow and the snake tightened painfully against his leg before morphing and twisting in grotesque undulations until a breathtakingly beautiful woman was pressed against him, her leg entwined around his, her arms wrapped around his neck.

"I never thought you had a weakness, my cold, cold horseman," Lucifer hissed in his ear. "I never thought you had a heart...until now."

❄ 9 ❄

Whether one was a human, an immortal, or a deity, there still remains nothing worse than being denied something one wants.

As one of the most powerful immortals known to the history of this universe, Lucifer, the morning star, the Devil, Satan, Old Scratch, Mephistopheles, The Lord of Darkness *her fucking self* was only ever denied two desires since the beginning of time. Those souls who were bringers of light and therefore were delivered to their respective heavens...

And Julian Roarke.

He wasn't the largest of the Horsemen, nor the most handsome.

Though his body almost shimmered with pale perfection, and his Gothic beauty was, indeed, rare and brilliant, she'd fucked bigger immortals. Stronger ones. More skilled. She'd had *Sidhe* orgies that lasted for weeks of mortal time. She'd banged kings, queens (sometimes both at once), Gods, demi-gods, fae, demons, angels, and just about everything in between. She'd done it all, from every position. She'd taken the form of a man and fucked all the things. As a woman, she'd been fucked by all the things, sometimes simultaneously.

She'd like to meet the being who would *dare* slut-shame Satan.

She'd had the other Horsemen. Once they saw what she'd done to Julian, they'd relented.

Nicholas Kingswood fucked like he wanted to pound his demons into her. Theirs was a power-play she'd likely never forget.

War's "sword" was one of legend. For a warrior, he approached sex with a strategy and didn't give up until he'd scorched the earth and wrung every last gasp of breath she possessed.

Having Death "come" for her, was one of the darkest, most satisfying moments of her life.

So what the Princess of Darkness couldn't figure out, was why she'd spent so many damned centuries lusting for Pestilence.

It *could* have been because Julian Roarke was one of two men to ever resist her temptations, she supposed.

She'd made certain that the other one was crucified.

Rejection was inconceivable to her. She was literally the most beautiful woman on the planet. Flawless. Victoria's Secret models sometimes sold their souls to have a hip-to-waist ratio to rival hers. Her blonde hair was more than twenty different highlights of shimmering gold. She had the thighs of a dancer, the ass of a yoga instructor, and the mouth of a porn star. She was sin personified. Sinning was kind of her deal.

And Julian Roarke never pitched even half a wood in her presence.

What the eternal fuck was she supposed to do with that?

She'd started with the usual seductions... innuendo, dancing, gifts, cajoling, enticing and so forth. She'd gone so far as to spread her legs on his bed once, and pleasure herself for him. And *She* did that for no man, for she was no man's object.

Julian had been unimpressed.

Then she'd gotten rough. Bonds, brands, curses, *ad infinitum*.

And *still* it came to pass, that Julian Roarke was the most stubborn motherfucker on the planet. Also, because of the nature of their existence, the Four Horsemen were out of her particular purview. Sure, they worked for her from time to time. She may be more powerful than they were. She could, and had, made their lives a living hell, but she had limited power *over* them. She couldn't break them. She couldn't kill them.

And she was unable to rape them.

More's the pity.

But after all this time, she'd had an ace in the hole, as it were. A dark, devious trick, of which she was quite proud, that turned Julian's own power against him. As one of the most deadly creatures in existence, he'd been created to control those powers. And she'd pounced immediately. He was different than the primordial men. He was no barbarian, nor was he politician. No conqueror, warlord, or tyrant. No artist, writer, musician, or bard.

Julian, was a scientist. A shadow. A silent observer of balance and life. While other men pitted their strength and skill against their enemies, Julian felled them with a single-celled organism expelled from his breath. While other dreamers looked to the skies to contemplate the vastness of the universe, Julian held a universe of his own on the tip of his finger, inspecting and comprehending every last nanobe.

The knowledge in his eyes fascinated and frightened her. He resisted her because he saw what lived in between the dark matter that comprised her being. She wanted to show it to him. Wanted to unleash it upon him. He was pure. He was good. He was rare. And she wanted him so much, it distracted her from her real purpose here.

And while he resisted her, she'd cursed him. Because why the fuck not use the darkest magics to isolate him from any warmth, any touch, and especially, any other woman.

So who did this de Moray bitch think she was? Lucy was glad she'd ruined their party. The moment the witch had made herself vulnerable, Lucy had used her influence to fuck with their good time.

Watching the tart gallop away on Julian's stallion, Lucy reached out and gripped Julian's chin, hoping to capture his undivided attention. "You're hard, Julian," she purred into his ear, fitting her hips tightly against his.

"Not for long."

She could feel the length of him against her, the size and shape impressive, but... losing its potency.

A familiar emotion speared her, and then was smothered by a tempest of rage that she hid behind a throaty laugh. It wasn't hurt. No one hurt the Devil.

She rubbed her body against his, drawing her long, sharp nail down the stubbled angle of his cheek, she seethed at the way his pale eyes lingered on the path that had carried that de Moray bitch away.

Those Druid descendants were more powerful than she thought.

"Do you remember the plague of Cyprian?" she purred in his ear, and delighted in the instant rigidity of his muscles. She knew that of all his memories of her, Cyprian was the one he most hated. That he most feared.

Julian's pale eyes darkened to the color of ripe blueberries as they gazed into the past. "I remember being entranced and charmed by the ingenuity of the Romans. I remember walking among them, watching them learn how to use medicines, and clean water, and discover galaxies, and create a civilization the likes of which the world had not yet seen."

"*Yes*," Lucy hissed, rubbing her hand down his throat and across the broad expanse of his bare chest.

The warmth of another's hand still lingered there. God how she wanted to fuck him.

How she wanted to hurt him.

"I remember how you trapped me there with your dark magic. How you used the Chymerian chains to bind me for twenty-five years."

"That's nothing in the life of an immortal." Lucy waved his pain away.

"That's a veritable eternity in a room with you." His voice dripped with sarcasm. "I remember that at the zenith of the plague, five thousand terrified souls died every day. How St. Cyprian was the only man who stood between smallpox and the world... and because of us both, he failed." Now his voice was hard and his cock soft. "I remember that I never hated anyone worse than I hated you then."

"You've hated me ever since."

He nodded, a quick movement of his sharp chin. "You would come to me whilst I was chained, rub against me, much as you're doing now, and offer to release me, to stop the carnage, if I would only submit to you. Lie with you."

"I asked you why you eternally denied me there in that pit." Lucifer bit his earlobe. "Right before I handed you that baby, I asked you *why*. And do you remember what you said to me while that infant died in your arms?"

With strong and sinuous movements, Julian disentangled himself from her grasp. "How could I forget?" he asked in a droll monotone. Though she didn't know why he bothered to. He knew she could feel his anger mounting. That when his heart had darkened and his blood seethed, she fed off those powerful emotions. As still and obsequious as Julian pretended to be, she alone knew the extent of his fury. She, alone, felt his pain.

This is what she wanted him to feel. This is how she would defeat the draw of the only woman who would ever get in her way. If Aerin de Moray was strong enough to survive his touch, she was strong enough to break Lucy's curse. If one of the de Moray witches could do that, then the four of them together might just have what it took to defeat her.

She either had to destroy them... or recruit them.

And destruction was *always* the more attractive option, wasn't it?

She crept closer to him, pleased to see the hesitation in his eyes and the circle of decay in the ground beneath his feet. "You told me that if you gave in to me, then a fate more horrible than five thousand daily casualties would befall humanity."

"So I did."

"And why was that, exactly?" she prodded.

"Darkness," Julian murmured, turning from her as though he couldn't bear the sight of her. "You know that my powers are such that they not only infect others, but others likewise bind to me on a molecular level. Were I to kiss you, were I to take any part of you inside of me, or put any part of me inside of you, your darkness, your cruelty, your *evil* would infect me. I would never be rid of it, or you. And to be eternally rid of you is the thing that I desire most in this world."

Lucifer let the acid in his words slide off her skin as she went in for the kill. "Darkness," she repeated. "Do you know how I'm going to win this, Julian? Do you know just who is my secret weapon? Do you know who will have to delve into the darkness that is a part of her soul, that is a singular component to her element? Do you realize, Julian, that which you abhor, and that which you desire are one and the same?"

Letting her fingers wave in the air, she stirred a wind to ruffle the uncommon locks of Julian's black and silver hair. "Darkness, Julian. Darkness and the Devil have always walked hand in hand, and guess which element I've always commanded? Guess which of the de Morays has my same penchant for darkness?"

Julian whirled back to look at her, a stricken expression shadowing his masculine features. "No," he denied. "Don't say it."

She didn't have to, but she couldn't help herself. "Aerin de Moray."

Aerin mowed down three zombies with her car, well, Tierra's car, before zipping into the Maison de Moray's drive. She'd left a peaceful Victorian mansion for a clandestine meeting with a forbidden would-be lover, and come home to the zombie-fucking-Apocalypse.

From a distance, they looked like neighbors filtering into a party, but from close up the undead were storming the gates.

She sprang from the car and made a running dive for the wrought-iron gate Claire slammed behind her as the horde reached it and poked their arms through in a parody of the TV walkers.

"Thank God, you're okay!" Aerin flung her arms around Claire.

"Why wouldn't I be?" she asked. "You know, except for the horde of zombies at our front door!"

"Where have you been?" Tierra demanded from the lawn where she brandished a shovel and rake like weapons, balefully eyeing the undead attempting to climb the six-foot iron fence.

"The corner of business and none of yours," Aerin answered. "Where's Tommy?"

"Tommy?" Claire echoed. "He's the least of our

problems." She turned to the crowd shaking the gate. "Get bent, you creepy fuckers!" She grabbed Aerin's hand and walked toward the garden where Tierra stood. "What do you think they want?"

"Look what I found!" Moira emerged from the shed, their trusty ax in one hand and a chainsaw in the other.

"Dibs!" Claire and Aerin both spoke at once.

"Guess again." Moira jogged up to them in her usual bare feet and cutoffs, weighed down with her lethal loot. "Chainsaw's mine, bitches. The Notorious RBG and I are fixin' to relieve some zombies of their civil liberties." She tossed the ax the very short distance between them and Aerin caught it and wielded it like a bat. "You ready to get your hands dirty, fancy pants?"

"I am now," Aerin said with a dark smile, wrapping her fingers tightly around the handy padded grip of the ax.

"Hey, where's my weapon?" Claire scowled.

"I got you a rake." Tierra handed the garden tool to her.

Clare dubiously inspected it with her nose wrinkled. "Gee, thanks."

"Let's not try not to use magic," Tierra said. "The last thing we want is to open another seal seeing as how this is the fallout from the last one." She looked around at the lovely gardens, anxiety wrinkling her delicate brow. "And keep them away from the garden, especially my peonies."

"Fuck your peonies, I'm keeping them from eating my face," Claire said.

"Yeah," Aerin agreed. Then stopped to think. "But also, let's try to avoid breaking the new windows."

"Says the woman who blew them all out in the first place," Tierra muttered.

"Shut up."

Moira stepped to Tierra. "Do y'all think Tierra

should be out here fighting, what with the baby and all?"

Tierra scowled and lifted her shovel. "Don't you dare try to make me sit in the house while you fight zombies."

The gate rattled as one of the denizens of the grave flung a leg over the spiked top, ignoring the fact that he impaled his taint as he began to scramble down the other side. A few of the ghoulish faces appeared almost alive, as though they hadn't been in the grave very long. Others barely had skin covering sunken skeletons, and ranged between several different stages of decomposition.

For zombies, they were all impeccably dressed. Nice suits, military dress uniforms, and colorful frocks that loved ones had buried them in.

"At least they ain't naked zombies," Moira observed.

"Yeah, because *that* would be the weird part." Claire rolled her eyes.

Cat calls and dirty words were flung through the iron bars as the growing crowd frenzied with panic because one of them had finally gotten through.

The one staggering at them now.

Aerin knew she was running out of time. She had to tell her sisters the information she'd gleaned from Julian. "These zombies are not just after eating our brains or whatever, they're after our souls. Our powers. They need to *die*...like, again." With that, she rushed the interloper, knowing that hacking his head off wouldn't stop him, but it would slow him down long enough for them to make a plan.

"What do you mean, they're after our powers?" Tierra chased after her, brandishing her shovel. "How do you know that?"

Aerin ignored her question, lifting her ax and holding it behind her like a batter waiting for a pitch.

The zombie, a man in his mid-fifties with an accountant haircut, gave her a bone chilling smile, even when she swung her ax. He moved at the last moment, and the blade missed his neck, but embedded in his shoulder, nearly hacking his arm off.

"I don't need all my limbs to kill you, girl," he said, reaching for the sleeve of her blouse. "I've killed plenty of women. You should see who's buried in my basement."

"Pastor Bill?" The note of horror in Tierra's voice was almost drowned out by the rip of a chord and the roar of a small but powerful engine. "How?"

"Always had my eye on you, little Tierra de Moray." Disgusting excitement flashed in his dead, dead eyes. "Always wanted to take you to the basement, I was waiting for you to ripen to the correct age, but I died before you hit puberty."

"Die again, you chicken-fucker!" With a war cry that would have impressed a kamikaze, Moira leapt past them all, sinking her chainsaw into Pastor Bill's head. Chunks of flesh and carnage flew everywhere like a blender turned on high with its lid left off.

Pieces of Pastor Bill hit Aerin's suit pants, and she fought the sour bile crawling up her throat.

Moira didn't stop until the man had been cut clean in half down the middle, his two parts melting to the ground.

"Well, if that doesn't stop them, then nothing will," Aerin said.

"Damn right." Moira revved the chainsaw engine. "I liked that more'n I should have."

Tierra made a strangled noise, and they whipped around.

"You going to be sick?" Claire asked. "Do you need to sit down?"

"No," Tierra looked at the pieces of zombie that was tossed at her feet. "Maybe. But I just can't believe this. Pastor Bill? He was always so nice to Aunt Justine and me. I can't believe he's a... that he did... that he's such a..."

"Such a *fuck*," Aerin spat on the corpse—one of the halves anyhow—the limbs of which were still twitching. "They all are." Sweeping her free hand to encompass the undead pressed against the locked fence, a few managing to climb half-way up the gate, she addressed her sisters. "The souls of all these corpses are in hell. They're the damned, only reanimated, and they're after us because if they consume the organs that contain our powers, they'll be granted them.

And if they consume the rest of us, they'll take our souls."

"Ew," Claire grimaced, then paled. "That's why you were asking for

Tommy?"

"Yes, he's one of them, Claire."

"Well, yeah, he's a zomb...he used to be dead, but he didn't go to hell. Tommy was a good man. It's my fault he's dead."

"How do you know all this anyhow?" Moira asked Aerin, the chainsaw idling in her firm grip.

Three identical, suspicious russet eyebrows lifted in her direction.

"We have zombies to kill," Aerin said, and turned to the gate, brandishing her ax.

"Aerin," Tierra's voice held a note of dangerous warning, one she'd never heard before. "How do you know?"

"Okay, I asked Julian!" Aerin flung her arms out, forgetting for a moment that she was gesturing with a very sharp ax. "What?" she asked in defense against their stricken looks. "He's all immortal and smart and shit. I figured he could help us out."

"Goddess damn it, Aerin, keep it in your pants around the ones who are trying to annihilate us, would you?" Tierra wagged her shovel in Aerin's direction.

"And I know I'm knocked up by Death, don't think I don't realize, but things are different now. I haven't seen him since... mostly."

"Point is," Moira cut in. "We can't trust a thing those Horsemen say."

"Julian wasn't lying," Aerin defended. "I would have known. I can feel when someone's lying, remember? He said that the blood of the martyrs is the fifth seal, and those who reap their vengeance and belong to their heavens will return there immediately. Those who are in hell are somehow being kept here. These zombies are *damned*...literally."

They were robbed of the time to absorb that information as the latch on the gate finally sheared under the weight of a horde that had now swelled to forty. Their voices weren't groans and snarls and hisses like on TV, but threats and words and voiced desires that should have been unspeakable.

Inside the phone was ringing. In the distance, sirens blared.

All hell had broken loose.

Luckily for them, the dead did seem to move like they were constipated octogenarians. Constipated octogenarian evil cannibals controlled by necromancy and driven by the promise of Druid power and a second chance.

Or whatever.

"Oh man," Tierra fretted as she tightened her grip on her shovel, "we've warded this house up, down and sideways. I can't believe they can get through!"

"Must not work on someone who's already dead," Claire said, swiping at one of them with the wide side of her rake. It knocked down the teenager with the already missing arm, but in moments, he was struggling to his feet again.

"Well, shit." Tierra backed away from an approaching tiny Asian woman who screamed threats, or demands at her in Japanese. "Get back," she warned. "I don't want to hurt you."

The woman grabbed for Tierra's arm, her teeth opening to take a bite.

"Don't you dare!" Tierra wrenched her arm from the woman's grasp and jabbed the sharp head of the shovel into the woman's mouth.

Gnawing on the metal, the lady just held out her wrinkly arms and did her best to snatch at Tierra until the earth witch actually drove the shovel through her head, knocking the woman down and separating every-thing above her sinuses from the rest of her jaw.

"And stay down!" she yelled.

Problem was, like the decapitated hippie from the afternoon, they didn't stay down. It reminded Aerin of a Monty Python movie, except when she'd relieved a kid in a marine uniform of all his limbs, no blood had shot out of cheap pumps.

"Don't fight me," he'd cajoled. "I'll do more with your powers than you ever could. I know where the danger is. Give it up."

"Go back to your grave, uh, soldier," Aerin pointed. "That's an order!" Maybe that would work.

He attacked her. And even when there was nothing left of him but a stump, his hands went all "Thing" from the Addams Family and finger-walked their way over to her, grasping at the hems of her slacks.

Reluctantly, Aerin had stomped the palms into the ground, staking them with her stilettos.

"Take that, you undead asshole." She paused, chewing on her lip and also a bit of shame. "Also... thank you for your service."

"This isn't working!" Claire called, swinging at a crowd of five zombies, barely holding them off.

One of them grabbed her hair, and Aerin lunged, fearing she was too far away to get to her sister in time.

"Speak for yourself!" Moira pranced over to Claire,

the chainsaw running on full speed as she began to cut through the crowd like a knife through butter. "Yeeeee-haaaaw!" she hollered.

Though, as efficient as the chainsaw was at cutting through flesh like butter, it seemed to merely create two halves of a corpse, and that came with its own form of chaos.

A hand closed around Aerin's ankle, causing her to stumble. She looked down to see the long half of Pastor Bill latched to her, his creepy-ass eyes and half smile staring up at her from the ground.

"Fuck. This," she hissed, and dropped her ax.

The moment Pastor Bill went flying over the fence on a strong gust of wind to land in the street, Claire dropped her rake. "Hell isn't the only place you can burn, you undead bastard!" Fishing a lighter out of her pocket, she flicked it open and curled her hand around it, creating beneath an expanding ball of fire. "Here goes nothing," she muttered and tossed it at a group of three corpses lurching toward her.

They didn't explode so much as immolate.

"Did you guys see that?" she squealed. "That was my first fireball."

"What did I say about magic?" Tierra scolded, whacking a rather chompy teenaged kid right in the kisser. "Open another seal and we're dead meat!"

"That's only if four of us use magic at the same time," Claire pointed out.

"Yeah, don't use any of yours," Aerin said. "Hey, Claire, behind you!"

Claire whirled around, creating another fireball with her hands.

Aerin lent it strength, feeding it with oxygen.

"Uh, y'all?" Moira's worried voice sounded from behind them.

"Get it," Aerin hissed. "Bomb that fucker."

"*Guys.*" Out of the corner of her eye, Aerin saw

Tierra wave her arms, but Claire didn't see. She hurled her gigantic fireball at the zombie and the thing melted, leaving only bones.

"Yes!" Aerin celebrated, high-fiving her sister.

"Stop with the fire!" Tierra yelled.

"Why? It's working."

"No!" Aerin and Claire turned to see Moira pointing at the three flaming zombies stumbling around the yard. One had just bumped into the shed, setting the hundred-year-old wood structure on fire. "No, it ain't."

❈ I I ❈

"I can do something about this." It took a second for Moira to reluctantly peel her fingers from the chainsaw. Closing her eyes, she flung her arms out, muttering an incantation under her breath. The sky over them darkened just as an armless zombie fireball set all the lavender and sage bushes ablaze, releasing a rather pleasant scent into the night.

Aerin swiped at three swarming crones and, out of the corner of her eye, she saw a zombie policeman in his dress blues reach for the chugging Notorious RBG. "Moira, the chainsaw!" she yelled.

Startled, Moira was still able to kick the undead 5-0 out of the way in time to retrieve her precious weapon, but not in time to focus where her summoned clouds would dump their contents.

Claire screamed as the freezing deluge drenched her, smothering her latest fireball and making a mess of her leather. Only one of five burning bushes were extinguished, and not even a drop touched the shed.

"What the shit, Moira?" Claire called shaking water off her hands.

Moira didn't answer until she'd carved through the cop and spat on his remains. "Excuse me, burning britches, but the only thing scarier'n a zombie is a zombie with a chain saw."

"Give Sandra Day O'Connor to me," Tierra ordered, staking someone to the ground with her shovel and advancing on Moira. "Then summon another cloud before the fire jumps to the house!"

"It's RBG, my personal hero!" Moira said, pulling the chainsaw out of reach like a recalcitrant child with a toy. "And she's mine!"

Aerin grabbed the chainsaw's handle from behind and relieved it from Moira's grip using the element of surprise. "Write your feminist manifesto some other time, for now we need some rain."

Moira threw a promise of retribution over her shoulder, but repeated her earlier spell, conjuring concentrated storm clouds.

Claire squished and squeaked up to Aerin, her wet leather making all kinds of unnatural noises. "You know how to use that thing?"

"Um... keep the spinning chain-y thing away from limbs I want to remain attached."

Claire grimaced. "Hand it over, I've always had an affinity for dangerous machines."

Glad to be rid of it, Aerin carefully passed it to Claire, who revved the engine and turned to protect Moira's back while she put out the fire that was quickly turning into a blaze.

Problem was, now the flaming zombies had separated, and one was headed for Tierra who was trying to pull her shovel out of a struggling zombie's hands, all the while dodging someone else's dentured chompers.

"Some help over here, Moira!" Tierra screamed as the smoldering zombie stumbled closer.

"I'm *trying*," Moira gritted out. "Do y'all know how hard it is to aim a raincloud?"

"Here," Aerin jogged around a collection of zombies dressed like a quilting circle and threw her hands toward the cloud. The wind positioned it over Tierra for the precious seconds needed to put out the fire.

One flaming zombie down, two to go.

Once Tierra's flowing silk, chiffon and lace dress was sopping wet, it clung to her like a second skin, and she stood in the middle of the grotesque chaos, shivering and teeth chattering, surrounded by more than six un-dead doing their utmost to make her their midnight snack. She looked panicky, and wriggled her fingers like her magic itched to escape.

Claire was doing okay with *whatshisface*, the chain-saw, and Moira had figured out how to empty a few of the grave escapees of their remaining liquid, effectively turning them into zombie-jerky. With no fluids to lubri-cate their movements, they quivered like dry husks of corn and blew over in a stiff breeze.

A stiff breeze Aerin was happy to supply.

But more of the hungry fuckers filtered through the fence. Two, it seemed, for every one they incapacitated. They were losing this fight, and if they didn't figure something out very quickly, they would lose everything.

Finally giving in, Tierra called roots and vines up from the ground beneath her, snaking them around the ankles and legs of her attackers and pinning them down.

Aerin stared at Tierra's stomach, only a tiny tiny bit bigger than it had been before. Not yet a baby bump, but if one had an eye for detail, they would tell that the lower belly was fuller, and her hips were beginning to widen.

And suddenly, Aerin was afraid.

Until an idea knocked her upside the head with such abruptness she flinched. It felt as though it had been flying through the nether and shot through her thoughts like a dart.

"Claire, don't use your magic," Aerin ordered.

"Why?" Claire quieted the chainsaw long enough to ask.

"Because I'm about to use mine." Dashing through the yard toward the house, Aerin called to Dr. Lecter, her vampire bat familiar. "Bring me the Grimoire!" She slipped a few times on slimy parts she'd rather not identify in her bare feet, fighting her revulsion.

Dr. Lecter appeared just as she reached the bottom of the porch steps, the heavy tome clutched in his wee claws. He flapped over to Aerin and deposited it into her reaching grasp.

"Thanks." The book felt warm in her hands. The blue rune-tattooed skin of its cover the temperature of a live body. It pulsed with power, power she craved. No, not craved. That she needed to save her sisters. *Yeah...* "Okay Grim," she addressed the book. "We're dying here... show me a spell that is effective against the undead."

Grim opened beneath her prompting, his pages flipping from front all the way to deep into the back of the book. Thunder clapped a warning out over the sound from the direction of the standing stones the moment Grim's final page settled into place.

"Is that the back of the book?" Teirra asked in a shaking voice, lifting her hands and clutching her fists as more and more vines and plants were called to her aid to immobilize the undead.

"I thought Grim's wards didn't work against these guys." Claire handed the chainsaw back to Moira, now that the fires had all been put out.

"This one will." Aerin grinned down at the page, dark swirls adorning its corners and the painting of a skull and a candle interrupting the dark, sinister letters. "All right, you zombie ass wads, prepare to become my bitches."

❄ 12 ❄

Lightning forked through the sky, and the rumbling answer of thunder crawled after it, a cold, loud wind shrieking in from the east.

"We're not...read... back ...Grim!" Tierra was saying something, but it was lost in the sounds of the approaching storm and the calls of trapped zombies and the power swirling, and the heart beating in Aerin's ears.

"I'm going to need some fire and a skull," Aerin called.

"Allow me" Claire jogged over with loud leather creaks. Once she reached Aerin, she swept an arm to the struggling horde. "I think we have more than enough skulls here.

"No!" Tierra lunged through her cadre of trapped undead, ducking and weaving their reach like a human pinball. "Those spells are necromancy," she yelled. "That's not what we do."

"That's not what *you* do," Aerin called back. "But nothing else is working. It's time to fight fire with fire." She slid a glance to Claire. "Er, death with death. Undeath? You know what I mean."

"I gotcha." Claire flicked her lighter. "I'm ready when you are." Aerin began the incantation.

"Without a soul or body of earth."

Tierra was almost to them, and Moira wasn't too far behind her, working backward and swiping at the zombies with her trusty chainsaw.

"Don't," Tierra cried. "Those spells are dark. We don't know what they can do!"

"It says right there," Claire argued. "Incantation to control the undead."

"We want them kilt, not controlled," Moira called over the ripping of the chainsaw as another one melted before her, his limbs scuttling on their own toward Tierra.

"I didn't see one of those!" Aerin yelled, then started over.

"Without a soul or body of earth. What once had life, but death has delivered…"

With discomfiting synchronicity, the head of each zombie, almost a hundred in all crowded in and around their yard, all swiveled around to gaze at Aerin.

"Those returned through unholy birth, out of the grave and ashes slithered…"

"Do you feel that?" Moira asked a chill visibly shaking her shoulders.

"Yes," Tierra nodded. "It's heavy… like a weight of something in the air, like it's trying to smother us."

Aerin could feel it, all right. It enveloped her like a cloak, settling around her like a robe of nobility. Power surged through her, tendrils of it snaking from her mouth and calling to the twitching undead on the lawn.

"I think it's working. Look, they've stopped trying to bite us." Claire pointed with her free hand.

"Heed me now, thou slaves of the past. Unchain your flesh from the grasp of
Death…"

"He's not going to like that," Tierra warned, reaching out for the book, though still a few paces away.

Aerin didn't care. She felt hard, like her skin would crack and her bones would splinter, so much power surged through her. It threatened to tear her apart, but in a decadent way. Like a sneeze, or an orgasm. A moment of pure sensation that rearranged molecules and expelled chemicals and threats, and breath.

Air.

This was right... it may not be good, but it was right.

"I can feel it too," Claire touched her shoulder. "It's intoxicating."

"It's dark!" Tierra cried. "Stop!"

"No." With a swipe of Claire's hand, a wall of fire leapt between them, separating Aerin and Claire from Moira and Tierra. The heat singed the air like a scream, and smelled of sulphur and terror, and pain.

"Claire?" Tierra wrenched her hand away just in time to stop it from being burned. "How could you?" her eyes shimmered with hurt. "We don't use magic against each other."

"Come to me, if your numbers be vast. And heed the commands upon my breath..." Aerin paused, readying to say the final words, wishing that her sisters could understand... that they could feel this. Power. Control. Knowledge and darkness.

But shadows could be good, couldn't they? The moon Goddess lit the nighttime, not the day. Death was a catalyst for rebirth, and hell balanced out heaven. This was Arma-fucking-geddon, and Aerin de Moray was never one to stand by and let things happen. She *made* things happen, and now she had an army of the undead to help them all. *"By the earth, the air, the fire and sea..."*

The last words caused her a bit of hesitation, but it was too late to stop now...

"By the power of darkness, which I call unto me!"

The undead knelt. The ones who were only bound

by their ankles dropped to their knees. The others who had no limbs, merely bowed their heads.

"What have you done?" Tierra asked.

"Oh don't get your panties in a wad," Aerin snipped. "Look at them now, they're harmless." They glanced over to the horde, still as stone and bowing as though at some macabre royal court.

"You can't stop us," Claire said in a strange, monotone voice.

Aerin looked over at her. "What? Stop who?"

"I see the future in the flames... and whatever path we two chose, the world will come with us. You can't choose for us. You can't stop us. If you join us, decide it is time to end it all, to rule it all, no one will be able to stand against us. Not the Lord of the Damned, not the Horsemen, and not the denizens and deities of the otherworld."

Claire's eyes were burning now, shadows crawling through the veins on her face like writhing black worms.

"What nonsense you talking, girl?" Moira demanded.

"Look what you did to her!" Tierra scolded. "You made her all evil!"

"That wasn't me!" Aerin shook her head in denial, but she snapped the Grimoire shut.

That seemed to slap Claire out of it and she blinked, her eyes and skin returning to normal and the wall of flames abating to nothing but a singed line across the grass. She rubbed her eyes for a second and then fluttered her lashes. "What?"

"Give me that!" Tierra snatched Grim out of Aerin's hands. "I'm so mad I could just... just... bury you!"

"You did that to Death, already," Aerin came back at her. "Time to get another trick. Besides, look at them. They're not trying to kill us anymore. I just did a good thing."

"Whatever you did," Moira rubbed at chill bumps on her bare arms. "It ain't in the realm of good."

"Yeah, but it was in the realm of effective, and *you're welcome*." She turned to Claire. "You feeling okay?"

"I feel great," Claire shrugged. "Though I don't know what happened just now."

"Progress," Aerin wrapped her arm around Claire's shoulder. "That was some powerful fire you just wielded tonight.

"Right?" Claire's eyes gleamed with pride.

"More like possession," Moira muttered, turning to Tierra.

They stood staring at each other, the charred line between them becoming a chasm, the distance growing from a few inches to a gulf of mistrust and suspicion.

"L-let's get hosed off," Moira suggested, an obvious attempt to break the sudden tension. "We'll think better without zombie guts and chainsaws. We'll figure it out."

"First of all," Tierra's eyes narrowed as her grip on the Grimoire tightened. "get these abominations of yours *off* of my yard!"

"So it's your yard now, is it?" Claire challenged. "I thought it belonged to all of us."

"You know what I mean."

Aerin put her hand on Claire's arm, hoping to soothe her fiery temper. "It's okay, Claire. I know exactly where to send them." A few lonely Horsemen could use some company.

As she turned to give the order, Aerin felt momentarily torn. It was a heady thing, having an army... even if they were mostly shriveled and gross. She didn't want her sisters to hate her or to mistrust her. But she didn't feel what they felt. She'd known what to do and she'd saved the day.

Why couldn't they see that?

She knew why. Because deep down, they understood

what Claire had prophesied was true... Tierra and Moira were both afraid. Afraid of their powers and afraid of their potential. They didn't know what she saw, hadn't been there when Julian had informed her what could happen if they decided to throw their hats in the ring for supremacy over the earth.

They'd only just heard the truth.

That they were powerful, and whatever they decided to do... No power in the universe, light or dark, could stop them.

❧ 13 ☙

<blockquote>
"Earth to release me from the land
Water to guide the task at hand.
Flame to hasten my course ahead.
Air to be the path I tread.
By earth, fire, water, and sky,
Goddess bless this broom to fly!"
</blockquote>

*T*hwack. Thick grasses muffled the sound of the new broom hitting the ground... again.

It did not, however, muffle the string of creative epithets spewing from Aerin's mouth. She couldn't concentrate, could barely even breathe.

She was angry. Angry at her sisters for the rift that had opened up tonight. Angry at their worried silence or their spoken mistrust of her. Angry with Julian for his strange actions today. For the violence that had erupted between them before he'd withdrawn from her.

Why make a deal to see her if he was only going to push her away? Was it some kind of Four Horsemen Jedi mind game?

"I thought you were afraid of heights." As though conjured by her tempestuous thoughts of him, Julian's cultured voice melted from the darkness before the rest of him.

"What are you doing here?" Aerin spun on him. "It's almost dawn."

His hands were linked behind him as he climbed the gentle hill to the edge of the drop where she stood above the churning ocean. It hurt to look at him for too long, he was that beautiful. "I had a feeling I'd find you here after all the madness in town."

Madness. That was putting it lightly. Frightened people. Walking dead. Chaos in the streets.

The world would never be the same...and a fourth of the blame was upon her head.

Or was it? Was all of this someone else's fault? It was certainly someone else's prophecy. They only thing she'd done wrong was being born.

Arguably.

Two of her three sisters seemed to think that she'd done something very wrong tonight.

Did Julian know? Could he sense the darkness inside of her? Did he realize that, even now, the undead were slowly converging on his Horsemen brothers at their cabin in the woods?

The assholes deserved it. Didn't they? The undead wouldn't *kill* the stubborn immortals... but they would certainly keep them busy for a bit until the sisters could formulate a plan of some kind.

The de Moray sisters were floundering, stumbling about like blind toddlers in an earthquake. That had to change.

Now.

Aerin used the action of picking up her discarded broom to reach out and sense his emotions.

"You're conflicted." She studied the stark angles of his face and deep, pale eyes that wouldn't meet hers. "And you're sad." It drifted to her on the sea breezes, his desolation. The darkness was after him, too, but he was better at running from it than she was.

"Always," he confirmed.

"Do you...want to talk about it? About what happened earlier?"

A small sliver of light kissed the San Juan Islands, visible from their northern vantage and they both watched it, side by side.

"I'm eternally lonely," he confessed. "My immortal existence seems without any other reason but to suffer, to inflict suffering upon others.

Can you imagine what that is like?"

She tried. She really did, and realized that her mortal brain, while it could sympathize, could not truly conjure the scope of reality to which he was referring. "No."

"I do not enjoy my existence. Killing for me is no conquest. No war. No chance at revelation or rebirth. Until you, I've gone longer than ten *thousand* years without touching another body and watching them putrefy and expire."

"I'm...sorry."

"Are you?" He turned to her then, pain lashing at her from his large frame. Making her want to curl inside of herself, to run and hide from it. What was he doing here? What was he trying to tell her?

"Of course I am, Julian." When others would have retreated from him, Aerin stepped forward, reaching out to take his face in her hands.

His bones felt raw and heavy against her delicate fingers. "What if your existence could be something else? What if all of this didn't have to be a battle between the eight of us? We could parlay, maybe. Your brothers. My sisters. We could forge an alliance, discuss our options, maybe even join forces. I mean, I know that there is conflict between the four of you. That Conquest and War might just be down for an Apocalypse, and that Death is against, for now. And, like you said, you've never really landed on one side or the other. So... let's hash it out. Make some fucking pro/con lists, an action plan, at the very least a peace treaty."

"Like an international summit? Or a board meeting?" His affectionate smile melted her, and his eyes were infinitely tender, and a bit too moist as he tucked a tendril of her hair that had escaped her bun behind her ear.

"Exactly." She smiled back at him, showing her pleasure.

"Are you saying, Aerin, that you are *for* opening the seals and ending the world, or against it? That you're not committed to fighting this?" He enunciated his words, his gaze boring into hers with an intensity she couldn't understand. He wanted something from her. He wanted the truth.

"I'm saying... we could discuss our options. That there's a chance my sisters and I are destined to bring out the Apocalypse for a reason... Maybe... maybe it's time." Aerin gripped her broom tighter as his hand dropped away from her, and all the emotion in his eyes flickered and died out, leaving them pale and cold.

"I know what you're thinking, Julian," Aerin forged on. "But if I've learned anything from life it's that things aren't black or white. There are no true heroes, there are no pure villains. Just people with agendas. What defines you is what you're willing to do to reach your ends."

"You think that because you have not lived long enough to learn that you are wrong." He retreated from her, physically and emotionally, taking several steps backward toward the tree line. "I have landed, Aerin. I have chosen a side."

She blinked. "What?"

"There is still too much left to be done. Potential unrealized. There is still hope for them, Aerin. And we can't take it from them. It's too dangerous, now isn't the time."

"Do you get to choose? Do you have the final say?" Aerin advanced on him. "All I'm suggesting is that we explore what might happen, what *is* happening. Five out of seven seals are open already and maybe—."

More shadows lurked in the trees. Big ones. Three of them. Each with a different emotional signature.

"Julian?" Aerin's eyes widened, unable to believe what was happening. "What is this?"

His hands shook though his eyes were like ice, and he curled his bare fingers into fists, blasting her with pain and fear and piling mountains of his regret on her shoulders.

"I'm sorry, Aerin," he whispered, as the three other Horsemen melted from the mists, dismounting their steeds and slowly making their way toward her in an arc. Trapping her against the harrowing drop. They looked like the warriors of yore, larger than life and handsome as sin. Like knights from a fairytale... or a horror movie.

"You disingenuous *motherfucker*," she spat, her heart shriveling with pain that was all her own. "You're here to kill me."

Julian closed his eyes and shook his head. "I could never."

"But I could." Nicholas Kingswood put a hand on Julian's brawny shoulder in a show of brotherly affection before advancing past him toward Aerin. "We all decided it had to be *you*."

"You're the darkest of the four, Aerin," Julian explained as his brothers closed in. "The one who could tip the scales in *her* favor... I can't allow that to happen. If she prevails, she might gain your soul along with your sisters'. Along with *everything and everyone* else. All hope would be lost, don't you see? I have to give humanity a chance. I've suffered this long for *them*, resisted her for this many millennia. That can't all be for naught."

"She *who*?" Aerin cried, backing away from the advancing Horsemen as they crushed the grasses and rushes beneath their heavy feet. Conquest with his light hair shining like sand slicked with blood in the pre-dawn light. The midnight tresses of War and Death. Wide shoulders, swarthy features, and lethal intent in their eyes. "Who are you talking about?" She cried out as a bit of the cliff fell away beneath her feet, and a buffet of wind seemed to press her forward, away from a deadly fall, but toward the men who would do her in. Rocks and four hard places...

Don't show them you're afraid.

"We cannot say her name," War stated.

"You can't tell me even though I'm about to eat it, here?" she demanded. "Jesus Christ, you guys."

"No." Julian shook his head. "The Devil."

That shut her up.

Julian walked forward with his brethren; the sight they made in the gathering dawn was truly something to behold. If Aerin wasn't so afraid, she'd be awestruck.

"You're... you're really going to let them kill me."

Julian looked away, the silver streaks in his hair flashing as the cresting sun illuminated them all. "If not for her, it would all be different. But I can't allow her to destroy the good that I see in you. That I—I *love* about you."

"Don't you *dare* say that word to me!" The darkness surged within Aerin, and with it, a power she hadn't before felt.

"Goodbye, Aerin de Moray," he murmured. "Knowing you has been my greatest pleasure."

"Fucking me would have been your greatest pleasure," she said coldly. "But I guess you've done that, in a more figurative sense."

The fear was gone. She looked down at the churning ocean and felt... nothing. A beast of pain gnawed at its cage in the pit where she'd thrown it, but it would soon be smothered with her signature chill. She wouldn't let it end like this, there was so much left to do. So, instead, she put her broom between her legs, murmured the flying spell... And jumped.

Instead of the waves and rocks coming up to meet her, Aerin paused in mid-air for a few moments, then shot ahead.

"*OhshitohshitohSHIT!*" she screamed as the calm water bounced the pink reflection of the sunrise and her own ridiculous image, straddling a kitchen implement and rocketing toward who-the-fuck-knew-where.

All those movies had been right... witches flew on broom sticks.

Who knew?

Flying would have been in-fucking-credible if she hadn't spaced one tiny detail.

Killian Bane had big, scary black angel wings.

Well, wasn't that shittastic?

She could feel the kiss of Death on the back of her neck, and she looked back in time to see him barreling after her like an avenging angel, grim intent set in his strong jaw.

"You'd better back off or—or—I'm telling Tierra on you!" she called, all mature and shit.

He laughed, and the sound speared fear through her bones. "Not if I catch you first."

With a flap of his great wings, he gained on her, and Aerin knew she was fucked.

She squeezed her eyes tight, waiting for the touch of Death. If only she could disappear. If only she was back in the kitchen with her sisters.

If only she could see them one. Last. Time.

Poof!

Or, rather... *CRASH!*

Aerin ran headlong into the refrigerator and clattered to the ground, the small branch of her broom feeling like an entire two-by-four beneath her aching back.

Oh man, that was going to bruise.

"What the hell?" Tierra shrieked, standing so quickly she knocked the kitchen chair over.

"You...you... just like... appeared!" Claire marveled.

"Anyone else think that was too wonky for words?" Moira queried.

"Holy shit, you guys!" Aerin stood on wobbly legs, adrenaline pushing away the pain that wanted to swallow her whole. Sure, the man she... er... Julian wanted her dead. In fact, all the Horsemen had decided the world was better off without her. She'd let her feelings be hurt later.

Because she could fucking fly!

"Holy shit on a broomstick!" Aerin exclaimed again, her heart pounding and her blood singing.

"What?" her sisters asked in unison, their eyes wide and disbelieving.

"We need to get that ax," Aerin said, picking up her broom. "We're making us all one of these, then I'm going to take you on one *hell* of a ride!"

TIERRA

TIFFINIE HELMER

❧ I ❧

> *"Do not fear death, my daughter*
> In time all will be made known.
> Stay close to your sisters and the earth;
>   for she will reveal her powerful
>   secrets.
>   by earth, air, fire, and sea..."

Tierra woke with a start, sitting straight up in bed as the whispers of the dead floated around her. She choked back the scream crawling up her throat and tried to fight the vestiges of the nightmare. Grief and depression threatened to smother her and tears seared the back of her eyes. Battling the need to cry, she embraced her surroundings with relief.

She was alone in the daylight. No ghosts weaved through mist, twisting around sentinel Standing Stones and morphing into the Four Horsemen, brandishing apocalyptic weapons, the arrow, sword, scales, and Death, silent and still, holding the scythe, a macabre extension of his hands.

Could her mother be trapped in the Standing Stones on Siren's Cry, her soul held prisoner by the Four Horsemen? Or had that been her mother speaking to her, offering up much needed advice and wisdom?

Get a grip, Tierra.

It was just her imagination on hyper drive because she'd been pierced by Conquest's arrow and died for a time in the stones herself. The same place her mother had died.

That made more sense, and didn't tap into the yearning for a mother she never knew. A mother she could use more than ever right now as she was going to be one herself. Lately her dreams were wicked and wild with no rhyme or reason. Somehow her memories, fears, and desires had combined with last night's midnight zombie raid and produced one hell of a nightmare.

No more ice cream before bed.

Zombies?

Had that really happened? She wished it had been a dream that she could wonder at and hopefully shake off. But it was too real, *too visceral*. She'd hurt...*them*—whatever *they* were—had a hand in killing those...*those* things. You couldn't really hurt or kill something that was already dead. Could you?

But Aerin. Aerin had done something. Something forbidden. Just how bad remained to be seen.

Jinx jumped onto the four-poster queen-size bed, with its handmade crazy quilt of silks and satins, and swiped at Tierra with a black paw. Not a concerned how-are-you-doing paw. More like a get-your-ass-out-of-bed-there-is-shit-to-do paw. Her familiar's eerie all-too-knowing green eyes glowed with judgment in the late morning.

Goddess, she was tired. So very tired. All she wanted was to sleep and to keep some food down. From all she'd read—with making potions and trying to figure out a way to stop the looming Apocalypse limiting her time—her symptoms were normal for the first trimester. Pulling an all-nighter to fight a horde of zombies, not so normal.

The black cat wasn't the only one upset about Tierra's condition. She wasn't too happy about it herself. It didn't seem fair that she'd remained a virgin all this time, waiting for that one romantic true love, and when she finally threw caution into the wind and slept with someone, she got knocked up. Being an earth witch, she should have figured she'd be extra fertile and taken precautions. But still. She'd slept with Death. How in any universe would he have a part in creating life? His job was to take it.

She didn't even know what she was pregnant with. Chances were good it wouldn't be a normal baby boy or girl. Not with a scythe-swinging immortal father and an elemental earth witch for a mother.

She reclined against the pillows and covered her abdomen with a protective hand. While part of her shared her sisters' fear that she carried a demon spawn or the Antichrist, the other part was already fiercely protective, and she knew she'd lay down her soul for the fluttering new life inside her.

Jinx gave a screechy, drawn-out meow that raised the hairs on the back of Tierra's neck.

"*Fine*, I'm getting up." She tossed back the covers and climbed out of the bed, feeling aches and pains from the fight of the night before. Muscles she hadn't used in a while protested with a vengeance. Swinging a shovel at zombies instead of using it to dig in the earth put a strain on the arms and shoulders. Some of her homemade tiger's balm would be called for today.

Gingerly stretching, Tierra ventured to the turret bay window and looked out over her damaged gardens. They needed help after last night.

She gave into the yawn that cracked her jaw and caught the steady stare of beady black eyes watching her from the branch of a hemlock tree.

Clever harbinger to stay just outside the protective perimeter of the wards.

Killian Bane, the Fourth Horsemen of the Apocalypse, the Grim Reaper, the Great Destroyer, Death himself, in his raven form, watching her.

Bastard never seemed far anymore.

She hadn't talked to him since the night she'd died, but she'd felt his black eyes burning a hole through her at odd times of the day and night. They'd probably have to talk at some point, as they were having a child together.

But not today.

Mentally she conversed with the stately evergreen, asking for a favor it seemed all too happy to give. With a flick of her finger, the pine branch bowed and released, flipping the raven off his perch. A deep throaty caw echoed like a sardonic laugh as the raven slingshotted away. *Take that, you demonic peeping Tom.*

Death might not be intimidated by her powers, but a pregnant woman was a force to be reckoned with. And she planned on kicking some ass today. She wasn't doing another midnight zombie brawl, or midday one, for that matter. They needed to find out, without Aerin using spells in the back of the book, how to kill—er, rid the world of the undead.

Grabbing another quick shower—she'd taken one before bed, but after the last twenty-four hours she didn't think she could get clean enough—Tierra dressed in a flowing sundress the color of apricots, adding her crystal bracelets that helped protect against evil. Cat's eye, agate, and topaz, which had Jinx meowing approvingly. The cat sat on the dresser next to the mirror monitoring Tierra's choices, and tossing her a few Tierra hadn't considered. But when Tierra added the jasper and moonstone for pregnancy, Jinx hissed.

What did it say when a witch's familiar was against protecting her child?

"Either tell me what you know or stop hissing," Tierra said, picking up the ancient scrying crystal that had helped deflect Conquest's arrow from piercing her heart, and slipped the golden chain over her head. She'd left her hair down, rather than taxing her sore muscles into braiding or putting it up. Maybe she could get one of her sisters to help her with her hair.

Jinx gave a mocking meow as if reading Tierra's thoughts.

Hmm...what if the cat understood her? She locked gazes with the feline, and its green eyes met hers, feral and shrewd.

This was no pet.

First on the list of chores for today: witches' familiars. What help were they? From modern-day fairytales to before the recording of the Brothers Grimm, the witch's familiar held some power or was a helpmate to the witches. And as each of her sisters had their familiars, too, it made sense that they would be useful.

Jinx purred and rubbed up against Tierra's arm. Well, she must be on the right track.

Gathering Jinx in her arms, Tierra ventured downstairs to consult the book and scare up some lunch. For the first time in a long time, she felt like she could eat and maybe keep it down.

That is until she reached the first floor and entered the kitchen.

Aunt Justine, Gwen, and the new coven member, Lucy, sat at the table having coffee with Aerin while Moira leaned against the wall. Moira's grudge against Aunt Justine wrapped around her like armor and added a pall of unease over the gathering. Those sitting at the table tried to ignore Moira's resentment for the perceived villain in their midst, but Aunt Justine still squirmed in her chair.

The overwhelming stench of sulphur assaulted Tierra's senses and her stomach churned. Could emotions put off scent? Was Moira emitting that putrid smell with her hatred of Aunt Justine? Lately, as her pregnancy progressed, smells were magnified tenfold. But this was rancid enough that the others should be able to smell it.

Jinx hissed at the guests, leapt from her arms, and scampered out of the room.

"There she is!" Aunt Justine exclaimed, her smile all white teeth, her eyes bright jade. "I'd know that jingle anywhere."

Maybe she should retire the ankle bracelet, but she loved their musical bells that sang of mystical places.

"Aunt Justine." Tierra swallowed hard and put on her welcome face, greeting Lucy and Gwen. Why hadn't anyone told her they had company? She would have stayed upstairs. Making small talk would require more than she had in her to give right now.

Especially coven company.

"Where's Claire?" she asked, looking around the room and not finding her.

"Claire's with Tommy." Moira folded her arms over her braless tank top, glaring daggers at Aunt Justine.

Would Moira ever get over Aunt Justine trying to kill her? Probably not. Justine didn't look very comfortable either squashed between Gwen and Lucy at the round table. Smart of her though, to not sit within scratching distance of Moira.

Claire's Tommy was another thing that needed to be handled. Tierra mentally added ridding the house of him to her list of chores. After last night, Claire had to know that Tommy was dangerous and not the boy she'd loved.

"Is that a good idea?" Tierra asked. "Tommy alone with Claire?" *Did no one remember the power-hungry zombies wanting to eat our hearts out from last night?*

"*You* want to tell Claire who she can and cannot see?" Aerin asked, glancing at both her sisters to gauge their reaction. "Yeah, didn't think so."

Well, if Miss Dark Spell isn't feeling her oats this morning.

"Tierra, you look as fresh as a ripe peach in that dress," Lucy commented, smiling and seeming sincere, but the hairs on the back of Tierra's neck rose again. "I swear each time I see you, your skin glows brighter. Please, join us for coffee and share with us your secrets. Aerin makes it just how I love it. Strong enough to wake the dead."

"Tierra doesn't drink coffee. She's more of a *tea*totaller," Aerin smirked, raising her cup to her lips.

"Tea is probably better for your...nerves anyway. Isn't it, dear?" Lucy asked with a knowing quirk of her perfectly penciled brow.

Tierra shivered. How did this newly transplanted Irish witch know about her condition? Had Justine told her? She'd asked her not to tell anyone until she figured out what she was going to do. Or could Lucy be hiding powers beyond the ken or the capacity of the other coven members? For now, Tierra pretended she hadn't picked up on Lucy's cloaked remark.

"Remember," Tierra said, "I'm in the business of making tea. It would make sense that I'm also a fan." Slowly, she inched deeper into the kitchen under the guise of brewing some, but in reality, it was to move away from the nauseating smell of rotten eggs that had her stomach twisting in fits. And she'd such high hopes of eating something today.

"That's right," Lucy said. "Your little shop. What was it called again?"

Oh, she knew the name. What game was she playing at? "Ambrosia's Brews and Charms," Tierra supplied.

"Yes, I remember now. Such a charming name. I need to make a point to drop in one of these days. Tell me, how *is* business doing with all the unfortunate happenings of late?"

"Wonderful." Aerin proudly beamed. "Ambrosia's is now a global marketplace. I've taken it to the clouds, so to speak. And while a lot of brick and mortar stores are failing, recent events have increased the sales of the alternative health tonics and teas Tierra sells."

"So very pleased to hear it."

Tierra set the tea kettle to flame, wondering what they were really doing here. This wasn't a checking-in-to-see-how-you're-doing visit. It was a checking-in-to-see-what-you're-up-to visit. It seemed too coincidental, this mid-morning meet after last night's lawn party. Couldn't be the use of dark magic on the air that would have reverberated through the countryside like sonic waves when Aerin read from the back of the book, could it?

She hoped her sisters had caught on to that, too. Moira looked fully aware of the undercurrents, while Aerin seemed to be enjoying Lucy and the others' company. Almost as though she was holding court.

"Yes, the Goddess has blessed us having Aerin and her talents here." Tierra attempted to change the subject, wanting it off her and her business. "Please continue with your conversation. I didn't mean to interrupt."

"You're not interrupting," Gwen said, her Barbie doll looks and plastic smile making Tierra's uneasiness flare further. "In fact, we'd love your insight."

Tierra swallowed again, wondering how long she'd last before she must excuse herself. "My insight on....?"

"Before you arrived, we were discussing last night," Lucy said. "So much going on and rather than put any stock in the rumors, we thought it would be best to come to the— well...source, if you will." *Rumors?*

Lucy continued, "It seems all of Port Townsend can't stop talking about a woman matching your description—and that of your sisters as you all look so much alike—seen flying on a broomstick over the Sound." Lucy tilted her head, raising her perfectly shaped nose into the air like a hound on the scent. "Know anything about that?"

She reminded Tierra of a purebred Afghan hound with her long, silky, platinum-blond hair, symmetric features that were so arresting they compelled you to stare. But if you gazed upon her too long, you might get bitten and lose part of yourself. This woman had power. Tierra could feel it coat her skin like humidity and see it shimmer like heat over a mirage in the desert. Claire had been enraptured with her and believed Lucy's power and knowledge would be helpful in thwarting the Horsemen.

Maybe it was the morning sickness, but Tierra was no longer so sure. Lucy made her nervous. What kind of witch was she? What kind of power did she have? Aerin appeared to accept her without a second thought also.

How did Moira feel?

Tierra glanced at Moira. Did Moira see what she saw? Could that be why she stood back from the group, more so than her desire to see the last of Aunt Justine?

"A woman flying on a *broom* over the Puget Sound?" Tierra questioned, filling the tea infuser with fresh-dried mint. The sharp, clean scent was refreshing, and she breathed it in, praying it would help keep her stomach from heaving. The best thing for that would be to lose their current company. "Sounds like a fairytale."

"Oh, no, it isn't," Gwen rose excitedly and rushed forward as though to make her point. "There is recorded proof of witches flying on broomsticks, but it seems the magic and science of it has been lost over the last two hundred years or so."

"Might have something to do with all them witch drownings those folks in Salem got up to," Moira muttered. "For the record, y'all let me get burned alive on anything less than hickory, we ain't sisters anymore.

Got it?"

"Make a note of that, will you, Tierra," Aerin said.

"Do you have any idea how useful that skill would be in the fight against the Horsemen if we can come at them from the air?" Gwen scooted forward in her excitement.

"One of the Horsemen can fly," Aerin said.

"Death," Lucy provided.

How did she know that? Nowhere in the book of Revelations, the Grimoire, or the Google Gods had it mentioned that Killian could fly or was known to change shape into a raven.

"Yes," Aerin answered. "So, I don't believe witches on broomsticks will stop the Apocalypse. If such a thing as flying on broomstick could happen," she added, though she looked like it killed her to stay quiet on her amazing achievement.

"Justine said that there was a spell in the book that explained how," Gwen pressed.

"Did she now?" Aerin drawled, gazing at Justine.

"Well, you know, I thought I did, but I was probably mistaken. Yes, I'm sure I was. Plus, there is so much information in the book...most written in older and forgotten languages. I'm just an old woman who imagines things all the time." Aunt Justine tried to smile but looked anxiously from Lucy to Moira as though she felt danger from both. But why would she fear Lucy? "Why don't you girls talk? I need a word with Tierra."

Thank you, Goddess. Who would have thought she'd thank her aunt for anything anytime soon?

"Sure, Aunt Justine." Tierra stressed the family relation in case anyone objected, and then wondered why she felt the need to. "Please excuse us." She gathered her cup and saucer of tea and turned toward the solarium. She attempted to keep her pace steady even though she wanted to bolt. Hopefully the overflowing clusters of flowering plants would help rid her nose of the stench that hung over the kitchen like a festering disease.

Tierra kept moving until she reached the purple-pink heliotrope. The vanilla and cherry pie scent complimented her mint tea, and she stood for a moment and soaked them in until her stomach stopped its persistent pitching. Once under control, she turned and faced Aunt Justine.

Justine's face was strained, the skin dark under her eyes and hung from her jowls as if she'd recently lost weight too fast for her body to adjust. Tierra looked deeper and noticed the weakened color of her hair, more gray and fading to a pinkish tint that really couldn't be called red anymore. "Are you okay, Aunt Justine?"

"No, I am not. I need to move back home. Now. I can't stay with the coven any longer. *Please*, you have to allow it." The please came out as a whisper and Justine glanced over her shoulder toward the kitchen.

They were far enough from the others to not be overheard, but Tierra lowered her voice just in case. "What's wrong?"

"Nothing is right. Nothing has been right since your...*sisters* arrived, and now there are dead men walking about. *Zombies*, have you heard?" Justine's lips twisted together in a sneer. "I can't bear to watch the evening news any longer."

"None of those are reasons to move back in."

Justine seemed to struggle with something and then ventured closer.

"Things...are different with Lucy in the coven."

"How? She and Gwen seem to be hitting it off nicely."

"Too nicely. They're thick as thieves," Justine muttered, though the words didn't hint of jealously. She focused on the pots with cheery bright yellow blossoms that Tierra had planted months ago. "Why did you plant so much St. John's Wort?"

If Justine thought this was a bunch, she should see what Tierra had cultivated out in the gardens and in the surrounding forests. In modern day, St. John's Wort was commonly used for depression and anxiety, but traditionally the herb was used to ward off evil spirits. Believers dried and hung the plant from religious symbols or iconic statues, and monks were still known to plant St. John's Wort around the perimeters of monasteries like their brethren had before them. Tierra figured it couldn't hurt.

Aunt Justine met her eyes. "You feel it, too, don't you?"

"Feel what?" She knew the answer before Justine spoke it out loud.

"*The evil*," Justine whispered.

Tierra narrowed her eyes. "What is happening at the coven?"

Justine glanced back to the kitchen and then grabbed Tierra's hand and strode to the farthest corner of the solarium. "Blood magic. Sacrifices."

"Forgive me if I'm wrong, but you were more than happy to experiment with blood magic and sacrifices mere months ago. Remember Moira and why she hates you?"

"This is *different*. There are unnatural...*activities* going on with the coven. Sexual, demonic rituals. *Black* magic."

Tierra felt Justine's fear as if it were her own and swallowed the bile that rose in her throat. "What about Moira?"

"That girl is as backward as the possum-eating people she came from."

"Not the right thing to say to gain my favor. As we had the same mother, her people are *your* people."

"That isn't what I meant, and you know it. You've seen how difficult she is."

"Difficult or not, she is my sister."

"And I am your aunt. I raised you, Tierra, and don't you forget it. I sacrificed the best years of my life to give you everything I could."

Except love. "You attempted to kill her." And who in the coven had attempted to kill Tierra's other sisters when they were babies? Would they attempt to kill her baby when the news was out? Lucy knew she was pregnant, of that Tierra was pretty damn positive. She laid a protective hand on her belly.

"I've told no one that you're with child," Justine said, clearly reading Tierra.

She shouldn't have been surprised. "So, you know then?"

"Of course I know, but I won't tell if you—"

"Are you threatening me?"

"No, of course not, but I can't promise to stay quiet as Lucy can *make* people tell her things."

"What have you already revealed about us?"

"Nothing, I swear."

"Except you've spilled secrets about the Grimoire."

"I told you, she *knows* things. Things she shouldn't. Things no one should." Justine grabbed Tierra's arm, her nails sinking deep. "You *have* to take me back in."

"It isn't just up to me. You must convince my sisters."

"Have I not been good to you? I've been running Ambrosia's while you and the others have been stuck here hiding out from those damned Horsemen. I've helped ward this house and tried to make amends. I can't help it if Moira is as stubborn as a rock. You need me."

It might be easier for Tierra and her sisters if Justine stayed at the coven, but if Justine truly felt threatened, the manor was the safest place to be.

No matter what she'd done, Justine was family, too, and Tierra couldn't turn her back on her. Justine had been born in Maison de Moray and had lived here all her adult life. If push came to shove, she might have more of a legal right to the place than Tierra did. Moira and Justine would just have to work out their differences once and for all.

"Let me talk to them," Tierra said, but first she'd have to throw up.

❀ 2 ❀

"Where the hell have you been?" Dru demanded, his sword clenched in one hand while yellowish-green ooze slowly dripped off the blade. In his other, he held a decapitated head by the hair.

"What are you, my mother?" Bane answered. If War wanted another fight, he'd gladly give him one. After Tierra had flung him from her view, beating the shit out of someone would go a long way toward improving his mood.

From the looks of the front yard, there had already been one hell of a battle, or rather a battle from Hell.

"You son of a bitch." Dru advanced, tossing the blinking head onto a pile of countless body parts. "Do you have any *fucking* idea what we've been dealing with while you were off spying like a pubescent teenage boy on your *witch*?"

"By the body parts littering the area, I would have to say zombies. If a horde of the undead pissed you off, your skills were in sore need of testing."

"Test this you brainless dogshit pain in my ass." Dru came at him with his sword raised, the blade glinting sharp and lethal in the sunlight wavering down through the treetops. War's sword had been shaped from indestructible steel—forged in the belly of volcanic mountains, honed on the skulls of demons, and blessed with aim the gods themselves would shy away from. It was a weapon to be wary of. Even for an immortal.

Death stood his ground while Dru held the sword at his throat. "I would have expected this behavior from Nick but not you, War."

"That's before I had to spend all *fucking* night battling the undead. One word. One goddamn word from you and they would've left us alone. If you had been where you should have been, and had commanded the army of undead back to Hell where they belonged, my night would have been free."

"To do what? Consult your maps? Drink? Or fantasize about a fire witch who is fucking her dead boy-toy."

"Shut your fucking mouth." Dru pressed the blade into the skin of Bane's neck, burning a line.

"Enough!" Julian said, flinging off a wayward bony hand scratching its way up his shoulder.

"Let the assholes have each other," Nick called over to them, swinging a zombie arm up and letting it rest on his shoulder like it was a bat. "Dru's right. Bane should have been here. I called him and the piss-for-brains hung up on me."

"And you know why," Bane defended himself. As much as he'd ever would.

"Well, *I* sure as fuck don't." Dru pushed him, yet Bane didn't budge. It was hard to get Death off his plot when he chose to put down roots.

"Drustan, lower your blade," Julian commanded. "This helps nothing. It's understandable that Bane would be watching over the...mother of his...offspring during the witches' fight with the zombie horde. Either one of us would have done the same."

"Well, he sure as shit can clean up the remains. Put them back in the ground."

"I second that," Nick said, throwing the mutilated arm onto the pile of body parts.

The bony hand Julian had flicked off his shoulder, attempted to crawl up his pant leg like a spider. Julian stomped it into the earth and wiped the offending ooze off the sole of his shoe onto a patch of grass. "I wholeheartedly agree with that suggestion. Bane, when you are finished cleaning up this...ghoulish pandemonium, meet us in the library.

There is much to discuss."

"Have fun, gravedigger." Dru flipped him off on his way into the cabin.

Someone had his cock in a twist. His comment about Claire's Tommy had hit closer to home than Bane had intended. Weren't they in a quandary? Four Horsemen brought low by four comely witches.

Bane turned and regarded the mutilated corpses littering the yard and adjoining forest beyond with the detachment required of the chore. The majority of the carnage still inched or crawled in whatever fashion it could. Talk about a mess. He should have been here, not watching out for Tierra who'd been fighting these same zombies. One word from him at her place, and they would have left. But he couldn't bring himself to intervene when he'd been praying for just one of the sisters to fall under the macabre onslaught. With Moira operating a chainsaw, it should've only been a matter of time before she'd hurt herself or one of her sisters. Yet, she'd surprised him, but not half as much as Tierra had, wielding a shovel like a warrior.

Though Aerin had been the biggest shock of the night. Did Julian know that his witch delved into the black arts? Had started on a dark path that didn't have many switchbacks? Could that be what he wanted to discuss?

Bane faced the remains of the zombie army, said a few words more ancient than Egyptian and watched dispassionately as the pieces and parts crawled, rolled, and carried themselves off to slumber once again to the silence of their graves. Once completed, and the surface looking much the way it had before, he turned and entered the cabin.

A double shot of Patrón waited for him on the table near the window, along with three very pissed off Horsemen. Julian sat in the leather, brass-studded armchair, nursing a rare vintage red wine. Dru stood sentry over his maps, swirling his Johnny Walker Red, while Nick cocked a hip against the wet bar, shaking a martini, most likely heavy on the dirty.

"What happened last night?" Julian asked, not looking at him.

"You know as well as I do. Aerin can fly. She'll be sharing that knowledge with her sisters as we speak."

"That isn't what I'm talking about," Julian said, taking a sip of his wine. "Who performed black magic and sent the zombie army our direction?"

"You know who."

"I need it confirmed."

"Aerin de Moray. Satisfied?"

"Never." Julian drained his goblet and reached for the bottle of Italian wine he'd placed close.

"We received a call from...you know," Nick said, pouring his martini into a glass. "*She's* been able to infiltrate the premises and hidden a fair amount of brimstone inside."

"We should see results of their exposure to the poison soon." Dru refused to look at him.

Brimstone.

That demon whore.

What would prolong exposure to elements from the depths of Hell do to Tierra and the babe? "Where did she put the brimstone?" If he had his way, it wouldn't be there long.

"She didn't say, but seemed especially proud of herself." Nick leaned back against the wet bar. He looked like a businessman who'd had a particularly bad day at the office. His gray suit was smudged and stained with bodily fluids. He'd lost his jacket some time ago, and his usually pressed dress shirt looked as though he'd been living in it for a week. Torn at the seams and frayed at the bottom, it hung untucked from his slacks. In Nicholas Kingswood's case the clothes didn't make the man, his arrogance and superiority over others shone no matter what he wore. He was a man to be cautious with. He'd shot an arrow into Tierra's chest, his aim true enough to have killed her. Bane had refused to take her soul, and that of her unborn child, *his child*. Without her sisters' quick thinking, he would've lost her and the miracle they'd somehow created. He didn't trust that Nick wouldn't try to kill Tierra again if given the opportunity.

"What did you find out?" Julian asked, reading Bane's yearning to wrap his hands around Nick's throat.

"About what?" It took considerable effort for him to turn his deadly stare away from Kingswood and focus on Julian.

"Whilst you were watching the witches, you observed Aerin perform black magic, and we all witnessed her fly. Did you see anything else?"

"Do you think black magic is how Aerin figured out how to fly?" Dru asked. "The undead she'd sent our way didn't even question her orders. Orders usurped from...you know. *She* commanded the undead to kill the witches and take their powers. So what did Aerin do to upset the order of command?"

"Flying on broomsticks is not black magic," Julian said, holding up his hand when Dru went to interrupt. "Not all witches who have flown in the past were bad. But flying in itself doesn't make a witch good or bad. She's just a flying witch."

"Which we don't need." Nick loosened his necktie and flung it off. "Gods, it's been hard enough to fight them on the ground. Airborne puts this battle on another playing field."

"Bane can fly, so can your arrow," Julian pointed out.

"Being able to fly doesn't mean they will own the skies. That takes skill and practice.

They don't have time for either."

"They sure as shit seem to learn fast and faster every day." Dru knocked back his drink and slid the glass aside rather than pour another.

"It's time we made a solid battle plan to take out Aerin."

Julian's breath caught, and he went suddenly still.

Dru pointed a finger at him. "You agreed. We all did. It's Aerin."

"You really should have fucked her when you had the chance, brother," Nick said. "It's a shame, good pussy like that going to waste.

She could've been your one and only. Want us to capture her so you can have your first fuck before we kill her?"

"If you want to continue to breathe out of any orifice in your face, keep talking." Julian's words were much more threatening because of the quiet, deadly way he'd delivered them, much like an unassuming virus that snuck in and killed in gruesome, unimaginable ways.

"Now that Aerin is aware of our plan, the sisters will band together and take countermeasures." Dru hiked up a pant leg and set his booted foot on the coffee table, leaning his elbow onto his knee. "This is how I see it. Now that she can fly, she's going to want to. It will be like a new toy for her to try and conquer. So we use him —" he pointed to Bane "—to capture her and bring her here. He can't help himself from watching the mother of his spawn, so we kill two birds with one stone.

So to speak."

"And the wards?" Julian asked, looking at each man in turn.

It was Bane who answered. "Do you really think your witch will stay within her boundaries when she owns the clouds?"

"You are out of your ever-lovin' mind!" Moira parked her hands on her hips. "We finally cleared this place of the bad juju, and you want to muck it up again?"

"She's scared," Tierra said. The discussion about Aunt Justine's request to return to the manor wasn't going well, not that Tierra had expected it to. And that damned sulphur smell stinking up the kitchen was making her sicker by the minute. It was late in the day, and she'd yet to keep any food down.

"We're all scared," Moira said. "The whole world's goin' to hell quicker than a greased gator."

"Now, wait," Claire interjected, pacing in front of the fireplace, her finger tapping her lip in thought. She'd returned from somewhere with Tommy hours ago. Supposedly he was out back helping Sunny's father, Basil, rebuild the shed that had caught fire last night. Tierra had been feeling too rundown this afternoon to check on their progress. "While Aunt Justine is about as comfortable to be around as wearing wet socks, it might be better to have her close. We'd have eyes on the coven that way. She does plan to stay involved with them, doesn't she?"

Tierra shrugged. "I don't think so. She seemed really shook up."

"Why would we need eyes on the coven?" Aerin asked, sitting in the Queen Anne chair with her knees crossed typing away on the laptop and yet somehow keeping track of their conversation. "They are on our side.

They want to help. Lucy—"

"Lucy is not what she seems," Tierra interrupted. "I don't know what she is, but I know she's dangerous."

"And how do you know that?" Aerin glanced up from her computer.

"I feel it." Tierra couldn't sit any longer and strode to the open window, but instead of breathing in the calming scent of lavender from her flower beds, she inhaled the stench of leftover zombie. How long would the odor stay? For that matter when would the next attack come, because sure as hell there had to be a limitless supply of undead wanting to eat them. They needed to be ready and not fighting over Aunt Justine.

"*You feel it?* I'm the empath," Aerin said. "What? Now that you're carrying death's spawn you're all-knowing?"

"Aerin, turn it down a notch," Moira said. "Be nice."

"I'm not nice. I'm honest and sometimes the truth hurts."

"Lucy knows I'm pregnant." Tierra rubbed her arms. Her skin crawled and for some reason her hair hurt. Everything in her body felt sore and achy as though she had the flu. She wasn't that out of shape, and last night's fight shouldn't have made her feel like she'd competed in a triathlon.

"Yes, she does," Claire confirmed. "She told me the first time I met her. She could feel the new life about you."

"*And* you were going to tell me this when?"

"I actually forgot, what with Tommy coming back and all."

"You forgot that this powerful witch from somewhere in Ireland figured out I was pregnant. Does she know who the father is?"

"Hey, it's not like you'll be able to keep it a secret long, anyway," Aerin said. "You'll be bigger than the house before you know it." She visibly shuddered at the thought.

"Aunt Justine knows," Moira said. "Dagblast it! She *is* going to have to move back in so we can keep an eye on her. If that thought doesn't taste like the back end of a toad."

"How do you know what the back end of a toad tastes like?" Claire asked.

Tierra wrapped her arms around her middle. "Please don't bring up tastes. Any kind of tastes."

"Tierra, what the hell's wrong with you anyhow?" Moira asked, laying a hand on her shoulder.

"Don't. Don't touch me" She jerked away. "Everything feels wrong, like I'm going to come out of my skin. Can't you feel it?"

The three of them looked at each other, then back at her.

Aerin shrugged. "I feel great." She shut down her computer and sat up straighter in the chair, taking more notice.

"If anything, I feel better than I have in days," Claire agreed.

"Well, I for one could use a walk," Moira said. "I must admit, the walls are gettin' mighty confining."

"Yes, that, too." Tierra breathed. "I haven't kept anything down today, and I swear I'll cry if one more of my flowers loses a bloom."

"Now, sugar, that's them pregnancy hormones talking."

"No, it isn't. Something isn't right. Not since Justine, Gwen, and
Lucy were here."

"I'm sure it's got more to do with the thought of Aunt Justine moving back in," Moira declared, trying to soothe. "That old bat—"

"Hey, no insulting bats," Aerin said. "Doctor Lector will take that personal and so will I."

"Speaking of bats, has anyone seen our familiars?" Claire asked. "Kai has been missing for hours. Usually he comes running when I call him."

"Cheeto!" Moira suddenly screeched for her fire-breathing teacup pig and ran from the room.

"Now you've gone and done it." Aerin slid a look at Claire.

"Where is that bat of yours?" Claire asked her.

"He's nocturnal. I never look for him until the sun goes down."

"Jinx hasn't reemerged since the coven was here," Tierra admitted, looking around for the cat, adding another worry to her growing list.

Moira ran back into the room. "I can't find Cheeto. If your bat has been feeding on him again, I'm crisping up his wings in a vat of lard."

"You know what lard's made of, don't you?" Aerin raised a brow.

"Oh, good goddess, please no talk of food! Especially greasy food." Tierra swallowed and closed her eyes, trying to focus on anything but the upset in her stomach.

"The familiars are probably fine. Just sleeping off last night's zombie bender," Claire said. "There's no reason to add more to our plate."

"Maybe you need to see a midwife?" Moira suggested to Tierra.

"You mean a *doctor*," Aerin countered. "A real MD."

"Women have been birthing babies since Adam and

Eve. Where were the doctors then?" Moira's hands were back on her hips.

"Nowhere, which is why the mortality rate for women giving birth was astronomical and like seven out of ten babies didn't survive their first year," Aerin preached.

"Be quiet! Just all of you be quiet. Please." Tierra deflated onto the cushions of the couch and buried her face in her hands. "It's too much. Zombies, covens, Horsemen, and goddess, *babies*." She couldn't take it anymore.

"Oh, Tierra, you poor thing," Moira said. "Want me to make you some soothing tea?"

Aerin folded her arms over her chest. "There is a way to take care of your condition."

"No. Don't mention that again—"

"Aerin's right, Tierra," Claire said. "Maybe this isn't supposed to happen. You are miserable. You look like death warmed over—okay, okay, not the best choice of words, but we are worried about you. What if this baby kills you?"

"It won't." Though she wasn't sure. She'd yet to find a case online or in Grim that addressed the topic of witches and the Horsemen procreating. Plenty about demons. So that begged the question: were the Horsemen demons? Were she and her sisters?

"We don't know that," Claire continued, pointing to Tierra's belly. "Death is that thing's baby daddy." There was silence for a minute as Claire's word sunk in.

"It'll be okay." It had to be. Tierra took a deep breath and nearly choked on the rotten-egg smell coming from the kitchen. "But if we don't air out this house, I will be moving out."

"I can help with that." Aerin jumped to her feet and stirred the air.

"Moira, let's make an ocean breeze to rival the air freshener companies."

"On it."

Fresh air with a hint of brine and sunshine circulated into the room, driving the hellish smell away, and Tierra breathed easier.

Claire sat next to her and took her hand. "There, that's better. Have you tried meditating lately? Close your eyes and think of your gardens."

Tierra moaned. "My gardens were trampled by zombies last night."

"Right, not gardens. Think of the Standing Stones."

"Where I *died?*" She looked at her in horror.

"Ugh, help me out here."

"Think of our mother," Moira suggested. "Remember how lovely she was, how much she loved us. She carried four babies. Lord love a donkey. What if...what if you're so sick on account of you're having more than one?"

"It's too early to tell," Aerin said, looking worried. "It's hard enough to think of one."

"Not helping," Tierra said, opening her eyes and getting to her feet. She had to grab the back of the couch as a wave of dizziness attempted to take her down.

Moira reached out and steadied her. "How about we go outside for a bit."

"Hey, we can practice flying our brooms!" Aerin jumped to her feet. "It'll be a nice break for all of us and something we need to master— and fast—anyway."

"Except the coven is watching and wanting to know how to do that very thing," Claire pointed out. "And something like that is best done under the cover of darkness."

Aerin waved her hand as though to shoo away a pesky bug. "I'm not worried about them."

"They could have spies on us right now," Tierra said. Tommy would be the perfect spy as Lucy gave Claire the spell to bring him back. No matter how they brought up the subject, Claire refused to evict him. Could he be what was stinking up her kitchen?

"I know a cloaking spell," Claire said. "I found it in the book. It just appeared. Funny, right? Get it, cloaking spell, *appeared*."

"A cloaking spell as in the Romulans?" Aerin asked.

"I love that you know that, and yes, just like that." Claire smiled.

"Sorta."

"We'll prepare for flight tonight then," Aerin said, nearly jumping in her designer heels.

"I don't know about flying," Tierra said. "My magic isn't as strong when I'm not connected to the earth." Remembering the night Killian enfolded her within his wings and lifted her off the ground still brought on bouts of anxiety. "What if the zombies or the Horsemen show back up tonight? We need to figure out a plan for both of those, and not be flying around like its Halloween."

"I can't *wait* to fly on Halloween!" Aerin exclaimed. "Besides, flying is a combat tactic. One we need to get better at, especially you."

"Death has wings," Moira said. "You need to fight flier with flier, so to speak."

"How much of that Horsemen repellant potion do we have stored away?" Claire asked. "I say we load up the super soakers and mount up. I, for one, am looking forward to flying again."

"I'd be lyin' if I didn't say I wanted to give it another go," Moira agreed.

Three eager and identical faces turned and looked at Tierra.

Well, at least it would get her out of the house.

$$\maltese \quad 4 \quad \maltese$$

Flying was for the birds.

Witch or not, she wasn't meant to fly unless assisted by an airplane equipped with seatbelts. Her sisters had taken to the air like fish to water—diving and swirling, cartwheeling and laughing, while Tierra was no more than a witch on a stick, feeling foolish, inept and to be perfectly honest, completely out of her element.

Before leaving the house, they'd found Claire's cloaking spell, which wasn't anything like what the Romulans used to hide under the nose of Captain Kirk. This charm muddled what others saw if in their midst, rather than truly hiding them. The spell consisted of weaving amaranth flowers and fiddlehead ferns into wreaths and wearing them around their necks. The dark crimson flowers were pretty and smelled like honey and complemented the sharp earthiness of the bright green ferns, but other than its visual appeal, Tierra didn't know how well it worked to conceal them. They should have given the invisibility spell a dry run before flying off into the skies around their house.

With each passing minute, Tierra's fear of discovery increased. Every rustle in the trees was another zombie horde bearing down on them, and each beat of a wing was Death swooping in to take her.

That thought was part dread and part desire.

The full summer moon glowed fever-red over the evening, and the nocturnal forest bloomed under its caress, expelling pollen into a sensual dance of temptation that caused her to ache in places she was better off not thinking about. Woodland creatures frolicked and fornicated, reveling in this midsummer's eve of enchantment, and suddenly the last thing Tierra wanted to be straddling was a branch.

She wanted to ride...*him*.

Death suddenly swooped in from the deepest shadows of the night, stealing her breath. Bare-chested, his skin glowing pearlescent under the moon, he mesmerized her in his fallen angel form. His blue-black raven wings outstretched to catch the downdraft and slow his heart-stopping speed as he aimed right for her.

Oh, good goddess.

Her heart dropped into her stomach and something like hunger roared to life.

Killian Bane touched ground on a whisper and looked straight at her, a cunning smile on his handsome face. A face so beautiful women through the ages must have competed and killed each other to gain his attention.

His eyes glowed obsidian in the moonlight, shivering and heating her simultaneously as they drank her in. She needed to run, but couldn't move under his arresting stare that missed nothing.

So much for the cloaking spell. He saw her just fine.

"*Tierra*." Her name tumbled off his lips like the final decree of judgment, as though she'd been sentenced and didn't even know she'd been on trial. "You're beyond the wards, *gazelle*."

Oh shit. She flicked her eyes to the side and tightened her hand around the broomstick, ready to brandish it as a weapon. How had she let that happen? She was mere feet from the line of protective wards. What had she been thinking? Oh yeah, wasting her energy and time trying to freaking fly. Now she'd pay for her carelessness.

"What do you want?" she demanded, wishing her voice hadn't squeaked.

"The same thing you do." His nostrils flared and he advanced a step toward her. "We have much to discuss, you and I."

She raised the broom. "I don't want to talk to you."

"I know." His lips curled into a satisfied smile. "You want to fuck me."

She swallowed, his words ringing true. *Goddess, please help me, because I fear I'm beyond helping myself.* Memories of his touch, his lips, his body against hers, inside hers assaulted her senses. She could smell him, and he was dark and earthy, dangerous and irresistible.

"The earth pulses with your need, *gazelle*. Did you think I couldn't feel it, hear it, wouldn't respond? Me, of all people."

"But you aren't really a person, are you?"

"Neither are you, my witch."

"I'm not yours." Tierra de Moray belonged to no man.

"And that is where you are wrong. You carry my child. Part of you is *mine*." He stood broad of shoulder and narrow of hip, tall and domineering, and if she didn't get away from him now, he'd have her, and she'd be lost.

"You need to leave." She took a step back, and his eyes flared. "Right now. My sisters—"

"Will never catch us." He lunged for her, tore the broom from her grasp and wrapped his arms tight around her. His wings flared wide, and before she could gather air in her lungs to scream, they were airborne.

Killian shot them straight up into the sky so fast that tears leaked from her eyes. Tierra could do nothing but hold onto him, her fingernails digging into his shoulders, her legs anchoring around his hips.

He groaned and nuzzled the side of her neck, his warning a whisper on the wind, "Don't let go."

She glanced down and wished she hadn't. Vertigo assaulted her and she gasped for breath to the point that her head swam with dizziness. Tightening her hold on Killian, she prayed, calling out to her sisters even though she knew they couldn't hear her. She was disconnected from the earth, from her power.

Fear needled in, sharp and furious.

What if he dropped her? He could so easily take her to the edge of the atmosphere and let her plummet back to earth, to her death. Hadn't she just come to terms with the fact that she wasn't meant to be in the air?

But more than being off the ground, more than not having contact with her sisters, it was Killian who truly frightened her. He was Death. Stories throughout history had mentioned him, legends, mythologies, fairytales. *The Bible*. He was the Grim Reaper and she a captive in his clutches.

And worst of all, part of her thrilled at it.

Demented. I am demented.

Their trajectory switched and the ground suddenly rose up to meet them. She screamed, finally finding her voice, certain she'd be hitting the earth and splattering all over it. She hid her face in the crook of Killian's neck, knowing she wouldn't survive another moment. He chuckled, the sound rippling along her nerve endings like he'd skipped a pebble into a pond. Before she knew it, her feet were on solid terrain.

Power returned, surged with such force that she gasped. Her head fell back on her shoulders, her mouth opened, and her eyes closed in the blissfulness of recoupling with Mother Earth.

He held her in his arms, his breathing raspy, and she

felt his arousal hard and heavy against her. She raised her head and looked at him, his dark, slumberous eyes holding her as captive as his arms. She wanted him and knew he read it in her gaze, the way her body leaned into his.

"*Tierra*." Her name was a tortured groan on his lips.

He reached up and tore the wreath from around her neck, the action breaking the spell he had her under. If she didn't do something now, he'd have her under him in the next heartbeat.

"Don't you *Tierra* me, you son of a bitch. How dare you do *that*? Pluck me off the earth, tear me away from my *sisters* and my—" She stopped herself before she revealed just how powerless she'd been soaring high in the sky. Instead, she raised her hands and moved the soil under him like a conveyer belt, shooting him ten feet back from her.

Now, that felt good, powerful and downright *satisfying*.

For added measure, she quaked the earth below him, ready to bury him six feet under liked she'd done before.

He flapped his wings once, hovering safely above the ground. "You will not *bury* me again," he growled.

"Want to make a bet?" *Ooh, this was heady stuff.* She hadn't let loose in a while.

He drifted her direction, moving those glorious wings just enough to keep his feet off the grass. Instantly, she felt small and defenseless below him. Maybe Aerin was right about the damn flying business.

"Let's call a temporary truce," he said. "We really do need to talk."

"You didn't bring me here to *talk*, and where the hell is *here* anyway?"

"Look around you."

She did and immediately calmed. "You brought me to the Standing

Stones? Why?"

"So you'd understand that I don't mean you any harm. You are more powerful here, Tierra. Truly if you buried me on this sacred ground, I'm not altogether positive that I could dig my way out of the grave."

"That's information you shouldn't share with me." She considered him quizzically.

"It makes you feel safer more powerful to be here, doesn't it?"

"Yes," she admitted.

"Then if I alight, you won't attempt to bury me?"

"No promises," she muttered.

He chuckled again, the sound sexy and completely disarming. She lowered her hands and gave him a nod that it was safe to land.

"I do love your kittenish side."

Kittenish? She was a damn earth witch, one that had kicked his ass a time or two.

"All right, more lioness. Better?" he asked, reading her easier than she'd like.

"State your case so I can go home. By that I mean *walk* home, not fly," she clarified. Her sisters had to be frantic with worry by now. She attempted to send a message to reassure them, but Killian stopped her with a hand on her arm.

"Don't. In fact, I need you to seclude them even further. You send out a beacon, it won't only be your sisters who will pick up the transmission. You have the ability to hide us from the world here in the

Standing Stones. It will be like we're the only ones on the planet."

"How—?" she started to ask and then instantly she knew. Felt the truth of it flowing in her veins. Twice now, her blood had been spilt inside these stones, shrouded in mystery and legend. Once when she'd been born in this very place, and then months ago when she'd died. She'd stood over her body, held the hand of her unborn child while Killian and her sisters fought to bring her back.

Tierra closed her eyes and called upon the vegetation thriving within the mist creeping along the forest floor and weeping down the sides of the cliffs. The locals called this area Siren's Cry because the wind whistled through the stones, sounding like a grieving woman. Moisture teared down the rock-faced cliff and pooled to the turbulent ocean below adding to the mystery.

As her mother had before her, Tierra had the flora fan the fog to the stones and choked the pathways with vines and thorns, canopying leaves and branches into a shield until she and Killian all but disappeared.

Now *there* was a cloaking spell. Finished, she opened her eyes and stared into Killian's.

"That was very well done," he said, a mix of pride and trepidation in his voice. "You are more tuned in to your power than I thought. I shouldn't be surprised that you and your sisters continue to astonish us."

"Should you be telling me this?"

"No, I shouldn't." He gave her a deprecating smile. "But I can't seem to help myself where you are concerned."

"Why? We're strangers."

"I wouldn't exactly call us strangers."

"Enemies?"

"I'd like to think we can get past both as we're going to be parents." *Parents*. She hadn't gotten used to the pregnancy word yet. Parenting with this man was beyond comprehension.

"Whether enemies or strangers, it didn't stop us from making love the day we met. And it won't stop us now." He paced toward her, and they started to circle each other in a dangerous dance mirrored by the stones.

"That isn't going to happen. It shouldn't have happened last time."

"I took your virgin's blood. Do you know what that does to a man?"

"Uh...no." Who knew men cared about that kind of stuff in this day and age? But then he wasn't from this day and age, and she needed to not forget that.

"No one has touched you but me. *Only me*." The possession in his eyes branded her skin.

Her heart thundered in her ears, and she knew he heard it, felt her excitement and fear, and fed on both. "How do you know I haven't slept with hundreds of men since you and I—"

"I would know if another man touched you."

"This is getting very antiquated," she scoffed. "Next, you're going to tell me that I can't sleep with anyone but you. Well, forget that, I can sleep with whoever I want to."

"Try it and whoever you choose to share yourself with will die." The last was said through his teeth.

"*What?* You can't do that. That's insane."

"I can and I will." He grabbed her and pressed his hand to her stomach. "You carry my child. We are destined for each other."

"I don't believe in destiny or prophecies. That's your delusion, not mine."

"How else do you explain me fathering a child? I am Death, Tierra. In all the lifetimes I have lived, and the women I have lain with, never did I need to worry about contraception. It took you, an earth witch, a *prophesied* earth witch, for me to be able to propagate. It's not only destiny, it's a fucking miracle."

"Or curse," she countered, feeling panic that never seemed far when discussing this subject. "Have you thought of that? We're pawns in the *prophesied* Apocalypse. I'm sure your fellow Horsemen are saying the same things about this child that my sisters are."

"You do not carry the Antichrist."

"Can you say that for certain, beyond a shadow of a doubt?"

A pulse throbbed in his temple and he took his time answering.

"No."

"*No!* You weren't *supposed* to say no! You were supposed to reassure me." She buried her hands in her hair, covering her ears. She'd give anything to have unheard what he'd just said.

Good goddess, if he didn't know that this...*child* she carried wasn't some evil seed, how was she to believe it? Based on how she felt most of the time, she probably was possessed by a demon. Case in point, she didn't do things like run off and cavort with strange men, and they didn't get much stranger than the Fourth Horsemen of the Apocalypse. And now she'd run off with him twice. Ever since she'd met Killian Bane, she hadn't been herself.

She'd given him her virginity because he was what? Hot? Convenient?

Well, not convenient, that wasn't the right word. He was *there*. Like a mountain that needed to be climbed, or an artesian spring to drink from, and she'd never had her thirst quenched. A woman ravenous and he was a mana from heaven.

Who wouldn't want to sleep with him? Look at him. Chest bare and chiseled, pale and perfect like a marble statue, but warm to the touch. And she so wanted to touch him. Reach out and stroke the downy softness of his feathers, feel the hardened muscles of his body.

Damn it, this is not helping.

"Tierra, listen to me. We will get through this. Together."

"No, we won't. We are on opposite sides of a very big war. One I wanted no part of nor did I ask for. And I'm compromised, possibly carrying something from *The Exorcist* or *Children of the Corn*."

"Stop this now." He took her shoulders in his large hands and gave her a hard shake. "I've seen our child's soul, remember? Demons don't have souls."

She was afraid to hope, to grasp for the thin thread he offered. "And the Antichrist, does he have a soul?"

"That I don't know. But consider this. What if our child—created out of darkness and light, life and death—is the one soul on the planet who can stop the Apocalypse?"

❄ 5 ❄

Killian smoothed Tierra's hair back from her face. Fear and hope warred in emerald eyes deeper and more mysterious in the light of the blood moon. Gently, he pulled her into his arms and offered her something he'd never given anyone.

Comfort.

Greedily, he took solace from her in return as he held her. He breathed in her intoxicating scent of blue moon roses, delicate and enchanting, with hints of lavender that soothed the beast inside him and tendered his touch.

Ever so lightly, he traced the shape of her face, over her sharp cheekbones, dusted with a spattering of fairy freckles, along her stubborn jaw, to her neck where her pulse throbbed under his fingertips.

Her heart beat in time with his.

Fast and frantic with need.

The ache in his soul burned unlike anything he'd ever known. She consumed him. Owned his conscious moments. He considered her in every action, and had damned his existence by dividing his loyalty between his brothers and this one earth witch. If she had any inkling of how much power she held over him, he'd be in deeper trouble than he already was.

"Kiss me, *gazelle*." He wasn't only asking for a kiss, and by her sharp intake of air she knew it. But he doubted very much that she grasped how hard it was for him to ask and not just take what he wanted, what he needed.

"I shouldn't," she breathed.

"But you will."

"*Yes*." She buried her hands in his hair and pulled him down to her.

He growled and took her mouth, tightening his grip, afraid she'd somehow get away from him again. His hands crushed the soft fabric of her apricot dress, gathering the material and lifting it until he had to break the kiss to whip it off and over her head. Quickly, he captured her mouth again. His tongue breached her lips, and he kissed her long and hard and deep.

The world's outcome became insignificant. The only thing that mattered in his existence was joining with Tierra again, completing each other, partaking of the paradise that she promised. He'd had no concept that part of him had been missing until he'd lain with her too many months ago.

Deepening the kiss, he kept it slow even though he wanted to rush, wanted to feast. Her soft gasps turned to purrs when he brushed the sides of her sensitive breasts and filled his hands with their newfound weight. The soft whimpering sounds from the back of her throat tempered his need and he marveled in awe at the subtle changes that her body had already made to accommodate the creation of his child.

He'd committed to memory the way she'd looked, felt under him the last time he'd been blessed to have his hands on her bare silken flesh. But now, her breasts were fuller and more sensitive, the nipples darker even in the limited light. He yearned to cherish, to discover what thrilled her, what she desired most, wanting to fulfill each and every need.

He didn't retract his wings, but instead curved them around her and fashioned a feather bed to lay her down upon the sweet summer wildflowers growing within the Standing Stones. Her burgundy hair fired red in the moonlight, splayed against the blackness of his wings with a bewitching contrast that had his heart swelling in emotion he couldn't name.

This was where she was meant to be, within the circle of his arms. Pregnant or not didn't matter. She was his. His match. His mate. And by the gods, it would take more than the end of the world to keep her from him.

Her gasps came faster, her hands clutching at him. Slanting his lips firmly against hers, he made love to her mouth. His tongue plundered, nibbled, and sucked, until her gasps became pants and her body arched in demand against his. Still he held himself in check.

He had to time this perfectly, needed her chanting his name as she took him within this sacred circle of stones. But gods, his blood raced and his desire to be inside her grew until it became painful.

Tearing his mouth from hers, he kissed and nipped where his hands had so reverently caressed. She twisted under him, helpless mewling sounds escaping her, causing his blood to thicken.

She arched under him, begging with her body for him to conquer hers.

His breath hissed between his teeth. He ripped off her lacy underwear and freed himself from his jeans, kicking them off so nothing would be between them.

Flesh to flesh, heart to heart, soul to soul. It would be. Had to be.

Pinning her down with the weight of his body, he positioned himself at her opening, and rubbed his shaft between her wet, silken folds. His eyes closed on a tortured groan at her wetness, proof of her desire for him, her readiness. How he wanted to taste her, carry her essence inside him. He wouldn't last. Not with her offering herself up to him so trustingly. He promised before the moon gave way to the sun, he would. This was only the beginning of how they'd share the passion and wonders of their bodies with each other.

But for now, he must stay the path. There was too much at stake for him not to. He focused on her pleasure with his hands, his mouth, and his body to bring her to a fevered pitch until she was mindless with need and writhed with it.

She begged, and her fingernails bit into his hips, leaving crescent marks to bleed on his flesh. He demanded in a guttural voice he barely recognized as his own, "*Say my name*."

"Killian."

"*Again*. My full name. Say it." He stroked the hot tip of his cock along her folds, his thumb sliding and flicking over the apex of her sex. His body strained, and his soul waited breathlessly for her to do what he commanded.

"Killian," she gasped. "Killian Bane."

"Say you take me."

"Yes, take me."

"No, say that *you* take me," he growled. "All of me."

"I take you. Oh goddess, please, yes, I take you, Killian Bane. *Now*."

"*And I take you, Tierra de Moray*." He plunged into her until he was seated as deep as her body would allow. Elation rushed through him like a wave of white heat, and he released a victorious shout he couldn't contain.

Tierra shuddered, contracting around him as she climaxed from his single thrust. Her head thrown back, her neck beautifully arched and offered up for his teeth to bite, her mouth open on a cry of surprise and ecstasy. Letting her ride out her pleasure, he drank in her expression, so similar to earlier when he'd landed them in the Standing Stones, and she'd connected with the earth, her power claiming her as he'd just claimed her.

He gave her a moment to catch her breath and then he took it away again and again.

❧ 6 ❧

Tierra lay on a wing and a prayer, floating on a plane of gratification so complete it couldn't be wrong.

Killian's fingertips lazily drifted over her skin as though he couldn't get enough of her. It was heady to have a man such as him worship her body, and if she wasn't careful, she'd crave his touch with the need of an addict. She tingled everywhere, on overload, higher than she'd ever been. She didn't think she'd survive another coupling. If she climaxed again, she'd burst into a million twinkling lights, become one with the stars overhead that had begun to wink out as the eastern horizon pinked with hints of the coming sunrise.

"How do you feel?" he asked.

The question caused her to laugh, and she curled her naked body into his. "If you don't have any idea, I don't think I can adequately explain."

An amused rumbled sounded in his chest. "I meant, are you well?"

"Extremely well." In fact, she felt better right now than she had in a long while. Locked up in the house her skin crawled and she had to constantly fight the ever-present nausea, but here within the stones and lying in Killian's arms, she felt beyond wonderful.

His hand covered the slight rounding of her abdomen. Naked, her body revealed the effects of their first time together, but clothed she probably had another month, maybe six weeks, until she'd no longer be able to hide the pregnancy. Luckily, she wore a lot of loose-fitting clothes, but she'd have to go up a size if she were to keep her secret a little longer.

"And the babe?" he asked.

"No complaints." Her heart swelled with sudden emotion. She wished they could stay here in this bubble. "Is sex always like this?"

"No. What's between you and me is magical." His voice held a note of reverence. "Tierra, I must tell you something."

"Must you?" She didn't want the moment to end just yet. Most likely what he had to tell her would make her angry and then she'd have to leave him, give up his touch, and take up her staunch position on the other side of the line that cut between them like a canyon.

He drew complicated circles on her belly with his fingertip. "This is important."

"Isn't everything lately?" she murmured.

"There is something...dangerous in your house."

"I know. Aunt Justine is moving back in." Her attempt at humor wasn't received.

"This is serious. An item...lurks inside your home."

"What? How did it get past the wards?"

"I can't say. No, don't ask. I *really* can't say. There is power in a name spoken aloud. Especially if spoken in a place as powerful and sacred as this."

"One of your fellow Horsemen?" The euphoria was definitely waning. She wanted to press, make him tell her "the what" if he wouldn't tell her "the who."

"So what the hell is this thing?" He stiffened, and she held up her hand. "You can't even tell me that? Cut to the chase and tell me what you safely can."

"The element in the manor is like poison. Haven't you been feeling ill?"

"Of course, I'm pregnant," she scoffed.

"More than symptoms consistent with pregnancy. Intense sickness, out of sorts, change of attitude. Pay attention to how you feel in certain rooms. Concentrate."

The kitchen. But how much of that was due to her aversion of food? Most of the worst bouts of sickness had been after encountering Tommy. Now it was her turn to stiffen.

"Do not touch it. Find it, get it out of the house, but do not touch it. Promise me."

Fear crawled along her skin, completely diminishing any leftover tingles. "Are my sisters in danger with it in the house right now?"

"The more exposure, the deeper and lasting the effects. You and your sisters will react differently depending..."

"Depending?"

"That is for you to discover. Find it, but whatever you do, you must not touch nor burn it."

Fire was the best way to destroy something. It was permanent, which was why burning witches had been so popular. "All right, any ideas on how to get rid of it?"

"I have the ability to dispose of it properly."

What? Didn't that make him look like the guilty party? He'd been hanging out in his raven form, watching her. Could he have somehow gotten it, whatever *it* was, by the wards? But then why would he be telling her about it now? "I can't let you into the house. My sisters would kill me." There would be hell to pay for being here with him now. But if she lowered the wards and allowed him into their sanctuary, she didn't even want to comprehend the repercussions of how her sisters would see such a betrayal.

"I will know when you locate it."

"How?"

"For now, it's best you don't know." He sat, pulling her up. "Come on, I'd better get you home."

Echoed voices from the past whispered over her skin, asking her not to leave. Not yet.

"Actually," she said, finding her dress and slipping it on over her head. "I'd like to stay for a while. I need a moment alone to collect my...thoughts before returning to the manor." More like come up with excuses, gather her defenses.

Dig in the earth, the wind whispered.

Aunt Justine would most likely arrive bright and early this morning. The woman was one of those irritating morning people and she would be making herself felt. Tierra should have been there to help smooth the way, but as the sun continued to rise, she didn't think she'd make it. The walk of shame would be hers.

"It's not safe to be on your own." Killian scowled. He retracted his wings and stood before her shirtless, struggling into his jeans. The ancient tattoo that covered his back depicted a hooded Grim Reaper hovering over the River Styx while fire and brimstone burned around the fallen angel. Somehow the tattoo must house his wings.

"The stones will protect me."

"And when you leave them? Nothing but peril awaits you out in the open."

Didn't she know it? She'd been alone when he'd grabbed her, and she'd probably regret what had happened between them later when he wasn't around to mess with her common sense.

But she couldn't leave this place yet. Maybe she never would. It was quite nice here. Peaceful and serene, and the surrounding forest could provide shelter and food. Part of her longed to disappear, to forget the worries and problems of this world and live life simply in nature. Alone.

"Killian, you know the history of this place, and what happened here. I need to stay and hear what waits for me. By myself," she stressed when he opened his mouth to object again.

By the way the vein throbbed in his temple, the set of his jaw, and twitching of his hands, he struggled not to argue or simply sieze her and fly off into the dawn. "I will take you home. Open the shield you secured around this place, and I will wait for you to finish." He glanced at the peaking sun. "Don't take long. We've already stayed longer than is wise."

There wasn't anything wise about what they had done this night and they both knew it.

"I don't want you waiting for me."

"That is the only option you have, *gazelle*. I will not leave you unprotected. Don't force the issue because you will lose."

He cupped the back of her neck, his mouth searing hers in a hard kiss. Releasing her as quickly as he'd grabbed her, his eyes showed determination and warned her not to test him further.

She shivered with the cold realization that this man felt he could dictate to her. Yes, they'd created a child, but his overbearing protectiveness needed some updating since it still languished in the dark ages. She was a witch with powers of her own, and she'd been able to take care of herself just fine for the last twenty-six years. Well, besides the Apocalypse thing.

Stewing with the need to set him straight, she pushed against his chest and surprised them both when she broke his hold. "I am not yours to command, and you'd be wise to remember it."

She linked with the shield she'd created over the stones. Vines of ivy snaked in and seized Killian, flinging him out of the Standing Stones, and sealed solid behind him. It all happened so quickly. Time slowed, and she saw everything in minute segments like a movie.

Whoa. She'd never been able to do anything like that before, but then she couldn't remember a time she'd been this angry. Could this be what Claire had talked about? That their powers intensified after losing their virginity? Tierra hadn't noticed anything other than the physical effects that losing her virginity had caused. Had she just tapped into her sexual power?

"*Tierra!*" Killian shouted, smacking his fists against the shield. It held against him.

She didn't like her name spoken in that tone, she decided. "Leave me be."

To make sure he did, she had the vines reach for him again, but with a frisson of aura, he transformed into his raven form and flew out of reach and out of sight.

All thoughts of Killian ceased as whispers amplified, revealing long-hidden secrets.

She didn't question what they wanted her to do. Last time she'd been here the voice from the grave had been her mother's. If her mother felt the urge to impart more information, she'd take what she could get.

The earth hummed, directing her to where it wanted her to go. The closer she got to the smallest of the eight stones, the louder and faster the ground pulsed. She was surprised the stones didn't quake from the vibration. Kneeling, Tierra held her hands over the area at the base of the stone. The soil was warm as though the sun shone on it, but the sun had barely crested the horizon. The heat had to be coming from what was hidden below.

Compelled by a force that seemed both ancient and familiar, she dug. The ground easily gave at her touch, and she wondered for a moment why she didn't just use her power to move away the dirt. The pleasure of the soil in her hands and the element of physically needing to uncover whatever had been placed here kept her digging. Roughly two feet down, her fingers connected with something hard and long. A root maybe, but nothing tall grew nearby. Feeling much like an archeologist, she carefully brushed the dirt away and revealed a wand.

Instantly, she saw the artifact for what it had been in its original form. A staff of ash wood offered to a powerful druid from the sacred Tree of Life, but over time wands had emerged. And this one—*hers*— was one of four.

The need for caution shivered over her. She glanced up and studied the forest beyond the shield. No sign of Killian or anyone else.

Nevertheless, she asked the trees and foliage to alert her to any interruptions. She carefully set the wand beside her, the overwhelming urge pushing her to continue in the treasure hunt, and remove more earth. Next her fingers brushed something metal. An electrical current shot up her arm and into her chest. She gasped and had to take a minute for the sensation to level out before reverently extracting the crown of pure gold shaped into the antlers of a stag.

Holy Mother of Earth.

She'd seen this before, drawn and documented in the pages of the Grimoire. In her hands, she held the golden crown of Malcolm de Moray.

The last known King of the Druids.

❀ 7 ❀

Oh, she was in trouble.

The wand lay on the ground by her side while Tierra cradled the pure gold crown in her lap. These artifacts were going to get her killed once she stepped out from the protective barrier of the stones. Items like these did not go undetected by other magical beings. She couldn't leave them behind, couldn't stop touching them since she'd dug them up. Could she rebury them and return for them later? She discounted that thought as soon as it formed. No way was she taking that chance.

At least she'd gotten rid of Killian. If he'd stayed... If he knew...

Thank the goddess, he hadn't. She'd be in more hot water than she was right now.

Think. Don't just sit here like a worried ninny. You're a witch for goddess' sake, and not completely without defenses.

There was also power in the wand and crown, but if she used it and it backfired, or was too much for her to handle, then what? Look what'd happened when she and her sisters had linked without fully understating the consequences.

Believe, the word whistled around her.

Tierra recognized the voice and the mystical quality

to the ring. "Mom?" She glanced around, searching out the apparition of her mother and found herself alone. At least as far as physical beings went.

A cool spectral caress cupped the side of her face. It wasn't an unpleasant sensation, more refreshing, like she'd soothed lavender and spearmint balm over her skin.

Claim your inheritance, daughter.

"Inheritance?"

The wand has claimed you, but you must claim the crown in order to make it yours.

Tierra looked down at the crown nestled in her lap. "What will happen if I do?" It would be good to have some answers first. All her life she'd made choices on instinct and emotion and look where that had gotten her. Single, pregnant, and fighting to stop the world from imploding.

Do not doubt yourself, my daughter. What might seem wrong now, when reviewed after time, can turn out to be right. You are such a result.

Did her mother know something? "What of my child? Do you know the outcome?"

The future has yet to be written. The heart is all that matters, in life and in death. Trust yours.

Trust her heart? She needed more than that. Her heart had gotten her into this mess. That and her libido.

A tinkling laugh sounded like crystal chimes ringing on a soft summer breeze. It was the most beautiful sound Tierra had ever heard and tears sprung to her eyes. "Please, tell me what to do."

That I cannot.

A tear traveled down her cheek and the cool touch returned to wipe it away.

Don't cry, Tierra. There have been too many tears. Return to your sisters, for you are stronger together than apart. What-

ever is to come, you must remain as one. By earth, air, fire and sea...so mote it be...

The wind suddenly wailed through the stones and Tierra's heart clenched, hearing the weeping of Siren's Cry.

Her mother was gone. Tierra swallowed the cry to beg her to return and wiped away the remaining tears that yearned for her mother's embrace. She needed to be happy for the brief connection and not want for more.

She picked up the crown and studied it. For whatever reason, her mother was part of this, had shown her the way to find her inheritance. That couldn't be bad, could it? Inheritances were like gifts, boons. Plus, her own mother wouldn't steer her wrong.

Slowly she raised the golden circle of antlers and set it on her head.

The same sensation that had shocked her when she'd been digging and first touched the crown returned and grew. From a seed germinating and breaking through the soil, it unfurled its leaves to the rising sun. Tierra gasped, embracing the flourish of new knowledge and power. Her senses went on hyper alert, and voices all around her could suddenly be heard. Not people. Animals.

The beasts of the forest.

She closed her eyes and tuned in to the new frequency. It felt natural, as though she'd opened a door that had always been there, but for some reason or another had overlooked it each time she'd passed down that particular corridor.

An eagle soared overhead and she melded with it, drifted along as though she were a hitchhiker. The eagle didn't seem to mind. In fact, it welcomed her and was proud to show her what he reigned over. The fear of being off the ground was replaced by an overwhelming sense of freedom.

Is this what Aerin felt when she flew, and Claire and Moira who had taken to the sky so easily? Untethered, liberated, and spirited?

From the eagle's eyes, Port Townsend glowed green and lush below her with Puget Sound sparkling like sapphires in the sun, showcasing the surrounding emerald islands. With a little nudge, she directed the eagle to fly over Water Street where Ambrosia's was already open for business and a few customers shuffled in to order their morning coffee, tea, and scones.

To the west, a seining boat crested the waves as it headed out to the fishing grounds, while a pleasure craft unfolded her sails and captured the wind. Tierra stayed with the eagle until it spotted prey.

She broke the connection, not wanting to share in its breakfast of shrew tartare. Opening her eyes within the circle of the stones, she froze, coming face to face with a majestic white stag that had silently stepped in.

The sun shone between his silvery antlers. He stood there like some mythical beast from the fairytale books she'd read as a child. His shoulders were massive, his stance regal and serene.

She blinked. He couldn't be real, but he didn't disappear.

According to myth and legends, the Native Americans believed that to see a creature like this was to invite you on a spiritual journey, and to follow where it led. The Celts suggested an adventurous quest with the gods and fairies of the otherworld—Tuatha Dé Danann —and a lesson to be taught since, to have come across the white stag, you must have transgressed. Well, she'd certainly done that last night.

The Christians believed the sacred animal was a symbol of Christ. But in other, older, more pagan beliefs, the white stag was not a creature of the gods, but himself a god, and represented the three creative forces of the universe.

Sex, life, and death.

Killian had pointed out that she, an earth witch, symbolized life, and he, the Fourth Horsemen of the Apocalypse, Death, and they'd created a life force together.

Could he be right and they were fated? Maybe she ought to rethink that fate/destiny aversion.

One thing was for certain, she needed to talk to her sisters, hit the books, and figure out what all this meant.

Grasping the wand, she shakily rose to her feet before the blessed beast. Her heart pounded and her mouth fell open when the stag bowed his head in a formal greeting and knelt before her like a loyal subject. Tierra didn't question the validity or safety of climbing onto his back.

From wherever he'd come from, be it through time or the otherworld, he'd arrived to see her safely home.

MOIRA STOOD ON THE FRONT PORCH, HANDS PROPPED on her hips, a worried expression painted on her face. She gaped when Tierra dismounted the white stag, her mouth falling open as the stag bowed before leaping off and disappearing into the forest that bordered one side of the yard.

"Where the *hell* have you been?" Moira asked, recovering quickly from the shock. "And since when do you travel by big giant bucks?"

"I'm having a bit of *déjà vu* here." Aerin joined Moira on the porch, Claire right behind her.

The look on their identical faces were full of condemnation.

And I thought I was in trouble before.

"It's not like she can get knocked up again," Claire commented.

"But she can get herself killed again," Aerin stated.

"Do you have *any* idea how worried we were?" Claire asked in a voice that wasn't open to excuses.

"The least you could've done is leave us a fucking message," Aerin said. "If you didn't have your cell phone, you could have used your magical powers or written something in the dirt so we didn't spend all night looking for your sorry ass and thinking the worst had happened."

"I'm sorry," she started, realizing how much she'd hurt them by not letting them know she was okay, or at least not dead somewhere.

"Damn right, you're sorry," Aerin said.

"Before we get to the reasons why you were out all night and didn't call, I need an answer," Moira said. "How the hell did you ride in here on a *deer*? And are you wearing a *crown?*"

Self-consciously, Tierra reached up and took off the crown she'd forgotten she still wore. The solid gold felt heavy in her hand. She should have a headache, but barely felt the weight of it until she'd taken it off. "It was a white stag."

"You can ride a white...*stag*, but can't manage a broom?" Aerin raised an eyebrow.

"You need to explain yourself, Tierra," Claire said.

What a picture she must make.

A night spent rolling around on the ground with Killian, digging in the dirt for her inheritance, and traveling miles on a wild, mystical animal through the forest from Siren's Cry. Sounded like she'd been on an acid trip. "Mind if I take a shower first?"

"*Fuck, yes!*" Aerin and Claire answered together.

"You think your walk of shame will wash off with a shower? Think again, sister," Aerin said.

"Fine." Her anger ignited, sparking against theirs. It was easier than dealing with her embarrassment and the hurt she'd caused them with her thoughtless actions.

"You three flew off to goddess knows where and just left me to fend for myself."

"It wasn't our fault you couldn't figure it out," Aerin followed up.

"We told you to stay within the wards and practice," Claire said.

"How hard was that?"

"Well, I got all turned around and ended up outside them. I didn't mean to. I just wasn't meant to fly. I'm an earth witch, and forcing me to do something before I'm ready, or willing, wasn't helping!" She'd felt like a child who couldn't ride a bicycle and all the neighborhood kids were making fun of her.

"All right, everyone calm the fuck down," Moira said in a voice meant to both placate and command. "Where did you go, Tierra? By the looks of you, we have a good idea *who* you were with all night. But how did you disappear so completely?"

"We couldn't even find you when we scryed," Claire admitted. "It was like you'd dropped off the planet."

"And with Death being able to move between realms, he could have taken you beyond our reach," Aerin said. "Did you think of that?"

No, she hadn't. "It all happened so fast. Killian appeared from out of nowhere and grabbed me."

"That fucking son of a bitch," Aerin muttered, obviously remembering how it had felt when Killian had come after her in his stealth-bomber winged-form. She'd poofed and ended up materializing in the kitchen —a new power that she hadn't been able to reproduce with any measure of control since. It seemed to be a "fight or flight" response to extreme fear, with emphasis on the flight.

"He took me to the Standing Stones," Tierra admitted.

"Why?" Moira asked. "It's not as if that place has a lot of pleasant memories for you."

"Such a romantic, that one," Aerin sneered. "But maybe fucking you where you died gets his rocks off." *Ouch. The gloves were off.*

"All right, chill your ass down," Moira said to Aerin. "I can help you with that if you'd like." Moira must be the middle child, the peacekeeper, or she just had the biggest, most forgiving heart of the four of them. "Death tried to save her, remember? He had a part in opening the

Fourth Seal, *his* Seal, because of it."

Aerin pursed her lips and looked like she wanted to reply, but held her tongue even though it appeared it would choke her to do so.

"Now," Moira continued, "let's go inside and discuss this like grown-ass women. We don't need to put on a show for whoever might happen to *overhear*. A bunch of pots callin' the kettle black will get us nowhere fast."

"It probably has something to do with her getting a piece of ass and us wanting some,"

Claire admitted. "With Death's bun in her oven, we're all in heat. And that's saying something coming from me as I'm always a few degrees above normal temp."

Aerin snickered. "You are one hot witch."

The tension lessened somewhat, and Tierra breathed a little easier.

"Ain't nothing being discussed until I have some coffee and biscuits on board," Moira said. "After a night of horizontal hokey pokey, I'm usually hungrier than a bitch with a litter of sucklin's pup. I'm sure Tierra could eat a horse, er that is, a farmer's market worth of organic vegetables."

"Don't forget tofu." Claire shuddered.

Actually, steak and eggs sounded good. She hadn't had meat since she'd become a vegetarian at the age of sixteen. And now that she could talk with the beasts, it didn't seem right to indulge in eating one. But the craving surprised and tempted her to give up the last ten years of healthy eating.

Moira held open the front door, and Aerin and Claire entered into the grand foyer. Tierra stepped up onto the porch to follow them into the house. The smell hit her as soon as she breached the entry. Burnt, rotten, suffocating.

"Where's Tommy?" she asked, covering her nose and taking a step back outside next to Moira.

"Not this again." Claire turned and fired at Tierra, her words searing. "I'm tired of hearing you complain about Tommy. Keep it up, and we'll both move out and you won't have to put up with either one of us."

Whatever is to come, you must remain as one. "No, Mom said we have to stay together."

"*Mom?*" Moira asked. "Just what in the Sam Hill have you been up to?"

"I have lots of stuff to tell you, but not inside the house. It's not safe." She took another step back.

"Are you insane?" Aerin asked, standing next to Claire, the threshold a line between them and Tierra and Moira, who stood on the porch. "It's the most pro-tected place in the world we could be right now.

It's warded out the ass."

"I don't think I can go in there." Now that she'd spent some time away from the manor, the smell seemed stronger and more repulsive. "I have informa-tion that someone or something dangerous got past the wards and is in the house."

"Aunt Justine hasn't arrived yet," Moira muttered.

"It isn't Aunt Justine."

"You forget about it being Tommy," Claire warned. "You've had it out for him since he arrived."

"Claire, do you remember how he showed up?" Tierra asked. "He isn't alive. He isn't the same man that you loved. He's something else."

"Every relationship has issues. Look at yours." She

scoffed. "Now there's a man who gives new meaning to the term dead-beat dad."

Aerin laughed. "Good one. How long you been waiting to use that?"

"A while actually. I have a bunch of them. Want to hear?"

"No. *I* do not," Tierra said.

"Later then, we'll compare notes," Aerin said. "I have a few of my own."

Tierra tried again with Claire. "Tommy isn't the same man that you loved, and in some part of your heart, you know that."

"You know nothing about it, Tierra, and if we want to keep this discussion civil, I suggest you drop it."

"Wait? So the relationship, for lack of a better word, between me and Killian is fair game, but you and Tommy are off limits?"

"Yes."

"Tierra's got a point, Claire," Moira pointed out.

"Killian Bane is the Fourth Horsemen of the Apocalypse," Claire sneered. "He is Death and our enemy. He tried to kill Aerin just days ago, and will no doubt try again. So, I have plenty to say."

"She's damn right," Aerin said.

"Tommy is..." Claire paused. "He's my lost love, my first love. I killed him, remember? Burned him up from the inside with my Fire, and by some blessing, I get a second chance to right that wrong. Has Tommy hurt either of you?" She pointed to Tierra and Moira, obviously secure with what Aerin thought of him. "Has he made any attempts to make you feel uncomfortable? He's been the perfect houseguest and is completely devoted to me. *He loves me.*" There was heartache behind her words, and Aerin reached out and laid a hand on her shoulder.

With her empathic abilities, she would pick up Claire's emotions stronger than Tierra and Moira, but there was no doubt to how much pain Claire was still in because of Dru's betrayal.

But what if Tommy was the danger that Killian had warned her of? He'd been conjured with a spell that hadn't set right with Tierra. She felt darkness around him, much like the zombies they'd been fighting, but different. How could she explain and get Claire to listen without taking offense?

Hurt and grief sliced through Tierra, and she blinked back tears.

She was losing her sisters. She felt it. A rift had appeared at some point, and it was widening.

❊ 8 ❊

A raven flew off the branch and headed deep into the woods toward the cabin that was more of a mountain retreat than a simple log structure. Bane had seen Tierra safely to the edge of the wards. Not that she needed him. Riding astride the stag, she'd been about as safe as she could be.

Landing, he morphed into a man and strode purposely into the house and found Nick in the kitchen.

"Nice to see you finally showed," Nick greeted, pouring coffee. "Tell me, brother, have you been sleeping in the devil's bed or a witch's?" Nick lifted the cup and calmly sipped, his actions belying the anger of his next words. "My money's on the witch. I can see from your face where you've dipped your wick. If you were fucking Lucy, the rest of us might get a break from her attentions."

"Where are Julian and Dru?"

"I don't know. It's like no one around here gives a flying fuck for the mission. Everyone is off either doing the devil's bidding or spying on a witch—obviously forgetting that we're supposed to be killing one."

"That just got a lot harder to do."

"Well, shit." Nick set the mug down on the granite counter with a smack. "What now?"

"Tierra has the King of the Druid's crown and staff, at least part of the staff. A quarter of it."

"Fuck. Wands? Do they *all* have their wands?"

"I have no idea."

"Familiars and now wands. If they figure out how to use them, we might as well call it. Game over."

Bane chose not to tell Nick about Tierra and the appearance of the white stag. But he couldn't keep quiet about the crown and staff. They'd all know soon enough even if Bane didn't inform them.

"Can we retrieve the crown?" Nick asked.

"No. She's already claimed it." He covered the pride he felt for the woman carrying his child, by grabbing a mug and filling it with coffee from the carafe.

"They have no idea, do they?"

"Not a one. Which will be our saving grace if we can keep them in the dark."

Nick suddenly went on alert. "Cover your balls. Hell's about to break loose."

"Hello, boys!" Lucy called from the front door, entering the kitchen a few seconds later. Dressed conservatively in a pink suit and ivory pumps and pearls, Lucifer looked more like a devoted wife of the fifties instead of the ruler of the Underworld. "I hope you don't mind that I let myself in. I thought it would be good if we chatted."

Bane knew why she was here. Knew she'd show soon after Tierra had left the protection of the Standing Stones and the world embraced the return of the Druid's crown and staff.

"Have a seat and I'll pour you some coffee," Nick offered.

"Thank you, Nicholas." She pulled out a chair and sat. "I'll take it strong and black. I've been choking down tea at the coven. Witches and their herbs, it's enough to make one want to slit her throat." She waited until she had her coffee and Nick and Bane had joined her at the table to start with why she'd come. "I haven't heard from you two recently and need an update. Dru's cavorting with the coven, and setting up that frontline nicely, and Julian's busy heading up an outbreak of smallpox in Africa. That continent is ripe for epidemics."

"Smallpox was eradicated," Bane said. If smallpox was set upon the earth again after decades of no one being vaccinated, it would decimate the population. He'd have to call up more reapers to transport the dead. The disease had nearly wiped out the Native Americans back in the 1600s when it had been introduced from the Puritans. So much for a New World.

"Do you think I would let mankind completely destroy one of my pet projects?" Lucy scoffed. "Maybe you need a refresher course of who exactly I am and the power I wield. You and I haven't combined talents since the days we inspired the Deuteronomy chapter in the bible and that piteous list of sexual immorality." More like horrified him.

"Now, Lucifer, take credit where credit is due," Bane said. "I had very little to do with that." He'd been more of a tool to be used, to shock, and sicken than a willing party. Somehow he needed to completely break those binds.

"True. It's sad that you aren't more bloodthirsty." She heaved a great sigh. "The places we could have ravished, the souls we could have taken, and the power we would have shared."

As if Satan would share anything. Bane wisely kept silent. One thing about Lucy, she liked to talk and loved nothing more than a captive audience.

"I'm sure you are aware that a few...relics have surfaced." The real reason she'd appeared. "I can't tell you how disappointed I was with this morning's revelation. It was all I could do not to release the hounds. The shockwave that went through the coven was enough to call in Dru to combat it. You know as well as I do what will happen if the Druids are allowed a toehold back on the earth."

Bane purposely kept his mind blank.

"I want to know how this happened," Lucy demanded when neither Nick nor Bane spoke. "Someone better start telling me what they know. *Now*."

Nick was the first to break the stinging silence. "From what my sources tell me, Tierra de Moray unearthed the Druid king's crown and a portion of his staff from the Standing Stones this morning."

"*Wands?* He fucking made wands from his staff? Why that irritating, clever son of a bitch." Fury turned her eyes to flames, destroying the demure and harmless appearance she'd attempted to cultivate. The devil did love her disguises. "Does Tierra know of her connection to the last King of the Druids?" She gritted this last bit out through her teeth. Lucifer and Malcolm de Moray had a history. He'd been able to stop Lucy's attempt to bring about the Apocalypse a thousand years ago, and she still held a grudge. It seemed like Malcolm had bested her once again and this time from beyond the grave. He'd been a patient man in life, but to wait a thousand years to play his hand? Impressive.

"By all accounts the witches are clueless," Bane imparted, keeping any inflection out of his voice and his expression nondescript.

"Five Seals are open," Lucy said. "I want the other two. The faster the better. From now on, your number one priority is the witches. Filter the rest of your duties to your minions and concentrate on the de Moray bitches."

"And what would you have us do?" Bane asked.

"If you can't kill them, convert them. *This is* the End of Days. I'm through waiting for my rightful place in the sun."

Separated by a threshold, Tierra and Moira stood outside on the porch while Claire and Aerin stayed inside the entryway. For a few heartbeats it seemed like no one was willing to cross over the sill.

Tierra broke the silence and offered up a compromise in regard to the house. "How about we gather in the solarium?" The solarium was light and airy with French doors that opened at both ends. The plants would hopefully help clean whatever putrid smell Tierra couldn't get past.

"I could use a drink," Aerin said. "It might be morning but as none of us have been to bed yet, I believe I'll have my coffee with a shot of whiskey."

Claire gave a jerky nod. "Sounds good. It's been a hell of a long night."

"How 'bout we be totally honest here and forget the pretense of coffee and just drink whiskey." Moira pointed to Tierra. "You're stuck with tea, but since the rest of us aren't knocked up, we can partake."

They ventured into the house, and Tierra held her breath. The manor needed a top-to-bottom spring cleaning. With everything going on, she hadn't had seen to it yet this year. She didn't have time now, but she had to find what Killian had warned her about.

Her stomach still rolled, but then she couldn't remember when she'd last eaten anything. At least anything that had stayed down. Through the entry, into the kitchen, and finally the solarium, Tierra looked for anything out of place or something that didn't belong. Nothing jumped out at her.

Once in the solarium, she opened both sets of French doors and fresh air blessedly wafted through. This was better. She could do this, though she felt guilty not helping her sisters in the kitchen as they gathered whiskey, glasses, and brewed tea for her.

Exhausted she yawned, sank into a patio chair, and set down the crown and wand she still had clutched in her hand on the table. She must have zoned, not really slept, but drifted on the fragrance of the flowers nestled into their colorful pots crowding the space.

Moira came in balancing a tray of fruit and scones with one hand, the other clutching a bag of pork rinds. "Here, I thought you'd like something to eat. Need to feed the little tadpole." Moira set the tray in the middle of the table. "Claire will be along shortly with the tea. You feeling okay? Your night out didn't...do anything?"

"I'm fine. Just really tired. Thanks for the concern and the food." Tierra eyed the selection of sliced apples, peaches, cherries, kiwi, and blueberry scones, then watched Moira tear into the bag of pork rinds.

Her stomach churned when the smell of fried pig skin hit her, but not in sickness, which was more disturbing.

"Did you find Cheeto?" Tierra asked, knowing Moira was careful about eating any type of pork when he was around.

"We found all the familiars hanging around the shed that Tommy and Sunny's father are rebuilding. Like a bunch of contractors watching over the progress. We tried, but we can't coax them into the house. Weird."

Aerin walked in with a bottle of whiskey and three glasses, and Claire followed behind her, carrying a teapot and a fine bone china cup and saucer.

"I went with the rose petal black tea," Claire said, setting the cup and pouring tea for Tierra as though she was offering up an apology for her earlier outburst. "That okay?"

"This is great. Thanks." Tierra raised the cup to her lips. The tea was one of her favorites. Sweet, floral, with earthy undertones. It was like sipping nectar from the heart of a rose, but today it didn't set well on her palate. Her eyes shifted to the bag of pork rinds, and she watched Moira popped one into her mouth and crunch.

"What?" Moira asked with her mouth full. "Do I have something on my face?" She brushed at her cheeks.

"It's nothing." Tierra picked up a scone and flaked off a corner. It was dry and tasted like dust. She washed it down with another sip of tea and knew she didn't want any more. What she wanted was too disgusting to think about. Her stomach rumbled with disagreement.

Aerin poured shots and passed them around. She threw hers back and winced slightly, letting out a breath. "So what happened, Tierra?"

Tierra looked at each of her sisters individually. "Killian and I, well we, uh..."

"We know you got your rocks off," Claire said, taking the bottle and refilling the glasses. "We can see that."

"How?"

"Your aura," Aerin said. "It's more vibrant and shimmers with satisfaction."

"Gotta give it to Death, he always comes for you. Or maybe it's best said, you always *come* for him." Claire's comment caused Aerin to giggle. "I have a million of them." She clicked glasses with Aerin.

"Don't listen to them," Moira said. "She's jealous 'cause she ain't getting any. That boy, Tommy, his cheese has done fallen off his cracker."

"No it hasn't. He has...cheese," Claire said. "I think."

"*You* don't know?" Aerin asked. "You've been hanging with him all this time and you *don't* know?"

"We're taking it slow. Besides this isn't about me, it's about *her*." She pointed to Tierra.

"It's about all of us. Killian warned me that something or someone has gotten by the wards. We need to take this seriously. Moira just mentioned that our familiars refuse to come into the house. If you don't want to believe me, believe them."

"Wait a sec," Claire said. "If he was willing to tell you that much, why didn't he tell you what or who?"

"Said he couldn't say."

"Like if he said who, they'd know?" Aerin asked.

"Yes, exactly that. Also, he mentioned all this stuff about there being power in a name. You know that feeling you get when you know someone is talking about you? Seems there might be something to it."

"Oh, there is," Aerin said. "I've dominated the cloud for a reason. I know things."

"Dru told me something similar." Claire grimaced as though saying Dru's name didn't set well on her tongue. She washed it down with another shot of whiskey.

"Did Death tell you where this thing is?" Moira asked.

"Just that it's in the house and that it would make us sick or possibly act out of character." She watched Aerin and Claire finish off another shot and refill their glasses. They were quickly on their way to getting toasted.

"Okay, we'll sweep through the house when we are done here,"

Aerin said. "Anything else?"

"I'm not to touch it, and we're not to burn it either."

"Then how do we get rid of it?" Claire asked.

"He said he could dispose of it," she answered weakly.

The three of them shared a look, but it was Aerin who spoke. "And you didn't think that was a ploy to get inside the wards?"

"I did at first, but not after."

"A.D. or B.C.?" Claire asked.

"What?" Tierra's attention was torn between the

conversation and the bag of pork rinds Moira continued to devour.

"After death—*la petite mort*—or before climax?" Claire explained.

Aerin quaked with laughter, causing her to grab her sides. "You have to *stop*. You're *killing* me here."

"Ha! I see what you did there." Claire and Aerin dissolved into whiskey-aided giggles.

"All right, you two have had enough, and I not nearly." Moira stood, reached over, and took the whiskey bottle from between Aerin and Claire and filled her glass to the top. "Why would Death care about something harmful in the manor?"

"Because Tierra carries his spawn and he wants her alive," Claire said. "It's Aerin he wants dead."

"Not just her," Tierra admitted. "He threatened to kill anyone I slept with."

"Oooh, that's soooo romantic," Claire said, her words slurring.

"It is not!" Tierra said.

"Very Heathcliff," Aerin agreed with a nod of her head that almost had her toppling out of her chair. "Obsessive, wrong, and politically incorrect, but you gotta admit, it must have thrilled you a little bit."

"The hell it did."

"Liar." Aerin snorted. "If Julian had said something like that to me, I would have blown him right there and then."

Tierra tried to steer them back to the original subject of conversation. "We have to consider that it isn't a thing in the house, but a who." She held up her hand when Claire opened her mouth. "Hear me out. Yesterday, Gwen and Lucy were here, Aunt Justine too. And Tommy is always here. They all had access past the wards. We need to divide them up and take a hard look at each one of them."

"It's not a bad idea," Moira agreed. "There are four of them and four of us."

Claire pointed at Tierra. "She doesn't get to investigate Tommy."

Fine with her. She hadn't been able to be in the room with him long before feeling the need to vomit. "I'll take Aunt Justine. I can be objective where she is concerned." She looked at Moira. "Or I can take Gwen." Lucy made her too nervous.

"No, I'll take Gwen," Claire said, her eyes narrowed to slits in thought. "There's something about her."

"I'll take Lucy," Aerin volunteered. "I want to get to know her better anyway."

"This is an information-gathering mission, not a let's-make-friends mission," Tierra said.

"I know," Aerin said. "But you have to admit, she radiates power. I'd like to know what kind. That leaves Moira with Tommy. I think that works as she's dealt with many...interesting characters."

"Hey, what do you mean by that?" Claire asked.

"Just that Tommy doesn't have a pulse. You have to admit that."

"Well, Julian oozes disease."

"Not to me, he doesn't."

"He would if he could and did, once upon a time," Claire said. "You were one sick puppy when we first met you after he infected you with his 'disease.'"

"Wish he would try and infect me again," Aerin muttered and grabbed the whiskey bottle from Moira, and tipped the bottle to her lips.

"So I could cut off his balls and feed them to him."

"I think you've had too much to drink," Claire said. "Give me."

"Not even close," Aerin said. "I see Aunt Justine."

"There ain't enough whiskey in the free world to make that okay," Moira said, holding her hand out for the bottle and refilling her glass.

"Are you girls *drinking* before breakfast?" Aunt Justine asked, censure heavy in her voice. She planted her hands on her hips just like Moira liked to do.

"Just move your shit along and leave us alone, old woman." Moira gestured with her hand as if she could shoo her away like a pesky bug.

"I would, but there is a strange...man in my bedroom."

"Oh, sorry," Claire said. "Tommy was staying in there. He'll be moved out soon."

"You have a...*man* staying in my bedroom." She said this like a man had never been in her bedroom before. Come to think about it, Tierra had never seen her aunt in the company of men. Only women.

"You gave it up," Moira pointed out. "It's now the new *guest* room. Understand. *Guest*, as in you don't stay long."

Aunt Justine ignored Moira. "I must warn you, Gwen and Lucy know you lied to them yesterday. You shouldn't have done that."

"What are you talking about?" Tierra asked.

"I take it none of you caught the news this morning?" Justine held her nose high in the air. "Apparently the world is not only having a rash of the walking dead, but—*aliens*—have been sighted over Canadian and US airspace. As there is *footage* of three humanoids on broomsticks who look a lot like you...four." She raised a finger to get her point across, but obviously didn't know which of the witches to blame. "Pockets of panic are breaking out all over the Northwest. When the video goes viral, which you know it will, witch hunters, scientists, and doomsayers will be all over this place. You will be found out."

"Guess, that invisibility spell doesn't work on radar," Aerin murmured. "We'll need to tweak it for modern day technology."

"Gwen will be back and I'm sure Lucy will be, too,

both of them wanting to know why you lied and how you flew. Lucy's a powerful witch, the likes of which I've never encountered. You need to be careful with her," Justine warned.

"We don't owe Lucy or Gwen or anyone else any explanations," Aerin said. "It's none of their fucking business."

"Don't be naive. The coven is powerful, and there is a hierarchy in place with Lucy in residence." Justine's eyes narrowed as she noticed the crown and wand on the table in front of Tierra. "Oh my goddess! *You* have them? Where did you find them? The coven is talking about nothing else except the Druid magic returning to earth. Otherwise I would have been here much earlier this morning."

Tierra wished she'd hidden the items before Justine had arrived.

Justine's jade eyes nearly sparkled with the need to tell someone of her discovery.

"No, you don't." Tierra jerked to her feet, grasped the wand and laid a hand on the crown. "If you are moving back in here, your loyalties must lie with us. You tell no one. *No one*, about these," she stressed.

"Tierra, this is a *good* thing and will benefit all the members of the coven."

"The only people I trust right now are my sisters. You asked to come home because you were frightened of the rituals the coven was preforming. I believed you. But if you feel the need to share this information, or anything else regarding us with them, leave right now and don't ever return. Those are the rules. This is not negotiable."

Justine's eyes widened and silence settled around the solarium as they waited to hear her decision. "All right. I'll agree to your terms. I won't tell a soul."

Tierra relaxed a few degrees, even though she badly wanted to gather the wand and crown and run for her room. She didn't trust Justine, and wouldn't until she'd proven herself. Going after Moira had been an act that Tierra couldn't get past, but Justine was family so she would give her the benefit of the doubt or enough rope to hang herself with. Either way, the truth would be known.

"I'll just go and help that...man in *my* bedroom move along," Justine said, and left the room.

"Well, I reckon, you done told her what for." Moira reached her hand into the bag of pork rinds.

Tierra couldn't take it anymore. "Give me those." She snatched the bag away from Moira and helped herself to a piece of fried pork skin. Euphoria exploded in her mouth and she shut her eyes and chewed. She was so hungry and this tasted so good. Even knowing what she ate, she wanted more.

A hush fell over the room. Tierra opened her eyes and found her sisters watching her, their mouths opened in shock.

"I don't want to hear it," Tierra said and stuffed her mouth with another handful.

"Not a peep," Moira said and shared a wide-eyed look with Claire and Aerin.

"I think we should make some coffee," Aerin said. "We need to sober up and sleep will have to wait."

"Yeah, we can sleep when we're dead." They all stared at Claire. "Hey, if we don't figure out what those things are—" she indicated the wand and crown "—why Tierra's craving pork, and what's hidden in the house, we'll probably be dead sooner rather than later."

"Don't forget the Horsemen and zombies," Moira said.

"And our mother," Tierra said. "She showed me where these were hidden. She called them my inheritance."

"Our mother?" Moira asked. "What did she say?

Did she ask about the rest of us? Do we get an inheritance, too?"

Tierra quickly filled them in on the brief interaction with their mother that had been comforting yet cryptic. "She warned me, warned us, '*Whatever is to come, you must remain as one.*'"

"That's heavy," Moira said.

They all digested that and then Moira asked about the wand and crown, "Who did they belong to before?"

"Malcolm de Moray, the last King of the Druids," Tierra answered.

"The Grimoire mentions him."

"We need to find out who Malcolm de Moray was," Aerin said.

"Well, considering the name, and the word *inheritance*, I think we can safely assume he was a relative," Claire said.

"This is the weird part." Tierra pointed to the crown. "It's ancient, formed in the Iron Age."

"And how do you know that?" Aerin asked, her tone skeptical.

"I know a few things," Tierra retorted. "Especially historical stuff.

And besides the metal kind of told me." She was an earth witch after all.

"The metal told you?" Aerin paused and thought about it for a second. "Really? That's badass, but come on, the Iron Age? Do you know how much the crown would be worth if it's really from that long ago? Not to mention, how the hell did it get to North America?"

"I know it came from the time period of the Druids," Tierra said.

"You're saying Malcolm de Moray was a relative *and* the last King of the Druids," Aerin pressed. "How is that possible? Besides, if it were even true, there is no way to know that we can trust him. Or that he has anything to do with this. We can't even be certain of the things we see inside the stones until we know for certain who or what they come from."

"I didn't imagine any of this. I know it, and our mother told me."

"Yeah, well..."

"You were there that night, Aerin, you saw her, too," Claire said. "Why don't you think the relics are from the Druids?"

"Because it doesn't make sense that those things would be given to Tierra from a Druid who lived over a thousand years ago. How did they get *here*?"

"There's an awful lot of folk tales and such about Standing Stones,"

Moira said. "Many believe they are portals."

"To another place?" Claire gasped.

"Possibly to another time," Tierra said gravely. "Malcolm de Moray's name and image is in the Grimoire, so are pictures of the crown and staff. I can't remember exactly what was written, and I know this sounds crazy, but until this mess is over, crazy is where we're setting up camp. When I touched the wand, I saw the staff that Malcolm had whittled into four wands. This one is mine. There are three others out there and they are yours. We have to find them."

"Well, hot damn." Moira sat back in amazement. "I sure wouldn't mind having one of those. What's it do? And why do you get the crown?"

"I have no idea what the wand does yet, but the crown is mine."

"If it's an inheritance," Moira said, "technically it would belong to all of us."

"The crown belongs to the next earth Druid, and I think that's me. The second I put the crown on, I could talk to the beasts of the forest. Something powerful earth witches have been reported to do, but I hadn't until now. I don't believe it's a source of power, more of a tool for knowledge."

"Let me see that." Moira picked up the crown and put it on. She waited a few heartbeats. "Yeah, I got nothing. Damn, that's heavy." She handed it to Aerin. "Here, you try it."

Aerin tried it on, shrugged when nothing happened, and gave it to Claire who shook her head. "Golden antlers really aren't my thing. I believe its Tierra's. I seem to recall pictures of a Mother Earth, and she was all decked out in garb like this."

"Wasn't that a shampoo commercial a long time ago?" Aerin asked.

"They had to get the image from somewhere," Claire said. "It would make sense that this thing belongs to Tierra. But I sure as hell want my own wand."

"Me, too. So how do we find them?" Aerin asked, considering.

"We need to hit the book and see what Grim has to say about them and the crown and our long lost relative Malcolm de Moray," Claire said.

"Great place to start." Tierra finished off the bag of pork rinds, and wondered if there was any bacon. "There is one other thing," Tierra said before everyone went their separate ways. "Aerin, we need to find you another wardrobe. Since the Horsemen are gunning for you, it would be best to leave your tailored clothes and designer heels in the closet."

"I've paid good money for my clothes. There isn't anywhere here in town open for shopping as Nick has bought up most of the businesses."

"There are clothes in the attic," Tierra said.

"You want *me* to wear hand-me-downs?" Aerin's thunderous look could have rolled trailer houses.

"Tierra's right. Though, them high heels did come in mighty handy fighting off that zombie the other day," Moira said. "You might as well have a target painted on your back with those fancy duds you wear.

You're welcome to anything of mine."

"Mine, too," Claire offered. "And I agree with the others. Every one of those horsemen will know which witch is which with you dressed like a Park Avenue socialite. But you mix it up and we'll confuse the hell out of them. Or they'll think you flew off somewhere. Either way, you'll be safer."

"If my only choices are gypsy hand-me-downs, biker chick, or Dukes of Hazzard, I think I'd rather be a nudist," Aerin griped.

"Come on. You know it'd be fun messin' with those four assholes. They've got it coming in a big way," Moira said. "If they can't tell us apart, their plans are as good as shot to shit."

"Agreed. You'll have to let your hair down, too," Tierra commented, enjoying Aerin's surly mood. Aerin was always so polished, not a strand out of place. It was time she came down from her lofty perch in the clouds and saw how the other...well, three-fourths lived.

"Someone is going to pay for this," Aerin muttered.

❅ 9 ❅

"How'd it go?" Bane asked Julian. The man looked paler, more tortured than normal.

"As well as one might expect," Julian answered. The expression on his face spoke of indifference, but Bane felt the misery emitting from him. Out of all the Horsemen, Julian's cross was the hardest to bear because he had compassion for the innocents he infected.

Bane had learned long ago to ignore the pleas of the dead. There wasn't anything he could do to save them. Lives were many times forfeited without right or reason, and he was only the transporter. The only life he hadn't taken was Tierra's by refusing to take her soul and that of their unborn child, giving her sisters precious time to heal her. His refusal to transport their souls would not have saved them from dying, but would have left them to languish as spirits with no destination. A worse sin in his experience, but a risk he'd been willing to take in order to save them. A completely selfish decision on his part, if he were to be perfectly honest.

"We expected you back much sooner than this." Bane filled a tumbler with tequila and was surprised when Julian asked him to pour another. There had only been a few times he'd seen Julian drink something stronger than wine. He hadn't wanted to see it again.

"Want to talk about it?" Bane handed him the glass of Patrón and settled into the chair adjacent to Julian's. His cravat was absent, his normally impeccable suit smudged and wrinkled, and Bane thought he noticed a tear in the fabric near the hem.

Dru and Nick entered the library before Julian could unload. He drank instead. "Gods, this is nasty poison. It tastes like dirt." He shuddered.

"Why isn't he nursing the grape juice?" Nick asked. "Did things go to shit in Africa?"

"I guess that all depends on your perspective." Julian got up from his chair and struggled out of his jacket, tossing it aside as though he didn't care. Bane shared a look with Nick and Dru when Julian reached into the cabinet for the bourbon. He held up the bottle—*The Devil's Cut*—and scoffed. "Seems appropriate, don't you think?" He grabbed a fresh glass, gathered the bottle, and fell into his chair.

"What the hell happened?" Dru asked.

"First, I have a question I want answered," Julian said. "One that I have been laboring with since this whole business began. Why are we doing this?"

Nick was the first to speak, "We took an oath—"

"And where is this deity who accepted our pledge, our obedience?" Julian interrupted. "Has anyone seen her in a thousand years, two thousand? We have been forsaken by the Goddess, seduced by the Devil, and, in my case, cursed."

"What is this, a pity party?" Dru asked.

Slowly Julian filled his glass with bourbon. He didn't answer until he'd drained it. "You haven't seen the suffering I have, been responsible for wiping out countless innocents. I don't want to do this anymore."

"So you're what, tucking tail? *Quitting?*" Nick asked. "Yielding to the wishes of that witch because you don't have the balls to kill her? This is *your* calling, *our* mission. It's not something you get to choose to set it aside when it gets tough."

Julian leapt out of his chair, the glass hitting and shattering on the hard wood. He grabbed Nick by the throat and slammed him against the wall. "Tough? You think where I have been, what I have been doing was *tough*? It was horrendous, unspeakable. *Inhumane*."

Nick eyes went to deadly slits. "You want a fight, I'll fucking give you one."

"You aren't human, Julian," Dru said. "None of us are. We're immortals, chosen by the Goddess to bring about the Apocalypse. It's our duty."

"Fuck duty." Julian released Nick back with a shove and reclaimed his seat, grabbing the bottle and drinking from the neck. "And fuck the Goddess if she even exists anymore."

"He has a point," Bane said from where he'd sat quietly taking in the interaction. "What about free will? Don't we have a right to choose? We've followed duty for a millennium, and now that the Goddess has forsaken us, and...the other...gaining power. Why must we do her bidding? Where is it written?"

"You know how this works," Nick spat, rubbing his neck. "The humans have given her power by their beliefs, their fears. She's been around for over two thousand years, propagated fear and damnation until they drank the Kool-Aid. We committed to bring about the Apocalypse. It's the reason we fell from Heaven, to act as guardians, protectors, and destroyers if called upon. We knew this day would come. I, for one, am fucking excited that it has finally arrived. The humans have ruined the earth and forsaken the feminine divine. They don't deserve to inhabit this planet anymore."

"So it's up for grabs?" Bane countered. "We just destroy everything, kill everyone, and then hand it over to someone like—"

"*Don't* say her name," Dru cautioned. "Not when you're talking treason. And it isn't up to us who takes the reins."

"Why isn't it?" Julian asked. "We were employed, if you will, by the Goddess. She's abandoned us and the earth long ago. I never gave my fealty to *Lucifer*."

They all three winced when he said her name aloud.

"I am beholden to no one," Julian finished.

"Stop this. We knew that bringing about the Apocalypse wouldn't be a fucking cake walk," Dru said, standing next to Nick and looking down at Bane and Julian. "Man up, you pussies."

"That's exactly what I'm doing." Bane calmly sipped his drink.

"What I've done."

"What are you talking about?" Nick asked. "What *did* you do?"

"Last night, when I lay with Tierra in the Standing Stones, I bound her to me."

"You...*fuck*." Nick buried his hands in his hair and stared up at the ceiling as if looking for divine intervention.

Divine intervention didn't answer.

The stench of over-priced perfume, much like a smoker bathing in toilet water to cover the smell of stale cigarettes saturated the air. Lucy slithered into the room on a whiff of sallow smoke that grew until it solidified into the image of a dangerous woman. Dressed this time as a dominatrix, her blond hair permed and ratted high around her like an eighties porn star, Lucy also sported metal spikes in her ears and a whip coiled at her hip. Killer high-heeled boots that reached midthigh completed the intimidating outfit.

"Hello, boys," she greeted, her lips exaggerated in a puffy pout and painted a deep blood-red. She eyed each one of them slowly, taking in their expressions and stance. "Do I sense contention among the ranks?"

Silence stretched until it was as taut as the string of Nick's bow. They each felt the arrow nocked and aimed to pierce.

Bane stood and faced Lucifer, taking her attention off his brothers.

"Nice outfit. Trying to make a point?"

"Subtlety isn't my strong suit, though I've dabbled when it fit my purposes." She ran her hand over the leather corset that thrust her cleavage up to her throat.

How did she breathe? Not that she needed to, Bane mused.

Lucy sauntered toward him, putting extra sway into her hips. "Tell me, my dark reaper, what have you sown for me today?" When he didn't answer, she waved her black silk-gloved-hand toward Julian. "To date, the scoreboard has Julian leaving you all in the dust. And here I thought brothers were competitive."

Julian lurched to his feet, turned his back on Lucy, and weaved his way to the liquor cabinet. He grabbed a bottle of vodka this time. Bane didn't think he cared what he drank, just needed the highest proof and most numbing of what was available.

"Yes, Julian, please pour me one," Lucy purred. "No ice. You know how much I enjoy the *burn*."

Julian jerked at her words, but he splashed a tumbler full and staggered on his way to hand it to her, cradling the bottle as if protecting its contents for himself.

She narrowed her kohl-rimmed eyes. "Oh, no, Julian, tell me you aren't plagued with demons. Africa hasn't taxed you, has it? Your work was so creative, that of an artist really. I couldn't be more proud."

"Go back to Hell." He fell back into his chair and took a long draw from the bottle.

Lucy threw back her head and laughed. The devilish sound grated, much like cloven hooves scraping down a tin roof. "Now, now, my pet. The havoc you have wreaked on my behalf makes me feel inclined to reward you. What would you like? Just tell me and I will make it happen. That is, besides that witch you fancy." Her tone darkened. "*She*, you cannot have."

Julian refused to look at her and lifted the bottle to his lips and gulped.

"Let him be," Bane said.

Slowly she swiveled her head on her shoulders without moving her body. No matter how many times he'd witnessed the trick, it was always disconcerting to see a head turn ninety degrees. He knew she did it to remind him of who she was. Basic horror 101.

But she didn't scare him. Not anymore. He had her number.

"You *dare* to order me about?" She aligned her body with her head and handed off her drink to Dru, who tossed back the vodka and set the glass aside.

"I dare much more than that." Bane took a step toward her, his shoulders squared, his eyes cold. "I've wanted to do this for over a thousand years. Once you enthralled me. Not anymore. I see you for what you really are."

"And just what am I, Killian Bane?" Her voice literally sizzled the air between them.

"A spoiled kid who didn't get enough of mommy's attention. You can play the victim all you want, throw your tantrums, and wreak havoc, but I don't believe in you anymore. So fuck off."

"*Bane*," Nick warned, flanking Lucy's side.

"Stay out of this," he ordered. "This is between her and me."

"You've chosen *her* side then?" Lucy asked in a venomous hiss acidic enough to strip paint. "That bitch who up and left you—all of you—to flounder without direction? Without a thought to your wellbeing, your future, your spirit. You would choose *her* over *me*?" she thundered.

"I'm not on your side or the Goddess's. I'm on mine."

"Does this have to do with those four witches?" She switched gears as quick as a Formula One driver. "Which witch has caught your *fancy*?"

He shuttered his expression, but Tierra's name popped into his head and Lucy snatched it out.

"I should have known it would be the earth witch." She smirked and then her eyes alighted with pleasure. "I hate to break it to you, Bane, but Tierra de Moray has been sleeping in another's bed. The bitch is pregnant."

"I know." Bane relished watching the smugness on Lucy's face fade in confusion when her arrow failed to strike its target.

"You...know? You're aware she's with child, and it doesn't bother you that she carries another's bastard in her belly?" she scoffed. "Well, I for one never thought of you as the progressive sort, Death."

He let the silence weave around them, heard his fellow Horsemen hold their breath for what he'd say next. Dru slowly shook his head and telegraphed, "Don't do it, man." Nick stood at Lucy's elbow ready to do her bidding, while Julian slumped in his chair like he didn't give a fuck about anything anymore.

"Tierra's child is mine." In all his years, Bane had never enjoyed saying a statement more so he repeated it. "It's *my* child that she will bear. *I* spilled her virgin's blood and *my* seed grows inside her."

Lucy's mouth fell open, and she deflated before his eyes like he'd taken his fist and sucker-punched her in the gut. Within seconds she had herself under control and raised her head to glare at him. Her eyes flared with the fires of Hell and she dragged in a breath that seemed to increase her size. But he knew it was an illusion.

A shrewd glint entered her eyes. "You will *pay* for lying to me. Death does not *create* life."

Bane smiled, not hiding one bit of his triumphant emotion. "He does when he lies with the most powerful earth witch since the last King of the Druids. Yes, I was there. I watched over Tierra as she claimed the crown and staff, witnessed the return of the Druids and the beginning of your end."

❧ 1 0 ❧

Tierra stumbled outside into the gardens, kept moving until breathing became easier and the debilitating nausea abated. Another moment in that house and she would die. The last week, she and her sisters had searched everywhere, taking the manor room-by-room, looking for whatever had been hidden in the house. They'd found nothing.

But something evil was hidden inside.

She trusted what Killian had told her, and if that wasn't enough, her physical reaction made her a believer. Aerin and Claire had tried to explain away her responses as morning sickness and that Tierra was being overly dramatic because of the pregnancy. That was a bunch of bullshit. This wasn't normal morning sickness. Didn't matter that her pregnancy wasn't normal either. She *knew* danger lurked in the manor.

It must be a person instead of an object. That was the only thing that made sense. A body could move in and out of the house, yet whoever it was had somehow confused the wards.

While Tierra was affected the most physically, even violently at times, the effect on Claire and Aerin was more subtle. They were more demanding, bawdier, and quicker to anger. Of course they didn't see it that way and were pissy with Tierra when she'd tried to talk to them. Moira, on the other hand, dissolved into tears at the craziest things, like the taste of fried chicken, Aunt Justine looking at her sideways, or the smell of magnolias. Moira worried incessantly and tried to help heal the rift developing between all of them to the point of exhaustion. Moisture bled from her eyes in unending streams, and if this kept up, Tierra feared Moira would drain herself dry.

Tierra had to do something. Things couldn't go on this way. Nightmares plagued her sleeping moments and sickness her waking ones. She'd lost weight, and her clothes hung on her thin frame. The weight loss made it easier to see her baby bump, and it was harder to hide her pregnancy.

She and her sisters had taken to studying the Grimoire night and day, but it had yielded very little. Almost as if it was hiding its secrets, not ready or willing to reveal them at this time. The location of the other three wands remained a mystery, too, which made Aerin more determined to find hers regardless of the means necessary. Claire was leaning the same direction, which fueled Tierra's nightmares of losing her sisters to darkness.

Hammering and the sounds of saws carried from the back of the property. Tierra turned in that direction to investigate. The shed that had caught fire during their last zombie fight had been completely repaired, so what were Sunny's father, Basil, and Tommy repairing now?

Tierra reached the edge of the stone steps that led to the lower perennial gardens where she did most of her commercial growing. A large section of forest had been cleared to make way for a beamed structure that was no more than a skeleton at this point. Tierra's eyes widened in shock as zombies weeded the long rows of perennials while another horde worked construction on the new building. Not only were rotted bodies operating power tools, but loose limbs and hands held nails in place to be hammered and operated the dummy end of tape measures.

Tierra found Claire and Aerin—who looked chic and sophisticatedly breezy in the old clothes they'd found in the attic—in the thick of working bodies and parts. Were they *directing* the mass?

"What the hell is going on here?" Tierra asked.

"Don't you love it?" Claire said. "This was supposed to be a surprise. Aerin had this great idea for a drying shed for the herbs and flowers that are in such high demand on the website. The shed isn't big enough for the quantities we need."

"But you're using zombies as...as...*laborers*?"

"Bet your ass," Aerin said, consulting her iPad. "We're getting shit done."

"We agreed," Tierra said, dread sinking in. "No more dark magic."

"*You* agreed." Aerin lowered her iPad and faced Tierra. The spark in her silver eyes said that she was more than prepared for the argument to come, relished it even. "Using the zombies as organic labor, if you will, is so much better than them trying to kill us every time we turn around." Aerin gestured to Tierra's flowerbeds. "Just look at your plants. They are thriving. Turns out no one knows how to mulch better than the dead."

"I don't want them in my gardens." Tierra shivered thinking of their flesh-rotten hands touching her plants and vegetables, disturbing the soil around their precious roots. "A lot of these plants are *consumed* in teas and medicines. Zombies can't be *touching* them. That's just...*gross*." And certainly wouldn't meet FDA regulations.

"Shh," Claire admonished. "You'll hurt their feelings."

"Feelings? Are you *serious*?"

"Yes, she is, and we don't discriminate in the work

place," Aerin continued. "Fighting and name calling is prohibited. We're resolute in providing a safe, non-combative environment. It doesn't matter what time period they lived in, what positions they held in society, everyone here is on the same playing field. Dead. Who knew dead would make for one hell of a great work-force? I've never had a better group of employees."

"And besides," Claire added, "they're stuck here for now. They just want a purpose."

"They *want* souls," Tierra stressed. "*Our souls*."

"They want whatever I tell them they want," Aerin said in a voice that chilled Tierra quicker than an arctic squall.

"Aerin, dark magic has a price," Tierra tried to reason. "One you might not be able to pay."

"You know what, I'm sick of this," Aerin said. "I did this for you, so don't judge me or tell me what to do or how I have to do it. I've been on my own a long time, sister. I can take care of myself, and I have enough money to buy small countries so don't lecture me on what I can or can't afford."

"You aren't doing this for me. This is all you. I want no part of it." Tierra held up her hands and stared at Aerin and Claire for a long silent moment. "And the price required will have nothing to do with money."

"*Tierra!*" Moira called. "It's Sunny. She says it's urgent." Moira hurried toward them and handed Tierra her cell phone that she'd left inside the house. "What in the hell is going on here? I've heard of the living dead before, but the landscaping dead is new to me."

"Hey, Sunny. What's up?" Tierra stepped away and greeted Sunny while Aerin and Claire made their explanations to Moira.

"I need you." Sunny's usually cheerful voice cracked over the line, heavy with stress. "I can't keep up with the customers today. It's like there's some sort of evil convention in town, and Ryan won't leave the supply delivery unless you sign for it, and we're nearly out of paper goods," she finished on a note of panic.

"You've signed for his deliveries before."

"I know, but with all that's going on in the world, people packing up and leaving without paying their bills, he refuses to leave the supplies without getting paid first. There isn't enough petty cash, and he won't take a check. I'm sorry, Tierra."

"Where's Aunt Justine?" Justine had been dealing with most of the day-to-day running of Ambrosia's.

"She never came in today. I figured you two were working together at the manor, or she's involved in the early morning coven gathering."

"What early morning coven gathering?"

"From what I've heard, they've performed a powerful ritual. A few of the witches have come in today and were real excited. I thought you knew all about it."

"No, I didn't." What was the coven up to? A trip to Ambrosia's would get her away from the dead heads and would hopefully help her figure out a way to deal with Aerin and Claire. They had to understand they were dealing with powers beyond their control. "I'll be right there." She hung up and tucked the phone into the pocket of her skirt.

"Where do you think you're going?" Moira asked. "It ain't safe for you to leave the wards."

"Sunny needs me down at the shop." And she needed to start living her life, not cooped up in a house that was slowly killing her.

"Let her go," Aerin said. "Out of all of us, she's the safest. With Death's spawn growing in her belly, none of the Horsemen will dare touch her. Besides the rest of us have work to do. Hey, you slackers!" Aerin rushed to herd two zombies standing off to the side back to work. One looked like a dried corn husk dressed in a Civil War uniform, and another, juicier one wore a three-piece pinstriped suit from the twenties. Both jumped at her words and rushed to do her bidding.

"You shouldn't go alone," Moira said, laying a hand on Tierra's shoulder. They both watched with dismay as Aerin had the zombies falling into line and doing whatever she wanted. One even saluted. "I'll go with you. I could use a break from this place, too."

"Suit yourself." Claire shrugged. "Be smart about it and take the squirt guns loaded with that Horsemen repellant."

"Claire, while we're gone can you try and talk some sense into Aerin," Tierra said. "She's drunk on power right now. She's not thinking straight."

"Actually, I think she's got the right idea. I'm tired of fighting for my life and worrying about yours. This is a happy compromise. Just look at the drying shed she's having them build for your herbs and flowers. And it's taking less time than a crew of humans. These guys don't need a lunch break and can work day and night without tiring."

While the drying shed would come in handy, Tierra didn't like the means used to achieve it. "Claire, she's practicing necromancy. That isn't good." In fact, it was very, very bad.

"Good isn't getting us anywhere, now is it? We're locked up in this house, stuck inside the wards, not able to leave or be who we are meant to be. What has good gotten me in this lifetime? Nothing." Claire answered her own question. "I'm tired of defending and fighting against these bumfucks. Afraid of Dru and his fellow Horsemen coming after me, and if the world is ending, I might as well live it up any way I can."

"You can't mean that, Claire. Remember that above all things, evil is seductive," Tierra tried again. "Can't you see that you are being duped into believing that this is easier?" When in the long run, the cost of dark magic would be more than they could afford to pay.

"You know what, Tierra, I'm sick and tired of listening to you preach."

"*Claire*," Moira scolded.

Tommy sidled up to them, holding a handsaw, blond and guileless as a surfer. He was the complete opposite of Claire's dangerous and fiery appearance with her dark red hair and sleeveless black leather vest and torn jeans. He draped an arm around Claire and drew her into his chest. "You okay, babe?"

"I'm just fine," Claire directed her answer to both Tierra and Moira. "Just fucking fine." She turned and walked away with Tommy.

"Tierra." Tears filled Moira's eyes once again. "We have to do something."

"I know." But what, she didn't have a clue. They had to figure a way to save their sisters and fast, before they were too mired in the muck to be rescued.

❧ 11 ❧

ater Street was deserted.
"Where is everyone?" Tierra asked. "Sunny said she was overwhelmed with customers, and where is Ryan with the delivery truck?"

"I don't have a good feeling about this," Moira muttered. "There aren't even zombies hanging around."

"That's because they're all being used as slave labor up at our place." Tierra parked on the street in front of Ambrosia's rather than behind the building. She left the car running, wondering if she shouldn't head home instead of entering the café.

Bells hanging from the door rang as Sunny pushed it open and hurried outside, her pile of pink dreadlocks spilling around her shoulders.

Tierra shut off the car and climbed out, feeling better once she saw Sunny. Moira did the same, but for some reason neither moved away from the vehicle.

"You're here! Hurry, there's a crowd inside!"

"Then why aren't you in there serving them?" Prickles of unease chased up her spine, and Tierra scanned the street. She felt...watched.

"Because you're out here looking like you're ready to bolt and I need you. Shake a leg, T. You, too, Moira. Where are the others? We could use them as well, but the two of you will do, now get a move on." She motioned for them to hurry, turned and entered Ambrosia's in another cascade of warning chimes that Tierra had hung and blessed when she'd opened the shop.

Tierra looked down the road again, half expecting to see a dried up tumbleweed cartwheel across the barren street. She turned back to Moira. "What do you think?"

"That we'd best hightail it out of here. I got goosebumps in places that ain't natural."

Tierra glanced back to Ambrosia's. The sun reflected off the windows, making it impossible to see what was happening inside, painting the building with variegated shades of red and orange. In a weird way the building looked like it was on fire.

"I think you're right." Tierra reached to open the car door and came to a quick stop.

Nicholas Kingswood stepped from the shadows, an arrow nocked in his bow and aimed at Moira. "Right you are, Tierra, but it's too late for both of you." Conquest continued in his confident swagger, closing the gap between them. "Ready to kneel and beg?" he asked Moira, a triumphant grin spreading across his face.

"Like hell." Moira drew her water pistol loaded with the Horsemen repellant that had sent Death flying away months ago in a sizzling fury of burning feathers and smoking skin. Just as she lifted the pistol to shoot, a heavy hand grasped her wrist from behind, disarmed her, and War held a sword to her throat.

Nick's grin widened. "Thought I came alone."

"You *would* need back up," Moira spat. "I've already proved that you can't take me by yourself. Didn't like the little bath I gave you last time."

"Behave, Moira. I doubt you want me to shoot your sister again." Nick swiveled the arrow's aim to Tierra. "Don't take another step, earth witch. You already know the pierce of my arrow. I wouldn't think you'd be too anxious to experience it again."

"She's off limits," Moira said, panic causing her voice to pitch an octave higher. "Death said hands off."

"I can shoot her without killing her. I'll just aim a little lower and take care of that...unexpected problem. Doubt Bane will give a shit about you then, will he, Tierra?"

Tierra covered her belly protectively with her hands. Conquest might not have pulled the bowstring, but his verbal arrow hit its target true enough. How many times had she thought the same thing?

Not now. Don't let him play on your insecurities.

Beneath her flowing skirt, the wand she'd strapped to her thigh pulsed with power, but she knew Conquest and War wouldn't give her the time she needed to release it. Then there was the matter of *how* to use it. She hadn't figured that out yet.

Mentally she sent out a call to Aerin and Claire and hoped they weren't so hindered with their dark activities to hear her. Not knowing what else to do, she relayed the message to the beasts in the forest and asked them to deliver it. If a herd of animals suddenly appeared at the manor, Aerin and Claire should take noticed that all was not right.

"What do you want?" Tierra asked.

"I'm pretty satisfied right now." Nick's cool eyes grazed over Moira. "*Very* satisfied."

"Probably on account of getting to hear yourself talk," Moira said. "Seems to be your favorite hobby. You and your second-string soldier have me, so let Tierra go. You only need one of us anyway."

"No, Moira," Tierra said.

"Don't worry about it, Tierra. These two are fixin' to learn they can't begin to chew what they've bitten off." Thunder rolled overhead.

"She is a mouthy bitch," Dru said, eyeing the sky

that had been clear one moment and now seethed with water-laden clouds.

"That she is." Nick chuckled, his focus centered on Moira's lips as if he appreciated that fact.

The door to Ambrosia's opened again and Sunny returned looking put out. "What are you guys doing?"

"Get back inside!" Tierra hollered. "Call Aerin and Claire. Hurry!" she added when Sunny didn't budge.

"Yeah, that isn't the way this is going to play out. And you two are taking too long." Sunny motioned for Tierra. "Best come in, like I said,

T. That is if you want Moira to keep her head."

"Sunny?" Tierra questioned, confused.

Sunny laughed. The sound rasped like high-pitched violin cords and was completely at odds with Sunny's more friendly musical tones.

Cold dread washed over Tierra. "You are not Sunny."

"Score one for the earth witch," the woman sneered. "Though it's been fun inhabiting her for a stretch. I do so love this pierced and tatted generation, so creative and open to suggestion. She really does think highly of you, T. I hope that's a comfort. Or not. I don't really care one way or the other."

"Who *are* you?" Tierra asked.

She moved forward as if taking the podium on a stage. "I am known by many names." Her voice amplified over the empty street and seemed to reverberate from everywhere—above, below and inside Tierra's own head. Moira's widened stare locked with Tierra's, obviously experiencing the same thing.

"Some know me by Deceiver," she continued. "Which is certainly true, along with the Destroyer, a personal favorite of mine. Then there is the Serpent, Adversary, Leviathan, Son of the Morning, and the Dragon." She gave an exaggerated sigh. "How I do miss the Dark Ages—picked that one up there—they literally worshiped me old school.

Idols, desecration, cannibalism, sexual rituals, virgin sacrifices." She sighed wistfully again, causing bile to rise in Tierra's throat.

"You'd be hard pressed to find a virgin in today's world," the woman continued. "Oh, wait. I did hear a rumor that Tierra was such a virgin. Is that really true? How did an earth witch, such as yourself, retain your virginity? And at your age? Unbelievable, a true miracle there. Witches in general are known for spreading their legs for just about anyone, isn't that right, Moira?"

"Bitch!" Moira spat. "How 'bout you kiss the north end of a southbound mule."

"Yes, I have been called that and worse. Most address me by the Devil, Satan, Lucifer, Beelzebub, though I must admit, that one isn't a favorite. Doesn't sound very attractive, does it? For the last few centuries, those *closest* to me have called me Lucy." The air shimmered and Sunny's body convulsed. She fell to the ground in a heap, and Lucy stepped out of her like she'd slipped out of a trench coat.

Moira gasped. "Holy jumping Jehoshaphat. That just ain't right."

"Sunny!" Tierra's heart pounded in her chest and tears sprang to her eyes at seeing her longtime friend crumpled in a heap on the sidewalk.

"Don't worry," Lucy said. "She'll wake up, eventually, and feel like she's been on a bender. This isn't the first time I've worn her. All the money stolen from the shop, yeah, my work. She's becoming really comfortable, almost tailor-made." Lucy kicked Sunny's legs aside and slithered closer to Tierra. "But you on the other hand, to be inside you with Death's child budding to life, now *that* is definitely something I'd like to experience."

Tierra shuddered with revulsion. *Holy Mother of Earth.* True evil stood in front of her and radiated out in nauseating waves. Her stomach lurched, and she swallowed the need to vomit. "Over my dead body."

Lucy had been in their house. Broken bread with them. Tried to act as a confidant, one that had seduced Aerin into thinking that Lucy was an ally. Claire, too. Killian had been right. But why the hell hadn't he told her that the *Devil* had been the one courting them?

Lucy smiled as though enjoying Tierra's scrambled thoughts.

Can she read my mind?

"I'm right surprised you can change in and out of them bodies so fast, old as you are," Moira said, getting her wits about her faster than Tierra. "And if you're lookin' to get some work done on account of those saggy tits, I can give you some numbers."

Lucy laughed and pointed at Moira. "*You* will be fun to play with."

She motioned to Nick and Dru. "Get her out of here. Lock her up with Justine. I'm sure the two of them will love the Hell out of that."

"No!" Tierra rushed toward Moira and came up quick when Dru yanked Moira's hair, pulling her head back and exposing her throat to the sharp blade of his sword. He nicked the thin skin above her jugular and Tierra froze.

"Hey!" Nick yelled. "Watch the blade! She's mine to taunt, not yours."

"Seems he's got a pretty big sword," Moira said. "Who knows? I might enjoy it more than your itty bitty arrow."

"Why the fuck would you want a few minutes alone with this *witch* is beyond me," War said.

Rain started to fall in fat drops and quickly turned into a curtain of water.

"Stop it, Moira," Nick muttered through clenched teeth, wiping water from his eyes.

"If you're afraid of a little water, asshole," Tierra

said, "let me provide you with some shelter." The earth trembled, and Tierra split open the asphalt under Nick's feet. He jumped aside as if expecting her to try and bury him. She hadn't thought Killian had shared his humbling defeat months ago with his fellow Horsemen. She should have known better.

Lucy reached out her hand and Tierra's airway closed off as if Lucy had her fingers physically wrapped around her throat. "Don't, Tierra. I'm much stronger than you, and the earth is *mine*. I fell from Heaven to make sure of it." Lucy's arm flew out to the side, and Tierra soared through the sky, landing on her side in the middle of the street a hundred yards away, the air knocked out of her as her ribs and shoulder took most of the impact.

"*Tierra!*" Moira screamed, straining in War's unbreakable hold. Water flooded from the sky, and waves pitched violently on the ocean, cresting over the pier.

"I told you *two* to get *her* out of here," Lucy growled at Nick and Dru. "What the fuck are you waiting for?"

Dru said something under his breath that Tierra didn't catch. He grasped Moira's arms, and restrained her hands behind her while Moira screamed Tierra's name. Her voice raised the tide, and seawater spilled over the wharves into the parking lots and inched toward them.

Horses suddenly appeared galloping down the road, one red, one white. Water splashed from their hooves and they pounded the earth in a symphony of cymbals and war drums heralding the end of days.

Tierra reached under the soaked fabric of her skirt and freed her wand.

"Oh, no, you don't, you upstart little *witch*." Lucy rushed forward and stomped on Tierra's wrist. "Want to play like that, do you? Let's see how you like this."

She slipped a chain over Tierra's head and secured it around her neck like a leash.

Suddenly the world went dark, lifeless, and deafening screams of the damned rang in Tierra's ears.

"Get it off!" Choking, Tierra lost her hold on the wand, and rivulets of water carried it out of reach. She clawed at the chain that seemed to have sealed itself to her skin, gasping for breath. A large stone the size of a peach pit hung from the chain, burnt, black, with a sulphuric stench. It acted like her own personal kryptonite and smothered, exhausted, and rendered her powerless the more she fought to free herself from it.

Lucy yanked Tierra's hair, pulling her head back. "Look. I don't want you to miss this. Watch and know that you can do *nothing* to save your sister. She will be dead by nightfall." *Moira*.

Spirited away on Conquest's horse, she was gone in a flash of snowy mane and razor-sharp hooves.

The rain stopped, and the ocean receded.

"It's just you and me now, Tierra," Lucy whispered in her ear.

"W-what...*is* this?" Tierra fought the choker and tried to send another urgent message to Aerin and Claire. It was hard to focus, to string her thoughts together, but she had to get through.

"Don't you recognize it?" Lucy asked. "You've been living with this and ingesting it for, dare I say, a while now. If we had the time, I would love to see what long-term effects brimstone would have to that brat you're brewing. But time, sadly is one thing that has always been in short supply."

Brimstone? Oh good goddess.

"*Ingesting*—how?" Tierra choked, her heart sinking at the thought of the damage the brimstone might have already caused her child. She knew the smell and the physical reactions, but this was much, much worse than the response to what had been placed in the house. "Brimstone is one of my favorite weapons as you never know how it will react with the chosen target. Its earth without life, stone that has burned in the fires of Hell until it fuses and becomes a small part of Hell itself. And obviously debilitating to you, which is interesting. I ground some of it into a powder and added it to your teas. All those precious teas you love so much and push on your coffee-loving sisters. I did have Justine add some to the coffee for good measure." Lucy chuckled. "She wasn't even aware of what she was doing. Impressionable, that aunt of yours. Now, Aerin, she seems to have responded well, don't you think? I couldn't be happier with the results. I haven't noticed its effects on Moira, yet. I will need to experiment more now that I have her under my care. But Aerin and Claire, they'll make a great addition to the Sisters of the Serpent. Yes, I'm sure you'll be thrilled to know that the coven has been renamed and restructured under my expert tutelage."

If Moira came into further contact with brimstone, it would surely kill her. At the manor, Moira had been full of tears, leaking moisture until she was exhausted. Tierra couldn't let that happen. Somehow she needed to overcome the effects and warn Aerin and Claire. They needed to rescue Moira before the brimstone destroyed her.

And Aerin and Claire had to be warned that the Horsemen were working with the Devil. At least War and Conquest were.

Tierra couldn't stomach it, couldn't believe that Killian had consorted with the Devil. Not the man she'd given herself to, had created a new life with.

She retched until she dry-heaved. Her head pounded as if there were a thousand hammering zombies inside it mashing her brains into oatmeal.

Silently she prayed for the Goddess, for her sisters, for...Death.

"Now it's time for my favorite part of my plan."

Lucy grabbed Tierra's arm and wrenched her to her feet as though she weighed nothing.

Tierra stumbled, and Lucy yanked her arm until it felt torn from its socket.

"Keep it together a little longer, Tierra. You're today's main attraction, and we don't want to disappoint the coven. You've stalled me long enough."

Lucy dragged Tierra past the crumpled Sunny and into Ambrosia's. The door shut with a tinkling of bells. The sound belied the darkness of the souls that turned toward them. Lucy supported Tierra in front of her with an arm across her chest while her other hand splayed over Tierra's slightly rounded stomach.

Another wave of sickness threatened to consume Tierra when Lucy licked her tongue up the side of her neck and nipped her ear. "You can blame Death for what's about to happen next. He's been a very, *very* bad boy, and his actions must be punished. The quickest way to do that is take away the one thing he has always coveted. Life." Lucy's hand flexed over Tierra's belly, and her nails dug into her skin.

"No," Tierra growled, finding strength from somewhere deep inside her. She tore Lucy's hand away and struggled in her hold.

Lucy merely laughed at Tierra's useless attempts to free herself.

The gathering responded to her laughter, and they began to chant in a language Tierra had never heard before. They swayed and writhed, naked, outside a circle of crushed brimstone where a Leviathan cross had been painted in blood. An infinity serpent eating its tail was anchored at the bottom with an inverted crucifix above. At the top of the cross, a thick wooden post had been bolted into the bamboo floor with wide steel plates.

Each of the twelve women—Lucy made thirteen —had the

Leviathan cross tattooed on their right breasts. The

marks were angry and red as if recently tattooed. A closer look revealed that the symbol had come from a hot iron branding their flesh.

"Meet the Sisters of the Serpent," Lucy announced, tossing Tierra to the greedy hands of the chanting coven. "Tie this witch to the stake and burn her."

❦ 12 ❦

Tierra! Killian rushed for the front door and yanked it open.

"Where the bloody hell ya off to?" Julian hollered, glancing up from gazing into another bottle of booze. He'd been drinking the cabin dry since he'd returned from Africa.

"Tierra's in trouble."

"Bugger. Aren't we all?"

Killian was airborne before his wings completely unfurled. Tierra's screams echoed in his head, and her pain clutched at his neck and scalded up his legs.

Honing in on her tortured cries, Killian flew toward Ambrosia's, dread filling his heart. Smoke spiraled into the sky, and he knew she was locked inside the burning building.

She couldn't die. He'd bound her to him. No one could take her life but him. As long as he lived, she did, but that didn't mean she couldn't be hurt, or the child.

He flapped his great wings, surging forward, praying to the Goddess that he wouldn't be too late.

⚓

Tierra screamed again.

Imprisoned within the ring of fire, she frantically fought against the chains binding her to the stake. She tried connecting with the iron like she'd so easily linked with the golden crown, but all that she could make out were horrific, nonsensical mutterings and shrieks.

"The chains were forged in the fires of Hell," Lucy supplied with a knowing smile. "You can't break them. Don't you think I thought of that, too, you ill-equipped, pitiable excuse for an earth witch. I had hoped this would be more challenging. You see, the victory is so much sweeter when it is."

The coven started to slowly recede, their chanting growing a little panicked as the flames shot higher, licking toward the four corners of the café, creeping up the walls in wicked strokes, and flinging ash and sparks to the floor only to be regurgitated by the fire.

Lucy laughed, her arms flung wide, directing the fire like a conductor in front of an orchestra. It flared, hissed, and smoldered, much like a beloved pet. The flames crackled and spat, reaching for Tierra with destructive fingers. Taunting and tormenting as it inched closer only to retreat and then hungrily begin again and again.

Smoke seethed and billowed across the antique tin ceiling. Heat intensified until the commissioned paintings on the walls melted, creating grotesque nightmarish images. Tierra gasped for breath in the smoke-heavy air, her lungs rejecting the pollution, producing rib-wracking coughs.

How did Claire stand this?

The windows burst and flames bellowed, greedily devouring the additional oxygen. The Sisters of the Serpent screamed and yelped, running outside to safety.

Lucy's laugh turned to a sadistic cackle.

"Why are you doing this?" Tierra gasped, fighting to

breathe. "Why not just kill me?" Why did she have to be burned?

"You have no idea, do you? Let me educate you, witch." Lucy stayed outside the burning circle, but dampened the flames in order to taunt Tierra further, dragging out the torture.

If Tierra could keep her talking and the flames from consuming her, she might be able to think of something to save herself.

"Burning a witch at the stake is traditional," Lucy said, "and in my opinion, not practiced near enough these days. It works amazingly well for destroying earth witches. Especially a *pregnant* witch." She spat the word pregnant as though it was offensive.

"Did you really think you could keep the father a secret from me?" she continued. "That I would let you live once I knew?" she sneered, sounding like a woman betrayed.

Confusion must have shown in Tierra's face, for Lucy suddenly changed tactics, her tone a mix of pity and scorn. "Are you aware that Death and I have a long and tempestuous history? Once upon a time, we were lovers, collaborators. We have followed and led each other through the Ages. Even Revelations speaks of our special bond in chapter six, verse eight: *'And I looked, and behold a pale horse: and his name that sat on him was Death, and* Hell *followed with him. And power was given unto them over the fourth part of the earth...'"* she quoted, satisfaction shining in her face as the barb took root inside Tierra.

Tierra had never asked Killian about his past relationships. Why would she, when she knew there was no future for them. Baby or no baby, he was an immortal. But to know that he had lain with the Devil, had done some of the same things to Lucy's body as he had to hers...

That, she couldn't stomach.

Anger and fear and the need to lash out stirred inside Tierra. The wooden beam she was tied to suddenly sprouted leaves and branches. Roots plowed into the floor, breaking through the foundation until it reached the soil under the building and burrowed into the earth.

Lucy's eyes widened in shock and surprise, but she couldn't be more so than Tierra. The power came from her core, her womb chakra, and her *child*.

The branches and leaves grew rapidly until the wooden beam resembled a weeping willow and cocooned Tierra inside the circle, providing much needed oxygen and crying tears of sap over the flames, causing them to sizzle and die.

"*No*," Lucy growled. "You tree-hugging bitch, you will not defeat *me!*" The fire flared, becoming a beast with teeth and claws. It attacked. Licking and slicing at the tree, swiping at Tierra and sizzling the leaves until they curled in on themselves, only to have new ones take their place.

The tree whipped its willows in defense at the advancing flames, and a frenzied dance began.

New branches grew between the links of the chains securing Tierra to the post until the iron groaned and the links gave way, freeing her of the bonds. She fell to her knees, coughing and clutching at the brimstone leashed around her neck.

"You can't do *this!*" Lucy screeched. "You don't have the *power* to resurrect the dead. That wood was *dead*. There is no heart core, no sap. I made sure it was kiln dried and dead. So how the *fuck* are you doing this?"

"She isn't doing it." Killian emerged from the billowing smoke like a dark angel from a horror film. "Our child is." Pride and satisfaction weighed heavy in his voice and reflected in his arrogant stance.

"That isn't *possible*," Lucy said, spittle flying from her mouth.

"Theoretically neither was the babe's conception."

Killian marched through the perpetual flames and grabbed Tierra, helping her to her feet. His raven wings enfolded her, adding another layer of protection against the furious flames that soared higher as Lucy's mood darkened. Killian's black eyes searched Tierra and his nostrils flared with anger. "You will pay for this, Lucifer."

"You *dare* to threaten me?" Lucy roared. Flames snapped and snarled up the walls to the ceiling, eating through to the second story.

"There is *nothing* I wouldn't dare for this woman and our child. You can't kill her, so give it up. She is *bound* to me. She is *mine,* and I am the only *being* who can take her life in this world or any other."

"Mark my words, Killian Bane, you have made an enemy on this day. You might have saved that witch from burning, but that brat is still in play, and the Devil always gets her due." Lucy flared, becoming one with the flames. The fire rumbled and the earth shook.

Killian tightened his hold on Tierra and shot through the fire-eaten cavity in the ceiling, bursting through the roof into the sky. He angled right and dove toward the ocean as Ambrosia's exploded in a black ball of fire.

❈ 13 ❈

Tierra went from blistering flames to freezing water.

Not just cold water, but saltwater that acted like acid, washing over the burns on her arms and legs. Just as quickly as she was dumped in the ocean, she was back in the sky, gasping for air. Killian shook the moisture from his wings, and Tierra squealed at the violent movement.

His hold tightened around her and he whispered in her ear. "I've got you. You're safe. Hang on to me a little longer. That's right, just like that." His lips brushed against her cheek.

She shut her eyes and let him take over. She'd have to deal with the fallout of today, but for a few moments she could float weightless in his arms and think of nothing.

Too soon they landed, and carefully he set her on her feet. She'd lost her shoes at some point, which wasn't surprising. More often than not, she was barefoot anyway.

Killian's voice rumbled over her. "Here, let me." His hands were at her throat, and he tore the brimstone choke collar from around her neck and threw it far, until it disappeared into the ocean.

Tierra inhaled with overwhelming relief. Power surged inside her and washed away the stench and sickness the brimstone had invoked. The earth embraced her as she connected with it.

Her head fell back on her shoulders and she closed her eyes in ecstasy.

"God, I love watching you do that." Killian drew her in to his chest, one hand cupping her face, tracing the tracks her tears had made, while the other rubbed the marks on her neck left by the brimstone. His lips lowered to within an air's brush of taking hers, a groan escaping him.

"What the fuck, Tierra?" Aerin yelled. "Ambrosia's is burning to the ground, and you're out here sucking face with *Death*!"

Tierra jerked in Killian's embrace and tried to move away, but he grabbed her arm and held her next to him, keeping that connection between them as though he couldn't bear to let her go.

Aerin and Claire ran up, their brooms clutched in their hands. Killian had landed Tierra just outside the wards. Her sisters came to a stop just inside.

Once again a line had been drawn between them.

"Are you okay?" Claire took in Tierra's sooty and singed clothing, the angry second degree burns on her exposed arms and legs. She narrowed her eyes at Killian. "Where's Moira?"

"She's not *here*?" Killian asked. "Tierra needs to be healed, *now*!"

"They have Moira," Tierra revealed. "War and Conquest took her.

They were lying in wait for us, along with Lucy—"

"Lucy?" Aerin questioned. "You must be mistaken."

"I'm not. She's Satan, Aerin, as in the Queen Bitch of Hell. She possessed Sunny, and she's the one who smuggled brimstone into the manor and laced the tea and coffee with it. She's been poisoning us with evil, and the other Horsemen are working with her. They also have Aunt

Justine." She turned to Killian. "We have to get them back."

Slowly, he shook his head as though in regret. "I can't help you with that."

"Why not?"

"They are not my concern. You are. You and our child." Briefly he laid a hand on her stomach, and then his eyes fell on Aerin and Claire.

"Everything and everyone else can go to hell."

"They concern me!" Tierra stressed.

"I hope Nick and Dru end this." His narrowed eyes looked at Aerin. "Succeed where I failed."

"I dare you to try and end me again, you douche weasel," Aerin sneered.

"If they kill Moira, the Apocalypse is over," Killian said flatly, facing Tierra again.

She slapped at his chest and tried to push him away, but he didn't budge. "You *bastard*. She's my *sister*."

"And they are my brothers. Nothing has changed in that regard."

"But..."

He'd fought the Devil for her. No, that wasn't right, she reminded herself. He'd fought the Devil for their child. He hadn't professed any great love for her, regardless of his talk of destiny when they'd made love in the Standing Stones. He'd only talked of desire.

But then did she love him?

How could she? She didn't even know him.

Tierra took a step back. The events of the Standing Stones sharpened in her memory. "Explain what you said to Lucy, that we are bound. What does that mean?"

"Bound?" Claire asked. "As in *married?*"

Married? Good goddess, no.

Killian ignored Claire and reached for Tierra. She retreated another step and entered the safety of the wards placed around the manor. His grasp brought him into contact with the wards, and he jerked back his hand like he'd been shocked with an electrical current. "Tierra—"

"I said explain."

"You *accepted* me, all of me, gave yourself to me as I gave myself to you. You are *mine*, Tierra, whether you like it or not. And I am yours." The words they had spoken to each other came rushing back.

"Say you take me."

"Yes, take me."

"No, say that you take me," he growled. *"All of me."*

"I take you. Oh goddess, please, yes, I take you, Killian Bane. Now."

"And I take you, Tierra de Moray."

"You tricked me." She swallowed. Desire to feel him inside her again warred with the need to bury him in the ground. How could she still want him after all he'd done?

His lips quirked as if knowing her thoughts. "Regardless of the method, promises were made on sacred earth. They are binding and unbreakable."

"You *married* her without her *permission*?' Aerin said.

"He'd impregnated her the same way," Claire added fuel to the fire.

"I will find a way to break them," Tierra vowed.

"You can waste your time trying, but a promise made within the Standing Stones can't be broken by time or death. Just ask your mother when you next converse."

"What the *hell* does that mean?" Tierra asked.

"Her secrets are not mine to reveal."

Anger and frustration driven by fear had Tierra lashing out. Suddenly her wand appeared in her hand. Last she'd seen the wand it had been carried away in a river of water rushing in the street during her showdown with Satan. She had to learn more about how the wand worked. For now, she shook the earth.

Killian laughed. "I hope our child receives your fighting spirit." His wings unfurled in a quick snap. Before he could take to the sky, Tierra had him seized with the vines of the forest and opened the ground below him.

"Go to Hell, Killian." Tierra flicked the wand, and the branches threw him into the opened maw and the earth swallowed him whole.

"Well, that's one way to get rid of an unwanted spouse," Claire said, when the dust cleared.

"It's going to be hard to get alimony with him being in Hell and all," Aerin commented and then shrugged at Tierra's crazed look. "Just saying."

"I didn't really send him to Hell, did I?" Tierra studied the end of the wand, horrified. She couldn't have, could she? Had she just delivered Killian into Lucy's vindictive clutches?

"Sure seemed like it to me," Claire said.

"We're a Horseman down," Aerin said with glee. "This is good."

"Do you think, if we kill a Horseman, will that stop the Apocalypse?" Claire's amber eyes narrowed in plotting. "Why haven't we thought of that before?"

"They can't be killed." Tierra's throat went dry. "They're immortal." But the statement came out in a whisper.

What have I done?

"They *were* immortal," Aerin said. "But what if we are strong enough to take that away from them? We're prophesied to end the world. If we have that kind of power, who's to say what we *can't* do?"

"Oooh, I like that," Claire said, the glint in her eye

turning into a flame and sending fear chasing up Tierra's spine.

"No, I don't like it. I don't want that kind of power." Or the responsibility that came with it. She just wanted to grow her herbs and make her teas.

Ambrosia's Charms and Brews, which she'd lovingly started years ago, was gone. Moira and Aunt Justine were in the clutches of Conquest and War. Aerin and Claire had embraced the dark side, while Tierra was at the top of Satan's wish list.

And, good goddess, she'd just sent the father of her child to Hell.

MOIRA

CYNTHIA ST. AUBIN

❦   I   ❦

Goddess of power, I'm stuck real hard
Turn these shackles into lard
If it's your will, so let it be
By earth, air, fire and sea...

Moira de Moray looked at her reflection in the crazed antique mirror on the ceiling overhead, seeing herself as she might be reflected on the surface of a brackish pond in Stump Bayou, the place she had once called home. Her lips moved only a little as she whispered the spell.

She closed her eyes and waited, attempting what she hoped was a reverent silence. When after a moment of unbearable stillness she opened one eye to peek at the mirror, she found she was still bound hand and foot by iron shackles to the bed of Nicholas Kingswood, better known as Conquest to whomever had scratched out the Bible.

"Damnation!" A deep metallic clanking was the only reply to her bitter oath.

Okay, so maybe spells weren't her thing. Lord knew she'd tried enough of them this morning to choke a deep-throated goat.

Please dear Goddess, I know I'm whiny, but could you

make my hands really tiny? She had thought—hoped?—that if she could slip her tiny hands of their cuffs, she could work her feet free, and once she escaped, one of her sisters might be able to reverse the spell. Even if they couldn't, for the chance at escaping the Four Horsemen of the Apocalypse—in whose compound she was now held captive—she was willing to consider a life with hands no bigger than a buffalo nickel. She'd just have to make more trips to carry in the groceries was all.

Please dear Goddess, I ain't fakin', turn these shackles into bacon. Now, *that* had been the real heartbreaker. Her stomach growled something fierce and she would have been more than willing to gnaw herself free. Technically, she knew the use of *fakin'* was a cheat on the rhyme, as much of her bayou patois had begun to fade these months with her sisters in Port Townsend.

Fading like her memories of a loon's mournful call just when the sunset sewed gold sequins on the bayou's surface. Or the whisper of a summer breeze threading through the Spanish moss outside her window in the shack she shared with Uncle Sal. Truth was, she'd been shedding herself like a snake shed its skin. Letting her sisters sand away her rough spots—and Lord knew there were enough of those.

Tierra patiently trimmed Moira's borders like she were a patch of overgrown herbs.

Aerin's breezy uptown parlance had filtered her own backwater blabber into something clearer, cleaner.

Claire burned off Moira's untended dead edges like autumn leaves, helping her find her own shape beneath beliefs that no longer served.

She could see the good in all of it, but wasn't sure she'd see her sister's faces again.

Moira huffed out a frustrated breath and gazed down the length of her tanned legs past her customary cut-off jean skirt to the metal cuffs at her ankles. She tried to draw her knees in, but judging by the chain's weight, the cuffs had to be made of lead or something.

Silver lining: if she did a few more leg lifts, that oughta count as her work out for the day, at least.

Her own irritated visage stared back at her when she flopped back on the pillow, which she was pretty damn sure was made of the finest goose down and covered in a pillowcase with a thread count in the quintuple digits. Nicholas Kingswood would have nothing less. The comforter beneath her bare thighs was no less silky and seductive in its buttery caress. These luxuries did little to allay the chilling effect of the rest of the room however, particularly the creepy-ass masks staring at her from their cases with blank shadow eyes. Helmets long since emptied of their heads. Swords and spears, still rusty with blood of the conquered. Newspaper clippings sandwiched in frames worthy of Baroque masterpieces. The word *surrender* featured prominently in just about every headline.

Trophies.

Trophies belonging to the man Moira sensed but didn't see. She smelled him on the sheets beneath her, that particular mix of expensive cologne, aftershave, and lust for domination. It was this last that eased her fear for her life.

Nicholas Kingswood could not help but come and lord his position of superiority over her before he allowed her to meet her end. And he would end her. Of this she had no doubt. In this way, he differed from his brothers.

Dru, War's own iteration, the blade and the bullet made in flesh, could not hide the lust for Claire rolling from him in heady waves.

Bane, Death on wings, as necessary and unstoppable as the sun's rising, collector of souls, broadcast to Moira a deep wound within his own immortal fabric: he couldn't bear the death of his own child, or Tierra who carried it.

Julian, embodied Pestilence in the dark, languishing form of the fiercely romantic vampires in books she'd swooned over on their back porch in the Louisiana summer heat, rocking herself with a broom handle in a hammock fashioned from old fishing nets. His longing for Aerin could pull the world off its axis.

But not Nick.

Oh, he wanted to bone Moira, sure enough. But the only reason he'd kept Julian's or Dru's sword from providing her a hasty introduction with her maker was because it was his right. He had been sent to kill her, and no other would bear her blood as their victory banner. Nick needed to own her, body to soul, bones to blood. Needed the knowledge that she *belonged* to him. And when he was through with her, a braid of her black-red hair might end up in the case right next to old *Creepy Eyes*.

"Well fuck that," she said aloud, readying herself to try another spell. Scarcely had she opened her mouth to begin an invocation involving motor oil and a llama when a sound snapped her lips shut.

Water. In pipes.

Someone, and Moira had a pretty decent guess *who*, had just turned on a shower. Close enough for her to feel the presence of moisture through the solid wood door to her left. Her chest went still, her eyes open in lidless concentration. The only movement in the entire stretched 'X' of her bound form were her lips, curving into a slow smile.

She'd been working on a little something. Something she'd been dying to try out. Delicious tingling stole over her, through her as each water molecule of moisture responded to her. Her cells, their cells, one in purpose. Only when she felt the wholeness of them heeding her call did she pull their heat into her body, leaving the water spraying from several shower heads at the body of Nick Kingswood at exactly two degrees above freezing. She thought the extra degrees especially magnanimous in light of all the general fuckery he'd dragged into her life.

"Fuck!" The hollered curse in that smooth, smoky baritone widened Moira's smile.

*And for my next trick...*a magician's voice announced in her head.

Moira beckoned the droplets to increase their pace. Just a titch. Say, about the velocity of a firehose?

They seemed all too eager to comply.

"Jesus fucking Christ! Holy fuck!"

And would the moisture collected around the glass shower door care to freeze, perhaps? she wordlessly requested. Just enough to prevent someone from opening it without a few solid body blocks, of course.

Not a problem.

Moira heard the squeaking of taps attempting to be turned off, then glass violently rattling. At this point, Nick's curses devolved into a language she didn't speak but could still take the general meaning of.

When it finally flung open, the wooden door followed almost at once, and Moira was confronted with the towering, naked, dripping frame of Conquest, with naught but a towel held to his admittedly impressive crotch.

"Good morning, Sunshine." Moira greeted Nick with her most beatific smile. "Well, don't you look like a drowned possum? Didn't your momma ever teach you to dry off while you're on the shower mat?"

Droplets hung jewel-like from the tips of Nick's disheveled hair, the exact color of a roux allowed to sizzle past brick brown. His eyes, usually the exact shade of sunlight through a good Tennessee whisky, had darkened considerably. Water droplets under her control only moments earlier willfully disobeyed her just for the chance to glide down the channels provided by his pectoral muscles, abdominals, and the dangerous ledge where his abdomen cut a deep "V" into his lean hips.

And the rest of him...Lord, but Moira couldn't let herself look for fear of what he'd see reflected in her liquid aquamarine eyes. She already knew what hid under that slate-gray towel, and he'd drop it in a second if the distraction would give him an advantage.

Seeing Nicholas Kingswood bare-ass naked would be enough to drive any woman straight past distraction and right over the cliff beyond it. Maybe she hadn't thought out this part of her plan so well.

"Problems with your plumbing?" she asked, sweet as sugared honey.

His chest rose and fell, his breath practically steaming from flared nostrils. He advanced to the bed with startling speed, drops of water falling from his body onto Moira's cheeks like rain as he seized her shackled wrists with hands equally unyielding.

His mouth hovered over hers. Close enough for her to feel his heated words against her lips when he spoke at last.

"While you are under my roof, I would advise you against provoking me."

"On account of you don't like what cold water does to your tally whacker?" This shot? A total bluff. Simple math told Moira that if he had both hands on her wrists, he had no hands on his towel. What she saw out of the corner of her eye hadn't been affected by the icy spray one lick.

Lick. Now there was an interesting idea.

"From this moment forward, every breath you take is given by my grace. As you are mine to destroy, your life is over the second I decide it's so. And understand this, *Moira Jo*—" An involuntary shudder worked its way up her spine with her name on his lips and her water on his body "—I am the only one in this house who has any interest in prolonging it."

"You want I should scare up a blue ribbon for you? Cheeto won one at the county fair once for Most Charming Animal. Can't say that it applies to you much, but I don't guess he'd mind sharing. Come to think if it, Nick Kingswood sharing a ribbon with a pig makes an awful lot of sense."

Nick's eyes darkened further at the mention of her familiar, a teacup pig that just happen to belch fire when stirred up.

Nick had made the mistake of shaking him up like a little tank of nitroglycerine and was relieved of his eyebrows for the privilege.

"You don't have any idea the danger you're in, do you?"

"What? You mean with the zombies, five seals out of seven more busted than a poker player on Sunday morning, two of my sisters seduced by the dark arts, the third knocked up with Death's spawn, Satan herself clamoring to turn me into some strappy sandals, and waking up chained to the bed of an apocalyptic horseman sent to destroy me personally?" Moira paused, allowing herself an unbroken gaze straight into those amber eyes as water drops now warmed by his body continued to rain down. "You're right. I don't have me the first god-damn clue."

Surprise softened the hard angles of Conquest's face. He hadn't expected her to understand. Most folks didn't when it came right down to it. For Moira, gifted with a large rack and about the worst backwater drawl a body could have, she'd encountered the same reaction all her life.

No one expected much from her, and she was happy to give them about what they expected.

From men, a *bless your heart*, and a pat a little left or right of her arm, grazing her boob. From women, the stony-eyed stare of outright dislike. "Then why do you insist on contradicting me at every turn?" Nick asked, his grip on her wrists tightening.

"Because I know you, Nicholas Kingswood." Moira leaned to the side of his face, his yet unshaven jaw brushing against her cheek as she whispered close to his ear. "I've tasted you. Remember?"

She certainly did. The heat of their mouths fused in the pouring rain, the ocean's tides coming in waves like their pleasure, her hand slick on his cock, convulsing around his fingers to the scent of salt air and sex. Her first—and to date—only orgasm. A fact that had surprised Nick almost as much as the tsunami-sized wall of water she had coaxed to launch him to the far side of the Puget Sound seconds after.

"Yes." His voice had lowered by several registers. The jugular vein on his throat rose and fell in time with the erratic throbbing of his heart. Moira kept her lips at his ear.

"You're a man who's used to getting whatever he wants. But you ain't gonna get it from me, Nick. No sir. I'm fixin' to give you what you *need*."

❧ 2 ❧

Nick Kingswood's blood burned hot beneath his chilled skin. At least he'd managed to rinse off the reek of smoke and brimstone still clinging to him after Satan's latest soirée before his shower had gone polar. He hadn't been particularly enthused to see Ambrosia's Brews and Charms go up in flames, as it belonged to him despite the protracted legal battle waged by Aerin de Moray, Moira's bun-wearing bitch of a sister.

Nick did not surrender his possessions lightly.

A tendency he applied to the water witch bound to his bed. The more she picked and poked at him with those made-for-sin lips, the more he wanted to shove something between them to silence her. Several options suggested themselves simultaneously, and an ache settled at the root of his cock.

Even with his hulking form dripping over her, Moira did not flinch. Didn't attempt to widen the distance he'd narrowed. Not she.

"What I *need?*" Nick repeated the word with a good measure more sarcasm than it had been spoken to him. "What I need isn't in your hillbilly head. It's in your skirt."

Moira raised her head from the pillow until her lips

actually brushed his before whispering between them, "Fuck off, *Conquest.*"

Nick clanged the manacles against the broad wooden headboard flanked by massive oak bedposts carved into replicas of the *Column of Trajan* in Rome, a battle he still harbored a lingering fondness for.

The spark of fear he waited for in her fathomless aqua eyes did not appear. Instead, he found pleasure there. Her pleasure at twisting him this way and that. Knowledge of her power to wring anger from him with a few carefully chosen words.

With effort greater than required to marshal the Imperial Roman Army, Nick arranged his features into a mask of vulnerability. Dark eyes widening, chest deflating, his very best down-turned, half-hurt frown.

"At least admit you want me as much as I want you," Nick pleaded. Moira's face shimmered into an impressionistic painting through the scrim of tears welling up in his own eyes. *Damn. He was better at this sensitive male shit than he remembered.*

For a split second, the water witch's gaze grew luminous, and if she'd had a free arm, Nick was positive she would have reached out to place it on his shoulder.

"Sure I want you," she said gently. "To get the hell out of here and see about fixing me some breakfast. Grits if you've got 'em. And I wouldn't turn my nose up if some butter and cheese hitched a ride as well."

Nick dropped the act and allowed a more natural, wolfish grin to occupy his face. "You may be a great healer, Moira, but you're a shitty liar."

He released her wrist and yanked up her skirt to expose her panties. Even from her vantage, she could see the dark moisture blooming on the light blue fabric. Nick traced the patch with a lazy finger, fighting the sudden rush of adrenaline. The edges of his vision rimmed red and the capacity for conscious thought retreated under the surge of sweet, drugging power. He was *winning*. Controlling the reactions of her body to his presence.

At that moment, he would have gutted a million men just to allow himself the pleasure of tearing the silky scrap from her and planting his cock in her velvet depths like a flag of possession.

No. Not yet. To do so would only be half a victory. She had not yet relinquished her will. She had not yet *surrendered*.

His eyes fell closed as he battled for higher brain function.

"For a water witch, you don't seem to have much control over the moisture between your legs." He let his damp fingers trail down the sloping muscle of her outer thigh. Nick liked this about his water witch—liked the way he could see how the hauling of nets heavy with fish had shaped her. Hardened her.

And now she hardened him. Painfully so.

Moira squeezed against her chains, fruitlessly trying to bring her thighs together, fighting the bonds as much as the traitorous body Nick felt boiling beneath his touch. Her stomach shuddered as he skimmed the edge of her panties, teasing the elastic with a finger. Lifting it, dipping beneath it, venturing upward to circle the bellybutton exposed by her short tank top.

"And these," he said, fingers brushing over the hardening buds of her nipples. He settled over her like a great, lazy cat, allowing his naked abdominals the bliss of contact with her bare midriff. "Might as well be a billboard." He pinched one lightly between thumb and forefinger and quickly brought his mouth to it, sucking her through the fabric while letting his teeth gently test it through the cotton fragrant with her wild scent.

Her hips arched off the bed, and Conquest could no longer refrain from sliding his hand under her skirt, pushing her soaking panties to the side.

"Water witch indeed." He explored her at his

leisure, letting his finger stray just shy of her aching bud until she was twisting, writhing, squirming...but not begging.

"Tell me you want me," he ordered, thumb hovering, ready to grant her entrance into the abyss.

"*No*," she panted. Perspiration rose on her brow, dampening the rich burgundy of her hair to spilled wine on his gray pillows.

"Three little words, Moira." He brought two fingers to his lips and licked them, returning them to her slick and sudden. Her gasp echoed among the masks and armaments. "I. Want. You." For a brief moment, Nick Kingswood wished the water witch beneath him shared his age, his knowledge, so he could make her utter these words in every language spoken by the tongues of men. He would make her come over and over, one descent into paradise for each admission.

How the delicate muscles in her jaw worked then, her teeth grinding beneath them against her will, treacherous as the sea. "Fuck you!" She bucked her hips away from him, but could not escape her bonds.

"No? Perhaps you require more direct methods of convincing." Nick moved between her thighs, running his hands up the firm flesh to pull her panties down to her calves. He brushed his lips on the inner flesh of her knee, and sudden pain shot through his head. Terrific pressure digging into his temples. Bright white blinding his vision. After a stunned moment, he reached up to feel his head and found that Moira had clamped him between her knees and was squeezing with enough pressure to crush a brick.

His fingers grasped her knees, expecting to pry her legs apart as easy as tearing fresh-baked bread. Not an inch could he move them, his biceps bulging with the effort.

A new sensation tightened in Nick's chest. *Panic?*

Surely not. Not he, who made potholders from the bears killed with his own hands.

"Eight time watermelon bustin' champion of Terrebonne Parish," Moira grunted. "You happen to know how much of the human body is made of water, Punkin?"

Nick searched for the number, wanting at least the satisfaction of knowledge to combat the sickening feeling of helplessness churning like a blade in his gut.

"Sixty percent," Moira provided for him. "Only I'd say you're at about a 52 on account of all the booze you swill. Alcohol is awful dehydrating, you know. Might want to lay off the martinis, Honeybuns."

"I. Am. Immortal." Exactly whom was he saying these words for?

"An immortal wearing a skin suit, in case you'd forgotten. Which means, 52 percent of that body is under *my* control now, Sugarbritches. And unless you back the fuck off, I'm like to splatter your immortal brains all over these here fancy sheets."

"Damn you, woman," Nick growled between clenched teeth and lips artificially pooched out, fish-like by the compression between her thighs. "You will surrender to me."

"When Hell freezes over. But hey," she shrugged as much as her restraints would allow, "maybe you can talk to that blond bitch, Satan who's leading you around by the dick. Maybe, if you begged her good and hard, she might do you a little favor. Throw you a table scrap."

"She doesn't own me," Nick insisted, the words somewhat garbled as they worked through puckered lips. Not at all the authority he had hoped to conjure.

"Oh, I beg to differ," a silky female voice interjected.

Nick didn't have to turn his head—not that he could have—to know Lucifer had arrived. The sudden infusion of her cloying, exotic perfume along with the gooseflesh riding the length of his spine and the sudden wilting of his cock was as reliable a predictor as an atomic clock.

Lucy slithered into his peripheral vision, clad head to toe in black leather and a boned bustier, looking every inch the dominatrix. Her blond hair brushed the tops of her mounded breasts in silky waves, her plump lips painted the color of drying blood.

"If it ain't Old Funbags McPeroxide," Moira said. Nick squeezed her ankle, trying in vain to signal the folly of this course. "I figured you'd show up at some point."

"Of course you did," Lucy said, a dangerous smile revealing even white teeth. "You're smarter than people give you credit for, that hideous mudbug-eating accent notwithstanding. And since you're smart,

I'll give you a little piece of advice."

Lucy approached the side of the bed, petting Nick's head as if it were a puppy pinned between Moira's thighs.

"You really ought to let him go down on you, love. It's just about the only thing that mouth of his is good for."

The Devil strolled over to the chair next to the bed and seated herself with a squeak of leather and the regal posture of a queen.

"Mind if I watch?"

❋ 3 ❋

Moira jerked her knees to the left, sending Nick Kingswood sprawling off the edge of the bed. He landed naked on the floor at Ol' Scratch's leather platform spiked heels. "He's all yours, Beelzeboobs."

"You couldn't be more correct," Lucy said, reaching down to drag a long, red nail down the length of Nick's chin. "He has been for ages, haven't you, *Conquest*? Speaking of, have you told Little Miss Moira who was your first?"

Nick shoved himself to his feet and retrieved his towel as Lucy settled further into the armchair, suggestively dropping one long leg over the arm.

"I don't recall asking." Moira yawned. "In fact, I don't recall giving a furry rat's ass where he chooses to dip his wick."

"Taking Conquest's virginity." Lucy sighed, her ice-blue eyes rolling skyward in fond recollection. "Now there's a night worth remembering." She let her head loll to the side and slid Moira a slitty-eyed wink. "He was a quick study. And hung? I keep a bronze replica of Conquest's cock in my boudoir for special occasions. It's not often that *I* have trouble walking the morning after."

"Yeah, well, I don't imagine walkin' on them cloven

hooves of yours would be all that easy even if you weren't spreadin' your legs for every horny, hump-backed, eight-legged demon oozing around the fiery depths of Hell." A little stab of victory spread warmth in Moira's heart when white spots appeared at the corners of Lucy's scarlet lips. She could swear she caught the flash of a grin on Nick's face as he made his way over to a walk-in closet twice the size of her entire shack back in Stump Bayou. "While we're on the subject," Moira continued, "do you have to have them boots made special? What do they call them guys that shoe horses?"

"Ferriers," Nick called from the closet. He leaned into view, a long, cut body clad in slacks that made his butt look like two scoops of ice cream and a white T-shirt that didn't so much fit as worship his torso.

"But shoeing cloven-hooved animals isn't customary in many cultures."

"Huh," Moira wondered aloud. "I'd have thought—"

A metallic *zip* prefaced Lucy's knee-length boot dropping to the floor. Her delicate, perfectly-shaped foot, toenails lacquered red to match her manicure, flexed at the cuff of her leather leggings. "Sorry to disappoint," she said.

Smaller than her own feet, Moira noted with instant dislike. Purtier too, though she'd always liked what she saw when she happened to look down while she was ambling barefoot down the oyster-shell backroads nearest her shack. Maybe there was something to these pedicures Aerin was always jawing at her about.

Thinking her sister's name awoke an ache deep around Moira's heart. They'd just started getting used to each other. Bonding over fried chicken and decapi-tatin' zombies and such. It had been weeks since Moira thought about sawing all the heels off Aerin's shoes or using one of them fancy suits she liked to make a patch-work quilt.

And now...Now she saw Aerin only through a shifting mist. The kind of dark, damp wall of fog the bayou would throw off sometimes in winters. And it was growin', this thing. Taking a little more and more of Aerin and Claire every day.

Moira was pretty damn sure the fair-haired minx admiring her own foot like it was the Mona Lisa had something to do with it.

"Well sure they look normal *now*," Moira said with exaggerated speculation. "But I bet if you shed that skin suit you've got aholt of, you'd be just as ugly as sin itself. Big old horns, fur, little black goatee, one of them chins looks like a ballsack..."

For a split second, flame flickered in Lucy's blue eyes, doused just as quickly by the sight of Nick Kingswood swaggering out of his closet, tightening his tie.

A small movement, but carried out with the same unstudied precision Uncle Sal used baitin' a hook. Something he could do with both eyes closed and one hand curled around the neck of a moonshine bottle.

She felt Nicholas Kingswood's age then. The dizzying sense that long before tightening his tie and picking up his briefcase, he'd closed the helmet on his suit of armor and hefted an axe.

"He's fun to look at, isn't he?" Lucy asked, her voice dreamy with admiration.

"Can't disagree with you on that point I s'pose," Moira admitted. Or, she could, but she'd be outright lying, something she tried not to do as a general rule. She remembered her first encounter with him within the confines of the airplane's first class cabin. Stealing glances at his long, powerful thighs and patrician profile from beneath her dark lashes as she'd feigned sleep. They sure didn't make men like that where she'd come from. Not Stump Bayou, where dentistry on long fishing trips as often as not involved a pair of pliers still smudged with engine grease and an extra slug of whiskey for the pain.

"But then, you've never seen him the way *I've* seen him." Lucy unzipped her other boot and let it fall to the floor before rising from her chair. Without her six-inch slut-boots, she looked diminutive next to Conquest's towering body and had to reach up to run her claws down the length of Nick's tie.

"Should we tell her about some of our more daring, exploits, darling?" Lucy suggested. "How I fucked you to victory in the Austrian-Ottoman wars? Or about the evenings we spent demonstrating every sexual position we'd invented for that Vātsyāyana fellow? Lovely little book he wrote about it, the *Kama Sutra*. Or perhaps how after the Iberian war, you bent me over a pile of the defeated and—"

"Is this the part where I'm s'posed to get jealous?" Moira asked. "Cause I got to tell you, all that yakkin' of yours ain't giving me much more than a headache."

Lucy's knuckles whitened as her grip tightened on Nick's tie.

"I think perhaps you ought to leave us for a chat, Nicky darling. A little...*girl* talk."

"These are *my* quarters," Nick insisted, brushing Lucy's hands from his tie. "I will not—"

"You will do exactly as I say, or I will make chitlins from this water witch's intestines before you've had the chance to break her will."

Nick's eyes drank darkness from the burnished cherry wood around him. Muscles bunched at his jaw. He looked to Moira, hoping—she suspected—for some kind of pleading *don't leave me alone with her* glance. She wouldn't give him the satisfaction, as much as her mind might be repeating that very thing.

So much for that.

He turned on the heel of his loafer and slammed the door on the way out.

"There now." Lucy sauntered over to the bed and seated herself cross-legged in the indentation at Moira's hip, casual as a college co-ed at a dorm slumber party. "You and I can really get to know one another."

Moira raised an eyebrow at her. "All I need to know about you I learned from Reverend Dupuis over the Sunday service pulpit. And just for future reference, girl talk don't usually start with threats of disembowelment. I ain't sure if you're aware, but the reason it's called *girl* talk in the first place is on account that the ones talking are girls. Not a prisoner chained to someone's bed and the Evil One acting like we're besties or BFFs or whatever the hell y'all call friends in these parts."

Lucy's delicate brows drew together in surprise. "Out of all your sisters, I had hoped that you and I might be able to understand each other best."

"How do you figure?"

"Well, we both know what it's like to be persecuted by other women, for one. You were born with the power to heal. I was created to maintain balance in the world. And yet, the very world we try to protect scorns us for the method we employ in trying to achieve our purpose."

Moira snorted. "Having your goons kidnap me and that backstabbing Judas Justine ain't quite the same as humping the hurt out of somebody."

"Perhaps." Lucy looked down at the pointed tip of one nail. "If you have the luxury of not knowing what I know. Your sister now carries within her an abomination that could be the ruin of not only this world, but countless others. As much as you and your sisters would like to ignore that fact, I cannot."

"Getting knocked up ain't the end of the world. Hell, where I come from, they have a maternity line of the caps and gowns on account of half the graduatin' class being—"

"Tierra's being pregnant isn't the problem," Lucy

said. Four inches of smooth cleavage just about pressed against Moira's cheek as Lucifer leaned in to adjust the pillows behind her shoulders. The extra support released a spot that had been gathering tension, and a pleasant burning slid down Moira's arm. "Men." Lucy's pale gold curls tossed as she shook her head. "Sometimes I think they haven't the slightest idea how to make a woman feel comfortable."

On this too, Moira felt herself agree, though she wasn't about to admit it.

"As I was saying," Lucy continued. "It's not Tierra being pregnant that's the issue. It's *what* she's carrying."

"I think they call them *babies*," Moira said. "And I s'pose they can be a kind of nuisance what with the spittin' up and the poopin' all the damn time and the hollerin' for a tit at all hours of the night. I sure seen some rough-lookin' offspring in my day too. When Skunky knocked up Ruby

Lee, I swear I damn near peeked in its diaper to look for a tail—"

"The antichrist!" Red blotches appeared high on Lucy's cheeks as she massaged her temples with slim fingertips.

Moira smiled inwardly. If there was one skill she had perfected under Nick Kingswood's liquid whiskey gaze, it had been the art of annoying the ever-loving shit out of someone bent on makin' you *ooh* and *ahhh* with their flat pronunciations of doom and disaster.

Lucy took a deep breath and arranged her features into an expression of concern as she began again. "Your sister is carrying the antichrist."

$$\textbf{\textit{\textasciitilde}}\ \ 4\ \ \textbf{\textit{\textasciitilde}}$$

Nick stormed across the vaulted expanse of the living room in the compound that had become their de facto base of operations since the First Seal's breaking. He strode straight for the front door, keys to his Ferrari 458 Italia grasped tight enough to dig into his palm.

"Where the fuck do you think you're going? And why does your head look like it got caught in a vice grip?" Dru had momentarily halted his pacing to glower at Nick from his post at the fireplace, now empty, but sporting soot-blackened stone walls as dark and impenetrable as the gaze War fixed on him.

"First, I have an errand to run. Second, none of your fucking business."

"What errand would that be, pray tell?" Artfully sprawled across the chaise like a poet in the severe throes of writer's block—or extreme intestinal distress—Julian Roarke, pale as the plague victims he had once infected, looked up from the heavy book on his lap.

"It doesn't concern you," Nick answered, his grip tightening on his keys.

"You've found a way to get rid of Lucy?" Dru suggested.

"No."

"You were on the point of disposing of the water witch and remembered that you had regrettably left your bow and arrow in the boot of your vehicle?" Julian pushed a silver-black lock of hair back from his sharp cheekbone with a gloved hand.

"No."

"You've devised a new solution to dispose of the horde of zombies that fucking bitch of an air witch sent to decorate our lawn like a bunch of undead plastic flamingos?" Dru asked.

All three men looked through the oversized floor-to-ceiling window to the thick underbrush and pine trees beyond their shared home.

Disembodied limbs hung from the trees like grisly garlands. Appendages clung to the branches and partially crushed or cleaved heads poked up through the grass like some kind of macabre Easter egg hunt. These remains seemed dedicated to stand—or hang, or loll—guard while their more intact colleagues had shambled off to accomplish an as of yet unknown request at their mistress's bidding.

Julian cleared his throat. "I would prefer you refrain from using such language when discussing matters pertaining to Aerin de Moray." The tone of Pestilence's voice suggested that this polite request was anything but. His pale blue eyes rose from the book on his lap to deliver a glacial warning to Dru.

Dru's shoulders squared within his fitted black T-shirt. "So you'll lead her into an ambush, but you'll get your knickers in a wad when someone uses *dirty words* in conjunction with her name?"

"Like you haven't *besmirched* Claire's name, Jules," Nick tossed out, hoping to fan the flames of their mutual dislike so he could inch unnoticed toward the door.

War advanced toward the chaise with thunderous steps. "You were talking shit about Claire?"

"I can assure you, I am not now, nor have I ever

talked—" Nick watched Julian's elegant mouth try and fail to shape itself into the vulgarity "—in a negative manner about Sinclaire de Moray."

"Really?" Nick prodded, daring another couple steps toward the door. "So what would you call that whole discussion we had about Claire's *ghastly unfeminine leathers* making her the ideal candidate for destruction? 'To rid the world of such an eyesore,' I believe you said."

The thick volume on Julian's lap slid to the floor with a heavy *whump* as Dru closed the space between them in three strides and hoisted Pestilence by his ascot, pinning him against the wall.

Nick chose that moment to make a break for it, but only got as far as the kitchen counter before Julian's voice froze him in place. "*Nicholas.*"

Dru's fist reared back in line with Julian's fine, aquiline nose, the muscles of his forearm bunched, cocked, and ready to deliver the blow.

Julian's expression remained unperturbed and stoic, even under the threat of violence. Nick had the displeasure of knowing his brother's lack of reaction had nothing to do with overconfidence or failure to understand aggression's finer points. Julian Roarke had simply seen suffering and death on such horrific levels that being punched in the nose didn't carry the emotional or psychic resonance required to physically move in self-defense.

"Should you desire a permanent case of testicular hemochromatosis, then by all means, continue, Drustan. But, I can assure you, I did not, at any time, make such comments about your paramour."

"What's he talking about Nick?" Dru asked, unwilling to wrest his gaze from Julian's lest his sack be stricken with plague on the sly.

"Fucked if I know," Nick said.

"You know very well which de Moray's choice of

clothing I find objectionable, and your efforts to mis-represent my statement is only further proof of your attempt to sow enmity between Dru and me so you can quit the premises unmarked."

Gods-damned fucking English accent. Julian Roarke could lend the reading of the *Malleus Maleficarum* an air of wholesome respectability.

"Do I need to punch this motherfucker or not?" Dru asked, pointblank, casting his dark eyes on Nick.

"Not," Nick admitted grudgingly.

Dru released Julian, who smoothed his ascot before settling back onto the chaise and retrieving his book. The few shoulder-length hairs that had escaped the queue Julian wore at the nape of his neck were likewise tucked back into place before Julian turned a thin vellum page. "Now then, Nicholas. Where were you off to in such a clandestine manner? Under normal circum-stances, I would assume you were off to a meeting with the water witch, but as she is presently chained to your bed, I'm going to presume your motivation lies elsewhere."

"I think you presume correctly," Dru added, circling Nick from a distance.

Julian glanced up at the grandfather clock near the mantel. "I wonder where Nicholas Kingswood would be hurrying off to at half-past seven in the morning. Were we not agreed that you would kill the water witch as soon as you *broke her*—if I may borrow your parlance?"

"We were," Nick said.

"And wasn't it you who said you'd have broken her before the clock struck midnight last evening?"

"He did say that," Dru confirmed, folding his arms across his broad torso.

"And when we expressed our doubts that this could be accomplished in such a brief timeframe without sig-nificant effort on your part, did you not say that the only *part* you'd need would be..." Julian hesitated, looking to Dru for back up.

"Right here," War said, cupping his package.

"Thank you, Drustan." Julian slid a leather bookmark between the large tome's pages. "Am I to assume that your plans went awry?"

"Gentlemen," Nick said with a heavy sigh, "have *any* of our plans for dealing with the de Moray witches up until this point *not* gone awry?" Both War and Pestilence remained silent.

"I was blasted by a thirty-foot wall of water, Dru had his sword stolen and has been thrown over for a zombie, the most lethal immortal in the world couldn't manage to off an east coast cloud company CEO, and Killian Bane, Death himself, has been cast down to *Hell* by the earth witch whom he knocked up. I think it would be fair to say that all our plans to date have been about as successful as the time Billy No-Arms Babineaux tried to jerk off."

A crease appeared between Julian's dark brows. "Did you...did you just employ a hillbilly colloquial anecdote? If you can't kill Moira de Moray, at least assure me you won't be adopting her ear-bloodying accent as well."

"Her accent is the least of our worries, *Jules*," Nick said, knowing how severely this irritated the refined scholar. "She's growing stronger. They all are."

"And would this explain the *errand* you felt compelled to undertake?" Julian asked.

"Since when did I need your permission to leave the house?" Nick's keys bit into the backs of his knuckles. "Did I sit there and give you the third fucking degree when you snuck off to let Aerin rape your encyclopedic brain about zombies?"

Julian lifted one eyebrow—his understated equivalent of complete, wordless shock.

"Yeah. I knew. We all knew."

Julian looked to Dru, who nodded his dark head.

"I'll be deuced." Julian shut his book sharply, the resulting puff of air rippling his loose silk shirt. "I thought myself fairly skilled in surreptitious machinations."

"Try planning a battle sometime." Dru had seated himself on the long leather couch, knees spread lax in their faded fatigue pants. "Covert maneuvers are *our* specialty, brother."

"Does walking across the goddamn living room and grabbing my keys seem like a covert maneuver to either of you? I just need to go somewhere."

"It's your hesitance to share your destination with us that has engendered our suspicions, Nicholas," Pestilence pointed out. "If it's a simple errand, why be so evasive regarding the details?"

Nick's empty stomach churned with an acid mix of rage and irritation. They weren't going to let this go. "Grrrss," he grumbled.

"Come again?" Julian asked.

"Yeah," Dru piped up. "I'm afraid we didn't catch—"

"Grits! I'm going to buy some fucking grits, okay? And some butter, and some cheese. You happy now, you nosy fucking pricks?"

"Aww," Dru mocked. "Conquest is going to make his water witch a nice breakfast. Are you sure you don't want to throw some biscuits and gravy in there too? I hear those backwater Southern broads eat that shit right up."

Nick had no recollection of having crossed the room or leaping onto the couch. His first conscious memory after Dru's comment was the sensation of War's teeth biting into Nick's knuckles through the flesh of his lip. His fist rained down again, connecting with Dru's cheekbone as an unforeseen haymaker caught Nick's temple, releasing firework bursts of a kaleidoscope cosmos behind his eyelids. He swung blindly then, but managed to land a solid right just below Dru's chin, rewarded with the hollow echoing crack of a trachea. War gagged, then coughed wetly.

Nick had threatened to punch people in the throat before, but never actually done it.

Dru's knee jammed upward, catching Nick's inner thigh, mere millimeters from a far more serious hit. Both of Nick's hands found the weak spot on Dru's neck and squeezed, releasing a rattling gasp.

"Get. The fuck. Off. Me." War choked through teeth coated in blood from his split lip.

"You will *never* again refer to Moira as dumb, you brainless *fuck*." Nick's thumbs dug deeper into the tanned, stubbled flesh of his brother's neck. "You understand me?"

"Now, boys. If you insist on engaging in these kinds of pissing contests, I demand that you at least make them useful."

That voice. Perhaps the only voice in all creation capable of freezing both War and Conquest mid-fight.

Julian alone did not look up, thumbing another page in his book.

"Nicholas, get off your brother, and go sit down like a good boy. I have a matter I would like to discuss with all three of you."

Nick grudgingly untangled himself from Dru and took a seat at the far end of the couch. Dru wiped the blood from his lip with the back of his hand and righted himself on the sofa. These dust-ups were neither unusual nor infrequent. Bring War and Conquest in close contact with one another, and they were just as likely to soil the field with each other's blood as they were their enemy's. The addition of females to fight about or fight over introduced an entirely different element. One Nick was neither pleased about nor eager to contemplate further.

No longer barefoot, Lucy beat a stern rhythm across the wood floor in her black leather boots. Rather than seat herself in the empty spot on the couch between them, she settled into Dru's lap like he was some sort of surly, tattooed armchair.

"Well, we seem to have a serious problem on our hands," she said.

"And other appendages," Julian tossed out, casting a pointed look at Dru.

"I'll let that slide for the moment, Julian, but I would suggest that you not test my patience today. I'm afraid it's rather thin at present."

"Moira decide against becoming your BFF then?" Nick asked. He'd had a vague idea of what Lucy might have had in mind when she'd dismissed him from his own room. When Moira had shot him a defiant look pre-departure, he'd had to fight off a fond—no, not *fond* —he immediately corrected himself. A *knowing* smile. If Lucy thought her odds would be better with a simple Southern girl than they had been with the power-hungry air witch, she was more wrong than tentacles on a housecat.

Jesus Christ. Where the fuck had that expression come from?

"She was...resistant, yes. But, she has some qualities I think we might find useful."

"Such as?" Nick asked.

"Such as, she considers her life to be worth far less than that of her sisters," Lucy announced casually as she picked threads from a hole at the knee of Drustan's fatigue pants.

"She told you that?" Nick kept his jaw from dropping by a sheer effort of will.

"She didn't have to," Lucy said. "I'm a woman. Women sense these things about each other."

"As do Leviathans, apparently," Julian muttered under his breath.

"What was that, darling?" Lucy asked, her attention shifting to him abruptly.

"Nothing." He offered her a frosty smile. "Just cross-referencing the Talmudic accounts of mythological beasts with the Apocrypha."

"Right." Lucy's red-lipped smile thinned considerably. "Perhaps you ought to limit your comments unless you have something useful to bring to this conversation."

"I beg your pardon," Julian said, hand over ascot. "Of course."

"As I was saying, the water witch's belief that her life is not as valuable as the lives of her sisters is something we might be able to work with." Lucy absently stroked the length of Dru's muscled thigh. "I believe we might be able to use it to solve *both* problems at hand."

"I was under the impression that stopping the Apocalypse was sort of the only problem at hand," Nick said.

"Which will be quite impossible for you to accomplish without the fourth of your number," Lucy explained. "Poor, poor Killian." She shook her head, a gesture utterly devoid of feeling. As always, Lucy appeared to Nick as a mask without a face.

"If he is indeed in Hell," Julian said, putting his book aside at last, "wouldn't it be within your purview to free him?"

"I only wish it were that simple. You see, residency in Hell is permanent, no matter how you end up there. Unless..."

Lucy let the word hang there, tempting them all to ask the question she had been dancing around since she sat down.

Nick obliged her. "Unless what?"

"Unless Death makes a deal with the Devil." Lucy's smiled broadened. Her canine teeth were sharper than Nick remembered.

"Luckily for him, I already have some terms in mind."

"He'll never give you his firstborn," Dru said, shifting his weight beneath her. "I wouldn't even bother with that one."

"Don't you think I know that?" Lucy's elbows folded under her bosom in a defensive gesture.

"Already asked him, did you?" Julian's ice-blue gaze came to rest on her face.

"Maybe," she admitted.

"So what is it you want that could somehow also solve the problem of the impending Apocalypse?" Nick asked, rising from the couch, considering mixing a gigantic martini though noon Pacific Time was yet four hours away.

"It's exceedingly simple, Nicholas." Lucy pushed off of Dru's lap and stood in the center of the room, equidistant from three of the Four

Horsemen. "I want the water witch's soul."

❧ 5 ❧

Oh, the expressions on those handsome Horsemen's faces.

Lucy allowed herself the luxury of a laugh on her way up Water Street. Coming from other women, it would have been a giggle. Coming from her, the malevolent snigger caused everyone within a half-mile radius to take a sudden chill. The religious among them crossed themselves or uttered spontaneous, silent prayers for reasons unknown to them.

The expressions in question had not been surprise at her admission that she wanted the water witch's soul. Knowing her for as long as they had, this revelation hadn't exactly been a shock. She was the Devil, after all. Souls were kind of her thing. Souls, and expensive leather handbags and shoes designers actually paid her to wear.

No. The surprise had come from her announcement that she was dead serious about making the pissing contests useful. Once she had explained that she needed their urine as part of a witch-repellant perimeter she'd built around the compound, they had all blinked at her, wide-eyed and embarrassed as frat boys who had just heard the words "cavity search" uttered by a particularly foxy police officer.

Of course, that usually ended in the foxy police officer being a stripper, and the frat boys enjoying a personalized exhibition of T&A that they mostly wouldn't remember after they binge drank themselves into oblivion and passed out under the coffee table.

Unfortunately, that would not be the case for her Nicholas, Drustan, and Julian.

A delicious late summer evening breeze lifted her blond hair from her neck, setting the leaves to whispering around her. It had taken her the better part of the day to secure a perimeter around the Horsemen's compound much as the de Moray witches had secured their vomitously quaint Victorian home against the Horsemen.

Using the *samples* from Nicholas and Drustan—Julian had predictably refused to participate in anything so vulgar—among many other elements difficult for anyone but her to procure, she had done it, and done it well. Like it or not, there was no way any of Moira's sisters would succeed in coming within a quarter mile of the compound where she and the old bitch Justine were being held, though she knew they would try.

And now, using a couple tricks she had perfected millennia before it even occurred to the de Moray witches' parents to hump bareback, she intended to uncover their plans for doing so.

She stopped on the corner just outside the witches' protective wards, purposefully standing in a shadow where only her vague outline could be seen. She wore a pair of cutoff jeans, a tank top that showed plenty of boob, and Moira's own cheap rubber sandals. The last, she considered a significant sacrifice on her part.

Now came the real fun. Using the voice she'd stolen from that backwater slut. Well, not so much stolen. It was more of a *copy and paste* kind of proposition.

Moira had brought it on herself really. Had made one too many sly jabs at her, the Lord of *fucking* Darkness herself. Instead of bonding over their shared abilities and proclivities, Moira had insisted on insulting and contradicting her at every turn.

Until Lucy broke Nick's bedside lamp over her head. An impulsive move perhaps. Not ideal in terms of attempts at future bonding. But, extremely effective in shutting her up. As was what she had done next.

With one hand pressed against the water witch's blood-sticky temple in a gesture almost motherly, Lucy had uttered the words that would allow her to borrow Moira's voice. She'd ended the rite by kissing the witch's pillowed lips and drawing the breath from Moira's own lungs. The water witch's voice had felt like smoke and silk sliding down Lucy's throat.

She had pushed the hair away from Moira's temple so it wouldn't become clotted, slowly licking the water witch's blood from her fingers. It had been there, she had tasted it.

The self-loathing. The self-hatred. The shame. The deep, ravenous desire for acceptance. The gnawing fear of rejection.

All hideously self-destructive. All perfectly useful.

It was while she walked from the Horsemen's compound toward the de Moray home that Lucy had considered how best to use this information, and now, she had a pretty good idea.

Shrouded in shadow, Lucy clicked from her own voice over to Moira's, an action that reminded her of depressing the tab of one of those multiple colored pens yuppies had been so fond of in the 80's. Now blue, now black, now red, now Satan, now a water witch.

"Cheeto," she whispered on the wind. "Momma's home. Come on, baby. Come see momma."

Lucy pinpointed the exact second when the tiny pig heard his witch's summons. A burst of eager porcine energy reached out to her, and she could almost hear his little hooves pawing against the front door of the house across the street.

"All right, for fuck's sake. Hold your fucking wad," she heard a voice say, muffled through the wooden door. *Aerin*. Vicious dislike flared within Lucy. How she wanted to punish the air witch, the one who had tasted *her* Julian.

It would have to wait.

The door cracked open, and a blur of pink shot through, scarcely heeding the warning called after him.

"Stay in the yard, okay? The last thing we need is someone flattening you into a breakfast patty before we can figure out how to get Moira back."

Once the door closed, Cheeto nosed his way through a crack in the fence and sped across the street, only to pull up short when his small hooves clicked to a stop at Lucy's feet.

"Gotcha!" She seized the warm body, which started to squirm the instant Lucy's hands made contact with his skin. She tried to speak to him in low, soothing tones, but the fucking walking pork chop *knew*. He *knew* she wasn't Moira and his anger at being duped vibrated through all three-and-a-half pounds of pork clasped between her glassy nails. "Ugh. Let's get this over with then."

She grimaced at the feeling of his wet snout against her palm, but wanted to hold his maw closed lest any ill-timed squeals alerted the sisters prematurely.

"Hold still little piggy. This won't hurt me a bit," she whispered close to his velvety ear. And just as she'd slid into Sunny's tattooed and pierced body, so she slid into the body of this tiny pig, Moira's familiar, who could come and go from the de Moray house as he pleased.

Space between the cells of her immortal matter shrank, sinking into and below the skin, the subcutaneous layer of fat. Her body fusing itself with the pig's until there remained nothing visible of Lucy.

Only after the process was complete did the memory of being cast into a herd of swine return to her. That hadn't worked out so well.

This would be different. She could feel it already. For one, Lucy found the intelligence of Moira's familiar encouraging. He lacked the wild self-will that had driven those stupid beasts off a cliff and into the sea below, where they had drowned, and she had evaporated to reassemble herself elsewhere.

But there was something else she hadn't counted on. Resistance. This fucking piglet was actually *resisting* her presence in his body. Only when she caused him pain equivalent to a cattle prod to one of his plump pink ham cheeks did the pig yelp and scamper across the street and back toward the house, where she intended to listen most carefully to every word spoken inside.

Lucy pawed the front door with a hoof, deliberately fighting for control. Cheeto's heart expressed a longing to curl up on the porch swing, where he could watch for his *real* momma, though he hadn't thought this in so many words. The pig's desires registered as a lower frequency hum, deeper even than emotions she'd felt run through some humans.

"In or out? Out or in? What's it going to be, bacon bit? Because if you come inside, you're staying this time." Aerin de Moray's Louboutin patent leather pumps appeared at roughly eye level in the opened doorway, and for a brief moment, Lucy considered seeing if Cheeto had anything in his abominable intestines to squirt at them as she passed. But then, she would likely wind up booted back into the yard, which served her purposes not at all.

She scampered in and toward the kitchen, where she heard female voices escalating in tension.

The cat dozing lazily in the corner chair startled to all fours the second she caught Cheeto's scent, her back arched, tail puffed like a bottlebrush, a low, deep growl issuing from her throat. A paw swiped at Cheeto's snout, lightning-quick, and Lucy felt the stinging pain of the scratch.

"Jinx!" the earth witch scolded, scooping up her familiar. "What in the Goddess's name has gotten into you?"

Luckily, Lucy didn't have to figure out how to feign porcine terror. Cheeto did that all on his own—quaking from curly tail to snout, hurt and surprise registering in his mind. He thought the cat a friend of sorts, didn't understand why Jinx would want to hurt him.

You're welcome, Hamlet, Lucy thought. *It's better you learn now. Cats have no friends. Just enemies who haven't yet outlived their usefulness.*

Tierra took the cat out of the room, leaving only the air and fire witch at the table. Lucy sensed their familiars were elsewhere, though they likely didn't understand the cause as well as she did. The budding darkness in them would be as easy for their familiars to sense as it was for Lucy, and they would continue to distance themselves until the transformation was complete.

Which Lucy dearly hoped would be soon.

She took the opportunity to examine them both at length. After all, the water witch's soul might be the most convenient, but was it the most desirable?

Aerin, all well-composed graceful angles in her tailored black suit, her hair twisted into an elegant chignon at the base of her neck, silver eyes staring into some middle distance where Lucy guessed Julian might be riding Archimedes through an endless moonlit pasture. Lucy's gaze lingered on the air witch's mouth, an exact replica of the one she had pressed her lips to hours earlier, only Aerin's were slicked with lipstick the shade of a good chianti at sunset. Those lips had tasted *her* Julian. Had drunk the dark passion of his tortured soul on more than one occasion. She'd be damned—okay, *more* damned—if she would settle for another woman's memories of the experience she wanted for herself.

No. Aerin de Moray's cold-hearted soul wouldn't do.

Cheeto twitched, uncomfortable with the hate radiating from his own body in searing waves. Lucy turned her attention to Claire before she gave herself away.

The fire witch—whose fashion sense most closely resembled her own—wore skin-tight riding leathers and a tank top, her burgundy hair spilling loose around her shoulders, amber eyes pulling lambent golden hues from the lighter she flicked open and closed repeatedly. Her soul blazed forth in unparalleled fiery loveliness, but fire and heat were both in plentiful supply in Hell.

This soul was definitely too hot.

"Are you planning on stopping that anytime soon, or do I need to take it away and get you a more suitable toy?" The irritation in Aerin's voice was palpable. The kind of tension begging for even the tiniest incentive to be unleashed.

Claire flicked the lighter opened and closed once again. "It's a free country, last time I checked."

"Yeah, but it's my lighter, and it's Gucci." Aerin snatched it from her sister's hand and slid it into her blazer pocket. "You want something to flick, go buy a Bic."

"Did part of your broomstick get lodged up your ass?" Claire asked, folding her arms across her chest. "You've been a grade-A bitch ever since you decided to play with your zombie puppets."

"You mean the zombies that rebuilt our shed and attacked the Horsemen after *I* kept them from gnawing on our souls? Would *those* be the puppets you're referring to?" Aerin challenged, her eyes flashing almost white.

"Yep. Those puppets." Claire leaned back in her

chair, parking her motorcycle boots on the table in front of Aerin's coffee.

Coffee showing no signs of poisoning from the brimstone Lucy had snuck into the de Moray house with Gwen's assistance. Had they found it, then? Lucy's already foul mood took a sharp right toward murderous.

"If I remember correctly," Aerin bit back, "you were the one who threw up the wall of fire so I could cast the spell. I'm pretty sure *you* are the only one of us to date who has used magic *against* one of her sisters."

"It's not the spell I'm objecting to," Claire said. Orange sparks wheeled deep within the tawny depths of the fire witch's eyes. "It's that superior attitude you've had ever since."

"If anyone deserves to have a superior attitude, it would be me." Tierra swept into the room, the edge of her skirt brushing the floor, wrists jangling with bracelets and beads as she balanced an array of glass bottles against her growing bosom. Below this, her gently swelling belly pressed against a loose-fitting lacy top in eye-frying green.

Tierra de Moray's soul had entirely too much fiber and not nearly enough mischief for Lucy's liking.

And yet, the attendant shame of Lucy's recent loss to the spawn created by Death and this witch stung far worse than the scratch on the pig's snout.

Defeated by a fetus.

Lucy was in the process of attempting to use Cheeto's limited tongue articulation to utter a curse toward that belly when Tierra bent down and scooped Cheeto up with one hand under the pig's rounded haunches. "Come here, you. I'll mix up a batch of my figwort and lavender balm, and your little snout will be good as new." Tierra deposited the pig on the counter, allowing Lucy a better vantage to the witches at the table.

Aerin had turned toward Tierra, her shoulders stiff

within her suit coat. "And why would *you* be more deserving of a superior attitude?"

"Um, hello?" Tierra answered, stooping to dig through another shelf packed with bottles of dried herbs and tinctures. "The wand? The crown?"

Lucy felt the teasing tone in Tierra's declaration. Her sisters did not.

"Oh, here we go," Aerin said. "She comes back from having a joyfuck with Death riding the Stag Express, an animal that was probably disease-ridden, by the way, and she thinks she's fucking Queen of the Forest and Winner of Magic. Now her baby daddy is in Hell, which I'm pretty sure is about a bazillion times worse than being in prison." She paused to take a sip of her coffee, which Lucy suddenly wished more than anything she had been able to poison. "Talk to me when you have more money than God and have made a tableful of hardboiled Russian businessmen weep their apologies and send you a fruit basket."

"For the Goddess's sake, Aerin. I was teasing. Trying to lighten the mood. There is no way we're going to figure out how to get Moira and Aunt Justine back if we keep pecking at each other like this."

The kitchen fell silent save for the clinking of glass bottles and the rustling of dried herbs. "Here we are. Honeysuckle, buckthorn oil, goldenseal, brimst—ohmy-hell! There's brimstone in my calendula!" The earth witch gagged as she stumbled backward, falling against the counter behind her for support.

Claire's boots hit the wood floor as she scraped back from the table. "*Jesus.* I thought you'd found all of it!"

"I thought I had, too." Sweat bloomed on Tierra's brow and she lurched toward the sink and heaved vibrant *Exorcist*-quality green vomit down the drain. "Get it...beyond the wards."

"I got this." The laid-back male tone was a direct

contrast to the tense feminine voices peppering the kitchen with panic.

Blond-haired, blue-eyed Tommy ambled over to the cabinet and palmed the offending bottle, pausing briefly to cast a suspicious glance at Cheeto before shuffling out the front door.

"See?" Claire asked in a defensive pitch. "Undead or no, I bet you're glad he's still around."

Tierra rinsed her mouth with tap water and flipped on the disposal, tossing in a few nearby lemon wedges for good measure. "We'll need to do another cleansing spell to rid the house of the toxic resonance."

"We will. Don't worry." Aerin hovered behind Tierra, her perfectly manicured hand looking like an indecisive bird. Wanting to land on her sister's shoulder, the small of her back, but ultimately falling dead at her side.

Lucy drank in the delicious waves of negativity, growing stronger with every breath. While her attention lapsed, Cheeto made a beeline for compost scraps someone had scraped onto a single plate on the nearby cutting board. He was already snout-deep in a mix of baked potato skin, some kind of fermented cabbage, and a slimy tofu-pudding skin when Lucy jolted him hard enough to send him somersaulting tail over hooves backward onto the stove, where he knocked a—thankfully cold— teakettle onto the floor.

"What in the several fucks was that all about?" Aerin asked. "It's like he had a mini-pig seizure or something."

"Probably shock from the snout wound," Claire proposed.

"Could one of you put him on the dining room table? I just need a minute."

Behind Tierra's back, Claire and Aerin played a quick round of Rock, Paper, Scissors, with Claire producing a rock to Aerin's scissors.

Aerin slipped on a pair of yellow dishwashing gloves, muttering a string of curses that made Lucy hate her slightly less before approaching the kitchen island to lift Cheeto and transport him to the table.

"Don't squeeze him too hard," Claire warned. "Remember what happened after the tofu wraps."

"What about the tofu wraps?" Tierra asked, a dark eyebrow rising in suspicion.

"Nothing," Aerin insisted too quickly. "Just that he got into your geraniums that day you made them for lunch, and I'm pretty sure they made him gassy enough to melt a new hole in the ozone layer."

And a good liar. Lucy hadn't been kidding when she'd informed Julian Roarke that his little air witch was indeed the most like her of any of the de Moray sisters.

Tierra rinsed a rag in cool water and twisted out the excess before applying it to the back of her neck. A thick lock of her hair had fallen loose from the proliferation of flowered clips and combs she used to hold it in a loose bun at the crown of her head. She ignored this as she sliced off a thin nub of ginger root and stuck it under her tongue.

Thus reinforced, Tierra spent the next several minutes grinding a poultice in an old-fashioned mortar and pestle, the muscles working beneath her golden-tanned skin. This was a woman unafraid of laboring with her hands, and one who clearly enjoyed being in the out of doors.

"You about done with your magic salad dressing?" Aerin called. "I'm pretty sure Moira's mini-hog is eyeballing me over here."

Lucy quickly turned her gaze elsewhere, snuffling at the used linen napkins. Because...food smells, right? That's something a pig would do. She paused, snout-deep in napkins when an alarming rumble rolled through the pig's intestines.

Don't even think about it, she ordered the pig in no uncertain terms. *You will not do* that *with me in your body*.

"Also, I think he's actually *listening* to you," Claire pointed out. "I swear he understood what you said just now."

The front door opened, and a pale, long-limbed Tommy made his way back into the kitchen, bending to plant a kiss on Claire's head. She reached up and gently touched the hand he placed over her heart. "Call me if you need anything else, babe," he said.

Again, he looked at Cheeto. Just a split second, but eye contact and recognition crackled between them. His wavy blond head shook as he ascended the back stairs, as if he were having an argument with himself.

"Here we are," Tierra announced, whisking to the table with her mortar and pestle.

Lucy/Cheeto trotted over to her dutifully, even sitting still despite the roiling protest within the animal's gut as the earth witch lovingly applied green paste to the pig's snout with her fingers.

"Trouble is," Claire asked, "what's going to keep him from licking it off?"

Aerin, seated next to Tierra, sniffed in the pig's direction. "The fact that it smells like ass."

"He's a pig," Claire said. "You've seen the shit he'll eat."

Talk about something useful, you babbling bitches, Lucy silently ordered them, the smell of Tierra's green concoction stinging tears to the pig's eyes as a stab of pain bunched in his rudimentary belly. Lucy shuddered inwardly. *How crudely these animals were made.*

"Then I'll make more," Tierra answered with a defiant tilt to her chin. "What I would like to know is, why are we bickering over lighters and talking about gaseous pigs instead of figuring out how to get Moira back?"

Because I own your sisters, Lucy thought. *Or I will, soon enough. Every day, Moira shrinks from their minds, little by little. As do you, earth witch.*

Both Aerin and Claire stared at the tabletop, chastened.

"We went on a reconnaissance mission earlier to the Horsemen's compound," Aerin admitted. "After we forced you to lie down for a nap."

"What in the Goddess's name were you thinking?" Blood flooded Tierra's cheeks. "Do you think I want to end up with all three of my sisters kidnapped, or shot, or burned at the stake?" The memory turned the earth witch's eyes the green of an uncut emerald. "The two of you out there alone with the Four Horsemen and Lu...," Tierra stopped herself, searching for a suitable substitution. "That bitch from Hell on the loose—"

"Three," Claire amended, a half smirk tugging at one corner of her mouth. "Technically there are only Three Horsemen on the loose since you gave Death a first-class ticket to Hell."

"That was an accident. Mostly." Tierra blew out an exasperated breath and set Cheeto on the floor at her sandaled feet. Lucy struggled to hold his body still against the cacophony of aromas beckoning him. The trashcan he could tip over. A potted plant just within reach. A scattering of crumbs under the chairs. How the animal could seek after more food with this hideous burbling in his guts baffled and disgusted Lucy in equal measure.

"Moira's there," Aerin reported. "And she's alive. I could feel her emotional signature from a mile away. One part smart-ass and three parts pissed off."

Tierra's sigh of relief was audible.

"But," Aerin continued, "since she's being held in a house with *Three* Horsemen and the Devil and she's still alive, my guess is they're interested in more than just killing her, or they would have done it already."

Claire nodded her agreement.

"Do you know where she's being held? Did you get close enough to see her?" Tierra's questions had an edge of desperation honed by residual guilt, perhaps, as it was during her own trial-by-fire that Moira was kidnapped.

Aerin and Claire snagged gazes.

"That's the thing," Claire began. "We couldn't even get close.

They've done something to the area around the compound."

"What do you mean, *done something?*"

Cheeto's keen ears picked up the sound of Claire pulling her riding leathers up to her knee. She gently peeled away a bandage to reveal a nasty scrape running the length of her shin.

"I have matching accessories on both elbows," Claire reported.

Tierra's intake of breath was sudden and shocked. "What happened?"

"I took my bike for a little off-roading, and when I got about a quarter mile from the house, something knocked me back about twenty yards."

"Ditto," Aerin chimed in. "I have a bruise on my ass the size of Cambodia. Even via the sky, I got about as close as Claire and was blown off my broom. Luckily, I caught a couple branches on my way down. I'm pretty sure my ribs aren't broken." She poked a polished nail at the waist of her suit coat and winced through an unconvincing smile. "See? Totally fine."

"This has to be that heinous hell-bitch's doing." Cheeto started as Tierra abruptly shoved her chair back from the table. She started digging through her cabinets and cupboards like a woman possessed...a condition Lucy knew the symptoms of intimately.

"Tierra?" Aerin asked with uncharacteristic gentleness. "What're you doing?"

The earth witch said nothing. Only continued her

frenzied piling of bottles and ripping handfuls of herbs from their respective spots on her shelves.

Claire rose from her seat at the table and put a hand on her sister's shoulder. Tierra merely slipped it off and commenced dragging out stockpots and delicate swan-necked distilling apparatuses.

"Tierra, *stop*," Aerin ordered.

"I can't." Tierra's voice was thick as mud, heavy with unshed tears. "I have to fix Claire's shins, and your ribs, and Moira's—" Lucy watched from her position under the table as the earth witch's shoulders collapsed and she broke into back-breaking sobs.

Claire wrapped an arm around her sister's shaking shoulders and cast a narrow-eyed glance at Aerin behind Tierra's back. Aerin took her time rising from the table, apparently as nonplussed as Lucy was by Tierra's hysterics, but eventually shored her sister up from the opposite side, wrapping an arm around her waist.

"This is *not* your fault, Tierra," Claire insisted.

"Claire's absolutely right. Any one of us could have gotten knocked up by their respective Horsemen and brought on the Devil's wrath." Tierra's sobs ratcheted up to one long, ear-stabbing keen.

Claire pinched Aerin's arm behind Tierra's back and shot her a glare as searing as fire itself.

"What I meant was," Aerin restated, "you were being attacked by
Satan. I'm pretty sure no one in that situation could have prevented Moira from being kidnapped. Or Ambrosia's from being blown to bits."

The keening transformed to a wail that had every plant within the house dropping its leaves to the wood floor. Lucy had to restrain Cheeto's body from rushing to snaffle them up.

"You. Are not. Helping. Sister," Claire hissed below her breath.

"I'm sorry, okay? I sort of fired the HR director who

ordered me to sensitivity training," Aerin whispered back.

"Then shut up and *hug*," Claire ordered.

Awkwardly at first, then with growing confidence, the wind witch's arms wrapped around Tierra's waist, mimicking the posture Claire had assumed.

"It will be okay, Tierra," Claire reassured her sister, tightening her embrace. "We'll find a way to get Moira back."

"We will," Aerin agreed. "We're much more powerful as four. I'm not about to let that moping Judas Julian rob me of such an important asset. And speaking of assets, Ambrosia's online earnings have totally outstripped the revenue from the physical location. I've been meaning to ask, did you have insurance on the store? We might actually *make* money on that old wreck of a building being reduced to ashes and—ow!"

Claire rewarded her sister with another pinch, high on the tender skin of her inner arm this time.

"I was just trying to say that there might be a silver lining to this whole thing," Aerin insisted. "We'll get Moira back, and we'll be better than we were before. Stronger."

Tierra allowed herself to be supported within the circle of their arms. "What would I do without you guys?" Her sobs had quieted to the occasional sniffle.

"Probably lead a totally normal zombie-free life," Claire suggested, which coaxed a contagious laugh from Tierra.

Waves of sickening sisterly love blasted Lucy like the irradiated shrapnel from an atomic explosion. A dark, gnawing pit opened in her stomach.

No. She'd divided them. Set them at odds against each other. Even moments ago, they had been at each other's throats. She could not allow this. She *would not* allow this. Couldn't *bear* it.

Lucy again summoned the electric pain she'd inflicted upon Cheeto earlier, and he shot out from under the table, emitting a terrific shriek and a burp of flames that flashed toward the bottom of Aerin's Armani pantsuit.

"What in the unholy fuck has gotten into that animal?" Aerin staggered backward, grabbing a kitchen towel to snap at the cuffs of her flaming pants.

Claire caught herself on the counter before the pig could plow her boots out from under her on his second charge around the table. "Are you sure there wasn't some mescaline or something in that goop?" she asked.

Tierra hopped up onto a chair and brandished a ladle, apparently not yet accustomed to keeping her wand on her at all times, a fact Lucy found herself immensely grateful for. "He might be having a reaction to the poultice. Maybe we should lock him in the shed. Just until the side effects wear off?"

"Side effects?" Aerin's voice had entered the higher end of the spectrum of human hearing. "Since when has fucking red glowing eyes been a *side effect?*"

Claire looked to Aerin. "If I didn't know better, I'd say he's—"

"Possessed." They all spoke the word at once.

A pregnant pause descended upon the de Moray household. That split second where each sister decided whether they were willing to sacrifice Moira's familiar for the chance to strike out at Lucy.

Lucy had no intention of hanging around to find out. Using a dizzying burst of power, she launched Cheeto's body through the plate glass window over the sink and greeted her mother night in a shower of tinkling shards.

The pig's body hit the ground hard, frightening him and jarring his intestines. The impact evicted a startled squeal and Lucy felt something else break free...something she fought to suppress so she could separate herself from the pig before—

FRRRRRRRP!

The audible flatulence blew from the pig's hindquarters, igniting in a jet of blue flame. Lucy fought against the sudden force of eviction, of this magic animal's natural reaction against her unnatural presence within it. All at once, she was rolling ass over teakettle across the lawn, landing in a heap at the curb.

Cheeto regarded her, his snout high in the evening breeze as he pranced toward the front door, his curly tail held aloft like a flag of victory.

Lucifer, Daughter of the Morning, the Adversary and Deceiver, stood and dusted herself off. Since this possession wasn't human, she didn't have to count it, right?

And if she didn't have to count it, she would never have to utter the phrase *exorcism by pig fart*.

Lucy held her blond head high as she walked across the street, the rhythmic slap of the water witch's flip-flops marking her passage.

Never had she been quite so grateful that she made her home in the bowels of Hell and *not* in the bowels of swine.

6

Moira awoke still chained to Nicholas Kingswood's bed with her cheek stuck to a glossy magazine and a headache fatter than the hemorrhoids on a hog. The serrated edges of newspapers brushed her bare thighs. Her calves and elbows bristled against the smooth, sharp edges of sensational rags that were always claiming Elvis up and moved to Boca Raton and was working as a short order cook somewhere.

Truth to tell, she'd slept on worse.

The bed of Uncle Sal's truck for one. That time Uncle Sal had damn near burned down the shack she'd grown up in trying to brew some moonshine with a Dutch oven and a healthy measure of lighter fluid. Camping he'd called it, as they watched the moon play hide-and-seek among the cypress trees and scribble the bayou with a disk of shimmering silver.

She'd woken up astride her share of men when healing them took a mite too much energy out of her and she'd collapsed mid-hump. Always awkward, waking up on someone whose nickname involved missing body parts or teeth you could count on one hand.

Then there were the times she'd awoken face-down on the bayou's surface, her hair tangling with the moss, startling some poor fisherman so bad he'd nearly filled his waders with last night's gumbo when he discovered she was still alive. She'd once floated as far as Lake Pontchartrain where a Coast Guard diver in a wet suit fished her out and insisted on giving her mouth-to-mouth long after she'd informed him she was just fine.

Just a few spells of sleepwalking, Uncle Sal had insisted, tears of relief funneling into the sun-weathered wrinkles at the corners of his tobacco-brown eyes. Moira hadn't the heart to disabuse him of the notion. To inform him that most of the time, she wasn't quite sure why she existed at all. That something deeper than the fossils below the bayou mud whispered nightly to her of sweet oblivion.

Until a much louder whisper had called her here to Port Townsend, where things had gotten awful weird, and according to the papers around her, the world was beginning to notice.

"Plague of fish descends on Port Townsend!" The *Port Townsend Leader* headline screamed. "Locals fear the worst in a chain of recent freak events."

"Rash of Violent Attacks Continues Across the U.S." Tagline: "Undead or Unexplainable?" This one? Only in the *New York*-goddamned-*Times*.

But it was the tabloids that sent cockroaches skittering through Moira's blood. Apparently, the *Washington Watchtower* had taken a particular interest in the de Moray sisters themselves. Almost as if they had been…tipped off.

"Sinister Sisters at fault for trouble in Port Townsend?" Below it, a picture of all four de Moray sisters scrambling to gather the downpour of fish. Whoever it was had caught Moira with both hands in the air, summoning moisture from the sky to keep the fish from drying out. From the angle and distance, the photo had been snapped hastily from across the street.

And it wasn't the only one.

A blurry shot of Aerin on her broom, coupled with the headline, "Witch Takes a Wicked Ride Through Port Townsend!"

But Lucy had saved the worst for last. Closest to Moira's face, unfolded so she could read the entire article, was a full front-page feature. Front and center, a candid photo of Tierra, blissfully trimming herbs in her garden, her growing bump clearly visible through her light floral sundress. "Witchy sister pregnant with the Antichrist?"

Moira skimmed the lines of type, blinking against her pulsing headache, her gaze snagging on a quote from "noted demonologist and modern-day witch hunter Reverend Bill Blanding:"

"I've been saying it for years but my words have gone unheeded. The end of days is upon us, and it is only if the evil among us has been rooted out and destroyed that we might enjoy another season upon the earth. The battle has begun, and I, for one, don't intend on staying idle while the Devil makes the earth his playground."

"Get your pronouns straight, you pig's pecker," Moira grumbled.

Numb shock tingled from her fingers and toes straight through to her hammering heart.

All this time, they'd been so focused on fighting the Horsemen and dealing with the plagues each Seal had brought about that they had been blind to a bigger and much more dangerous picture.

And the question that came with it.

What would happen if the world knew who they were, and what they had done?

The implications of this thought had only begun to tease the edges of Moira's mind when the door rattled once on its hinges, flying open under the power of Drustan Geddes's boot. Expletives that would have made the saltiest catfish noodler blush to his britches streamed from his lips as he hauled a shrieking, biting Aunt Justine into the room and slung her into the chair Satan had occupied earlier. Before she'd decided to redecorate by busting a lamp over Moira's head.

Her aunt's arrival was about as welcome as a rash of ass boils before a ten-hour tent revival.

Up to this point, Moira had pert near forgotten that murderous hag had been nabbed too. Probably on account of she'd hoped Justine had died of fright the second War had slung her over his massive shoulder. Moira had never been that lucky.

Justine glared at her captor, hatred burning bright in her green eyes, her graying red hair wild and face pale with rage.

"Accuse *me* of foul deeds when *you* are the one poisoning our coven and cavorting with the Devil herself!" Aunt Justine spat in the face of War, and Moira had to grudgingly give her a couple points for accuracy as the wad hit him square between the eyes. He wiped it from his face with the back of his hand, and for a split second, Moira thought he might use the same hand to deliver a stinging blow to Justine's cheek.

He froze, charcoal-dark eyes seething with black flame as he gripped both chair arms instead and shoved his face within a hairsbreadth of hers.

"Say what you will, *witch*. I may have slaughtered men without number in battle, but at least I can confront whatever gods may be knowing I didn't attempt to *murder* three newborn babes."

Justine's face turned to ash, her expression stricken and scorched. Her mouth drew into a tight, white line as her gaze fell to the torn fabric of her dark, shapeless dress.

Dru took a step back and looked from Moira to Justine and back again. "'Divide and conquer,' Nick said. 'It will be the best strategy,' he said. I should have fucking known better."

"Because you underestimated what a royal red pain in the ass that ol' harpy can be?" Moira asked, hoping she might flatter herself into an ally.

"Because I fucking invented that strategy. And in this case, divide and conquer isn't going to cut it."

"How's that?" Moira summoned what she hoped to be a look of genuine curiosity.

"Because two bitches in Nick's room means no bitches in mine." He turned his broad back to them and stormed toward the door.

"Hey, Mister?" Moira called after him.

"What?" Dru asked through gritted teeth.

"Look, I know you're War and all and probably know what it feels like to pave garden paths with the skulls of your enemies, but could you please, *please* not leave me alone with her?"

"You should be thanking me, water witch, for allowing you the company."

"And I can certainly see your point," Moira agreed quickly. "Only I hate her guts and she hates mine, so probably we'd be better off separate. See?"

War's slow smile sent prickles of fear straight up the back of Moira's neck.

"Well then, I'll be sure to leave you two together for a long, long time. Give you plenty of opportunity to work out your differences." With that, he quit the room, slamming the broken door behind him.

Moira exhaled through her nose and thought she might have seen just a touch of steam. "Fan-fuckin'-tastic. Kidnapped. Chained to Conquest's bed. Busted upside the head with a lamp by Satan, and now I'm stuck in a room with Aunt Just-give-me-a-minute-to-kill-these-babies."

She waited for a sharp-tongued rejoinder of the kind Justine had just flung at Dru, but nothing came. Justine remained silent.

"You know what really chaps my ass?" Moira continued. "I tried to be a good person, you know? Didn't steal. Didn't lie. Never killed nobody. Didn't hardly cuss." Moira's reflection in the mirror above her head confronted her with a shrewd expression. "Okay, maybe that last one was a lie. But of all I ever done, I can't quite figure out what I did to deserve being locked up in a room with *you*."

Deafening silence filled every corner of Nick's cavernous quarters.

When Justine finally spoke, the sound was so low, so quiet, that at first, Moira wasn't sure she'd heard right. "Come again?"

"I don't," Aunt Justine whispered. Only then did Moira see the fat tears sliding from her aunt's red-rimmed eyes, landing like salty polka dots on the fabric of her dress.

"You don't *what*? Make any sense? I'll vouch for that right here and now."

"Hate you," Justine said. "Never have."

She spoke the words so tentatively, so carefully that Moira felt each one must have clawed their way up her throat.

"So the killin' and all, that just a hobby for you, then?" Moira asked. "Back where I come from, women of a certain age take up knitting or canning preserves. Hell, even bingo, if it'll keep you from turning the chicken-carving knife on your family."

Justine shifted in her chair, the iron shackles binding her wrists and feet making the movement more difficult. Her eyes grayed as they took in the newspapers and magazines surrounding Moira on the bed. Then she was staring past them, looking at nothing at all, fresh tears turning her eyes to glass, spilling crystals down her cheeks.

"I never wanted this." This phrase wasn't so much spoken as *torn* from Aunt Justine's throat on a harsh cry that gave Moira pause.

Her reply was gentler than it might have been even five minutes earlier. "You think I did?"

"I *loved* my sister." Aunt Justine had begun to sway forward. Slowly, gently, in time with her sobs. "I loved Mirelle more than *anything*." Her throat closed over, and the tears came faster then, streaming hot down Justine's chin and neck.

All at once, Moira could feel the deep well of pain they sprang from. Justine had loved her sister. She meant it. She felt it as deeply as anyone can feel anything.

"We knew of the prophecy," Justine continued. "We thought—*I* thought—we could keep you safe. Keep you hidden, until you were strong enough to show the world you were good. You were...good." Justine's face contorted into a mask of such grief that Moira's own vision began to blur with tears.

"But when you were born, and she was dying..." Justine shook her head violently, casting salty drops off her cheeks. "He promised.

Promised that if I gave him the babes, he would save your mother's life."

"*He*?" Moira asked, interrupting. "Who's *he*?"

Justine ignored the question entirely, sobbing openly, hiccupping air like a child. "I would have done anything for my sister. *Anything*. Do you understand?"

Moira looked into her aunt's watery eyes and saw there something she had never seen before. Something she thought Justine incapable of entirely.

Love.

Love of the kind Moira felt for Tierra. And Claire. And all right, tell the truth and shame the Devil because Moira hated that bitch anyhow, for Aerin, too.

"Is there anything you wouldn't do to save your sisters?" Justine asked, desperate now, searching Moira's face for salvation, for forgiveness.

The woman who had tried to kill her, now turning to her for absolution.

Butter-thick irony clogged Moira's chest. No matter what animosity she held for the old bat, Moira knew Justine's question had only one answer. She had known it the second she'd stood awkwardly on their front porch for the first time, ambushed by Tierra's embrace.

Until that moment, she had never, in her life, been hugged by a woman. Granted acceptance. Been fussed over and cared for by a nurturing female presence. And each new arrival had wrapped her in another layer of warmth that only a sister could give. Her blood. Her family.

Was there anything she wouldn't do to save her sisters?

Moira returned Justine's soul-rending stare and spoke the only answer that was true.

"No."

"Then you must understand." Justine slid out of her chair and clanked to the floor, kneeling as if in prayer. "I would give anything to take it back. To take away the hurt I've caused, the damage I've done. No one should have to choose between saving the ones they love or saving the world." Her face fell forward, muffling her continued sobs.

Moira *almost* wished she had a free hand so she could pat her aunt on the shoulder or get her a hanky before her dress turned into one giant snot rag.

Instead, she decided she ought to try for some answers while the layer of ice between them had been melted away by tears. "If family means so much to you, then how come you tried to kill me?"

Justine lifted her face to meet Moira's questioning gaze. "Because I knew once you four found each other, they would be coming for you." She cast a meaningful glance at the door Dru had kicked in. "And what they would do to you could be far, far worse than any quick and merciful rite the coven could perform."

"Well you didn't have to treat me like a sack of vomit-dipped dog shit from the moment I set foot in the house," Moira insisted. "If you were planning on offin' me anyway, the least you could have done is be civil before you turned me into a human pin cushion."

Aunt Justine's gaze fell to the floor. "No," she said. "I couldn't."

"Why not?" Moira challenged.

"Because if I let myself love you, there's no way I could have...could have..."

"Stuck a dagger in my guts to save the world?" Moira finished for her.

Justine nodded. "Don't you see? When Mirelle died, Tierra was the only one of you left. The only one I could save. I fought for her. Bled for her. I couldn't bear the thought of losing her too. But now..."

"Now we're right smack in the middle of a cluster fuck of Apocalyptic proportions."

"I would have given my life if it could have saved Mirelle. And if I could trade places with any of you, I would. If my death would suffice to end this, I'd march to the gallows this very second."

Moira had to look her in the eye again, to anchor herself in the truth she found there.

"But I can't." The grief overtook Justine then, little rivulets working down the furrows a lifetime of self-flagellation had dug into her cheeks. "I can't take back what I've done. I can't bring Mirelle back. And I can't stop what's begun."

"No," Moira agreed. "You can't." *But I can.*

She sank into these three words like a warm bath. Her whole body melted against the bed, slack-limbed and relaxed. For the first time in her whole life, she felt...peace.

Oblivion had sought her all her days, and now she

knew why. She was the one meant to die. And in her death, Tierra and her child, Aerin, Claire, and the world would be made safe again.

Healed, the way she'd always done.

And at last, at long last, she could finally heal herself. End her own pain. Bring to a close the decades-long debate in her head of why she'd been made at all.

The colors in the richly-appointed room suddenly radiated vibrant hues. The sun's warmth from the parted curtains made its way into her very soul until she was nothing but light. Complete. Whole. Perfect in her purpose.

"It will be all right, Aunt Justine," Moira said, surprising herself with the serene quality of her voice. "You just hush a while and rest. Everything's gonna be just fine."

Justine shook her head miserably. "How can you say that? How can you know?"

"Because I'm Moira Joule Malveaux de Moray," she answered, treating Aunt Justine to the widest grin she could muster. "And I know shit."

Her aunt's somber pallor cracked for a split second, and for a brief moment, Moira saw a much younger woman. A woman not borne down by a lifetime of guilt and self-loathing, of crushing blame and dread. A woman Moira might have resembled had Mirelle de Moray survived.

"Now don't think this excuses that whole attempted murder thing," Moira chided. "Might take me a bit to get over that still. I tend to get a little sensitive about people trying to kill me."

"I understand," Justine agreed. "And for what it's worth at this late hour, I'm sorry." Her voice broke on the word. "I'm so, so sorry, Moira."

"You keep bawlin' like that, you might could float us both out of here, bed and all."

Justine stifled a burp of sudden laughter through her tears just as the door to Nick's room swung open again.

"Drustan!" Nick roared. "What the fuck is *your* ward doing in *my* quarters?"

The sound of boots shuffling in the hall preceded War, roughly brushing past Nick into the room. "Because any longer and that bitch was in infinite danger of defenestration," Dru mumbled.

"You been reading Julian's big word books again, brother?" Nick asked.

"Really? You're going to give me shit *now*?" A vicious smirk slashed across Dru's face as he stepped back and looked Nick over head to foot.

And then Moira did the same.

Nicholas Kingswood was wearing an *apron*.

Nicholas Kingswood was wearing an apron and carrying a *tray*.

Nicholas Kingswood, Conquest, bender of wills and destroyer of civilizations was wearing and apron and carrying a tray laden with plates, a steaming mug of coffee, a rose in a slim vase, and a napkin shaped like a swan.

"Shut up and get her the fuck out of here," Nick ordered.

Drustin grudgingly crossed to Aunt Justine and pulled her up by the chain binding her arms behind her back, grabbing the chain between her feet for good measure. By the time he lifted her, she looked like someone had put her in one of those kinky sex swings... which, now she was thinking about it, Moira was almost sure Nick had hidden away somewhere in one of the many closets this room seemed to boast, if the mirror overhead was any indication.

Justine cast Moira one last meaningful glance. Worried. Guilty. Gutted.

Moira shook her head and smiled just as her Aunt was carried out the door. "That's all over now, Aunt Justine," she called after her. "Water under the fishing dock."

Nick kicked the door closed after him and still managed to walk through his own room like it was lined with the backs of peasants, apron or no.

"Don't think I'm gonna believe you've gone all domesticated on account of that apron. You and I both know you're only wearing it because you're too vain to get butter on that expensive tie you got there." Moira nodded toward the tie in question. Gray silk, more carefully tailored than Moira's hand-sewn prom dress, which was her only basis for comparison. Uncle Red's wife had her standing on a beer keg for the better part of a week while she measured and cut, sewed, and cursed. And also drank a fair amount of hooch, which probably accounted for one sleeve being a good six inches longer than the other. All the better to keep Lester Beliveau's sweaty palm from clutching her shoulder.

At least on one side.

"Here I am, bringing you three-cheese grits, coffee, homemade biscuits and sawmill gravy, and you're trying to provoke me?" Nick set the warm tray across Moira's legs.

She had to swallow against the rush of saliva that flash-flooded her mouth as the inviting scents of eggs and sausage tickled her nose.

Nick made quick work of clearing the newspapers and magazines from the coverlet, dumping them into a pile in the armchair. When he came to the side of the bed where the remnants of the broken lamp littered the floor, his eyes flicked to Moira, tightening with laser-like focus on the spot near her hairline where her skin felt stiff with dried blood.

The affected expression of congeniality fled Nick's face like a child's chalk drawing washed away by a downpour, his emotions all running together like the smudged pastel colors. Courtesy and rage. Pride and bloodlust.

"What the fuck happened here?" Nick did not blink as he waited for Moira's answer.

"I think I might have called your friend something like *Loose-Britches the Slutty Soul Sucker*. She wasn't especially appreciative of my creativity."

Nick knitted together curses in several languages while stalking off to his bathroom. Moira heard the tap running, but refrained from any spontaneous practice of water tricks, still hoping to gain access to the breakfast waiting on her thighs.

Nick returned and seated himself next to her on the bed, first applying a hot washrag to loosen the blood on her wound, then a cold compress to relieve the pain.

That Nick would know of battle wounds and how best to care for them made perfect sense to Moira. Why he would take the time to tend to her when her death was his ultimate goal did not.

The contradiction left her searching for familiar territory, which the tray helpfully provided.

"You fold that napkin yourself, did you?" Moira asked, looking at the perky linen swan investigating the bowl of cheese grits.

"I certainly did," Nick said proudly, tossing the washrags on the floor among the glass shards.

"How many YouTube videos did you have to watch before you got it right?"

There it was. The reddening of his skin just where his thick, brick-brown hair met his forehead. His whisky eyes darkening. That wicked mouth taking on a cast of cruelty Moira found far more arousing than she should. Lord, but he looked fine when he was angry.

"I was *taught* how to fold napkins by an exceptionally accommodating chambermaid at an all-night soirée given by Louis XIV, if you must know."

Moira craned forward toward the tray and regarded

the mound of green stems piled atop her omelet. "How come there's weeds on my eggs?"

Nick's color darkened from red to a charming mauve, and Moira had to bite back a smile.

"Those are *motherfucking radish microgreens*, and they are a *motherfucking garnish*."

"Ohhh," Moira said, feigning ignorance. She'd known that of course, as men far wealthier than Uncle Sal had found their way to her in Stump Bayou. Men smelling of leather and aftershave who had taken her as far as New Orleans to wine, dine, and '69 her. She'd healed them from impending heart attacks mostly, these men. And from the occasional spunk sack or ass cancer, and that Gonnaherpacephal AIDS they picked up from hookers sometimes. "Fancy. I might even like to eat it. Trouble is, some asshole chained me to this bed."

"Oh, but I've thought about that already," Nick said felicitously, picking up the spoon and scooping up a bite of the grits. Cheese stretched in tantalizing strings from bowl to spoon. "Open wide for me."

The grits were hot. The request was hotter. It brought to mind the exact length and girth she'd first snuck a peek at on their unintended flight together and let slide beneath her rain-slick palm when they had near-devoured each other on the dock. Moira was no stranger to men, but she *would* have to open wide to accommodate Nick Kingswood.

Very, very wide.

"You have got to be out of your mind." Her throat had gone dryer than a nun's twat. She eyed the dew-beaded glass of orange juice with growing lust.

"Come on, Moira. How bad do you want it?" Nick hovered the grits close enough for the steam to warm her mouth then dragged the spoon slowly, suggestively across her lower lip, at which point she snapped her jaws over it like a starving jackal.

"Thif doen't meam I like you," she informed him, her mouth closed around the spoon. Moira's eyes rolled back in her head as the buttery, cheesy, creamy grits melted on her tongue.

First came the memories.

Then came the tears.

Her ten-year-old self, grasshopper-skinny legs pulled up under her T-shirt to keep them warm. Sitting at the simple wooden table in their tiny shack's galley kitchen over a bowl of cheese grits Uncle Sal had made just for her. The fragrant steam curling into her face. Her uncle seated across from her, drinking muddy black coffee and poking a thumb hole in one of last night's biscuits to squeeze a golden pendant of cane syrup inside. He'd have preferred the grits, but there hadn't been enough for both of them. There never was, it seemed.

Nick paused with the spoon halfway to her mouth. "What is it?"

"It's kind of fitting," she said, head sunken into the pillow, feeling the twin streams slide down to dampen the hair at her temples. "That this should be my last meal."

"Last meal?" Nick asked. "What the fuck are you talking about, woman? You haven't surrendered. And until you surrender—"

"I surrender," Moira said, lifting her head to look Nick square in the eye. His volcanic amber and hers roiling ocean. "I need you to kill me.

Tonight."

7

Many had begged Nicholas Kingswood for death —a state he had gloried in delivering to them at the time of his choosing and by methods varied and cherished. The many weapons in his cabinets of curiosities bore silent witness to this.

Why then, did Moira's request fill him with sudden, unbearable rage?

'*Why?*' was a question he had asked himself more in Moira de Moray's presence than in any other circumstance he could resurrect in all his long years.

Why had he gone and purchased grits, microgreens, and *lard* for fuck's sake, when he could have simply made a minion of some simpleton in range and had it done for him?

Why had he commandeered the kitchen and spent the better part of an hour in front of a cast iron skillet whisking and sautéing? Cutting biscuits and gentling eggs into perfect custard creaminess for an omelet when he could have just picked up cheese grits at least five different places in town?

Why did it matter that he did these things with his own hands? That no one else be allowed to acquire and prepare these things for her? *Why* did he...

Care? A foreign voice in his head suggested.

He rejected the notion outright. No, not *care*.

Control.

He wanted to own every ounce of pleasure she derived from eating the food upon her lap. To arrange the plate the way *he* wanted it arranged. To deliver it to her when *he* felt it should be delivered.

And Moira would die when *he* decided she should die. She was, after all, *his* to conquer. He alone had been entrusted with the task, and he would not be commanded by anyone on this earth, above, or below it, to execute her before he was ready.

Not even Moira herself.

"You got locusts in your ears or something?" Moira asked. "I said, I surrender."

"No," Nick said. "You don't."

"Yes, I do. Honest to Goddess, cross my heart and hope to die."

The last part was true. Nick knew that much. "Surrender not accepted. This isn't the way it's supposed to happen."

"Yeah? Well I was supposed to work the Thursday night shift down at the HooDoo shack before I was summoned by some magic spell and learned that I'm one of four identical sisters prophesied to end the world. Life don't always work out the way it's supposed to, does it, Sugar?"

Nick boiled beneath his shirt collar, feeling his jugular vein throb in time with a heady mixture of anger and arousal.

"What happened to the woman who was too proud to allow me to buy her a drink on an airplane? The woman who spilled water in my lap to make it look like I pissed myself just for her own amusement? The woman who conjured a wave to drive me halfway to Canada after I'd just given her the first orgasm of her life? The woman who had the balls to put up a fucking fight?"

"She's fucking exhausted, all right?" Moira surged up to the extent of her chains and the coffee and juice sloshed over their edges, threatening to spill. "She's tired of hateful looks from every female on the planet. She's tired of people always wanting, always taking. She's tired of being a problem and never a solution. She's tired of being afraid." Her body sagged back against the bed, burdened by the weight of her words. "I said I surrender and I mean it. I. surr-en-der," she said, drawing out each syllable of the word as if speaking to a small child.

"You surrender?" Nick repeated, his voice dangerously low and quiet. He set the spoon back in the bowl of grits, noting the whiteness of his knuckles on the handle.

"You want me to get a note pad and spell it out for you? I give up. I give in. I'm done."

"*Fuck* your surrender!" Nick abruptly upended the tray, sending it toppling off Moira's outstretched legs, the orange juice and coffee painting brief arcs across the air before the glassware shattered on the floor. The silverware clanged among the shards.

Her smart mouth hung open in a perfect "O" of disbelief and shock as he leaned over her, gripping the headboard but not touching her as he brought his face close enough to catch the scent of rain and wild muscadines in her cascading hair.

"You don't know the meaning of the word, Moira de Moray".

"Trust me, Mr. Kingswood. I'm from the South. If there's one thing we know how to do, it's surrender."

Another thin attempt at levity. Nick refused to be distracted.

"You think you can throw a few cowardly excuses at me and I'll clamber to obey like one of your hang-dog backwater boyfriends?" A cracking sound heralded the headboard splintering beneath his grip. "You couldn't be more mistaken."

"Let me get this straight. Just this morning, it was all, 'Damn you woman, you will surrender!' And then I surrender, and now it's all 'You don't know the meaning of the word!' Would you tell me what the hell you want from me so we can move this along?"

Anger bloomed roses in her cheeks, the precise color of an ass slapped good and hard. A dark thrill rolled down Nick's abdominal muscles and drove blood into his cock.

"I said I wanted you to surrender to *me*. Not to the self-destructive thoughts in your own head or some half-baked savior complex you've convinced yourself is for the greater good."

Moira's ever-shifting oceanic eyes took on the dangerous blue-gray of waves whipped into a squall. Resentment radiated from her with the force of the tsunami she'd sent to rid herself of him the last time he'd dared speak a truth she didn't want to hear.

"Yes, you *tasted* me that day on the dock, Moira," Nick continued. "But I tasted you, too. I know what you hide beneath those smart-ass quips and your *I don't give a shit 'bout nothing* exterior. You may hate me because I'm an arrogant bastard who wants to own you, dominate you, and make you beg for the pleasure I want to give you. You may even hate me because you know that I'm willing to carry out what I was created to do even when my brothers are not. But here's the real kicker." He cupped her chin to turn it toward him, wanting to observe the delicate and subtle shifts in her fathomless eyes. "Deep in the engines of your mind, whatever loathing you may harbor for me *pales* in comparison to what you feel for yourself, and when you say 'I surrender' what you *really* mean is that you want me to relieve the burden of being you."

His verbal arrow had hit its mark. Blood drained

from Moira's face into some internal wound—one he'd had to cut through a lifetime of scar tissue to hit. And yet, behind the hurt, a small, blue flame of anger flickered, waiting to be fanned into rage.

The airless space between them vibrated in violent silence, the kind of preternatural quiet that only the last seconds before battle could bring.

"You want me to play executioner now that you've become your own judge and jury, Moira, but I am not yours to command."

"I'm not commanding you to kill me. I'm asking you. And pretty damned politely, too. But if you're *unable to perform*, I'd bet one of those brothers of yours out there just might be. I'd bet that big ol' hunk Dru would be more than happy to—"

A resounding crack as loud as a gunshot echoed through Nick's chambers, and the headboard behind Moira split down the middle. "None of my brothers would dare touch you. You belong to *me*."

"Then finish what you started when you shot the arrow that nearly killed my sister."

The pleading note in her voice scraped against his resolve like nails on the inside of a coffin, a sound Nick wished he did not know.

"I've got to think there would be something in it for you," she continued. "I mean, you'd get to be the one who ends the Apocalypse. Doesn't that get you a gold star or something?"

"I don't give a *fuck* about gold stars," Nick answered, lowering his mouth close to her ear. "But we can talk about the *or something*." He allowed himself to drink in this image of her, beginning with the wine-dark hair spilled on his pillow and ending in her delicate, shackled ankles and bare feet. "I *will* end you, Moira de Moray, as you ask, but on one condition." He savored the momentary flicker of fear in her eyes.

She was right to be afraid.

"What?" she asked.

Her ear was as warm and silky beneath his lips as a sun-rinsed shell on the beach.

"I will fuck you until you understand the true meaning of the word *surrender*. Then, and only then, will I kill you, Moira de Moray." He nipped at her earlobe, gratified by the involuntary answering shudder rolling through her body.

Moira turned her head and blinked at him. "I'm about to die, and you're really going to use that as an excuse to extort sex from me?"

"Absolutely," Nick said.

The disbelief written on her features amused and delighted him. If she believed this request depraved, she had much to learn about his tastes and sensibilities.

Teaching her would be a pure pleasure.

"Well, Moira?" Nick dragged a finger across the fullness of her breasts above the line of her tank top. "Yes?" he asked, pausing to draw an 'X' directly over her heart. "Or no?"

❦ 8 ❦

Is there anything you wouldn't do to save your sisters?

Aunt Justine's question rolled through Moira's head like thunder.

Moira hadn't necessarily reckoned that saving her sisters might include agreeing to do the horizontal hokey-pokey with one of the Four Horsemen of the Apocalypse. With Conquest himself, no less.

Not that she hadn't thought about it. Hell, she'd finished what they'd started on that rainy, windblown dock at least a hundred times in her mind, in dozens of dreams, and even a couple times in the hot respite of the claw-foot bathtub.

A girl had needs, after all.

Of course, it was damn near impossible to look at a man like Nick Kingswood and *not* think of what he'd be like in bed. Broad shouldered. Lean-hipped. Muscles cut by the gods' own chisel. But for Moira, it was more than that.

It was his liquid caramel eyes climbing the muscle of her thigh the way a general traces a territory to be conquered. His arrogant smirk and the knowledge it hid. Silent promises made by his sinfully sensuous mouth. The way he made any space he occupied belong to him with the brusque movement of his powerful body.

A powerful body now leaning over her, blotting out the world and making her dizzy, leaving her only with his question and the few breaths she could sneak into her tightening chest past her thundering heart.

She didn't look him in the eye. Couldn't, for fear he'd read the answer already written there. "What if I said yes, but had a condition of my own?" she asked.

"Name it," Nick ordered, his voice thick with desire.

"I want these shackles off," she said. "Since this is going to be my last time, I'd prefer not to be trussed up like a chicken for Sunday dinner."

When he didn't answer, she dared a look in his eyes and had to bite her tongue to stifle a gasp.

Nick's eyes glowed unnatural saffron orange.

Something had caught fire inside him.

How many had seen this same hue before meeting their end?

"I promise I won't try to escape or nothing, if that's what you're thinking. Girl Scout's honor," she claimed, even though she'd never in her childhood been accepted into a troop.

"Feel free to try and run from me, if it pleases you," Nick invited. "But I can save you some effort by letting you know now that you would not succeed."

"And what makes you so sure?" Moira challenged.

"No one ever has."

Why the finality of these words caused heat to gather between her thighs, Moira couldn't say.

Nick's chest rose and fell in deepening breaths. "So we have an accord then? If I unchain you, you agree to let me *fuck* you?"

Taking one steadying breath, Moira nodded.

"I need to hear you say it." Nick loomed above her, perfectly still, unwilling to make a single movement until he had extracted from her the words he wanted.

"Yes," Moira said.

"Yes *what?*"

Lord. This conceited motherfucker wanted her to say *all* of it. *In for a penny*, as Uncle Sal would say.

"Yes," Moira repeated. "If you unchain me, I agree to let you *fuck* me." Feeling irritated and more than a little brazen, she'd put as much emphasis on the word as he had. "In exchange for killing me," she added, purely to make certain they were clear on expectations. "I'll be damned if it doesn't sound like I'm getting the raw end of this deal."

Nick leaned close to brush his lips over her ear, releasing a riotous wave of goose bumps down her neck and shoulders.

"It will be more than your end of the deal that's *raw* by the time I'm done with you."

Moira was certain Nick could hear the rush of blood pounding in her ears as he planted a kiss on her wounded temple that was as tender as his words had been brutal.

Warmth spread into her cheeks and down her neck, tightening her nipples into painful buds beneath her tank top. And she waited. Waited for him to go retrieve a key. A crowbar. A butterknife. Hoping for even a moment free of his presence to mentally steel herself against whatever he had in store.

It was not to be.

Nick reached for the cuff at her wrist and pulled the metal apart, bicep and pectoral muscles straining against his finely tailored shirt, the shackle yielding with only the briefest sound of protest. It fell to the bed at her shoulder, and she looked up at him, knowing her face most likely bore a dopey mix of wonder and disbelief.

Only when Nick's index finger gently urged her bottom jaw closed did Moira realize her mouth had been hanging wide open.

"Show off," she retorted, feeling a little burst of

pride that she'd been able to subdue him earlier when such feats were within his repertoire.

He leaned across her body and repeated the same process on the shackle holding her other wrist.

Moira drew her arms into her chest, glorying in the feeling of unrestricted movement. She rolled her wrists and rubbed the pink, damp skin where the cuff had been. A thousand pinpricks needled her hands.

"Seems like an awful waste if you ask me," Moira said, filling the room's dense silence with insubstantial words.

"I didn't." Nick rose and walked to the foot of the bed where he broke the band around her left ankle as quickly as he had the others.

"I mean, you're just going to have to get you a new set next time you need to chain someone to your bed," she babbled. "Uncle Sal used plenty of chains down in his shop, and these don't look like the kind that'd be easy to replace is all."

"That's because they're irreplaceable." Nick rent the last band binding her to the chains but kept hold of her ankle with his hand. "A gift from the Marquis de Sade."

He gripped her opposite ankle, and for a moment, Moira thought it was to relieve the tingling as she had done for her own wrists...until Nick pulled her roughly to the end of the bed.

Splitting her legs, his hips plowed into her inner thighs with bruising force. Already, his desire hardened against her thin panties, the heat of it radiating through the fabric separating them.

The barrier disappeared as quickly as the shackles had, torn and discarded. As were her skirt and tank top in the seconds that followed.

Nick's eyes burned brighter as she lay naked on the bed before him, devouring every detail from breasts to belly button to the thatch of hair between her thighs.

"Roll on to your stomach," he ordered.

"But aren't you going to—"

He gripped the backs of her knees, rotating one leg over, flipping her onto her face. Nick's fist fastened around the hair at the nape of her neck. He yanked just hard enough to send a tingle of mingled pain and pleasure down Moira's spine.

"When I give you an order, you will obey me, Moira."

"*Obey* you? We didn't say nothing about—"

What happened next stunned her with an embarrassment she hadn't felt since her girlhood, when Uncle Sal took her over his knee for borrowing the fishing boat without asking.

Nick *spanked* her.

A hard, stinging slap on her right ass cheek. Moira bit down on the bedclothes to keep from crying out. She'd be damned if she'd give him the satisfaction of knowing her body answered with an unexpected clench of pleasure.

"You will do as you're told. Do you understand?" he demanded.

"I said you could fuck me," she ground out. "I didn't say you could—"

"You've spent enough time punishing yourself." His voice was as hard and sharp as a blade's edge. "Now, I will do it for you."

Another slap scorched her ass and, frightened by the rush of moisture between her thighs, Moira kicked out as hard as she could, unbalancing Nick just enough to wriggle from his grasp. She rolled to her back, scuttling backward to the headboard away from this dark part of herself as much as from the man who made her confront it.

The second she caught Nick's enflamed gaze, panic fluttered in Moira's heart as she saw her own mistake. She had run. Like prey.

Nick lunged for her, launching himself from the end

of the bed, his full weight coming down on her before she could find purchase against the cracked headboard. With her free hand, she slapped his face hard enough to feel the indentation of his cheekbone beneath her palm.

He caught her wrist in his iron grip, pinning it to the mattress as she bucked beneath him.

Whatever power she had enjoyed over him earlier had evaporated the second she had voiced her agreement to his terms.

"There," he growled into her ear. "There's the fight I was talking about. Without opposition, there can be no conquest. And oh, Moira, am I ever going to enjoy breaking you."

Had she heard that right? Was he saying that he actually *wanted* her to fight him?

"Fat fucking chance," she spat.

"You think it's just me?" Nick challenged. "You think I'm the only one who wants it this way?"

"What the hell are you talking about, you sick fucker?"

Nick rolled her out from under him until they were on their sides, her body held fast to his, his powerful legs wrapped around hers. With his hand still fastened on her wrist, Nick forced her fingers down to her own sex.

"Feel yourself," he whispered, forcing her legs wide with his own. "Feel how wet you are for me."

Moira's fingers slid into the slippery folds, shocked to find them drenched with her own desire. He guided her hand over the sensitive nub at the apex, and her body jerked with unexpected pleasure.

The knowledge came in the quickening of her nerve endings and the delicious ache scribing his name on the inside of her thighs. *This* was conquest. Coming up against an opponent who knew her so intimately, even her own strengths could be used in the fight against her.

A force so ancient, so brutally wise that yielding is not a requirement. She would be owned. Assimilated. Absorbed.

Nick brought her hand to his mouth, sucking each finger clean of her arousal with wicked, languorous movements of his tongue. "You may lie to me all you please, but your body will always speak the truth."

His truth was wedged between the cleft of her buttocks, pulsing in time with the beating of his heart. Nick shifted his weight until she was facedown on the mattress once more. He grabbed a handful of her hair and wound it around his wrist, effectively pinning her cheek against the smooth coverlet even as his forearm snaked under her hips and pulled her up to her knees.

The sound of his belt buckle clinking and his zipper opening flooded Moira with another anticipatory rush.

Moira could not stifle her gasp as his smooth, hard length glided through her folds, coating himself in her moisture before he buried himself without preamble.

And when he was inside her, Moira knew she had never in her life been *fucked* before. The fierceness of their joining tore from her a cry of violent wonder. At his strength. His precision. At the beauty of his savage need to possess not just her body, but her mind, her soul, her thoughts, and her will.

How the feeble, sweaty pumping of men without number, even those whose bodies she found attractive were obliterated the second Nick's cock rooted itself in her body.

One hand tightened in her hair, one clutching her hip, Nick halted where he was, his breath tickling her back as he held her still.

Still enough that she could feel his wild pulse within her.

Still enough that the beating of her own heart searched for and syncopated itself with his rhythm, the throb of their separate life forces coming into alignment here at the beginning of all things.

Nick's hand left her hip to plant itself on her lower back. He withdrew from her, inch by glorious inch before moving into her again. Deeper this time. Slower. The precise opposite of what she had expected their encounter to be. Empty of the blind, bruising force she had been shoring herself up against.

No.

Nick's every stroke was a primeval exploration. And only when he knew her, knew where her most secret places dipped and bowed, did the real conquest begin.

Using muscles Moira didn't even know a man could own, Nick's hips moved in rhythmic eddies and currents, pushing himself not just inside her, but like a tide within her. Filling her to his hilt and then beyond it until their bodies joined at every possible angle, deeper, more elemental than the soft earth yielding and molding around a tree's insistent root.

Nick made her an extension of his own body. Angling his hips, angling hers, using the maximum attenuation of his broad back to build leverage each time he returned his cock to her in full, leaving her to mourn its absence each time he retreated.

They moved this way for hours, it seemed. Perhaps days. Time, like language, was just another casualty to their coupling. Moira found herself incapable of speaking in anything other than ecstatic cries, guttural moans, inarticulate pleas and demands. Nick spoke to her in languages she had never heard and yet somehow understood, using the same tongue to lick the sweat from her spine when it pooled there.

Somewhere between her first climax and her twentieth, Moira understood.

Were her life not slated to end before this side of the world saw the sun, Nicholas Kingswood would for ever own her. This is what he had meant. Not that he would simply call her his.

He would *make* her his.

Would explore her and pleasure her so thoroughly that no man, mortal or otherwise, could even hope to compare. He would claim her by the elemental fusion by which worlds are made and unmade. Just as he made and unmade her now.

She would surrender not because he'd forced her to, but because giving herself over to him was as effortless and involuntary as breathing.

Nick couldn't stop.

In all his long years, he had fucked and been fucked by mortal women, goddesses, nymphs, and every manner of whore, courtesan, and paid lay this world could offer. He shoveled them like coal into the eternally burning furnace of his lust. His need for conquest in *all* arenas. His never-ending, damnable need for domination.

But never had he been so enrapt, so possessed, so... bewitched by any creature in this realm or any other.

He had intended to fuck Moira good and hard, to make her come until she begged, sate his own need, then deliver his end of the bargain.

And at every turn, she had thwarted him.

Moira had pulled him down, down to pleasures deeper and more incendiary than the volcanic lava erupting from the Earth's core into the ocean's darkest fissures.

Surprise was an irksome, inconvenient emotion Nick thought he had long ago done away with. Tonight, Moira had taught him differently.

With her, there would be no satiation. He could fuck her for a thousand years and it would never be enough. He had no idea how long they'd been here. Had lost count of how many times they'd come in synchronization. Her ability to replenish fluids and his bottomless appetite left them endlessly devouring each other again and again.

Witch or no, she occupied a human body, did not have the benefit of the immortal strength and stamina that had won him many a battle. And yet this water witch proved equally insatiable. This he hadn't counted on. This he hadn't planned for.

For as long as she had lived, she had used her body to heal those in need, never taking for herself the pleasure he had derived from his every encounter. Now, with the prospect of her life coming to an end, she was not only taking from him all she had ever missed, but also all she might yet have enjoyed.

Sitting astride him, her head thrown back and her breasts swaying in time with the bucking and rolling of her hips, Moira fucked him like a woman desperate to compress a lifetime of pleasure into one heated night.

Damned if Nick didn't want to give it to her.

But he knew things she did not. Knew that the Devil had set her sights on Moira's soul. Knew their time was short, and if he was to help her without making her a meat sacrifice to Satan, he had to stop.

They had to stop.

Before the consequences of their rapture included the world's end.

Just once more.

Gods be damned, but he needed to feel her come for him, around him, *just once more*. He needed to render in his long memory the rapturous pleasure on her beautiful face, a look of bliss and contentment that he had put there.

He rolled her over onto her back, taking in the pink flush from her breasts to her cheeks, the sweat-dampened hair forming Botticelliesque curls around her face. He looked at the lips he'd swollen with kisses, the reddening patches marking her body like a map of where he'd been. Her aquamarine eyes had darkened with carnal knowledge he alone had imparted. Her face slackened by pleasure—pleasure she had finally taken for herself.

She had not needed to speak the words. Her body had surrendered to him again and again.

Fierce pride swelled in his heart...and cock.

He fit the backs of her knees into the crooks of his elbows and planted them back by her shoulders. From this vantage he could reach her mouth and breasts while fucking her at an angle that would have them visiting constellations in short order.

Moira's lazy smile loosened into an open-mouthed gasp of pleasure—a sound Nick found more heavenly than any angelic choir. The friction building between them was a close second and about as near to heaven as he was likely to get.

Her nails scored his back, working all the way down to his buttocks, which she grabbed, pulling him toward her at an even more rapid pace. Surprise number two.

Number three arrived seconds after in the form of a directive given in that honeyed drawl.

"Don't you hold back, Nicholas Kingswood." She rose from the pillow and nipped his earlobe. "Not this time."

He drove into her hard, almost losing himself within her when she folded forward to bite the swell of his trapezius muscle to muffle her moan. Tasting the sweat of his neck. Clinging to him, arms binding him to her with a power no incantation could hope to match.

"Take me," she whispered, coupling the demand with a sharp tug of the fingers threaded through his hair. "Take everything I have left." Never in his life had Nickolas Kingswood been given an order.

Never in his life had he wanted to obey.

Until now.

And with that, the last fraying thread of his carefully-guarded control broke altogether.

Vicious need took him then, and her with it. He fucked her with the mindless abandon of the animal his title implied. The *Horseman. Conquest.* The blood, and battle, and speed, and brutality all unleashed upon the body of this water witch, his sworn enemy, bringer of the End of Days.

All hers to command.

"*Nick*," she panted. "Oh, Nick, please. Harder."

Harder he could do. He held fast to her hips, his cock the weapon of her choosing, giving her the thousand deaths she'd wished for since she recognized her capacity for destruction.

Faster too, he gifted her, delving into her at the pace of Magnus, his warhorse, adopted when the scent of blood flared his nostrils.

The first twinges of her orgasm quickened around him. Her muscles fired in random jolts like an electrical grid tasked with unmasking the divine.

His own release raced to meet hers as if summoned like a mate through the darkness.

How gloriously she came apart before him. Her eyes jeweled like the sea at the sun's rising, her body melting into his, her going liquid as currents of pleasure broke over her in wave after wave.

Nick was lost at the sight of her. Growling her name in a primitive prayer. His seed poured into her as together they broke open the sky, the cosmos spilling out for them alone.

For that moment, the Apocalypse was only the ashes of a word scattered on the wind, and Moira was no more than his lover, and Nick was no Horseman, no assassin.

Because gods help him, he no longer knew if when the time came, he could let his arrow fly.

❈ 9 ❈

"**H**ey! I's wondering where these got to." Moira was tempted to slingshot the lacy red thong hanging from her index finger at Nick, but wasn't sure he'd return it if she did. "You want to tell me exactly how in the hell you have a pair of my underpants in your possession?"

Nick sauntered toward her, fresh from the shower, clad in naught but a luxury cotton towel. "The same way I have a pair of your cut-offs and tank top in the bottom drawer there. I took them."

Moira held her own towel to her chest, her wet hair raining droplets onto the Persian rug beneath Nick's antique armoire. Sure enough. She recognized her worn cut-offs and her threadbare Hoo-Doo Shack tank top folded neatly among Nick's boxer briefs.

"I'll be damned," she said. "I'd assumed Tierra had thrown them out sometime after I moved in. She isn't a fan of my sartorial leanings, you might say."

"The outfit you wore when we first met on the plane," Nick offered in explanation. "I like souvenirs." He indicated the lighted trophy cases containing the weapons she had stared at for hours on end earlier.

"I didn't figure you for the sentimental kind," Moira teased.

"If by 'sentimental,' you mean, *considered killing everyone on the airplane so I could fuck you right there in your first class seat*, then yeah, I was feeling sentimental as hell." Nick took a step toward her and brushed her dripping hair from the back of her neck. "When you live as long as I have, you choose the moments worthy of remembering."

"I get you. Believe me, there are plenty of memories I'd rather not have. Like the time Skeeter Robicheau got caught behind the Piggly Wiggly tryin' to have his way with a loaf of day-old French bread. I mean, I know it was probably nice and warm from being in the dumpster in August, but—"

Nick held up a hand. "I'd rather not add that visual to my collection, if you don't mind."

Moira let her towel drop to the floor and stepped into her panties, a peace offering in lieu of the image she'd just foisted on him. "What I want to know is how you got into the house to raid my drawers. We have wards in place."

"The only question I am equipped to answer with your body on display like that is whether I want you to sit on my face before or after I take you from behind." Threads of glowing gold were returning to his eyes as they fixed on her breasts, his arousal beginning to tent his towel.

"Don't you start that stuff, Mister," Moira warned. "You yourself said we didn't have much time on account of that evil bitch wanting to eat my soul and all."

"But it's not your soul I'm interested in eating." Nick hooked a finger in the strap of her panties and tugged downward, but she slapped his hand away.

"It's cute that you can be all playful and not an asshole after a fuck-a-thon, but if it's all the same to you, I'd like to get this over with." Moira shrugged into her tank top and shimmied into her cut-offs while Nick retreated to his walk-in closet to don his usual attire of slacks and button-up shirt.

"No need to dress up on my account," she said. "The funeral won't be for a few days after my body is found. *If* my body is found. And I'm

pretty sure murder ain't a tie-wearing kind of occasion."

"Depends on the murderer." Nick flashed her his knee-weakening, wicked grin.

Moira had to look away before she took him up on his offer of one last hurrah.

"Where the hell are my sandals?" she asked, going to her hands and knees to search under the bed.

"I think the selfsame consumer of souls might have borrowed them."

"It's not enough the bitch wants my soul. She's got to take my shoes too?" Moira used the bedpost to pull herself to her feet, only to have them swept out from under her.

Nick had scooped her into his arms as if she didn't weigh any more than a half-empty sack of potatoes.

"Guess I'll have to carry you then. The gravel in the driveway is sharp. Wouldn't want you to cut your feet."

"I'm not fixin' to be princess carried to my own martyrdom," Moira insisted.

"I wouldn't have to carry you anywhere if you didn't insist on being taken to Siren's Cry. I could shoot you right here and save us time. In fact, we might be able to get in a couple more fucks before—"

Moira punched him as hard as she could in the solar plexus, gratified by the sudden *whoosh* of air exiting his lungs. "Are you *really* suggesting that you kill me here just so you can get your rocks off a couple more times?"

"And yours." Nick managed to shrug even with Moira in his arms. "We get to fuck more. You still die. Makes excellent sense, if you ask me."

"You really are a bastard," she said, unable to keep the wonder from her voice.

"Have I ever claimed to be anything else?"

"Listen here, you toad scrotum-suckin'—"

"*Shhh*," Nick urged. "Think you can keep that smart mouth shut for the length of time it takes to walk from here to the front door?"

Moira smiled, and tweaked his nipple as hard as she could through his shirt.

"*Fuck!*" Nick growled.

"Shhhh!" Moira lifted her finger to her lips in an exaggerated gesture of censure.

Nick's eyebrows lowered like storm clouds as he paused with his ear to the door, listening—Moira supposed—for some sign of War or Pestilence. After a moment, he silently turned the door handle using the same arm braced under the backs of her knees.

All right, so this wasn't exactly the heroic march Moira had pictured herself making, but she had to admit it wasn't altogether unpleasant, being carried by Nicholas Kingswood. His muscled forearms deliciously brushed her calves, his heart beat against her shoulder, his warm body was a living cradle for her tired limbs.

Nick inched the door open and they were down the hall, across the living room, and out the front door with a speed and grace that superseded anything in Moira's experience.

Moira pulled the heady scent of velvet night into her lungs, the signature mix of salt air and damp, mossy verdant life she'd grown to love in Port Townsend. It settled on her skin, moist and cool where her body didn't touch Nick's. Far away, the ocean's lullaby called to her, every spent wave whispering *hush* as it foamed onto the sand.

Only the sound of Nick's shoes crunching on the gravel and the beating of her own heart within her ears interrupted the heavy silence. "Where are we going?"

she asked, when Nick had walked them far beyond the driveway and out to a dirt road.

"Her Royal Darkness set up a witch-proof perimeter, but I can get you out, but doing so requires that we be *mounted* to pass over the boundary. Also, escaping works better if She-Devil isn't in the immediate proximity."

"No wonder none of my sisters showed up," Moira said, a tightness in her chest loosening with the revelation. "And what do you mean by *mounted?* I thought that's what we were doing all afternoon."

"If I didn't know better, I'd say you were *trying* to goad me into fucking you on this forest floor so you can get your soul devoured by Satan. I don't know how long she'll be gone, Moira. I know only that she's not in the vicinity for the moment, and if you really want to go through with this, we need to move now."

Her body bounced in time with his long-legged strides.

"How do you know that ol' Serpent isn't here?" she asked.

"Because the soul-sucking maggot queen of the infernal realms has a pretty unmistakable astral resonance," he answered. "Also, I don't smell the blood of virgins."

"But you didn't seem to mind planting your flag between her demon thighs, according to her."

"I didn't know what she was then. None of us did. Well, except for Julian. He always was the brains of the operation. Refusing her landed him the curse of never being able to touch a single living creature without destroying it."

"'Cept for Aerin," Moira pointed out.

My sisters. All at once her heart filled with an ache large enough to split her chest wide open. Images unwound through her mind like an old-fashioned film reel. Tierra jangling into the room, all scarves and swaying fabric, smelling of herbs and earth and all things clean and good. Claire slouching at the kitchen table in her leathers, warming Moira with her easy smile and cinnamon-scented kisses on the cheek.

And Aerin. Lord, how they picked at one another. But Moira had long suspected it had more to do with similarities than the petty jabs about clothing and diction. A common wound they didn't have to acknowledge if they didn't get close enough to share. Stubborn pride keeping Moira from letting Aerin know just how much she'd wanted her approval. And Aerin's smooth-as-glass exterior, against which all things emotional and maudlin left unwelcome smudges. Fragile, glass was, beautiful and ethereal as the air that gave the molten particles their shape.

What she wouldn't have given to hug each one of her sisters one last time.

Last. This one word stuck in her mind and attached itself to everything she now smelled, thought, felt, and did. The last time she would watch the moon glow over the bay. The last time she would smile, laugh, feel the hot water of a shower slide over her skin.

"Here we are." Nick stalked into a copse of trees. A sleek, white car lurked within the shadows, its exotic headlights shaped like nostrils flaring in the darkness.

"Hol-ee shit," Moira gasped as they drew closer. "Is that a Ferrari

Italia 458?"

Nick halted abruptly. "You know cars?"

"Are you kiddin' me? I worked in Uncle Red's shop since I was big enough to hold a socket wrench. Back home, I drove a '69 Plymouth Barracuda."

"Keep it up, and I'll spread your legs on the hood of this car," Nick warned.

"Hey, it ain't my fault you've got the libido of a two-peter jack rabbit. I just miss tearing up the back roads, hearing the Badger growl..."

"You'll get to hear Magnus growl. I don't think he'll disappoint."

"Wait a minute," Moira said. "*This* is Magnus? I thought when you said *mount*, you meant he'd be an actual horse."

"Why have only one horse when I can have 600?" Nick asked.

"Can't argue with that logic," Moira admitted.

Nick walked around to the passenger's side, and with a flash of headlights and the requisite beep, the door opened, and he deposited Moira in the buttery black leather seat.

When Nick slipped into the driver's side and turned the engine over, the low, throaty growl sent a reckless rush of adrenaline down Moira's spine.

The very air between them felt electric with possibility, thick with the new intimacy between them, saturated with the sensual scent of leather, Nick's aftershave, and the man himself. The immortal sent to destroy her.

"Fast." Moira ran her fingers along the leather dash, marveling at a display that seemed more appropriate to a spaceship.

Nick caught her hand and slid it downward, but surprised her by guiding it to the jutting leather stick shift instead of his crotch.

"Wanna shift?" he invited her.

"Does a woodpecker shit splinters?" she replied.

"For our purposes, I'm going to assume that's a yes. Shall we?"

As it turned out, they worked the powerful machine much like they had worked each other's bodies—with a precision that seemed born more than learned.

Nick had opened the moon roof, allowing the wind to whip her drying hair into a frenzy as they navigated the frontage road circumscribing the bay at speeds neither would have dared in the daytime. Only when they neared the turn off that would send them up the winding road to Siren's Cry did Moira downshift, hesitating as her heart decided to rent a condo in her throat.

From this spot, she traced the treacherous lines of Siren's Cry as it jutted out above the ocean, calmer tonight than most in her recollection. The shadows of monoliths were barely visible beyond the thick gathering of trees. The Standing Stones.

Where they had seen their mother.

Where Tierra had discovered her crown and wand.

Where she would die so her sisters could live.

She damn near hit her head on the Ferrari's roof when Nick Kingswood wrapped his hand around hers on the stick shift. The same current that had shocked them both so on their first meeting still leapt between their twined fingers.

"You take over," Moira insisted. "I don't think I can." Nick nodded, understanding.

He guided Magnus expertly up the winding road, braking and downshifting in perfect time with every curve, much as he had reverenced her own body with a skilled and masterful hand.

Magnus slowed to a halt a ways down the road from the stand of trees beyond which the Standing Stones kept their silent vigil.

They sat together in the car, staring out at them in silence.

Moira searched inside herself for the stillness she had felt earlier that afternoon, looking into Justine's tear-stained face and knowing the answer. The same blessed peace found her again, warmed her chilly heart and expanded in her chest, filling her with light, and lightness.

Nick did not urge her out of the car, didn't so much as speak a word until she turned to him.

"Okey dokey," she said, wrapping her fingers around the car door handle. "Let's go."

He reached across to block her exit. "Keep your ass in that seat."

Her heart fluttered within her chest. After all this, was he truly going to try and stop her?

Did she want him to?

"The least I can do is open the car door like a motherfucking gentleman before I shoot you through the chest," he said.

"Oh," Moira replied, unable to summon any other cogent response.

She remained seated until Nick walked around to her side of the car and opened it, offering her his hand, which she accepted.

He didn't drop it as together they made their way the final steps over the dew-dampened grass, through the trees and out into the clearing where the stones stood tall beneath a sky full of stars.

Stars. Praise the Lord for a night without clouds so she could die beneath a moonlit sky with stars wheeling overhead.

She resisted the urge to count every blade of grass beneath her bare feet, capture a handful of leaves and smell them. To roll and glory in every last sensual detail she could greedily drink from these last few moments.

Moira allowed herself to reach out and place her palm flat against the nearest stone, feeling beneath its cooling surface the sunlight it had absorbed. She rested her cheek against the gritty warmth, looking at the lights of Port Townsend across the bay. Moira had no spells memorized for this moment. Instead, she resorted to an old-fashioned prayer of the kind Uncle Sal had always insisted on muttering over their steaming plates of dinner.

Please, watch over them, dear Goddess. Please, keep my sisters safe. Let this be the end. And let the end be good.

She turned to Nick and nodded, beginning her final trek toward the edge of the cliff.

Scarcely had she taken two steps when she was hauled backward by a hand grasping the back of her cutoffs, dragged into violent collision with the body of Nick Kingswood, hard and unyielding as the Standing Stones.

His mouth crushed hers, his lips a brand that would send her to her death marked.

Claimed.

$\maltese$ 10 $\maltese$

Moira opened to him like a flower drinking the rain, drawing what nourishment it could of the last of its little season. Nick moaned into her mouth, his tongue sliding over hers not with conquering force, but with urgent need, unguarded passion, painful longing.

She answered him in kind. Tasting him as she had their first time on the dock. Their first kiss and their last pressed together in a memory more voluminous than the ocean backdrop to both. Moira took all he was willing to give in the velvety exchange, hands twined around his neck, binding her to him now because there was no forever. No next time. No tomorrow.

He deepened the kiss, one hand plunging into her hair, fingers curling into a fist in the sensitive strands at the nape of her neck. Moira relished the miniscule darts of pleasure firing from her scalp down her neck, tugged by the hand of Conquest, fully alive in her body and devouring every sensation as it came, desperate for each second she could steal.

Her breasts flattened against his chest as he palmed the round swell of her ass before sliding down her thigh, lifting it over his hip. His desire pressed against her, the very throb of life itself.

Somehow, Moira knew Nick did this not for his own pleasure, but so she could feel, this one last time, just how much she was wanted. Just how much she was needed.

And she did.

Not just wanted, but wanted by a force as old as the world itself. Wise as he was impulsive, arrogant as he was tender, brutal as he was gentle. Ruthless as he was considerate. Nicholas Kingswood was as beautiful a death as Moira could imagine, and at last she ended their kiss, knowing the time had come for another deadlier part of this immortal to be buried inside her.

They both came away panting, but Nick did not release her, opting instead to hold her face in his cupped palms so she couldn't look away even as she struggled to hold the tears at bay. Her hands remained planted on his chest and she shut her eyes tight to memorize the sensation of his wild heart leaping beneath her fingertips.

"Brave Moira," he whispered, running the rough pad of a thumb over her swollen lower lip. "Are you ready?"

"I am." She looked up into his eyes, darkened to burnt umber by night's veil. "Question is, are *you*? Or are you going to pull me back for another bout of tongue twister?"

"Don't." Nick spoke through a tightened jaw, his forehead creased in concentration. "Don't tempt me, Moira. I could take you again. Right here, right now, this second and every second after it. I could fuck you while the world burned around us, and the only thing stopping me is knowing that you're strong enough to walk toward that cliff."

She realized the time for her wise-ass rejoinders had truly passed.

Her time had truly passed.

She was almost over.

"I'm sorry," she whispered. She felt her eyes filling

with tears again, the faces of all those she loved swimming on the backs of her eyelids when she pressed them shut.

Nick kissed her forehead, his hands splayed over her temples, letting his lips linger there until she closed her hands over his wrists and squeezed.

He thumbed the tears from her cheeks and dropped his hands to her shoulders, making sure she looked directly into his eyes before giving his instructions. Moira could not decipher what emotion lived in the amber depths of Nick's gaze at that moment, nor read the thoughts spooling through his immortal mind, but knew on some instinctive level this night would take something from them both.

"Walk toward the edge of the cliff. Don't turn until I tell you to." The urgency in Nick's voice dismantled what little defense Moira had left, and she could no longer stem the tide of her own fear in these final moments.

She drew a shaky breath and nodded before turning away from Nick, mechanically taking the first step, then the second, unable to keep herself from counting each as she moved toward the last step she would ever take.

Behind her, Nick spoke an incantation and the Earth beneath her feet shifted and trembled. Clouds appeared over her head where there had been none, circling above them like water around an unplugged drain. *The bow and arrow.* Nick was calling his weapons to him now.

"Now, Moira!" he ordered in a voice that seemed to come from everywhere and nowhere at once. She halted in place, close enough to the cliff's edge to see the ocean spit and spray against the jagged rocks below.

When she did, she understood why Nick had asked her not to look until he bade her to.

The Nicholas Kingswood she knew was gone.

What remained was no longer a mere mortal, an arrogant business mogul destroying and overtaking paltry sections of the earth at will. He *was* Conquest, Horseman who would bring an end to the Apocalypse. Here, and now.

Light swirled and leapt around him like lightning in a glass jar. Smoke billowed and swirled as the clouds overtook the sky completely. Through the miasma, Moira could make out three points of light: the fire-orange glow of Conquest's two eyes, and the sharp silver tip of his arrow.

Moira stared at it, waiting.

Conquest hesitated, the inner struggle evident in the outer manifestation of energy crackling and leaping, the fire in his eyes dimming like dying coals.

Please, Moira silently begged. *End this.*

Conquest's eyes closed, dousing the coals to the twang of the bowstring and an arrow's brief, whistling scream.

Pain exploded into Moira's chest as the razor tip pierced her clean through. She felt intense pressure. Shock. Sorrow.

Relief.

Moira staggered backward, driven by the arrow's speed and force. One bare foot found the earth's crust. The next, only air.

How absurd, the last thought her mind supplied before she plummeted toward the ocean and the rocks below.

I never did get to finish those grits.

❦ 11 ❦

> "Earth is our body.
> Fire, our soul.
> Air, our breath.
> Water, our blood.
> Flesh, knit to flesh.
> Vein to vein.
> The Goddess blesses you.
> Be whole again."

Moira nodded with appreciation, eyes still closed against the chilly water. *Now* that *sounded like a real-ass, honest to goodness spell*. She ought to write that one down. She could have saved an awful lot of critters with a spell like that.

Now wait just a gods-damned minute, she thought.

How in the hell was she thinking anything? She was dead. Like, Apocalyptic arrow through the heart, fall from a hundred-foot cliff, land on the ocean floor-dead. Real dead. Super dead. Deader than a corpse's pecker dead.

Her back still stung from the reverse belly-flop she'd done when hitting the water's churning surface. Ethereal blue light pried her eyelids open, and Moira found herself surrounded.

Cod, steelhead herring, spiny dogfish, sea otters, starfish, and even an orca whale had drifted by to examine her intrusion into their realm.

She felt scorn in their judgy, goggled eyes.

What the hell are y'all lookin' at? Half of y'all aren't even vertebrates. She reached out to their pure and simple minds as she had with Old Methuselah, elder statesman of the catfish colony back home. *Nothing to see here.*

But perhaps she was wrong about that.

Moira glanced down at her middle, where Nick's arrow still skewered her like a cocktail wienie on sample day down at the A&P.

She'd never had much of a mind for math, but by her rough estimate, she had at least twelve inches of the arrow's feathered butt end sticking out of the second "O" in *Hoodoo Shack* on the front of her tank top and another twelve jutting out of her back, ending in the arrow's pointed tip. Which left at least eight inches of the arrow still inside her body, puncturing all kinds of organs she'd planned on using ripe into her dotage, when her love of beignets and Irish butter gave her the 'Beetus and a four-alarm heart-attack sent her toppling off a barstool.

She took a gander at her surroundings, all illuminated by the same otherworldly glow whose source she couldn't find. Kelp forests moved in the water's caress with balletic grace. Fish swam idly by, seeking food or mates. She spotted an ancient, barnacle-crusted lobster and gently picked it up by its tail only to have it squirt a foul jetstream of curmudgeon crustacean invectives into her mind about other things she could dip in butter and shove into her mouth aside from him.

Fish back home had been a lot friendlier—that had been for damn sure, not banging on about *sustainable* this and *Washington Department of Fish and Wildlife* that.

Moira's hair, black against the glowing blue, floated around her in an amorphous cloud. She touched it, then her face, to test the solidity of her body before examining her hands and finding them raisiny beyond recognition. Sea creatures were insulting her left and right for invading an area protected by the National Oceanic and Atmospheric Administration, and judging by that weird-ass blue light, she was shot through, sure as shit, underwater, but somehow alive.

And speaking of that weird-ass blue light, just exactly where *was* that coming from—

Moira's scream released the remaining oxygen in her lungs through a cluster of iridescent bubbles when someone gently tapped her on the shoulder.

She whirled around in the slow motion movement the water would allow.

There was a woman in the water.

A beautiful woman emitting an eerie blue glow. A woman whose gossamer garments floated about her like something Moira had seen in ads for washing machines or tampons.

Eyes the exact shade of aquamarine as hers looked upon her kindly from a porcelain-pale face surrounded by a veil of hair a shade darker than hers.

Not Mirelle, her mother, but the resemblance was keen enough to smart.

An angel? Come to welcome her sorry, sodden behind to heaven?

If this *was* heaven, Reverend Dupuis was more full of shit than a manure truck.

The woman's smile widened. "This isna heaven, I'm afraid. And I've been accused of being many things, but an angel was never one of them." She winked at Moira, her full lips curving in a mischievous smirk that only enhanced the lyrical lilt of her Scots accent.

"How come you can talk underwater?" Moira asked, realizing her own words were not distorted as she had expected them to be.

"Because lass, like you, I am a water druid. My name is Morgana de Moray, sister of Malcom de Moray."

Moira recognized the name instantly. Malcolm, who had written to them in the Grimoire. Malcolm the Earth Druid king whose crown and wand Tierra had found.

"I'm guessing you don't just hang out down here all the time, so would I be correct in postulatin' that your presence here might have a little something to do with my being turned into a human shish-kabob by Conquest?"

"Yer postulating would be correct, Moira de Moray. I've come to pass along to you certain relics in my possession that are now yers to command."

"You know, I'd rather walk on my lips than to criticize, but those relics might have come in handy before I went and got myself killed so I could end the Apocalypse."

"Ah," Morgana said. "But it is precisely that act which qualifies ye to wield the relics to which I am referring. Yer willingness to lay down yer life for yer sisters. Self-sacrifice is a rare and beautiful thing, Moira, but as noble as yer intentions might be, ye're needed here."

"But I thought my being here was the problem in the first place. The seals. We keep opening the seals. Mostly on accident. And the Horsemen said that only one of us had to die to end it, and I thought, on account of I'm a screw-up, and nobody much wanted me around in the first place—"

"The Horsemen doona know everything, Moira." Her lovely voice held a hint of mystery, of knowing. "Although Julian comes pretty close," she added. "Very studious, that one. But I suppose one has to find other ways to occupy one's time when one can't..." She paused, searching the briny depths like the right words might be hidden in a nearby treasure chest. "Well, when physical pursuits aren't a primary priority."

"So there's really a chance that we might not end the world?" Moira asked. She hated the childlike hope in her own voice. Hated how vulnerable it left her to disappointment.

"The world's fate has not yet been decided. Many factors are in play. Machinations beyond yer comprehension. Much is yet to be revealed. But I can tell you one thing, Moira de Moray." Morgana floated closer, her silken garments cocooning them in a single cell. "Yer sisters are stronger *with* ye than *without* ye. If ye truly wish to avoid the world's end, ye *must* stay together."

This revelation pierced her with a pain sharper than Conquest's arrow. She knew Morgana referred to the growing divide between them. The invisible, dark rend that had been born of Aerin's necromancy, widening as they continued down dissenting paths.

Morgana's pale, slim hand came to rest weightlessly on Moira's shoulder. "Only together do you have hope of defeating the many forces seeking to destroy ye."

"Many?" Moira asked. "You mean the Horsemen and that walking mattress what eats souls with her coffee and dresses like a fetish hooker?"

"Not only they," Morgana warned. The hand on Moira's shoulder rose, index finger pointed as Morgana circled it in the water three times. The circle she had circumscribed flickered like a television screen seeking to land on a clear signal.

Moira sucked in a lungful of water when the image finally cleared. Their lovely old house in flames. An angry, torch-bearing mob sending up victorious shouts. Claire lying on her back, glassy eyes aimed skyward, her chest mauled open to an angry, red cavern. Tommy's face hovering above it, blood smeared around his lips like jam. Aerin and Tierra under attack, their strength waning but refusing to help each other. Their separate efforts as an approaching mob backed them toward the smoldering ruin of their house. Burning stakes had been erected in the corner of their yard, ready and waiting.

"No!" Moira pushed her palms against her eyes to block out the image. "No, this can't be happening."

"It isna." Morgana passed a hand through the water to disperse the vision pool. "Not yet. This is only what will happen if circumstances are allowed to continue down their current track."

"How do I stop it?" Moira pleaded. "I'll do anything. Just show me—"

"*Live*, Moira. Live, and claim yer birthright."

In Morgana's left hand appeared a long, slim, silvery wand inscribed with patterns of cresting waves. In her right, a delicate crown inlaid with runes of cobalt and aquamarine, its four spires resembling lacy coral.

Moira reached her hand toward the wand and felt a vibration travel through the water the second her fingers wrapped around its handle. A new, crackling energy surged through her, every cell in her body leaping with recognition of something long missed. Gripping the wand felt like the embrace of an old friend.

With her other hand free, Morgana wrapped both around the crown, looking to Moira, who knelt out of instinct. All chatter in Moira's head died away the second the crown slid into place. Never had her mind been so free of negative static.

Moira finally broke the reverent silence with a question as profane as this experience had been sacred. "So, now that I have a wand and all, is there anything I can do about this?" she asked, gesturing to the arrow still jutting from her chest. "It's going to make things real awkward come swimsuit season."

"Ye're the one with the wand," Morgana urged. "Try it."

Moira hesitated, looking from the wand to the arrow. "You see, I'm not so good with the spells."

"The wand doesna strictly require them," Morgana explained. "Though it can enhance spells when used correctly."

"You see, I'm not so good at doing things correctly, either," Moira said.

"Just try, Moira. That's the only way ye're like to learn."

"Here goes nothin'." Moira pointed the wand at the arrow in her chest, closed her eyes, and tried to concentrate.

"Arrow of Conquest, in me lodged, git on out like I had dodged.

My normal chest, return to me,

By power of earth, air, fire, and sea..."

A brief, searing pain slid through Moira's chest, but when she peeked down, the arrow had vanished. "I'll be a badger's ball-sack! It worked!"

Morgana bore the expression of someone who had just licked a battery acid-flavored lollipop. "Well, that wasna very conventional...but I suppose times do change. Do you know the spell for returning to yer sisters?"

Moira stood in the thick cold sand at the bottom of the sound and clicked her bare heels. "Uh, there's no place like home?" she said querulously, pointing the wand at her feet.

"Ach!" Morgana sighed. "These legends become so distorted over time. First of all, they werna ruby slippers, they were Malachite. And Toto wasna Dorothy's dog, he was her mate. An alpha shifter with a schnauzer fetish. Doona even get me started on Glinda—"

"Sorry," Moira said. "I didn't mean to bring up a sore subject."

Morgana massaged her temples. "Perhaps ye ought just study the Grimoire. Given yer position, it would be for the best."

"I can do that," Moira assured her, hoping Morgana

didn't think her heir a total dud. "Anyway, I can't go straight home. There's a stop I need to make first."

"Very well." Morgana took both hands in hers and whispered a blessing in a language Moira was unfamiliar with. When she was done, Morgana opened her eyes and laid a hand against Moira's cheek. "May the goddess guide ye," she said.

And then she was gone.

❧ 12 ❧

The wind whipped through Nicholas Kingswood's hair, emitting a melancholy howl as it scraped across the jagged cliff. He didn't know how long he'd been standing here, staring out at the heaving waves, searching for some sign of Moira.

All the while he kept his vigil, an utterly foreign urge kept returning to him—the overwhelming desire to punch *himself* in the face.

Was this what self-loathing felt like?

Nick had never in his unnaturally long life had to contend with it. Nor with the distasteful bedfellows self-loathing kept for company.

Guilt.

Shame. Regret.

Doubt.

All signs of a theory he had never personally sub-scribed to. This notion of *conscience*.

Yet, the desire to hurl himself off the cliff after her was undeniable. Part of him would welcome the pain of his broken body as a way of sharing what he had inflicted on her.

It was that part he had told to shut the fuck up several times without success.

Nick had fought many battles, but none of them

had taken place in his own head. As it turned out, he was a formidable opponent.

"Oh, Nicholas. I thought Julian was the Horseman who specialized in staring forlornly off windswept cliffs."

The sound of Lucy's voice, at once sensual and sarcastic, set Nick's teeth on edge.

"Lucifer," Nick said by way of greeting.

She sidled up to him in a squeak of leather and wrapped her arms around his waist from behind in a Heimlich hug.

"Tell me, darling," she said, her cheek pressed between Nick's shoulder blades so he could feel the words grate against his spine. "How did the water witch get past the barrier I erected?"

"I took her," Nick said. It didn't do to bother with deceit when chewing the fat with the Mother of Lies.

"Indeed." Her fingers slid down his hips and into the front pockets of his slacks. "And after I made my plans for her *painfully*—" she squeezed Nick's cock "—clear. One might think you were openly defying me."

Nick grabbed her hands by the wrists and peeled them from his person, turning to face her. Facing Lucy was always safer. "Is it my fault if you were too busy chasing your latest rejection from Julian to be present to collect her soul?"

She refused to rise to his deliberate provocation.

"But I was present, Nicholas. Waiting right down there in the shadows of the rocks." Darkness complimented Lucy's features in a way the daylight never could. Threading pale white-gold strands through her hair, turning her eyes to sapphires and her lips to red velvet. "Trouble is, there was no soul to collect."

"I know Moira can be a bitch sometimes, but I'm almost certain that she had a soul," Nick retorted.

"You know that's not what I meant. How can I collect a soul when *you* failed to kill her? You had *one* job,

Nicholas." Lucy poked her blood red-lacquered finger-nail into his chest to illustrate her point.

"I'm pretty sure my arrow was forged in the fires that made the world and tempered with the blood of infinite warriors. I shot her point blank through the chest." An unwelcome stab of sympathetic pain tight-ened behind Nick's sternum. *Sympathy pains?* What in the everlasting fuck was wrong with him?

"What the fuck else do you want from me?" Nick turned away from the cliff and stalked back toward his car, wanting the distance from Lucy.

Lucy's long-legged gait easily kept pace. "Perhaps to choose a location where the water witch wouldn't be falling to her death in *the*

ocean. The very place she could be healed from such a wound."

Nick halted in his tracks. "Moira's not dead?"

"Please," Lucy sneered. "Don't act like you didn't know. We know each other far too well to play this game. Not only is she *not* dead, she's inherited Mor-gana's wand and crown."

Nick's heart galloped in his chest. "How do you know?"

"Oh, little signs," Lucy said, picking at her finger-nails. "There's a halo around the moon, the sea has gone quiet, and she destroyed the entire compound with a flash flood and got away with that wretched aunt of hers."

"She did *what?*" Nick had to bite his tongue to keep from grinning.

Conquest, destroyer and decimator, *grinning.* For the gods' sake. What was next? Cartwheels? Affirma-tions? Mercy?

"You heard me correctly, Nicholas. She destroyed the compound. Dru and Julian may well be somewhere in Canada at the moment.

They've yet to make contact."

"That's unfortunate," Nick agreed, working as much gravity into his voice as he could muster as he found the remote in his pants pocket and beeped the car to life.

Lucy waited expectantly for Nick to open her door. Not because she was accustomed to being treated like a lady, but because she was accustomed to such menial tasks being the work of her many slaves and minions.

She slid into the passenger's seat, propping the wickedly sharp heel of her leather boot on the dash. As soon as Nick settled himself into the driver's side and closed the door, she grabbed him by the tie and pulled him across the armrest separating them.

The sapphires in her eyes turned molten orange, and the breath exhaled from her mouth scorched his nostrils with the scent of brimstone.

"Let me make one thing abundantly clear to you, Nicholas. If I suspect for one second that you are plotting against me, I will introduce you to levels of pain your immortal brain can scarcely fathom. Death openly defied me and is now rotting in Hell for the privilege. Bane's current circumstances will seem like a vacation in Eden compared to what I would do to you. Do you understand?"

Nick nodded. "I understand."

Coward, the unwelcome intruder in his mind accused. *A real warrior would tell Lucy that he would suffer her torments a thousand fold before he'd see Moira's beautiful soul shoe-horned into the twisted, empty cavern of the Devil's clutches.*

"Good," Lucy said, releasing her grip on his tie as her forked tongue darted out to taste his lips. "Perhaps you should find us a hotel for the night, Nicholas. I don't think you'll find your prior accommodations serviceable any longer, and we have much to discuss. But I think I'll fuck you first." Brazenly, she stroked her hand over Nick's crotch. "I'll not talk to you with the taste of the water witch on your lips."

Try it, the foreign voice in his head challenged. Not even the consuming kiss of Hell's eternal flame itself could burn Moira's intoxicating taste from his memory.

And for once, Nick found himself in agreement.

"We can talk, but my days of being fucked by you are over," Nick remarked.

Lucy's grip on his cock tightened, hoping for signs of arousal she didn't find. "You and I both know you love a grudge fuck, Nick. And

who better to take out your rage upon than me?"

Myself.

Stupid fucking voice of reason speaking the mother-fucking truth all the gods-damned time.

Nick didn't bother to argue. His thoughts had already wandered onto new territory.

Magnus peeled out of the dirt lot down the path from Siren's Cry, and Nick gunned the engine with a renewed sense of vigor.

Moira was alive.

Moira was alive, and armed with a weapon as powerful as his own.

If he had thought her a worthy opponent before, he was certain the next contest of their wills would prove...orgasmic.

Nick allowed a grin to take over the side of his face Lucy couldn't see.

He couldn't fucking wait.

"Hey, y'all. What's for dinner?"

Moira and Justine stood in the kitchen doorway of the de Moray house, waiting for their presence to register.

Tierra looked up from a saucepan and shrieked, the spoon she had been holding clattering to the floor as her hand flew to her mouth.

"Moira! Justine!"

Moira braced herself for the patented Tierra tackle-pounce-hug she was about to receive. Her sister didn't disappoint. Moira's and Justine's heads knocked together like a pair of bobble-head dolls as Tierra dragged them both into her embrace at once.

"Thank the Goddess!" she wailed, burying her face in Moira's neck while simultaneously squeezing Aunt Justine's spleen up to her throat. "You're alive! You're home! You're...soaking wet. What on earth happened to you? How did you get away? How did you—?"

Moira held up her hand. "It's a long story. Maybe we ought to wait until Claire and Aerin are here so I only have to tell it once."

"Claire! Aerin!" Tierra hollered at an eardrum-piercing decibel. "Get down here, now!"

Moira heard the shuffling of footsteps overhead, followed by the creaking of stairs announcing her sisters' descent.

"Holy balls," she heard Aerin mutter. "Whatever the fuck this summons is for, it better not involve kale."

"Or tofu," Claire replied. "If I ever come across the asshat who first cultivated the soybean in the afterlife, I'm going to burn his testicles to cinders."

They rounded the corner simultaneously and froze in the doorway.

"Look!" Tierra enthused, whipping off her apron. "They're home."

Moira hadn't been expecting either of them to rush her the way Tierra had. Neither had she expected the narrow-eyed scrutiny she met instead.

Aerin folded her arms across the blouse of the button-down shirt she was only allowed to wear at home since the Horsemen had unanimously decided she was the pick of the litter as far as the killing was concerned. "How do we know it's *really* her?" she demanded.

"Good question," Claire agreed. "A certain bitch who shall remain nameless has gotten awfully good at borrowing bodies lately. And besides, I don't think the real Moira would have brought Aunt Justine back with her."

Irritation needled Moira as she stood there in their warm and cozy kitchen. After having surviving a day as Conquest's captive, patching things up with an aunt who'd tried to kill her, being shot through the chest with an Apocalyptic arrow, inheriting her crown and wand from some watery tart, destroying the Horsemen's compound, and saving Justine, being asked to prove her identity was just about the last damn straw.

"We buried the hatchet while we were both captives, once and for all," Justine reported. "That's why Moira came back to save me."

"The Moira *I* know would have buried the hatchet in the back of your head," Claire pointed out.

Moira pulled up a stool from the counter and plopped onto it. "How exactly would you like me to prove my identity?"

"What if she told us something only Moira would know?" Claire suggested.

"Well there's a short list," Aerin snorted.

"Would this help?" Moira lifted her tank-top and retrieved her wand from the waistband of her cut-offs, setting it on the kitchen island.

Tierra, Claire, and Aerin gasped in unison.

Even in the pedestrian light, it glowed iridescent like the inside of a clamshell.

"Where did you get that?" Tierra asked.

"Same place I got this." Moira motioned to Justine, who handed her a canvas bag. Moira reached inside and withdrew the intricate crown, holding it up so the jeweled points caught the light before delicately depositing it on a kitchen towel. "It didn't exactly go with my outfit, and truth to tell, I kinda felt like a fool wearing it."

"You didn't answer the question." Aerin took a step closer, looking like a defense attorney inspecting exhibits entered into a court case.

"Where did you get these?"

"Morgana de Moray gave them to me."

"Malcom de Moray's sister?" Aerin asked. Out of all of them, she alone had studied the Grimoire with Talmudic zeal. "How is that possible?"

Moira shrugged. "She just kinda showed up after I fell from the cliff at Siren's Cry and sank to the bottom of the—"

"Back the fuck up," Aerin ordered. "You fell off the cliff at Siren's Cry? By the Standing Stones?"

"Yup. Of course, I'd just been shot in the chest by Nick's arrow, so my balance wasn't so great at the time."

Three sets of eyes widened to the size of duck eggs.

"You were shot?" Tierra fluttered over to Moira and put the back of her hand to her forehead, examining her from one angle, then another to check for other injuries.

Moira put a hand up her own shirt stuck a finger through the demonstrative hole in her tank-top. "Right about here."

"But that's right over your heart," Tierra observed. "How did you survive?"

"I think it had something to do with these here fancy accessories," Moira said, gesturing to the gleaming objects.

"So, after Nick abducted you, he took you up to Siren's Cry just to shoot you?" Claire had abandoned her place in the doorway and seated herself on the stool next to Moira. "Why wouldn't he have done it at their compound? Seems like that would have been a whole lot easier."

And now it was fixin' to get awkward.

"Because I asked him to," Moira admitted, staring down at her own bare feet. "Shoot me, that is. But only if he would do it where we had seen our mother."

"*You did what?*" Tierra's voice had risen a couple of octaves and color flooded her cheeks.

All three of her sisters were gathered around her now with Justine close in the periphery. "I figured it only takes one of us to die to end this. Tierra's knocked-up. Claire's all fiery and full of life. Aerin's all smart and rich. I can't see much that I bring to the table aside from fried animal innards."

"She's Moira all right," Aerin said sharply, rolling her eyes.

"How can you be so sure?" Claire asked.

"Because only Moira would say something so absolutely idiotic."

Moira looked into her sister's silvery eyes and thought she saw just the *hint* of a glassy sheen.

"You are an extremely valuable member of this...*team*

and contribute considerable...*skills* to the conglomerate." Aerin tucked a single stray hair back into its bun. "So, from now on, we would appreciate if you don't attempt to remove yourself from the operation."

"Gee, thanks, Aerin." Moira said, dropping an arm around her

sister's waist. "I love you, too."

"Speaking of love," Claire cut in. "Here's the real test."

They all followed her gaze to where a small, pink pig had paused in the doorway.

Her heart overflowing with a sudden burst of joy, Moira slid off her chair without hesitation, slapping her hands against her thighs. "Cheeto! Come here, baby! Come to momma!"

The little pig hesitated for all of a millisecond before launching himself across the kitchen and into her arms. Moira hugged him tight, relieved beyond measure to have his warm, squirmy body pressed close to her heart.

"Who's the bestest wittwe piggy ever?" Moira cooed, kissing the pig's moist snout. "Who is he? What's him's name?"

"Well, I think that answers that question," Aerin affirmed.

"But not all the others," Tierra reminded them. "Why are you both soaking wet?"

"I sort of had to destroy the Horsemen's compound to get Justine away from them," Moira admitted. "Which reminds me."

She set Cheeto down at her feet and resumed her place on the stool.

"While I was chained to Nick's bed——"

"You were chained to Nick's bed?" Claire asked, leaning forward, cheeks flushed with lurid excitement. "Kinky."

"Not until later," Moira continued. "But what I was saying—"

"Wait, wait, wait." This time, Aerin had spoken up. Her cool mask of professionalism had slipped from its moorings just enough to reveal the passionately curious woman beneath. "Are you saying that you and Nick...?" Her perfectly plucked eyebrows rose with lascivious insinuation.

All eyes fixed on Moira.

Lord. There was no easy way to say this. "Yes. Okay? We had wild gorilla sex for hours on end on account of that's what he asked for in exchange for killing me."

Now it was their mouths, not their eyes wide open.

"But that's not what I was trying to tell you," Moira insisted, quickly losing her patience. "I saw newspapers, magazines, there were pictures and they all—"

"How big?" Aerin queried.

"The newspapers? I don't—"

"His cock," Aerin supplied, earning her a stern look from Tierra.

"Are we talking Economy, Standard, Full-Size, SUV—"

"Aerin!" Tierra scolded.

"Oh, hold your water, Tierra. Claire only pretend-fucked Dru. Julian is more conflicted and emotional than a dumpster full of teenage girls, and you fucked Death and wouldn't give up a single detail. I just want a few juicy tidbits."

"You ever seen one of them Hummer stretch limousines?" Moira asked.

"*No,*" Claire said, not in negation, but in disbelief.

"Yes ma'am. And what's more, he can come about eighty-seven times in a row. Or something like that. I stopped counting after twenty." Moira turned to Aerin. "And if you make any crack about my running out of digits to count on, I swear to the Goddess I'll never give you another detail for the rest of our lives."

Aerin made a silent gesture of zipping her lips.

"Good. What I was trying to say is—"

"You used protection, right? Please tell me you used protection." Tierra ran her hand over the small rounded mound of her belly.

A worm of fear wriggled into Moira's gut. "Not exactly...I thought

I was going to die anyway so—"

"And *how* many times did you say he came?" Aerin's voice was shrill as a whistle. "You could have like a hundred loads of Nick's supersperm conquesting the shit out of your ovaries right now."

Moira slapped both hands down on the kitchen island. "Listen to me. Even *that* won't matter if we don't figure out a way to deal with this shit."

Aunt Justine handed over the bag, and Moira upended it, dumping the magazines, newspapers, and tabloids out for her sisters to see.

Tierra gasped, spotting her own image attached to the antichrist headline. Aerin followed soon after. Page after page of witch hunters, religious radicals, and amateur exorcists. All angry, all determined, all driven by the deadly combination of fear and ignorance.

"Do you see now?" Moira asked, waiting for her sisters' eyes to find hers again. "Morgana said that the only chance we have of defeating this Apocalypse is to stick *together*."

Moira held out a hand to Tierra, who took it, and offered hers to Aerin. Moira didn't miss the split second of hesitation before Aerin clasped it, and offered her other hand to Claire, who accepted it and waved Justine in to complete the circle.

"We can stand together, or we can fall apart," Moira emphasized by squeezing the hands in hers. "But the truth is the truth, and we have to reckon with it at the end of the day."

"What's that?" Tierra asked, her green eyes aglow with worry enough for two.

Moira looked around the circle, her own face repeated like a funhouse mirror save for the eyes glowing green, amber, silver, and faded jade.

"The truth is this. They know who we are. Where we are. What we are, and what we can do. They *are* coming for us. And soon."

ABOUT CYNTHIA

Cynthia St. Aubin wrote her first play at age eight and made her brothers perform it for the admission price of gum wrappers. A steal, considering she provided the wrappers in advance. Though her early work debuted to mixed reviews, she never quite gave up on the writing thing, even while earning a mostly useless master's degree in art history and taking her turn as a cube monkey in the corporate warren.

Because the voices in her head kept talking to her, and they discourage drinking at work, she started writing instead. When she's not standing in front of the fridge eating cheese, she's hard at work figuring out which mythological, art historical, or paranormal friends to play with next. She lives in Colorado with the love of her life and three surly cats.

Cynthia loves to hear from readers.

Visit her: http://www.cynthiastaubin.com/
Email her: cynthiastaubin@gmail.com

ABOUT CINDY

Amazon bestselling author Cindy Stark lives in a small town shadowed by the Rocky Mountains with a kindle of kitties, working her way toward official Cat Lady status. She writes fun, witch cozy mysteries, emotional romantic suspense, and sexy contemporary romance. She loves to hear from readers!

Cindy loves to hear from readers.
Visit her: www.CindyStark.com
Email her: CindyStark19@gmail.com

ABOUT KERRIGAN

Kerrigan Byrne is the USA Today Bestselling and award winning author of several novels in both the romance and mystery genre.

She lives on the Olympic Peninsula in Washington with her wonderful husband and Willow the Writer Dog. When she's not writing and researching, you'll find her on the beach, kayaking, or on land eating, drinking, shopping, and attending live comedy, ballet, or too many movies.

Kerrigan loves to hear from her readers! To contact her or learn more about her books, please visit her sites:

Kerrigan loves to hear from readers.
Visit her: www.kerriganbyrne.com

ABOUT TIFFINIE

USA Today Bestselling Author Tiffinie Helmer is always up for a gripping adventure. Raised in Alaska, she was dragged "Outside" by her husband, but escapes the lower forty-eight and returns to her beloved Alaska every chance she gets.

A mother of four, Tiffinie divides her time between enjoying her family, throwing her acclaimed pottery, and writing of flawed characters in unique and severe situations.

Tiffinie loves to hear from readers.
Visit her: http://tiffiniehelmer.com/
Email her: Tiffinie@TiffinieHelmer.com